thE LiStENERs

HARRISON DEMCHICK

Cover design: Rachel Stark
Layout: Tracy Copes
Author photo: Mallory Henson

**bancroft
press**

Published by Bancroft Press
"Books that Enlighten"
P.O. Box 65360, Baltimore, MD 21209
410-358-0658 | 410-764-1967 (fax)
www.bancroftpress.com

Library of Congress Control Number: 2012949915
ISBN 978-1-61088-081-7 (cloth)
ISBN 978-1-61088-082-4 (paper)
ISBN 978-1-61088-083-1 (mobi)
ISBN 978-1-61088-084-8 (epub)
Printed in the United States of America

*To my parents, who never once questioned
my crazy dream to write.*

PSA

All borough residents are to return to their homes immediately . . . Once inside, they are not to leave their homes, for any reason, unless otherwise directed by a law enforcement official . . . Residents are to shut and lock windows and doors for the duration . . . Bottled water will be provided . . . Stay tuned for further instructions . . .

All borough residents are to return to their homes immediately once inside they are not to leave their homes for any reason unless directed by a law enforcement official residents are to shut and lock windows and doors for the duration bottled water will be provided stay tuned for further instructions

*allboroughresidentsaretoreturntotheirhomesimmediatelyonce insidetheyarenottoleavetheirhomesforanyreasonunlessotherwise directedbyalawenforcementofficialresidentsaretoshutandlock windowsanddoorsforthedurationbottledwaterwillbeprovidedstay tunedforfurtherinstructions***OBEYTHEQUARANTINEOBEYTHE QUARANTINEOBEYTHEQURANANTINEOBEYTHE—***

Quiet. Quiet. I hear nothing.
You can always hear nothing.

first part

The Knock

The knock stabs at the air so hard it bleeds. The sound lingers like the endless vibration of a tuning fork, cascading from loud chime to low, insistent hum, from the plaster of the ceiling to the space between the hairs of the egg-white carpet.

The woman grips the collar of her pink, stringy bathrobe as she shuffles to the door, which shakes again on the strength of three heavy raps. When she speaks, she chokes on her own words.

"Who's there?" she says.

Through the door, the response is muffled but tough. "Police," a man says.

Kneading her shirt between her knuckles, the woman takes a cautious step back, the heel of her tense right foot rising above the deep red stain that never would come out, and says, as loudly as she can (which isn't very), "I don't believe you."

The door does not reply. It only stares, accusing and cruel.

And then its face breaks in from the back with a horrible crunch, plaster and wood collapsing as the door propels open, its doorknob bashing into the wall like a battering ram. A bearded man charges forward through the gap, aiming a night black pistol directly at the woman. She stumbles backwards, tripping over her own heel and falling down onto the carpet. The man who stands in front of her is not a police officer. And he has only one ear.

"Stay down!" the man says. "Stay down!"

"Is anyone else here?" The second man, broad and black, steps through the cracked and broken doorframe. He waves a similar gun around the room in a rainbow arc. He, too, has only one ear, his right, with only a flat wide bandage where the left ear used to be. And as he aims, his alert white eyes scanning the room in a perfect sweep, a third man squeezes in behind him.

Except the third man isn't a man.

The third man is a boy.

"My—my husband's a police officer!" the woman says, now on her hands and feet in some sort of crab walk, scuttling away. "He'll—don't—"

"We know," says the second man.

"Stay down!" says the first.

"Is Detective Joel MacDonald home?"

The boy, small and skinny, disappears behind the second man, his eyes looking down toward his shoes, gray and worn, the start of a hole by the toes of the right foot. He holds his own gun to his side, cold against his thigh, where the only person it can hurt is himself.

From somewhere comes the creak of a door, descending like a nervous violin.

"No, no, he's—he's not here!" cries the woman.

"Then we'll wait," says the second man.

"Mom?" The voice is a new voice, a girl's voice, cutting through the clamor, but only for a moment. The second man, the alert man, spins around, his gun pointed in a perfect bee-line through the head of the teenage girl standing just outside the apartment's stuffy little hallway. "What's happening?" says the girl.

The boy, who wears a torn white undershirt, does not look at the girl. He looks instead into the small kitchen only a couple yards away, staring as if it's some oasis in the faraway distance. A silver scrape in the white counter glows just slightly white under the hum of fluorescent lights. He stares at the scrape until it seems to be a living thing, wiggling and wriggling, and he squeezes his own thumb so hard his knuckle cracks, and consequently he doesn't see the second man pointing his gun at the girl, or the girl turning toward the boy with the sad white eyes of recognition.

"Danny?" says the girl.

That breaks his concentration. Now, the boy, whose name is Daniel, glances her way, but it's a half-look at best, tilting from the corners of his quickly blinking eyes. His breath catches halfway through the exhale, like a thin shirt on a sharp twig. And when he pulls it free, it tears a little, just a little.

"Hi, Katie," he says.

The Traffic Light

This happened earlier:

There is a room, one long forgotten now, with a bumpy white ceiling and red *Daredevil* posters lining pale blue walls. It has a close-cropped blue carpet and a closet door on its third handle. It has an alarm clock, wailing as it sits on the chipped silver radiator, which echoes the alarm in an atonal ring.

The kid underneath the once fluffy blue covers, fourteen and scrawny, covers his face and ears with a white pillow so that the dream, desperate to make its way out of his head and into some sort of oblivion, cannot escape. Already, the dream is hard to keep hold of, but it's something sunny, and most critically, it includes people—other people who aren't him. That's the important thing. That's why he shuts his eyes and holds on tight, even as the alarm clock on the radiator announces 7:10 in bright red LED and loud, resounding beeps.

But each *beep* pounds the dream like a hammer on a nail, each smack forcing it more decisively through his skull until the hole is big enough that not even the pillow can keep it there. When he reaches over the radiator to the alarm clock and switches the thing off, its blare coming to an anticlimactic close, he finds himself staring upward at the cloud of nothing that fills the instant silence.

The fact of the matter, the stupid, back-breaking fact of the matter, is there's no school. There's no need to wake up at 7:10. There's no need to deal with the alarm. But yesterday, when he turned it off and tried to sleep indefinitely, he found himself awake at the same time anyway, the absolute silence far more deafening than the broken blare of a ten-year-old alarm clock on a rickety radiator could ever be. The alarm itself proves no more restful, though, than the silence had. His eyes are open. His ears are open. He's no better off.

Getting out of bed for some reason—loudly, not rolling out but climbing to his hands and knees, forcing the rattling metal *creak*—Daniel tries to hold on to the dream, or the memory, or whatever it was. Bits and pieces hover above his head like clouds, and when he grabs for them, his hands pass right through them. What he gets are flashes at best, sensations at worst. Little photographic flashes of kids on a playground. A little box of apple juice, yellow like the sun. Anxiety, but the old kind, which makes it the good kind. And Katie—Katie was there, too.

Daniel does not look at the picture tucked into his bed frame. Instead, he pulls the blue covers off his back—they match the walls, as if he ever cared—and steps down onto the carpet, trying to make it more of a stomp than a step. The neighbors won't mind. He isn't even sure if they're there anymore. The baby hasn't cried for a week at least.

The sun pouring in through the window tries to make up for everything. It dodges the bed almost skillfully, but then, that's what Daniel always liked about the room. On a weekend, or during the summer, he could stay in the dark as long as he liked, the transition in the morning on his own time, suddenly and completely. As he thinks about it, he wonders if it is, in fact, summer. Normally, the lack of buses would be a dead giveaway, except now, there wouldn't be buses anyway. As Daniel steps into the trapezoid of sunlight formed by his bedroom window, he finds himself staring outside. The moment he freezes is the moment the silence returns.

Outside Daniel's window stands a traffic light. It still works. The light is red now, and it's the same red as the LED display on his alarm clock, which now features a prominent 7:14. But as he watches the traffic light, he sees it flip to green, then, ultimately, to an underappreciated yellow, and eventually back to red again. It's a strange thing to watch a traffic light every morning for maybe three weeks, without ever seeing any cars pass through. That's not to say there *weren't* cars, at least for a time. In fact, there are cars now, parked awkwardly against the curb, maybe three he can see right out in the middle of the road, doors opened and abandoned. But most are parked—the news anchors and the doctors had said not to drive, and the gas stations probably ran out of gas anyway.

There were motors, at least, the first week or so. There were a lot the first day. But by the second week, the most Daniel ever heard in one day were seven, and by now it's been at least a week since the last one. Sometimes he heard sirens, but whether sirens or motors, he never actually saw the cars, police or otherwise, and he never saw motorcycles or buses. He ran to the window once when he thought one might be passing down Rentwood, but if it did, he missed it. He heard them until he stopped hearing them. He heard them until there was nothing left to hear. He doesn't know where they went. The motors only ever seemed to go in one direction. They certainly never came back.

The cars are lined up along the side of the road now, collecting dust and pollen from the stunted little trees lined up along the sidewalk, which rise like giant anthills. Sometimes a bird poops on them. Otherwise they don't move. The island outside is urban, relentlessly urban, and the tall brick wall across the street is the clearest sign of that. The island was born kinetic. That the cars would be as silent as the traffic light, that the light itself would be out of a job—that no one has gone to dinner or work or even to *school* for weeks . . .

Pushing himself off the window and away from the sound of cars *not* driving, of motors *not* running, of horns *not* honking, Daniel heads to the bathroom, past his mom's bedroom, which no one has slept in for three days. (The first two days, Daniel checked, but today he doesn't bother. He can't.) In the small, white bathroom two rooms down, Daniel reaches behind the curtain for the shower knob, but the moment he starts to twist it, he pulls his hand away, as if the knob is a boiling teapot. For all the news has been saying, maybe it is. At least twice in the first five days, he turned the shower on by accident, and his mom, listening like a deer for the crunch of a hunter's boots, came running to stop him before he touched the water or breathed it. He never told her, but a little got on his fingers. It didn't seem to do any damage.

Maybe it never could have. After all, they don't know what's causing it. They don't claim to. But, hey, it *could* be the water. It could be the water as easily as anything else, and better safe than sorry or dead. So they said, "Don't shower. Don't bathe. Don't use your sinks. We'll bring you water." But they didn't bring much, and eventually, they weren't bringing any at all. At that point, using the water that way seemed outright wasteful, so Daniel stopped bathing at all, no matter how dirty and dusty he felt. But he still brushes his teeth. He uses the bottled water, what little is left. His mom will have more when she gets back.

But Daniel has plenty of deodorant. He has floss—enough for months to come. He has shirts, pants, and underwear, even if it's all gotten a bit grimy at this point, so he can at least look presentable for the inevitable audience of no one. Katie would get the joke if the phone lines weren't down, and if she wasn't so many blocks away, and if it was safe to take that first step outside and look for her.

The traffic light flips from green to yellow to red. The world does not react.

Daniel stares at himself in his smudgy bathroom mirror.

Silent House

Sometimes Daniel turns the TV on, loud, and doesn't turn it off all day.

". . . offered no indication of the situation beyond Crawford Street," says a woman, whose hair is made-up and her suit dry-cleaned and who probably showered before driving, outside of all places, to work this morning.

Daniel sits at the tan counter in the kitchen, eating a breakfast of Cheerios and water—Cheerios, because it's the only breakfast food left in the apartment, and water, because there isn't any milk left, and you've got to have cereal with *something*. The TV, a little old black one sitting awkwardly against the wall, picks up what little it can, but the image and sound have been inconsistent at best ever since Daniel's mom accidentally shoved it to the floor while making herb potatoes, so when Daniel reaches forward and turns the volume up—as loud as he can, louder than silence could *ever* be—only half of it is talk, and the other half gibberish at best and silence at worst.

Some military official is on camera now. Maybe he's a captain or a colonel or something. The reporter holds a microphone to his face. The words "everything we can" filter in between bursts of pointless static. An insistent squiggly gray line covers the old man's eyes and face, so all Daniel can see is the jerking mouth, changing into the reflection of a million funhouse mirrors. "You'll know something when we do," he says, with confidence.

Behind the captain or colonel or something is some square, brownish building, and in front of that a little circle of a road with a short, stubby tree. Daniel passed by it a bunch of times in the back-seat of his mom's Toyota, just a little bit past the bridge and into the body of the city beyond. It used to be pretty close. Now it's an out-side interview in an outside place with not even a single trace of one of those biohazard suits the doctors wore before they left. Daniel starts to imagine what might be beyond the camera. There's prob-ably a crowd of people, walking around and breathing the air and whispering to each other, "I've seen her on TV." Probably a couple of them work in offices. They have briefcases and handkerchiefs, and one is so distracted that he forgets he's late for work. His boss will be pissed. A couple other kids play soccer right behind them, and one almost kicks the ball into the camera by accident, but the other stops it just in time.

Daniel turns the volume up. He slams his palm into the side of the screen until the jagged black and gray lines veil the entire image. The sound transitions into a steady white noise. The picture could be anything, and maybe it is.

Daniel takes a bite of his Cheerios. They're soggy. He chews it just the same, and as he closes his eyes, he imagines milk, the whole kind, or even chocolate milk, which would be great. So he swallows it all the way down, feeling it slip and slurp down his throat, and that's when he hears the *pop*.

His spoon freezes above the bowl, a little droplet of not-choc-olate milk dripping back into the bowl with an indistinguishable splash. Daniel quickly turns the volume down, and as he does, he catches the much louder second *pop*, as sharp and sudden as a bal-loon left floating against a light bulb. With a metal clang, Daniel's spoon drops to the side of the bowl, then sinks into the water. His eyes turn toward the window on the far side of the living room, which faces the red brick building next-door. The sun catches the nearest window on the opposite end of the street, but from here, the view reveals nothing. Sliding off his stool, Daniel tip-toes out of the kitchen and into the adjoining living room. Floorboards creak beneath his feet. His mom's record collection sits organized against the wall, and her necklace, thrown off just before she last left, lies in a sprawl on the table. The table is a dark, leathery rainforest green, which folds and crinkles at the corners.

As Daniel squeezes his hands against the cool window, he hears it again, louder than before. He presses his face against the glass, staring down onto the narrow street below. It isn't empty. Down the block, passing by the boarded-up shop where Mr. Gomez used to work, is a man—maybe. It's hard to see. Three stories down and almost a whole block away, the figure walks forward with something of a limp, its (his? her?) left leg dragging its right one along. Pebbles part for its dangling toes. The top of its head is mostly bald, what little hair there is circling around the back in a thin ring. Its right arm, poking out through a badly torn short-sleeved shirt featuring some cartoon cow, is stiff and straight, as if it doesn't have an elbow, instead just a long stick of a thing protruding from the shoulder.

Its right hand holds a gun.

The arm rises into the air, still completely straight, and the gun, pointed forward, fires so loudly it cracks Daniel's eardrums even through the glass. With a loud whine, the bullet ricochets somewhere out to the left, but it doesn't seem to hit anything that can feel it. The figure shuffles forward, and Daniel, staring, imagines the sound of a maybe-limp foot scraping against concrete. Its face is wrong somehow. It's red where it shouldn't be red. And just as the word *boil* sears itself into Daniel's mind like a sunburn, the man or woman or thing in the street turns, its face pointed up and left until its ambiguous, lumpy face, and maybe its eyes, are looking straight into Daniel's own window.

"You!" it says.

Daniel blinks. His fingers squeak along the glass.

"It's all your fault!" it cries.

Before Daniel can even begin to consider what that might mean, the thing turns its whole body, and the arm rises again—the stiff arm, the bad arm, the arm with the gun. It's aimed at the window now. For just a moment, a frigid frozen moment, the arm remains there, like the barrier of a railroad crossing. It doesn't shake at all. Neither does Daniel, though he wants to.

There is a gun pointing at him.

The gun fires, its pop drowned out immediately by the crash of shattering glass and the scream in Daniel's throat. Daniel jumps back, tripping to the floor, shielding himself from the thousand scattered pieces of what used to be his window. He sees them on the floor, jagged and sharp; he feels them on his neck and back; and as he crawls away, his breathing loud and hard and fast, he sees on the back of his eyelids the thing and its railroad-crossing arm and its blood-red funhouse-mirror face.

His heart pounds into his ribs like a boxer's fists into a punching bag, and it's so loud he hardly hears the second sound, the one that might be a pop but maybe isn't. As the light static from the TV hisses in incongruous monotony, a piece of glass weaves its way into Daniel's left hand, but Daniel doesn't notice, crawling under the counter in the kitchen where the thing outside can't get to him. The angles are all wrong. He squeezes into the wall as tightly as he possibly can. He pulls his hands to his cheeks. His left cheek shoves the shard deep into his flesh.

Now he feels it. Now he cries out, but he doesn't look at it. Instead, he looks at what used to be a window, glass tinkling down from the top. A breeze finds the opening and pushes through, and it won't shut up. It hits Daniel's face. He shuts his eyes and tries not to breathe it in. He feels the hot blood racing around the wound in his hand. He sees the boil and the thing with the gun. When Daniel coughs, his eyes burst open, landing on a fragile piece of glass rattling in the broken window. It looks like the one in his hand. He crouches down and vomits.

As Daniel holds himself up on one hand, one arm, and two knees, trying not to look at the remains of his breakfast, something pounds against his door. It pounds again, and it pounds again. Instinctively pushing himself up and away from the mess he's made, Daniel scurries back from the door, but he hasn't gotten far when the voice calls out, "Police. Open up."

Daniel stops mid-scuttle. He stares at the door. It shakes in its hinges when whoever on the other end *knock-knock-knock*s again.

"Anyone in there?"

Daniel opens his mouth to respond, but the first thing that comes out is a cough and just a little more vomit. He clears his throat, then manages, "Yeah . . ."

"Open up."

Slowly, unsteadily, Daniel climbs to his feet. The floorboards squeak in resistance. Wincing, Daniel pulls the glass from his hand—it clinks as it hits the floor—and he holds the wound tight. "Are you . . ." Daniel coughs again as he steps closer to the door. "Are you—"

"It's safe. We got him."

The door has not been opened for a long time. It hasn't been opened for someone coming in for even longer—too long, in fact, given how long it's been since the last time someone went out. As he reaches for the deadbolt, Daniel's skinny fingers dance, shaking around the metal before they finally get a good grasp on it. With the idea of *safe* playing around in his head, Daniel unbolts the door, unlocks it, turns the knob, and pulls it open.

"Thanks, kid," says the first of two officers. He carries a duffel bag. He has a scar on his right cheek, a curvy little thing that widens at the top like a firework. Daniel imagines the blade of a knife carving through the flesh. Blood pounds against the wound in his hand. The other officer is shaped very much like a bulldog, big and squat and muscular, with wide, fat cheeks that flop down along the sides of his chin. Maybe he's smiling—his big, round eyes make it look as if he is—but his mouth is covered by a white surgical mask. Both their mouths are. The white stands out against the pristine blue of their uniforms and the still shiny copper badges pinned against their chests.

"Can we come in?" says the second officer.

Daniel notices he's shaking and tries to stop. The wind whistles through the window. "Yeah," he says, taking a little step back. "Yeah."

The first officer takes the lead, his dark eyes scanning the small room—the half-eaten cereal on the counter, and the regurgitated other half on the floor. They dart to the flickering light of the screwed-up television and the carpet of glass lining the floor. "Are you okay?" he says.

"Um," says Daniel. He glances at the window, remnants of glass zigzagging around the open hole in a wildly uneven circumference.

"Tough luck," says the second officer. With what might be a frown, he glances at Daniel's hand, then tugs a sheet of paper towel from the almost empty roll on the counter. "Keep pressure on it," he says, handing the towel to Daniel.

"Did you know that man?" says the first officer. He kneels down and lifts a shard of glass, as if he's studying it for fingerprints.

"No," says Daniel.

"He said, 'It's all your fault.'"

"I didn't know him."

"Mm-hm." The first officer nods, and then, with a slight grunt, rises to his feet. "A lot of them say things like that. They get sick, right, and they don't know what's what. Disease messes with their minds."

"They're nuts," adds the second.

"They're nuts. Don't worry about it."

"Okay . . ." says Daniel. The beaming sunlight cast through the shattered window projects a strange, jagged shadow pattern on the hardwood floor, like a giant mouth full of sharp, razorblade teeth. As the cool wind blows through the opening, Daniel imagines tiny little particles, a quiet red dust, flittering in and riding the currents, settling into a thin, grainy sand on the floor. Then he turns away and looks at the officers' surgical masks.

"Your mom here?" the first officer says. "Dad?"

"My mom went to get some toilet paper," says Daniel.

The police officers pause at this, the first one gazing at Daniel, the second specifically not. "When was that?" says the first.

"Three . . ." Daniel swallows. "Three days ago."

The officers look at one another, then back to Daniel. "Listen, kid," says the first officer, tracing his scar with a fingernail, "you know about the Give and Take?"

Daniel shakes his head.

"Give and Take is kind of a trade, see?" The officer crosses his arms as he says it, affecting almost the tone of a teacher talking down to a little kid. Daniel looks out the window. He's not a little kid. He's fourteen. "We're collecting all the guns," says the officer, "so *that* . . ."—he points to where Daniel's already looking, just as another shard of glass falls forward and out the window—". . . don't happen." He sniffs. "And in return, we deliver food and supplies right to your door. That sound okay?"

Daniel glances back at the counter, where soggy Cheerios are drowning in lukewarm water. "I guess," he says.

"Any guns here?"

"My mom has a gun."

"Get it for me?"

With a small nod, Daniel steps away, wood groaning quietly beneath his feet. It's a short way down the hall to the room, where the door stands slightly open. A little shadow-slit fills the gap. Outside the door, Daniel listens closely for the squeak of bedsprings, the sigh without an audience, the rumbling and rustling of drawers—for anything except the long, slow, high creak of the door nudging open, and the total, aborted silence behind it.

This will be the first time he's checked today. What if she's here? What if she's not?

He rests his fingertips on the door.

The nudge. The creak. The silence.

A hazy aura of light flows into the room through the window on the left, but it's not much. The room is not dark but dim, and the covers are halfway down the single bed, folded at odd bends, every flap and every sheet exactly where it was yesterday, and the day before, and the day before that when his mom climbed out of it in the first place.

There's no one here. There's no one here. There's no one here.

Daniel breathes in scattered little bursts. Sliding his feet along the furry blue carpet, keeping his eyes down, he makes his way to the old cabinet drawer and pulls it open. The gun is there. He's never touched it. His mom drilled that one into his head just fine, and Katie's dad, a police officer himself, echoed the point. The gun is there in case there's a burglar in the house, which you need to be ready for in the city when it's just the two of you.

But nothing's worth anything anymore, and it's just the one of them.

Dropping the paper towel, lightly blotted with blood, on the counter, Daniel lifts the gun by the handle, holding it between two fingers. The barrel scrapes against the thin wood. Daniel holds it at a distance, as if it's contaminated, which is funny, really, because it's one of the only things he can be absolutely sure is not. He leaves the orphaned bedroom behind and heads back out into the living room by the door, where the second officer, the heavy one with the bulldog cheeks, flips through Daniel's mom's record collection.

"You know how rare this is?" says the second officer, pulling one album the whole way out of the shelf. The record is *Cold Spring Harbor* by Billy Joel. It's the original, Daniel's mom once told him, before they fixed the speed and screwed it up. "This is pretty rare."

The first officer takes the gun from Daniel's hand. "Thanks," he says, dropping it into his duffel bag.

"You . . . you need to put it back in alphabetical order," says Daniel, eyes on the second officer.

The officer gives him a look. Then he drops the record into the bag, and goes back to the shelf. "I love this one!" he says, tugging another one off its perch, but it's in the bag before Daniel can see what it is.

"Necklace," says the first officer. He jerks his head toward the living room table, where the green necklace lies splayed across the wood.

"Oh, Gina will love that." The second officer walks over, reaches down, and scoops it up in a meaty paw. He glances back over to his partner, who's opened the duffel bag like a big basketball hoop. In some kind of alley-oop, the second tosses the necklace into the bag, where it jingles pleasantly against the metal of the gun. Daniel stares at the officer but says nothing. The officer returns his look.

"Tip," he says.

Daniel's mouth opens and closes.

"Head out?" says the first officer.

"Think so."

As the first officer reaches for the knob, Daniel manages a scratchy, barely-there "Wait." They both stop and turn. "My mom," says Daniel. In his head, he hears a nudge and a creak and a nothing. He sees an empty room she must eventually return to, the way a clock must eventually strike 7:10. He should focus on that. He should leave it alone. But the words are already halfway out of his mouth. "You think . . ." says Daniel. He has their attention now. "Um, my mom," says Daniel. "You think maybe . . . maybe she'll be back soon?"

As he turns the knob and opens the door, the first officer's eyes widen a little. "Out there three days?" he says. He cocks his head to the side. For a moment, it looks as if he's going to say something else, and in that moment, anything is possible. But then, without another word, the officer steps out the door, his bulldog partner following right behind. The door slams shut behind them.

A breeze whips through the window like an off-key whistle. It will never be quiet in this apartment again. That's what Daniel wanted, right?

Daniel hugs himself tightly.

The Door

This is what they said. They said: It might be the water. They said: It might be the air. They said it spread too fast for it to be anything but contagious. They said to protect yourself through separation—you from other people, you from the outside world, blocked by shut doors and locked windows and shirts and pants and mothers. Or something like that. They did not say how fast it all falls down, like a ring around the rosie. Ashes, ashes.

If the air is poison, the shattered window is a one-way needle into Daniel's bloodstream. It's already carved out an entry. So when Daniel retreats to his room—shuts the door, double-checks the windows, even checks his walls for cracks—it's the last line of defense from a strike so insidious and invisible he wonders if he'll even know when he's dead. He wonders if he'll care. He wonders if anyone else will know. He wonders if there's anyone left alive who knows his name. On another nameless morning in the last safe room, far from the hiss of the television and what little food remains (and he still hasn't finished his breakfast), he wonders a lot of things.

The walls close in. Daniel opens the closet for some extra space. He pushes aside the nice shirts, the ones his mom made him wear at some point before she left him here to die, and pulls from the bottom of the closet a short box of comic books. He flips through them until he finds an issue of *Daredevil*—the man without fear. Clutching it tightly, he retreats to the corner, by the radiator and the alarm clock dead-set on announcing the time some twenty-three hours from now, where the window's light casts just above him, barely brushing by the photograph caught in the bed frame.

There was a week last September when Katie decided she was going to be a photographer, but not with some digital camera or,

God forbid, her cell phone. She found a bulky old instant camera in the antique store past the bridge and carried it everywhere, grinning wildly as she stole moments from a history now turned outright foreign. But this picture is not one she took. Daniel's mom took it, the one with the two of them grinning—Daniel shyly, Katie gleefully. Katie snuck mutant bunny ears—that's three extended fingers—behind Daniel's head. Daniel and Katie are shoulder to shoulder. They're joined at the hip.

The phones went down shortly after the quarantine went up. The cell phones and smart phones lost their signals. The internet went offline and stayed that way. The news anchors, from their vantage point outside, insist that phones aren't down *everywhere*, but they might as well be, and it's not as if anyone can just shoot over to the internet café across the street and see if they still have a connection. Or maybe it all works fine. Maybe there's just no one to talk to. Maybe the phones are pretend like the photo is pretend, capturing things that don't exist anymore, like Daniel and Katie and mutant bunny ears and happiness.

The door rattles. That's the breeze, hitting it just so. It always does that in the summer when Daniel's mom leaves the hallway windows open. Apparently a bullet through a sheet of glass has the same effect. It's as if the wind is water, waves washing into the door in splashes tiny but constant. There's a crack of open space between the carpet and door. This room is not waterproof. Poisoned water, acid rain, washes up and over broken shards of grass and runs down the hall, and this room is not waterproof.

The Daniel in the photograph smiles.

The Daniel whose skeleton wants to crawl from his prickly skin continues to read. He reads about a man without fear in a world without plague where rescue is one page away. He reads as slowly as he can make himself read, staring so hard his eyes cross and the figures blur and pop out of the paper. He reads until it's real enough that he can jump outside, preserved in the pages as the tide rolls in. He shuts his eyes and he squeezes his hands and he's isolated from isolation.

"What did they take?" someone says.

Comic book panels shatter like a window. They come apart in Daniel's herkyjerk hands. His back slams against the corner and he struggles to breathe, coughing heavily as he glances to his right and spots the two men staring at him through the door, which they've carelessly opened. One is black and big; the other white and wiry. They stand in the tide, surgical masks, like those the police wore, wrapped around their head, not hooked around their ears but tied in a knot in the back. They have to be.

The men have no right ears.

"It's okay," says the black man. His left ear juts out. It's asymmetrical.

"Go away." Daniel pushes himself against the radiator. He coughs on his words. The water goes down the wrong pipe. "Close the door."

"Kid. Kid. It's all right," says the black man in a deep, calm voice. He smiles. "We're not here to hurt you. We're here to help."

"We're here to hurt *them*," says the wiry man in a needling little voice. "Followed them up." He talks with his hands, like he's clawing up the air and shoving it away. His loose silver watch slides up and down his wrist. "The cops. The fucking cops. They think they're in charge 'cause they got the power. Yeah, *now*, but they don't know, they don't—"

"Shut up," says the other one. Turning back toward Daniel, he says, "You know who we are?"

The thing is, Daniel does. The first time he learned about them was from Katie, who found out from her dad. He even saw them once, from the second-floor window at P.S. 128, passing through the dead brown grass by the derelict buildings bordering the playground, itself a remnant from when the high school was an elementary school. They were too far away for Daniel to see what Katie told him was there, or more precisely what wasn't. They were too far away to see the dirty white bandage where a right ear used to be.

"You're Listeners," says Daniel, quietly. He doesn't know much more. He knows Katie called them a gang. He knows there were crimes. And he knows the glint of light from the top of the big man's pants indicates a gun not unlike the one he just surrendered to the police.

"I'm Derek," says the black man, pointing at himself. "That's Terry."

"Yo," says Terry.

Daniel doesn't budge, but Derek seems to brighten. His eyes are big, the whites very white, his smile broad and clear. "Kid," he says, softly and surely, "it's okay." He laughs. Daniel didn't think anyone did that anymore. "We're the good guys. Okay?"

Derek steps the rest of the way into the room. His weight creaks on the floorboards beneath the carpet, so loud he might fall through. Daniel wonders how he didn't hear them come in. Maybe he just wasn't listening. Derek now stops no more than a yard from Daniel, then sits down on the bed. The bedsprings protest. "What's your name?" he says.

Unsteadily, Daniel pulls his knees into his chest, rocking away from the wall. "Daniel," he says.

"'Daniel,'" Derek repeats. "It's a good name. Strong name."

The other one, Terry, stands in the other corner, tossing his own dull green gun up into the air and catching it with a smack in his palm. The same part of the gun—the butt, covered by thick white masking tape with something written on it—lands always in the fleshy palm of his hand.

"And what's hers?" says Derek.

"What?" says Daniel. He hears the dull smack of skin as Terry grabs the gun from the air.

"What's *her* name?" says Derek. Daniel follows his eyes to the picture.

"Katie," Daniel says.

"Who's Katie?"

"My best friend."

"Yeah. Yeah." Derek leans forward. "Bet it's been a while since you've seen her, huh?"

It has.

"Where does she live?" says Derek.

"Rochester Avenue," says Daniel.

"Long way off." Derek sighs. "Long way off."

On the floor lies the fractured comic book, torn halfway down the spine. It sinks now in a sea of blue carpet. But then they're all drowning, with the window smashed and the door wide open. Can't they feel it? The water rises like mist and stabs Daniel's lungs, but if he holds his breath and closes his eyes, maybe it all goes away. If he holds his breath until his face is as blue as the carpet, maybe he can get what he wants. It always worked for Katie. Maybe if he sits here long enough, eyes closed, breath held, until he suffocates instead of drowns, he'll believe so strongly those final few moments that it might as well be real.

"Daniel?"

"Go away," Daniel whispers. He lifts the comic book and tries to determine where he left off.

"You can't stay here."

"Close the door."

"They'll come back," says Derek. "Maybe those two. Maybe people like them. Maybe another one of the sickos that shot out your window, right? If you don't let them in, they'll break down your door. If you don't give them what you want, they'll take it. They control you and they know it. Do you hear me?"

"Go away."

"Derek—" Terry starts, but Derek stops him with a hand.

"Daniel. Listen," says Derek. He readjusts himself on the bed, and the springs yell. "It's a scary world out there right now."

"Scary as fuck," says Terry. "That's how scary."

"They've trapped us here, Daniel. Fort on one end, ocean on the other, nothing but nothing in the middle," says Derek. "But if you stay here, you're even more trapped than the rest of them. You don't have to die, and live, and *be* all alone."

"I'm not," says Daniel, dropping the comic. "My mom will be back soon. She'll be really mad if you're still here."

"Daniel—"

"And if I'm not here when she gets back, she'll be really worried." Daniel hugs his legs.

With a sigh, Derek clasps his hands and leans down toward Daniel. "I had a mom," he says. "Dad too. We all had a lot of things. But nothing is what it used to be. You know that. I know you do."

"You're Listeners," Daniel says weakly.

There's a pause. "Yes," says Derek.

"You're criminals." That's what Katie's dad said. Her dad has a badge and a gun, like the police who came in and stole things and left him here to die.

Climbing to his feet, Derek turns around, leans against the wall, and slumps to the floor, right next to Daniel. Even leaning back against the wall, Derek sits straight and broad. "That's a lie," he says quietly. "Not an intentional lie. Not the kind born of malice, but of misinformation. Like a rumor people believe because a friend said it." He glances vaguely through the open door. "You have the TV on back there. How many lies have they told about life here? The police hurt you. We did not. Is that a lie?"

After a moment, Daniel says, "No."

"It's not," says Derek. "This is what we do. We filter through the lies, on TV or on the radio or on the internet, or from teachers—or from the cops who stole from you. Or even from good people. Like Katie."

"She wouldn't lie," says Daniel. He shifts left, leaning into the corner.

With a quiet sigh, Derek says, "You're right. I can see that in her eyes. But just because you don't mean to lie doesn't mean you tell the truth. When a lie is repeated often enough, even the best people, the smartest people, believe it's the truth." Then he leans his head down and, sideways, looks Daniel in the eyes. "When I tell you you won't survive here, that's the truth." He pauses. "When I tell you your mother is dead, that's the truth. I'm sorry, but it is."

Daniel winces at that. But he knew it too.

"I want to help you find the truth in the lies," says Derek. "When you listen closely, the one voice that's clear, the one voice that's really there—that's the truth. You just have to learn how to *listen* for it." He points to his one ear.

The hand that appears on Daniel's shoulder is strong and warm. When he looks up, its owner looks at him with eyes big and bright and unflinchingly sincere. The door may be open, but things can move out as surely as in.

"I need to leave a note," says Daniel. "In case—"

"Of course," says Derek.

As a glance passes between Derek and Terry, now waiting quietly in the corner, Daniel climbs to his feet, passes through the open doorway, and into the living room once again. It's all still there—the shattered glass, the half-finished cereal, the front door that looks to have been kicked open. Daniel raids the drawers by the half-broken television for paper and pen. The paper comes quickly—the back of an old Chinese takeout receipt. But Daniel opens cabinets in search of a pen. He shoves aside bowls. He checks the refrigerator.

When he turns around, he sees Derek's eyes on his. Trembling, Daniel says, "She'll know, right?" He sniffs. "She'll know?"

Derek nods. She'll know.

The Maze

The streets are like the house you grew up in: familiar, yet never exactly as you remember. You've changed, it's changed, and all that's left is the distance between the two.

The sidewalks on the city streets are empty now. So are the roads, though the occasional car is parked awkwardly in the middle. A lone soda can blown by the breeze rattles louder than the loudest motorcycle engine.

When a left turn leads into what might once have been the slums, even the passing familiarity fades and Daniel, breathing the naked air for the first time in weeks, can do nothing more than follow Terry as Derek watches his back. Daniel wears a surgical mask around his mouth. So do Terry and Derek, though theirs aren't strapped to their ears, but tied behind their heads. The elastic bands blend into the bandages covering the spots where their respective right ears used to be.

They walk. For an hour, they walk the streets of the small borough, but it feels like so much longer after weeks where the longest trek was from the bedroom to the refrigerator.

"Are you okay?" says Derek early on.

"Where are they?" Daniel says.

"Don't know," says Derek. "Sometimes you see them. Sometimes you don't."

The TV news had suggested otherwise, but then Derek did say the news was lies. Only in the first few days would the news channels show pictures of the sick people staggering through the streets, videotaped at a distance from helicopters, but the sick people certainly looked to be everywhere. It was as if you couldn't step outside without being attacked. That's what the healthcare workers in the biohazard suits had said, too. But now, most of the walk is absolute silence, minus the resounding echo of footsteps on abandoned streets. When Daniel looks down the road, the rough gravel extends into infinity, or at least to the docks, where they said on TV army boats keep an endless vigil. In the other direction is the bridge, which he heard has been blocked off, with no cars, buses, or people allowed in or out.

In the middle is nothing. Daniel couldn't run from that if he tried.

Eventually, a parking lot appears up ahead, but there aren't many cars in it. A few are parked toward the front. Underneath a few plastic shelters, shopping carts press together, the wind pushing them into one another. The rattle of metal on metal fills the air as the building behind it begins to take shape. Soon Daniel recognizes the building, a supermarket. Terry is leading them to the Food Garden. Daniel wonders if they have any toilet paper.

The Food Garden building is flat and squat. The wall at the end of the parking lot is glass, or at least it looks like glass. The sunlight reflects off it brightly, illuminating nothing that isn't already illuminated and hiding everything inside. That's why it looks so dark in there. Daniel spots the slight red outlines of checkout counters and a glowing blue plastic grocery bag. A firework sign in the window advertises five-dollar whole roasted chickens on Fridays.

In front of Daniel, Terry's legs pound against the ground with a bizarre intensity, an unrelenting consistency, as if he has a grudge against the pavement. He's tireless, even as Daniel's legs threaten to collapse beneath him. As Terry steps ahead toward the supermarket, his fingers clench, clench, and re-clench the green-framed gun in his hand, until, in an instant, he raises it and spins right, holding the gun firmly in an outstretched arm.

"Hey, five o'clock," he says.

Before Daniel even has a chance to follow Terry's eyes, much less turn around, the shot leaves the barrel, setting off an ear-shattering explosion and a tiny puff of smoke. In the distance, a red-faced figure slumps to the ground in a muffled huff.

"Hole in one," says Terry.

Derek, fingering his own pistol, pushes it slowly back into his pants. The shot rolls on like a rocket in the distance, but in seconds it's gone. Once Terry turns them back toward the supermarket, all that remains are the footsteps. Three pairs of feet tap against a parking lot built for a crowd that no longer exists, or at least one that has lost its capacity for food-shopping.

Listen, listen, listen: nothing.

The lights are off, but the electricity works. The muted slide of the automatic door is proof positive of that. But all the light comes from outside, and it doesn't spread very well, catching only the tips of the aisles but fading well before the end. As Derek, Terry, and Daniel step into the building, the absorbent plastic renders their footsteps monotonous, and Daniel, his eyes adjusting, can't make out a thing.

Then Derek whistles. "Phwi-*phwew*!" is what it sounds like. "Phwi-*phwew*! Phwi-*phwew*!"

From somewhere out in the darkness, someone "Phwi-*phwew*"'s back.

They walk down what might be the center aisle. Daniel's blinking eyes begin to adjust. Bags of chips lean back on the left side of the aisle. They border cheese crackers. A bag of pretzels, slightly dislodged, shoves some nachos. All Daniel has had to eat today is half a bowl of waterlogged cereal. His stomach rumbles. His legs tremble. His eyes catch on something else up ahead: a glowing red "EXIT" sign, casting a slight halo around itself. Terry passes into the back hall of the supermarket, and as he does, Derek taps Daniel's shoulder and points to his right. In the corner is a man, difficult to make out, crouched and armed. Then Derek points in the other direction, and Daniel sees another man in the same position. Derek lets loose something of a half-whistle, and the arm of the figure on the left juts forward with something resembling a salute.

Beneath the exit sign, Terry pushes hard on a set of double doors. They part wide and moan softly. Daniel follows through the gap, Derek right behind him. On the other side, dim little emergency lights, affixed to the top of both walls, shine just enough to reveal a heavier door on the right. When Terry knocks on it, a metal clang shoots through the door and around the passageway.

A small, muffled voice emerges through the door. "Password?"

it says.

"Brian is a fucking queer." Terry grins.

There's a pause. Then, the voice says, "That's not the password."

"How about, if you don't open this fucking door—"

"All fall down," says Derek, leaning in.

A latch clicks, and then the door opens, revealing a small plateau illuminated in dull red. The top of a skinny staircase hides right behind it. A twenty-some blonde guy in a green shirt holds the door back against the wall as Terry, Daniel, and Derek pass through. The blonde guy is very tall, and so skinny he looks almost anorexic. He doesn't seem to have shaved in days.

"You're a bastard," says the guy.

As Terry's chuckle expands against the stone walls, as the tall guy in the green shirt shuts the door again—the metal latch is much louder on this side—Derek, stepping into the lead, beckons Daniel down the stairway. The single flight of stairs leads to another door. This one opens easily with the twist of a knob. Derek steps aside to let Daniel in.

Immediately, Daniel is inundated by the sound of more voices than he's heard in one place in a very, very long time. In the massive, cavernous room, the entire length and width of the supermarket without the aisles around to clutter up the space, there are at least thirty men, some lying in bunk beds, a couple arm-wrestling, five sitting cross-legged in the corner playing poker. Their voices are indistinct, echoing like those around an indoor swimming pool. The walls are a cool, concrete gray. Descending lamps illuminate in strained, inconsistent fashion. A refrigerator hums out by the near wall. Daniel spots an office in the far corner, and a set of what look to be adjacent hallways, by which a couple men strap on goggles and grab a couple guns from a rack.

Every man here has only one ear.

On the left, Daniel catches his two-eared reflection on the mirror hanging from a nearby wall. The mirror marks the end of a much smaller alcove, wherein Daniel finds seven kids like him. A dark-haired kid in black shorts sits on one of the nine beds, tapping away on a PSP. Most of the others try to watch. All the kids have two ears.

"What do you think?" says Derek.

The kids, absorbed, don't seem to notice Daniel. No one does.

Too many voices make too much empty noise, joining with the drone of lights and the hum of the refrigerator. It's impossible to filter through the sounds and pick up even a single sentence or word that makes sense. It's a maze where someone's pulled out the walls—a maze where the end is so easy to find, no one even wants to look for it.

"There's someone I want you to meet," says Derek. He grabs hold of Daniel's hand and pulls him into the main room, navigating through a sea of Listeners. They begin to notice him now. A Noah's Ark of eyes begin to land on him, *two by two by two*, as his feet tap against the floor. That's where Daniel stares, until the grip Daniel has on his hand brings the feet to a halt.

"Adam," says Derek.

Very slowly, Daniel cranes his neck upward. A man in his thirties stares down at him, smiling brightly above a slight paunch and beneath a head of curly red hair. When he smiles, it's from ear to ear—ear to ear because, like Daniel, like the kids, but entirely unlike the other adults, he *does* have two.

"Ah," says Adam.

"This is Daniel."

As Derek smiles, Adam shakes Daniel's hand. Daniel offers no resistance.

"A pleasure, Daniel," says Adam. He squeezes Daniel's hand just a little too tightly. "There's a home for you here."

~~~~~~~

The room may be huge, but it's still mostly a simple room, and it doesn't take all that long to get settled in. Port-o-potty's in the corner. (We call it "Shit Creek.") Your bed's here, with the other kids, right next to Zeke's. Hey, Zeke. This is Daniel. Etc. etc. And then Daniel sits on a bed too stiff and too off-white, eating from a bag of Doritos and sipping a welcome-to-the-Listeners Coke while staring into the blank wall and trying to see through it, outside and along the same roads they traveled and all the way back home, where the broken window isn't really all that bad when you think about it. Maybe he can fix it. He got an A in Tech Ed.

The gray walls remind him of a garage, the kind where your

bare feet turn to ice as they pit-pat across the rough and dusty floor. Without any windows, and with the generator humming loudly—Daniel can hear it, but no one else seems to notice it—it might as well be winter, even if it's nearly summer. He shivers.

For a moment, he imagines what this place would really be like in the winter—this whole place, this city. The sky is a ghostly white, the piling snow covers the ground uninterrupted by footsteps or snowplows or salt, and the only people around to brave the cold, the only people with the guts to go out there, are too sick to know any better. Instead of curling up on the couch with Mom or dodging pillow strikes from Katie, Daniel squeezes back onto an ice-cold brick wall, the mist rising from his hyperventilating lungs, while a bunch of one-eared men he doesn't know ignore him. The snow piles high, he can't leave, the food is almost gone, and his home of TV white noise and soggy cereal and his room with the lock that doesn't work are so far away he can't even remember them, buried as they are under little flakes of white and red fluttering in through the broken window.

"Hey, Daniel," someone says. Daniel turns. Zeke, the scrawny black-haired kid playing with the PSP earlier, pulls a comic book from underneath a pillow and slumps down on the bed beside the one on which Daniel sits. With a slight flip of the wrist, Zeke nudges the comic forward. "Want it?" he says.

Daniel glances at the book. It's *Uncanny X-Men*.

"Have any *Daredevil*?" says Daniel.

"Probably, upstairs," says Zeke. "There's a spinner rack." Daniel starts to get up, but Zeke grabs his shoulder. "No, man, you don't go up alone. You gotta ask one of the Listeners, and only when they're already going up, okay? Gotta do it at night so *they* can't see you through the windows."

"Oh." Daniel looks down at his shoes. He imagines his toes are cold.

"What's it like out there?" says Zeke.

Quiet. And empty. "I don't know," says Daniel.

"Haven't been out there for, like, two weeks," says Zeke. "You don't get to go out till you can listen right."

Daniel looks at him. Zeke wiggles his right ear.

At that, Daniel's eyes drift down toward the cover of the comic.

He wonders if it's a one-part story or if it's only part two or three of four or five. Then he might never know how it ends.

"You see any of 'em?" says Zeke.

"What?"

"Sickos." With a grin, Zeke scratches a little cut beneath his ear. "See any sickos out there?"

"Yeah," says Daniel, even though he's never heard them called *sickos* before. "Two." Both dead now. One tried to kill him. In the back of his mind, a shot rings out, a window shatters, and razor-sharp glass cuts into his open hand.

"Me, too. One of 'em killed the other one." Zeke nods. "Then Adam saved me." Zeke looks at Daniel. "Did you meet Adam yet?"

Daniel nods.

"He's so cool," says Zeke. "He's our dad."

Daniel doesn't have a dad—just the memory of a tall, featureless man who disappeared a few months after Daniel was four. Maybe he looked like Katie's dad, even if he didn't act like him. As Daniel spots Adam speaking with Derek and some other Listener far across the basement, he tries to fit him into the ambiguous shape he remembers, but it's an awkward fit at best.

Eleven o'clock is lights-out. Without a window, and with only a few dim emergency lights leading to the stairwell, there's no such thing as sight, but that's okay as long as they can hear. Daniel, though, can't hear, not above the breathing and the snoring and all those creaking beds. There's supposed to be an alarm clock to his right. There's *always* an alarm clock to his right, and it always goes off at exactly 7:10, so he can get up at just the right time and stumble, half-asleep and only wearing underwear, into the shower. Then he turns the faucet, really fast so none of that first-early-morning-shower ice water gets in, and he lets the hot water, the *real deal*, hit against his face and fly off in a mist.

He uses soap. He *always* uses soap. Mom always buys the store brand, and it's too light and breaks apart really easily, but it still gets him clean, even though it smells kind of like chalk. He puts shampoo—the green kind—in his hair. Then he gets out and dries off and puts his underwear back on, and brushes his teeth, always in that order. When he gets back to his room, it's 7:32. It's almost always 7:32. He times it, and the numbers are there in big bold red.

Then he puts on his shirt and the same pants he wore yesterday, and he goes into the kitchen, where Mom is sticking in an earring and taking off a necklace and putting it on and taking it off and saying, "Come on, come on, it's time to go," as if he's the one moving slow. He pours himself a bowl of Cheerios with some milk, as much as he can put in, until every little O is completely drenched. Then he eats it all as fast as he can—four minutes is the best he's ever done, not counting drinking the rest of the milk out of the bowl, but that only takes a few seconds.

His mom drives him to school. She *always* drives him to school, every weekday, and the traffic is a mess because there are so many cars and don't they know how to *drive*, Mom says, honking the horn in the car, which she always parked on the curb, which is back there even right now on the wrong side the building, and he's never going to see it again . . .

It was right there! It was so close. It was there in the light and the sun, and here in this pit, this prison, this underground bunker of one-eared men with guns guarded by armed sentries at the doors, with a supermarket up above and miles and miles of distance from here to there, that one car, that Volvo with the slightly cracked windshield and the right passenger window that won't roll down all the way, is so far away he can't even imagine it, much less see it.

But it could be a dream. It could be in his head. Once, he had a dream where he was stuck on a hot air balloon for three months, living on the jelly and bread he'd packed in a picnic basket before the balloon flew away. And it felt like three months, even though it was only a few minutes, so these three weeks, these . . . damn . . . three weeks, they *could* be . . . it's *possible* . . . and in just a few minutes, or any second now, that phantom beeping will break into his head, and his eyes will open.

It'll be 7:10. Like always.

He'll stumble to the shower. Like always.

He'll feel hot water and use chalky soap. Like always.

And as the water rushes down his body and drip-drops to the floor, the dream will fall down with it, swirling and sloshing at the bottom of the tub before the whirlpool pulls it down into the pipes.

Because you don't remember your dreams.

Please don't. Please don't.

Wait for it.

Listen.

"Beep," whispers Daniel, very very quietly. It's so quiet that maybe he's not making a sound at all. "Beep, beep, beep, beep . . ." He closes his fists. His nails dig into his skin, and his eyes shut hard. "Beep, beep, beep, beep," he whispers, his lips opening just a tiny bit to let the words out.

"Beep, beep, beep"—squeezing the tears, gripping the covers—"beep, beep, beep"—arching back, ramming the pillow—"beep, beep, beep"—pushing his eyes shut so hard that only sunlight, the sunlight through his window at 7:10, can get through.

Transition

These are things that happened in the days following the initial quarantine.

First thing: A five-block buffer zone was established between the thin strip of land leading into the borough and the rest of the city, and all city residents from those areas were evacuated safely. The evacuation was mandatory. Business owners complained, but they stopped for the most part when military officers stormed the buffer zone and threatened to shoot them.

Second thing: City residents were advised to stay out of the buffer zone and not to re-enter for any reason, under any circumstances. Business as usual continued beyond the buffer zone.

Third thing: World religious leaders advised believers to start praying to God very, very hard.

(All this was reported on the news. You probably read about it.)

First Respite

The Apocalypse Is Here

You ever see those guys, holding up signs at the side of the road when you're trying to speed through downtown traffic to make it to the office somewhere near on time? Those homeless guys in a Salvation Army grab bag with the kind of frantic stare that makes you think they're looking right at you, and only at you? *The Apocalypse is here!* Nuts, right?

Ha-ha! I used to think so too, you know, and I even remember throwing a coffee cup at one of them when he didn't get off the road fast enough once the light changed. (The cup was empty.) And I drove right on by and I never thought anything of it, but lately I think, we really should.

You really should.

See, they seem nuts, but let's look at them a different way. Let's look at them logically, like a businessman. These are guys out on the street, no job, no way to get food, and what do they do? Do they beg? Are they asking for work or cigarettes or food or whatever it is you expect the homeless to ask for? No, they don't do any of that— they just stand by the road with a sign that can't help them in any way, at least not obviously. So why do they do it? They do it to *warn* you. They see what's coming, and this is the only way they can let you know in time, and maybe get themselves some redemption in the process.

I'll tell you, every guy with a sign on the side of the road has something he's got to make up for—sometimes something big, sometimes something small, or lots of somethings small. They've all got a story.

Mine starts about two months ago, up on the twenty-second

floor of the Bentford Towers, which is really just one tower. Of course, anyone who's taken the tour knows how Bentford went bankrupt before he could finance the other two that were supposed to be built. This was in the 1970s, I think. The tour groups never bothered us, so I never really heard much about it.

But anyway, the twenty-second floor is Xavier Advertising. You know Xavier Advertising. Well, okay, maybe you don't. It's easier for me because I'm in the business. I've gotten pretty good at listening to ads on the radio or watching them on TV and figuring out who did them, just based on the little things: the flow of the words (ReWind always goes with this descending dactylic structure), the order of testimonial to straightforward advertisement (I always like the ad wedged in-between actors pretending to be customers, but that's not how Public does it), and the kind of comedy (we're always big on puns, which I don't like, but Mike loves puns).

You've heard our ads—StayClear Antiperspirant, for example. You probably use it, but that slogan? "Stay smooth, StayClear"? I wrote that. I liked that one. Mike gave me a five percent raise for it.

Oh, but that's not the point. This was, I think, a Tuesday, and I'd just gotten into my office up on the twenty-second floor. It's not the best view, basically a straight shot of the slightly taller Fillmore building, but it's a nice office, and it's in a corner, and sometimes at around three in the afternoon, the sun bounces right off the Fillmore and into my office, and the blinds make this really neat visual near the door, a bunch of white and black lines, light and shadow, like a good kind of prison. I think it'd be a great visual for an ad, but I don't know for what product.

I'd just gotten into my office, and I'd dropped my briefcase on my desk, and put my jacket on the coat hanger, with the sleeves knotted around a second hook so it wouldn't fall off, when Mike walked in, without knocking or anything. I like the guy, but he's always been rude that way, and I hope he realizes it's important to knock when the horsemen come. But he was kind of distracted, so it's okay, I guess. I try to forgive people now.

"Hey, you hear?" is the first thing he said—not a "hello" or a "how are you" or anything, which doesn't show respect, and I'm pretty sure God doesn't like that. Anyway, I hadn't heard and didn't know what he was talking about, and he said that the whole city past

Crawford was quarantined—that whole borough—and that everyone for almost five blocks past there was being evacuated, which I guess is something I would have heard if I'd been listening to the radio instead of a Queen album. (I don't like listening to the radio in my own time. It's too much like work.)

And my first thought was, that's a lot of lost print advertising, which definitely wasn't right, but that's who I was then. I wasn't a bad guy, but I probably wasn't good enough, which is why I had to be more proactive.

The Apocalypse is here! The Apocalypse is here!

I don't want you to forget.

So the quarantine was really bad news, but the worse news was, Fox lived inside the quarantine. He'd called in this morning and said he wouldn't be able to make it into work until they let him out of the borough, which he said might not happen for a couple weeks. He actually lives down there, only about ten minutes away by car on a good traffic day, but there really aren't any of those.

Fox being stuck is the part I was really worried about. He used to be a car salesman and got really good at knowing what people have to hear to buy something, and I'm good at writing it up, so we work as a team for a lot of things. I have to admit it—he's the one who suggested "smooth" for the StayClear ad (I was going to say "dry"), because even though it doesn't make much sense for antiperspirant, he knew people would find it appealing and wouldn't think about it much. We'd worked on a lot of different ads and even written a couple jingles (he could write a decent melody if he had to), so he was a pretty good friend, and it was going to be tough to keep on producing without him for a couple weeks.

Especially after last week.

See, last week, he'd been out sick and I'd gone over to his computer to find the notes we'd written up for Mydosol, which is one of those drugs we had to sell without being able to say what exactly it does or who it's meant to help. (I like those. They're fun challenges.) I couldn't find the notes, and I wondered if he'd e-mailed them to me. Anyway, long story short, I got curious and went through his inbox, and found a couple messages with some computer tech guy he was working with to smuggle some money out of the company. A little off the top of our profits, month in and month out, and he'd been doing this for a couple years now, almost since he'd joined Xavier. Now, this was pretty surprising, because I had no idea, and I'm pretty smart. Mike clearly didn't know, either, but he isn't.

So, naturally, when he came in the next day, I called Fox on it, and confronted him, and told him he was taking money away from all of us. And that was bad, you know, in a moral kind of way.

I should make this clear now: I've never been a religious kind of guy, per se, but I always believed in God and Jesus and that kind of stuff. I went to church a few times a year, but the whole thing never really grabbed my interest as much as it should, except one time when the pastor was delivering a sermon and I realized a sermon would be a really funny way to advertise a sale at Pat's.

But when I found out about this quarantine, and how Fox was stuck in it, and so soon after all the stuff with the stolen money, I had to wonder, was this God's response? Was he punishing Fox for the theft, which, again, is definitely wrong according to the Bible? It made sense—after all, he'd decided to keep fifty percent of the stolen money, and I was only keeping ten for staying quiet. (The computer guy got forty.)

I still don't think I would have made the connection between the quarantine and sin if it wasn't for all the pundits I heard talking about it that way on the news. One of those big-name big-congregation preachers, Paul something or other (I don't think he's the same denomination as I am), was on one of those Fox News shows (not about Fox, that's just a coincidence) going on about how a plague is one of the signs of the Apocalypse, and how the people inside the quarantine, who, apparently, still had cable TV, should repent before the end. And he wasn't the only one: I also heard it reported that the Pope hadn't ruled out God's wrath as a possibility, and some other things I can't remember.

(I'm not supposed to listen to the Pope, I know—I'm not Catholic—but it's the same God, I figure. Especially now.)

So I decided to visit the pastor, whose name is Lawrence, sometime during the week, just to ask a few questions. I knew he came in on weekdays, because it was on weekdays that I used to go to those anger management classes, which he ran. (Some court-appointed thing—I got a little mad when the girl at the desk at a hotel in Reno dropped an important call from Mike, and I grabbed the neck of her shirt, you know, just to make a point. I overreacted, I admit it.) I used to wonder what Lawrence did on the weekdays, but even before the classes, I realized, logically, there's no way you can make a living on a one-day-a-week job, and even if you could, you'd be bored as hell, so the guy was probably in during the week for private meetings or sermon-writing, the other things God people do. (Preaching should be a daily thing, but I didn't realize that then.)

He had a bit of trouble recognizing me—I'd shaved the beard and tried to smile a lot more—so I had to remind him of my name, which is Saul. "Nice biblical name," he said, and I'd forgotten that there's a Bible Saul, too. I wondered if my parents knew that. Anyway, I asked him about the quarantine, and I told him about Fox—not about the money, though. I didn't want to get him into trouble. I just said Fox had maybe done something that would be a sin, and I left it at that. And Lawrence said lots of people had been in asking about the quarantine, and he was planning to talk about it in his sermon on Sunday, and I should come. It had only been a little over a month since the last time I went to church, but these, I guessed, were probably special circumstances.

"It's possible," he said, when I pressed him about whether this plague, the sickness everyone was getting, could be a God thing. "Calm down. There are lots of natural things in the world, natural phenomena," the pastor said, "but behind all of it is God, His law, His way. The world is guided by Him. Good and bad. Everything has its reason." So it made sense, then, that God could be punishing Fox, and that was enough to get me a little nervous, given this is the first big thing that's affected someone close to me. And when you really think about it, the quarantine was just ten minutes away, so this was really, *really* close to me, especially on Godly global terms.

I also asked Lawrence if this could be more than just a punishment and genuinely the Apocalypse. And he grinned and put his hand on my shoulder and said, "We're not finished yet," which he meant as a no. That came as something of a relief, and I thanked him and left.

But on my way back to the office, I thought, how would he know? Like any preacher or pastor or reverend or whatever, this is someone who talked to God every day, and who did good every day. How would he know if too many people were being bad, and if most people were evil, and if the world had gotten so horrible and sinful that it really was about to end? I didn't remember that much about the specifics of the Apocalypse, and I probably should have asked him while I was there, but what I remembered was something about the world becoming hell, or hellish, while the good people were whisked away to heaven.

So I thought about it logically. Inside the quarantine, people were getting sick, and dying, and killing before they died. The news reported on this. People were moving far away from the quarantine because they didn't want to catch the disease.

Isn't that hell on Earth? People stuck inside their homes, not able to go outside without catching some lethal virus?

And pestilence was definitely one of the four horsemen of the Apocalypse, I knew that much. (Did they actually come on horses, or was that just a metaphor?) A really contagious plague like the one killing people in the quarantine definitely counted as pestilence, and I think another of the horsemen was death, which was clearly also happening. But then again, the others weren't (I thought), and, also logically, it couldn't be the Apocalypse if the quarantine was going to be over in a couple weeks, at most. It was just a scare. A warning. I'd go to church and be a better person and Fox would be fine once the disease was cleared out. And that's the end of that.

Still, the whole thing got me kind of nervous, so when I got back to my apartment, I opened one of the boxes that was still taped shut from the move and dug around for the Bible, which Lawrence had given to everyone during the class. I found it near the bottom, next to a 45 of *Sheer Heart Attack* and above an old *Hustler*, which I'd kept for the novelty, really, because it came out the month I was born. The Bible was surprisingly thin and lightweight, and I appreciated that, because it takes a lot of talent and skill and energy to get your message out there in a short timeframe. Very efficient. God was like an ad exec. But when I opened it up, I saw the type was tiny, and the pages were so skinny they might as well be tissue paper, so maybe it wasn't that efficient after all. Couldn't be, really, given that a pastor like Lawrence could preach a whole year and still not get through the damn thing.

I flipped through the pages and tried to find something about sin and the Apocalypse, and it took me five minutes because it was buried right at the back. Always the last place you look. I tried to scan through it, but the language was all "hath" and "overcometh" and that kind of archaic language, which strikes me as a waste of time, because religion shouldn't just be for liberal arts Shakespearean scholar-types. It should be for anyone who wants to appreciate God. Limiting your audience is just bad marketing. I wanted information, and the book was making it hard, so I threw it against the wall, where it left a tiny mark right below the window.

I crawled over to the window and picked up the Bible. I'd been to a friend's kid's Bar Mitzvah once and they kissed their bible, so I did that. Didn't mean any harm—I was just scared, I guess. We all were. I hadn't done anything wrong, at least not seriously wrong on heaven-hell terms, and besides, this would pass. I put the Bible away.

I nearly forgot about all that God stuff, until about two weeks after, which is the longest Fox and the news had said the quarantine was likely to last. Mike had Fox calling in every day so we knew he was all right and safe and working on some great new ad ideas he'd share with me as soon as he got back. (You can't write together over the phone. You've got to be in the same room. It's all about chemistry.) That was pretty smart of him, and it meant we didn't have to just sit there and worry about what was going to happen to the guy, because we knew right from his mouth. The phones stayed up, which, if I'd still been thinking about it, would have made me more sure this wasn't the end, because you have to imagine you wouldn't be able to phone people during the Apocalypse. There'd be interference or something.

Anyway, after two weeks, Fox stopped calling. He'd called the last few days, and he was telling us about how the healthcare workers were leaving, and the quarantine wasn't likely to let up at all anytime soon. This was really frustrating, and I washed my hand in the sink (I'd punched the wall, which hurt) and I picked up the phone and asked if there was any way he could get back, and if there wasn't, if he could pitch me some of his ideas so we could get some kind of collaboration going, even if it wasn't ideal. I also asked him about the deal, which was code for the money (it's okay, I can talk about it, I gave it back), and the phone connection cut out before he could answer.

I don't know if that meant the phone lines were down or what, but the next day, he didn't call, and he didn't call the day after that, either. Mike spent a lot of time in his office, and I yelled at him and accused him of knowing something, but I'm not really sure what I meant. I was frustrated—it happens to the best of us. Maybe he couldn't call, or maybe he wasn't even around to call anymore. No more cameras were allowed anywhere near the quarantine, and no news was coming out of it, except from some *Tribune* columnist writing from the inside, although I never read her columns. Mike mentioned them.

I guess *her* phone worked.

So between the columns and the rumors, not to mention the quarantine itself, we all had to imagine things were pretty bad in there. The TV news kept rerunning the clips of sick people, tied down in hospital beds (exclusive footage from before the health-care workers evacuated), trying to hit or bite people. Their heads were all red and blotchy, but they weren't allowed to show that in detail on the news after the first time, because it was considered obscene. Someone posted the pictures on the internet.

Things were pretty bad, and they were *staying* pretty bad, and that's how I got to thinking about the Apocalypse again. I always think about things logically, and logically, if the doctors and nurses and disease people were leaving, that meant there was no cure, and not only that, but they were so far away from a cure that it didn't pay for them to stick around. So the disease was going to run its natural course, and nearly everyone inside the quarantine was going to die, Fox included.

And if they had to evacuate the five-block area immediately outside the actual quarantine, that had to mean they were worried about the virus spreading by air, which meant we could all be infected, and probably would, soon. There were rumors of sick people on the good side of the quarantine line, but nothing concrete. Just the same, it was only a matter of time, wasn't it? If this was a disease that couldn't be cured, it probably couldn't be stopped, either, so maybe the quarantine wasn't just a warning, and wasn't a punishment for the sinners on the other side. Maybe it was a sign of things to come. Maybe it was punishment for all of us.

The Apocalypse is here! The Apocalypse is here!

That's what I started to think, and on the drive to work the next day, I saw another one of those homeless guys with a sign that said exactly that. Actually, it said "The end is nigh." That's need-lessly confusing, I think, because we don't use the word "nigh" and most people don't know what it means, so I simplified the message. The Apocalypse is here . . . but I wasn't sure just yet. The evidence seemed to point that way, and no one had any other good explana-tion for the plague, but I still didn't know if it was definitely the case, and even if it was, what should I do about it?

I didn't go to work and, instead, drove down to the church, where I found Lawrence talking to some guy in a stupid jacket. I asked him if he was sure this wasn't the Apocalypse, and he said he couldn't talk now, which was, I think, totally insensitive, given how clearly nervous I was, and how my collaborator and friend was prob-ably dead, but he insisted I wait outside. Total lack of urgency. Some people need actual help.

But while I was waiting, it occurred to me that maybe he was angry because he was nervous too. I can relate; I'm generally pretty even-tempered, but if I'm worried about something, I can get a bit heated, even a little bit unreasonable. And why would he be ner-vous? He'd be nervous, I think, for the same reason I was nervous, because really, what was bigger than the plague? What was more deadly and more nearby than the plague? And then I took it a step further and realized, weren't lots of people acting strangely? Panic was reported on the news, and I'd heard a couple of guys at work talking about actual shooting going on around the quarantine; you could hear it if you got close enough.

So I left the church, got back into my car, and took stock of things, which is a logical thing to do. What, I thought, did I know? I knew there was a deadly plague killing people on the other side of a massive quarantine. Everyone knew that. I knew that covered pestilence and death, and probably also famine soon. War (I'd found out online the fourth horseman is war) was trickier, but I thought of what happens when people panic after earthquakes or blackouts and that kind of thing, when people start rioting and hurting one another, and I guessed that, too, could be happening inside the borough.

So, four for four. What else? The disease couldn't be stopped. Fox was in there, and he'd definitely sinned. Everyone would be in serious danger if the disease got out. People were panicking, and people were nervous, including one guy who had a direct route to God.

Then I remembered the homeless people and the signs, like the one that had brought me here. What if they knew? What if they'd known all along, and this is what they were warning us about? For the first time, I saw the homeless men as part of a grassroots advertising campaign, bringing the message directly to the people. It was a good idea, but it'd be better if people didn't think they were crazy. I'd always thought they were crazy.

I was wrong.

I realized then and there that it *was* the Apocalypse, and if it was, people had to be warned. People had to be saved. They had to know what was coming and change their lives so they'd have a chance of making it to heaven once the rest of the world became hell.

I was part of an advertising firm. I could help.

God would probably like it if I helped, but that's not why I did it.

By the time I got to work, it was a little bit before 11, which was late, of course, but late for a good reason. As it was, I'd made it just in time for the full staff meeting we held every morning. Mike grabbed my sleeve as I walked into the board room and asked why I was late to work, which under the circumstances was an entirely pointless thing to think about. I was late for work—hardly a big deal when the world is coming to an end and you have to get the word out.

But Mike was entirely focused on meaningless crap that day, standing up there like a sandbag in front of a tsunami. He was all "profits" this and "StayClear" that, and seemed a bit pissed off when I wasn't listening, but he did ask if there was something I had to say, which there was. When he said that, I leaned forward and clasped my hands like I always did when I was going to say something important, and I said, "I think we need to start a campaign to spread the word that the world is coming to an end."

Nobody responded to that immediately, and I realized I'd made a slight mistake—the rest of them didn't understand the situation yet. I'd spent so much time figuring it out for myself that I forgot I might have to convince the rest of the staff. "It's the Apocalypse," I clarified, but that didn't help, so I started to explain. "Let's look at it logically," I said, "like a businessman. Just a few miles from here, we have this—"

Mike, who can be a rude bastard sometimes, interrupted me, but I told him to shut up and continued. "We know the plague is God's way of punishing sinners," I said, "but how can we *tell* people? What's the most effective way to—"

Somebody asked if I was serious, which is a dumb question because it's obvious I was, but worse, it was another interruption, and you can't make a good pitch when someone's interrupting you. That's why you put commercials in the middle of music and not the other way around.

"It's a fact," I said, "that people are sick and dying over there, and we have a direct connection between that and sin, so this is damn fucking obvious and I can't believe we're *debating* this—"

"Saul—" Mike said.

"It's gotten one of us already, and we've all sinned like Fox did, so it'll spread and come for the rest of us if we don't . . ."

"Saul—"

". . . let people know and give them time to change their ways and beg forgiveness, and we need an ad campaign to tell them that, and I think we should use a jingle," I said.

Mike just looked at me for a while. It's really a jerk thing to stare. "Why is Fox a sinner?" Mike said.

"Because of the money we stole," I said.

And that's how I lost my job. In retrospect, it was probably a bad move, because I think I could have convinced the group to go ahead with my ad campaign. ("The Apocalypse is here" is catchy, and there are lots of things you can rhyme with "here," like "near," as in, "The quarantine is very, very near, and that's a sure sign the Apocalypse is here.") And I also shouldn't have said it, because it wasn't really true. I didn't steal the money. I just took ten percent for keeping quiet about it, which I didn't end up doing, so you could argue that I didn't do anything wrong at all. That's what I told Mike, but he was all moronic about it and told me he'd bring in the cops if I didn't give it all back immediately, to which I replied, of course, that I didn't have anything yet. So I just told him about the computer guy and left.

I no longer had Xavier to support my campaign, so I had to think up another approach. That's part of advertising, too, of course— attacking on multiple fronts. It's a well-managed military campaign, but I'd always done it using Xavier's resources, and it was going to be tough to find another front without my company. But I'm a smart guy, and I came up with something pretty quick.

WMPX had a morning radio show, pretty popular, called *Steve and the Man in the Morning*, which was largely paid for by our ads, so they owed us a couple favors. I was pretty sure Mike wouldn't go around telling everyone I'd been fired, so I called up Bartholomew (who goes by "Steve" on the air) and asked for a slot so I could send out a special message from Xavier.

It sounded all right by him, and I think it was a Friday morning, a couple of days after I'd lost my job, that I went into the studio. The Man (some little guy in sunglasses who refuses to be called anything else) led me into the studio, showed me to a little stool, and gave me these giant headphones, like in one of those booths at an amusement park where you record karaoke. We went on the air, and Bartholomew introduced me as "one of our good friends from Xavier Advertising," which was really nice of him. He's one of the good ones. He probably won't suffer in the Apocaylpse.

But anyway, I had the floor, so I gave my message. "With thousands of sinners stuck inside the quarantine," I said, "suffering from a plague that can't be cured or stopped, we all need to be aware: With the quarantine line so very very near, it's hard to deny the Apocalypse is here." I felt I made a much better case in the studio than I did before, and I'm sure someone out there was listening, but the producer, some bitch named Felicia, pulled me off the air. When I couldn't get on any other stations, I realized Mike had started telling people he'd fired me, which was really a lousy way to stay out of hell.

Square one is a lousy place to be in the middle of an ad campaign. Square one is when you have a product and no one knows about it. Square one is when the clients and product manufacturers are riding you the hardest, when you're under the most pressure to send something terribly clever through the airwaves or onto your customers' TV screens. God was the biggest client I'd ever had, and I didn't want to let him down, but there wasn't much I could do without the resources of my company.

I was trying to work out this problem at a bar one night, but I'd had a couple too many and wasn't thinking straight, besides which there was a very talkative guy next to me who seemed to have had quite a few more. He was shooting off a bunch of nonsense to the bartender about his girlfriend, all "breakup" this and "restraining order" that, and when he said "for Christ's sake," I found myself thinking about Lawrence, and preaching, and religion.

Lawrence, of course, was an awful preacher, couldn't even break off his damn pointless conversation to talk to me about the end of the world, but that was just it. I was angry because he didn't take the time to sit me down and look me in the eyes and tell me what I should do to make my life better, to make the world better, and to save as many people as I could when the quarantine broke down and its sickness and disease and death made its way past the borough and into the city. The jackass hadn't done any of that, but I could. He didn't have the message.

I did.

He doesn't know how to reach people.

I do.

So when the guy sitting next to me at the bar said something about tracking her down and "teaching her a lesson," I turned to him and said, "That won't help you when the horsemen come." (I wanted to make sure I was dramatic so I would get his attention.)

"Shut up," he said. That's a piece of crap thing to say to someone, especially when they're trying to help you.

"The end is near," I said, and I explained to him that we all had to be better people so that God would save us when He destroyed the world, and that any moron knew that.

"Mind your own fucking business," he said.

I tried to be more persuasive and, long story short, I found myself in a holding cell in a small neighborhood police station, a little dazed and a little bloody but otherwise all right—in the physical sense, anyway. But otherwise, I couldn't shake the feeling I hadn't helped that guy at the bar, and stuck in a cell, I couldn't help much of anyone at all.

But I wasn't alone. There was a black guy in the cell with me, maybe around thirty, and I didn't notice it at first because I was holding onto those gray bars, like if I held on long and tight enough I'd squeeze an answer out of them, but the guy was holding a Bible.

Some coincidence!

I asked him if he'd read it, and he said, no, he'd walked out of some gay pride meeting and a guy wearing a cross and a black hat gave it to him and called him a sinner. He'd gotten mad and punched the guy, and naturally that's a lot like why I was here, and I said so.

His name was Dew, and he seemed nervous, bouncing around on his bench, squeezing the Bible hard because he didn't know what else to do with it. So I thought, maybe I should give it another try. Maybe I should help him.

I told him that, as far as I knew, there was nothing wrong with being gay—I couldn't remember anything in the Bible about "thou shalt not be gay," definitely not in the parts I'd read—but he did have to try to become a better person, because the end was coming, and everyone had to repent.

He asked if I was a preacher. I said I was.

Since he didn't have anywhere else to go (though I think he'd have listened to me anyway), I laid out the whole argument I'd worked up, the one that kept getting interrupted everywhere else I tried to make it. And I wanted to be as convincing as possible, so I told him about Fox, too, and what he'd done to deserve God's wrath, and I thought it was an okay thing to talk about since the scheme hadn't worked, and Fox was dead, anyway. That was what happened to sinners—I saw that now, and I got Dew to see it, too, I think.

After just a few minutes of talking, I started to feel like someone else was listening in, and I was right. In the next cell down—I couldn't see anyone in it, but Dew said he saw a couple hands poking out—was, it turned out, the guy who'd punched me, the guy I'd kicked and hit with a mug. He wanted to know if it was really true—all the things I was saying.

I said it was.

The cell across from me had a homeless guy in it—an old man, dirty, a little smelly, but smelliness isn't a sin. He asked, is it really the end?

I said, "With the quarantine line so very, very near, it's hard to deny the Apocalypse is here."

They asked if there was anything they could do. And there was, of course. They could tell their friends, their family, and anyone else they could find. They could warn them to change their lives for the better, and in doing so fix their own lives, too. They could do anything in their power to remove sin from their lives so that, when God came, He wouldn't know they'd been sinful and would let them into heaven.

Dew asked what should be done, specifically.

"Be nicer to people," I said. The guy in the next cell suggested maybe I could try that, and I almost told him to shut the fuck up, but then I realized, maybe he was right. Maybe I did lose my temper a little sometimes. It couldn't hurt to be nicer to someone, which is why I've been so calm and cool in explaining all this to you.

I'm like that. I'm a better person now.

When they released me from the holding cell the next morning, I realized something: A preacher and an advertiser are really the same thing. They both have a message to get across and they both try to do it in the best, most effective way possible, to the widest audience possible. So with the end of the world coming, and with almost no one aware of it, I knew what I had to do.

I had to become God's ad man.

I also realized—and this is the thing to keep in mind when you start spreading the word—that people listened best when I was talking right to them. Dew, the angry guy, and the homeless man listened because I told them, calmly, what was coming, and now there were three more souls that would be saved. And I've got to assume that gives me bonus points with God.

But anyway, now I spread my message directly to the people. Some of the time, I walk along the street, pick people who look angry, or sad, or distressed, and talk to them. Most don't listen, but the important thing is that I try. The rest of the time, I walk along the street with my sign, which says, "The Apocalypse is here! The Apocalypse is here!" (I still use my jingle, but it's too long for people to read it on a sign.)

People think everybody on the side of the road is crazy—homeless guys in a Salvation Army grab bag—but they're homeless only because they're devoted. They're not crazy—they're spreading the word. The signs are everywhere. You can't miss them. So if you're still a sinner when the plague breaks free, then, frankly, you deserve what's coming.

With the quarantine so very, very near, it's hard to deny . . .

The Rift

Somehow, it's almost worse when Katie's mom looks up at Daniel. When Katie does it, she doesn't know what's going on. But her mom thinks she knows *exactly* what's going on, and when she looks up at Daniel and tries to meet his elusive eyes, she *blames* him. He's certain. But she doesn't truly understand, and Daniel feels bad for her. She doesn't understand how they saved him.

"Daniel?" says Katie's mom.

"What are you . . ." says Katie, trailing off as she spots what Daniel is hiding from her. It's not that he doesn't want her to see or know— it's that she won't understand the mark. She won't understand why he wears it proudly, because she's still a victim of the lies she was told. She doesn't know how to hear, and she won't understand why he does, and that's why he faces right, not left, and barely looks at her. It's the reason he keeps the right side of his face parallel to the busted door. But Katie is perceptive. She's always been perceptive.

And when she sees the flat white bandage covering the spot where his right ear used to be, she gets it. "Oh, God," she says.

"Katie, go to your room," says her mom.

"Don't go anywhere," says Derek, his gun still locked on Katie. "That's an order."

The eyes of the bearded man dart left toward Katie as he keeps his pistol trained tight on her mom.

But Katie ignores them both, staring unflinchingly at Daniel. "What are you *doing*, Danny? What happened? What—"

"Shut up!" yells Derek, his taut arm steady and straight, his finger brushing along the trigger. There's a ragged edge to his voice that Daniel's never heard before, something alien to the brother who saved him twice. And as soon as he says it, Derek turns to Daniel and opens his eyes wide, as if to say, "I'm sorry."

But of course he'd react that way, after everything they'd done to him. No one could go through that and not be angry. Still, as Daniel keeps his aimless eyes around the vicinity of the broken door, something in him trembles, and he knows exactly why: Katie is scared and confused, and Daniel doesn't want her to be.

Katie's mom trembles, too. Daniel's never seen her scared. He tries not to see her now, but as her outstretched fingers grasp strands of carpet, her arms shake and her eyes, seeing the gun aimed at her daughter, turn hard as steel.

"I want you to listen very carefully," says the bearded man. His name is Loren, and he tries to look Katie's mother right in those eyes. "When—"

"No," she says.

"When will your husband be home?"

"I don't have to tell you anything! I don't have to tell you anything!" she cries, and with that, she pushes herself forward and lunges at Loren, her stiffened fingers curved into claws, but Loren catches her arm and pushes her right back on her butt. Katie cries out.

"Hm," says Loren.

Daniel's M-1911 is limp at his side. The door is still open. It's so wide open it'll never be closed again. They could run right now, the both of them, he and Katie, but it wouldn't be in the same direction. Her mouth agape at the sight of her mother back on the floor, Katie doesn't know what's happened to the world out there. Maybe she watches the news, maybe she listens to the radio, but she doesn't know. If she knew, she wouldn't ask what Daniel is doing, or why. She'd know, and she'd know he's right.

But how do you tell your best friend who her father really is?

Loren glances at Derek, and Derek at Loren. "Get up," says Loren, pushing the barrel slightly closer to the woman on the ground. But she doesn't answer—she only stares at him with those cold, furious eyes, rocks gone molten. "Don't make this hard, huh?" Loren says, stepping forward and placing the barrel lightly against her cheek.

And now she moves. The fire fading, her arms trembling again, she starts to push herself to her feet. Grabbing her arm, Loren pulls her the rest of the way up. Katie's mom yells, "Let go of—"

Then the barrel of the gun is on her lips. "Shhh," says Loren.

Meanwhile, Derek glances slightly away from Katie, his arm still straight and his body, as always, alert. He turns to Daniel, who's done everything he can not to watch this, but failed. With his free left hand, he pats Daniel's shoulder and says, so quietly only Daniel can hear, "You can do this."

The rest of the message is in his eyes. Daniel can hear it—now that he knows how to listen. *We have to do this. I know it's hard. I hate it too. But it will all be all right in the end. You know it will.* And Daniel does.

As Katie's mom, pushed by Loren, moves toward the right hallway, she manages one parting glance at Daniel and catches him unawares; eyes meet, something hollow and endless in hers that Daniel can't turn away from. It cuts through him like a knock in a silent room, a cold "How could you?" blowing out the air vents. Derek lowers his gun and follows Loren. Loren glances back Daniel's way and says, "Girl's all yours." Katie's mom is finally out of sight, but when Daniel blinks, he sees her still.

He rubs his arms to push the goose bumps back down, and he does everything he can not to blink. In a moment, the only people in the room are Daniel and Katie, the best of best friends, joyously reunited, except even further apart than when Daniel was trapped in his apartment. He wants to tell her. Her gaze is unyielding, and he wants to answer the question, the why, like a prisoner trying to negotiate a plea during a police interrogation, but it's such a long way from there to here he's terrified Katie will never understand. He examines the floor, he studies the walls, and he says, "Let's go to your room, Katie."

"Danny!" says Katie.

"Please," says Daniel. For the first time, he looks up at her and meets that gaze, that question. It's like when one of them, usually Katie, would say something so off-the-wall that a silent stare-down was the only response. But actually not like that at all.

He wants so badly for her to hit him with a pillow that he can't breathe. Right in the stomach. Take that. He wants to retaliate. He wants to see a movie and make up stories and kick her butt in one-on-one soccer and he wants, oh God oh God he wants the context to be any other context but this. When Katie breaks their gaze, when she turns around and leads Daniel toward her room, he almost jumps on her back, and she almost laughs, and all he's trying to do is save her and all of them and, if she only knew that, she would understand she would she *would* oh God she would.

Soldiers of Destiny

Morning comes, but the sun does not.

There was a dream, but there's nothing to wash it away, so it dries and cracks into little bits. Daniel awakes and feels them on his body, these brittle paint chips, and with his eyes only half-open, he brushes them off his legs.

He gets up slowly, and sits on the side of the bed someone called his, head leaning down, hands lying on his skinny bare legs, white and pale.

The floor is cold. His bare feet touched them.

Stupid.

∿∿∿∿∿

The microwaved pancakes are all right, but the sausage patties are awful. When Daniel attempts a bite, his taste buds rebel, and the too-old chunk of ground meat falls back into a sea of syrup.

"Hey," says someone.

Glancing upward, Daniel sees a Listener with a long, chubby face and a too-small black t-shirt. As Daniel's fork prods the outline of the pancakes, the man points at Daniel with one finger and says, "You are Daniel."

"Yeah," says Daniel.

"Quentin," says the man. Daniel takes another bite of pancake, and as he does, Quentin takes a seat next to him on Daniel's bed. The legs of the bed scrape slightly against the cement floor. "Hey," says Quentin, "you know the secret to dealing with the microwaved sausage?"

Daniel doesn't. He just stares.

"Purge," says Quentin. "I'm kidding. Joke. But seriously, drown it in syrup and it almost tastes like food."

Daniel stares at the half-chewed piece of sausage skeptically. He wishes they had Cheerios down here, and he misses milk. Maybe he'll ask Derek later if he can go upstairs and get some.

"Zeke was pretty freaked out his first few days, too," says Quentin. "So I'll tell you what I told him. It won't be like this forever. When we save this place from the cops, when we set the borough free, when the plague dies down, we'll make this a better world for everyone. And with a better world"—he points to Daniel's plate—"comes better sausage." Quentin stares ahead blankly for a moment as if he's imagining it. Then, he pushes himself up off Daniel's bed and spins around, walking backwards into the further reaches of the alcove. "We're all in this together," he says, pointing both fingers Daniel's way. "Daniel." Daniel watches Quentin turn around again and high-five Zeke.

Daniel takes a bite of pancake.

What it feels like, strangely enough, is a math problem, with variables. It's hard to make sense of it otherwise—the series of numbers and letters. What can *M-1911* mean, all grouped together like that? And how is it that the equal sign is followed by an angular silver pistol? What kind of variable is that?

"This is an M-1911 pistol," Loren had said. His beard was trimmed close to his face, and somehow it made his eyes seem small—small, but focused, as they passed from two-eared kid to two-eared kid. "Standard issue." His voice was commanding, and when he held the pistol in his hand, it looked not like some variable, but like the absolute answer.

But now, in Daniel's hand, the gun is heavy and hard, like a rough, gray stone, and even touching it feels as if he's betraying Katie, and her dad, who first taught them about guns six years ago, and again at least three straight years after that, until he was absolutely sure they got it. Wrapped around the handle of an M-1911, Daniel's hands are liars. Traitors.

It's not like that for Zeke. His fingers wrap around his Berretta perfectly, and when he fires down the hallway that is not a hallway—the hallway that is, in fact, a firing range—the bullet goes where he wants it to go. His arms are straight and confident, and his eyes never move from the target at the back of the hall. Daniel wants to look anywhere but there.

At the back of this makeshift firing range, a long piece of yellow construction paper hangs from an old greenish mattress. On the paper, someone's drawn, in black marker, the outline of a man with a big red dot on his forehead.

"That is a sicko," Loren had said. It's the same word Zeke had used, and it sounds to Daniel like a carnival attraction. *Sicko the Clown. The Amazing Sicko and the Ring of Fire.* He imagines some perverted big-top where the colors are sharp red, the tent implodes, and Daniel's the only attraction—come see the freak, the amazing two-eared boy, the sideshow attraction who can't even hold a gun right.

In fact, Daniel hid from the gun at first, kneeling down in the far left of the group behind a big kid named Pip, or something strange like that, while Loren waved the gun, the math problem, the "M-1911 pistol standard issue," in the air before him. "There is no cure. There is no treatment. And if you go out there, they *will* try to kill you. They will try to *kill* you."

Daniel remembered a red-faced, stiff-limbed man with a gun all his own, a million pieces of shattered glass on the floor and one in the hand, and a breeze that wouldn't go away.

"You need to know how to defend yourselves," Loren said. "Against the sickos or anyone who tries to hurt you. If there is *any* sign of infection, even a single boil, you must fire—!" Then Loren spun around and fired one piercing shot down the middle firing lane, and a small hole instantly appeared in the chest of that crude construction paper outline. In Daniel's mind, it bled, imaginary drops of red rolling down the paper like drops of water along the rim of a bathtub, dripping down and pooling on the floor.

Now, Daniel grips the gun with both his shaking hands, and flinches every time a shot rings out. Loren's words sound and resound in Daniel's scared-as-shit little mind: "It's got to be instinct. It's got to be perfect or you'll never survive out there."

"Shoulder," mutters Zeke, standing next to him, aiming carefully.

Daniel's skinny hands shake. The gun tilts badly. The construction paper person breathes. "We're all in this together," it whispers.

Then Daniel kills it.

Throughout the day, the boys take turns on the firing range. Daniel's shots are accurate. Loren says he's a natural. At night, Derek takes Daniel up into the supermarket, where they walk slowly down the center aisle. Daniel holds a green plastic basket—a rolling cart would make too much noise—while Derek squeezes a dim pocket flashlight, blocking the light with his left hand so it doesn't shine through to the outside.

"No one knows why it's happening," says Derek, tossing a bag of Cheetos into the basket. "Loren thinks it's terrorists. Terry's sure it's a government conspiracy." His hand stops on a big red bag of chips. "Barbecue?" he says.

"I don't like barbecue," says Daniel.

"What do you like?"

"Salt and vinegar."

"Seriously?" Derek shrugs, then reaches up to the next level. "To each his own." He grabs a bag of salt and vinegar chips and flips it into the basket.

Derek is nice. This place is cold all the time, and the cold sits in Daniel's stomach like he's swallowed a giant ice cube that won't melt, but Derek looks him in the eyes and puts a hand on his shoulder, and for a second, it's like the cold isn't there, or at least not so much. For a second, he can hear the beeping of a distant alarm clock, and for a second, he can choose to ignore it. Then Daniel thinks of his dad. It doesn't happen often. He remembers only a few things, like the time Dad brought home a bouncy ball and threw it as hard as he could against the back wall. It bounced through the kitchen and right into his mom's Diet Coke, which spilled all over the new floor.

But Daniel doesn't remember his face. Just someone bigger than him.

"Anyway, whatever it is," says Derek, "it's got us trapped like rats on this island. And the people on the outside—they'll never be able to prove, one hundred percent, that it's gone. They'll *never* let us out. So the question is, how do we react?"

He had two ears, though. Daniel remembers that much.

Derek examines a bag of pretzels. "The thing about Adam, Daniel?" he says. "He's a *prophet*. The plague, the quarantine, the tyranny of the cops—he saw all of it coming. And he built this place, the compound"—he points to the floor—"so we'd be protected when it all happened. And he had us prepare for it."

The word "prophet" is big and wide. You have to listen pretty hard to hear God. Daniel thinks of the basement, all those one-eared men in close, uncomfortable quarters, eating microwaved sausage and going to the bathroom in a place called *shit creek*, and tries to reconcile that with Adam the prophet.

"What did you do?" says Daniel.

"Hm?"

"To prepare," Daniel says. "I mean, Katie . . . what she said you guys did . . . her dad's a police officer, and she said he said—"

"Listen, Daniel," says Derek, kneeling down by Daniel, switching the flashlight to the other hand and blocking the light. "I'm not going to deny we did some things," he says. "You know that. But we did what we had to, to survive in the world to come."

Derek looks him in the eyes. He always looks him in the eyes. But when he says the Listeners did "some things," he includes himself, and Daniel finds himself imagining everything those things might be.

"But you've got to understand," says Derek. "The cops?" He looks to the outside, toward the window, where Daniel can just barely make out a streetlight hovering over the parking lot. "*They're* the bad guys. Even Katie's father is a bad guy. Everyone trapped inside this borough is *reacting*, and *they're* reacting by terrifying people into submission. Filling their minds with half-explanations and quarter-truths . . ."

Daniel looks down toward the floor. Derek sighs.

"A couple of the guys checked out a house a few days ago, okay?" says Derek. "Adam keeps a police scanner on him. He heard about some kind of disturbance. Loren went, and he found this woman, young woman, handcuffed"—he grips his wrist to demonstrate— "to a furnace, crying her eyes out. Her boyfriend was knocked out on the floor, blood everywhere. The cops—they beat the man." He looks away. "And they raped the woman."

With that, Derek climbs to his feet, transfers the flashlight to his right hand, and starts scanning through the bags again. He pushes aside a bag of some chips Daniel can't identify.

"Why?" says Daniel.

Derek shrugs. "Power," he says. "But it's not theirs to have."

"It's yours?"

"It's everyone's," says Derek. "Equally."

Daniel glances right. "Why aren't there any girls?" he says. "I mean, if everything's equal—"

But Derek cuts him off with a laugh. "We're a brotherhood," he says, smiling. "That's the way Adam saw it. It's the way he knew it'd have to be. He *knew*. So it's not happpenstance that brings us here. It's design." He looks Daniel right in the eyes. "This is what we were made for. You know what that makes us?"

Daniel shakes his head.

"That makes us soldiers of destiny."

That's how the days go, and they *do* go, though day and night are indistinct when you almost never see the sun. In the mornings, sometimes they fire at the targets. Sometimes they work on their reflexes. Sometimes they practice striking as a unit—Terry's in charge of that one, teaching military hand signals, and how to get out the first and only shot while turning a corner. And sometimes the uninitiated just pass the time, playing Texas Hold'em while kneeled on both sides of a bed, their knees a little sore at the end of it but their time effectively killed. The first few times, Zeke invited Daniel to play, too, but the fourth time he stopped trying.

Instead, Daniel sits on his bed, reading the issue of *Daredevil* he found upstairs for the twenty-third time. He tries to pay attention to every single word, and imagines how the art would play out in real life, like a movie. That is, he tries to make the experience last as long as possible, because inside these walls, a long way from home, a longer way from Katie, and as far away from his mom as possible, time is all he has. He can never get to sleep at night, so he's always tired in the morning. And the thing of it is, he wants to sleep—more than ever, he wants to sleep, so he can dream forever, unrestrained by a beeping alarm clock. But it's not just the police and the *sickos* and Mom and Katie who can't find him down here—it's sleep. It's dreams. So maybe it's not those things that can't get in. Maybe it's Daniel who can't get out.

One evening, maybe, the Listeners pull a flat table, sort of like a dentist's chair, out into the middle of the bunker, and dim the lights very low. From a comfortable enough spot in the corner, Daniel watches them work. They place a little stool nearby and, atop it, a cup of something—Daniel doesn't see them pour it, but a red-haired Listener walks it over carefully, as if he's afraid it's going to spill. Everything is quiet as they work, unusually quiet, the way a church is quiet—where, if you make a single noise, close your book too loud or sniff too hard, you feel like all eyes will be on you.

It's worse when everyone listens this well.

Once it's all set up, the Listeners, still in silence, begin to gather around the table. Glancing to his right, Daniel sees the uninitiated follow suit, and he wonders how they know. A tall kid named Greg or something hits Zeke on the shoulder, and Zeke grins.

"You should see this."

When Daniel looks up, he finds Derek standing beside him. Derek head-gestures upward, and Daniel climbs to his feet. Although Derek tries to lead him into the crowd, it's already too thick to get a good view. Daniel doesn't know if he wants one. He's been hiding in the corner—yes, hiding and watching—but he can listen too, and he knows what this is.

"Initiation," whispers Derek as one of the other Listeners leads Zeke toward the table. It's Zeke who lies down upon it, and as he does, the door to the office opens, and Adam steps out, solemn and focused.

Father. Prophet.

The Listeners part like water for a wake, and for a half-second, there's just enough of an opening through the crowd for Daniel to make out a foot-long sheath held tightly in Adam's right hand. When Daniel glances up toward Derek, he finds him standing tall and smiling—just a little. Now the silence is nearly total—just scattered breathing and the slightest hums from the lights and the refrigerator. At first, Daniel sees nothing through the crowd, but then the sheath emerges overhead, held up to the light as Adam reveals what's underneath—a long, curved, and very, very sharp-looking knife. The knife catches the light and reflects it onto the dark ceiling.

Then he speaks.

"In a world that grows darker, always darker, louder, deafer . . ." His voice booms through the room like an organ's chord, filling every corner and every space, but *softly*. On pure instinct, Daniel steps back. Derek glances down.

"Why do you do it?" says Daniel, his voice flat and insignificant next to Adam's.

"Do what?" whispers Derek.

Daniel cups his right ear, and Derek releases an almost silent laugh.

"One ear, so that we may hear only the voices of our brothers," says Derek. "We filter out the lies"—he slices through his nonexistent right ear—"and hear only the truth."

"One ear, so that we may hear only the voices of our brothers," Adam booms.

Daniel looks at him. "But Adam has two ears," he says.

"Two ears," says Derek, "to protect us from those who wish us harm."

In the center of the crowd, Adam's raised knife looks so sharp Daniel expects the air to bleed. The knife shines in the lamplight. It hovers above Zeke, who's totally invisible through the crowd.

Derek's eyes turn back to the ceremony.

Daniel's close.

ᴧᴧᴧᴧᴧᴧ

At night, the children's alcove is one person fewer. One bed has been moved. Six kids, not seven, sleep. One by one, they all go away. One by one, the room will shrink. Daniel lays awake in bed, again, and wonders if someday he'll have this place all to himself. Or if he'll be next.

We're all in this together.

Slowly, so the bedsprings don't give him away, Daniel sits up, his bare feet smacking against the floor. He stands. He blinks. His heart pounds against his ribs so hard it hurts. Stepping forward, Daniel looks up at the mirror hanging on the wall, and yes, a mirror reveals little without light, but though Daniel may not be able to *hear* yet, he's learned how to see in the dark. It's easy when your eyes won't stay closed.

In the mirror, Daniel sees himself, in his underwear—the same underwear he wore yesterday, and the day before, and the day before that. They gave him another pair so this one could be washed, but he won't wear it. Daniel sees himself, thin and trembling, and he looks at his chest to see if he can actually see it bumping-thumping, but he can't. He *can* see his face, though, his wide-eyed face, mostly shadows in the bare illumination of emergency lights. He sees his eyes. His nose. His mouth.

His ears.

Daniel cups his right ear. His mirror-image cups his left.

And that's how it's going to be, isn't it? Isn't it? That's how it's going to be, once he's trained for a new life, but here's the problem: He wants the old one back. He wants the old one back more than he wants to breathe, and a hell of a lot more than he wants to hear. So he closes his eyes—closes them tight—and sees himself on his couch one weekend, watching TV with Katie. It never mattered what was on. A little flutter fills the corner of his eye, and a hint of a giggle fills his ear, but before Daniel can turn, the pillow has already hit his face, knocking his head back into the cushion. Climbing to her knees, Katie, still giggling, raises the pillow above her head again, and just as she's about to slam it down, and just as Daniel prepares to catch it and turn the tables, his eyes open on a smudged mirror in a desolately lonely place. They never stay closed.

Though that one memory may be gone, the life he used to have is still there. Because she's out there. She *is* out there. Maybe his mom isn't, or at least not the way she's supposed to be, but Katie didn't go anywhere. She didn't leave for toilet paper. Katie is *out there somewhere* and Daniel is not alone, he is *not* alone, he is *not alone*.

In the mirror, reflected-Daniel still covers his left ear. With a hard jerk, Daniel pulls his hand away from his face and steps back, almost stumbling, from the mirror.

Shot by shot. One by one. Ear by ear. Shot by shot one by one ear by ear bed by bed by bed by—

No.

No. No. No.

Unsteadily, Daniel's legs crisscross and he turns around, his feet landing on his pants, which lay by the side of his bed.

Daniel leans down and picks them up.

He puts them on.

Runaway

The knob turns easily. More importantly, it turns quietly.

It opens without creaking.

Daniel steps through without breathing.

A hidden generator hums all the way through the stairwell, but once Daniel is through the door, he closes it as fast as he safely can to trap the sound inside. He turns the knob all the way before the door shuts, so there's not even a click—the same thing he used to do at night back home, when he got up to go to the bathroom but didn't want to wake his mom. But slipping past the sleeping Listeners is the easy part. Daniel peers up to the corner of the concrete stairway, and the only hint of the landing up top is a dull red light cascading against the stairs. And Daniel knows, or thinks he knows, that there will be someone there, sitting by the door. There has to be someone there to listen for the password, and warn everyone downstairs in case of . . . what? In case the sickos get in? (Would they *knock*?)

So what now? Charge up the steps, tear through the red, and try to get the latch down and the door open before the Listener (who, let's face it, is sitting *right there*) has a chance to react? That doesn't happen. That can't happen. He'll grab his arm and push him back and throw him to the cold gray floor, plans revealed plainly in the ruby spotlight.

Or Daniel could walk up slowly, hands held high, and lie. "Derek sent me up here. He wants some Cheerios for breakfast tomorrow. I'll grab 'em and come right back."

Or he could just ask. They never said he was a prisoner. They never said he couldn't leave if he wanted.

Very softly, Daniel raises his foot up onto the first stair.

He hears nothing. The generator mutes the sound.

So he steps again, and again, and again, his head bobbing higher and higher as he approaches the corner. And when he's almost there, he presses back against the wall, just like Loren and Terry taught, and waits one second, two seconds, three seconds. Then he spins around in one motion, storming onto the plateau with his eyes focused straight above the next set of stairs, right at that door, that chair, and the one-eared man sitting atop it.

Sleeping.

Daniel slumps back into himself and takes himself up the next four steps, where he stops and stares at the man in front of him. Sleeping with his arms folded, the man loosely grips a revolver. A stubbly almost-beard contrasts sharply with his skin, which is tinted a sunburned red in the light. Breathing quietly, Daniel feels the goose bumps prickling along his arms. It's not cold, but there's a chill just the same, crawling over his ears and past his shoulders and all the way, creepy crawly, down his back. He's frozen in place. He sees the others discovering him like this in the morning, a soldier's statue frozen halfway through the battle. In a small jerk, he throws his fist in the air and tries to prepare himself. He forces back the pounding of his heart, the way they taught him to do, and focuses on the here, the now, the mission.

Then he charges, racing up the rest of the steps and reaching for the door, tugging the latch aside with a shockingly loud metal clang. As he draws the door open, the chair beside him scrapes against the floor, the Listener's eyes shoot open, and though he cries out and reaches for Daniel, Daniel, man, Daniel is *gone*!

He's gone through the opening and out into the market, gone with a sharp left and a hard push through the double doors, gone down the center aisle in the supermarket. The sentries might be pissed, and they might be moving, but it's too late—don't look, don't look, just run and run and *run*. Sneakers squeak against a plastic floor, and streetlights outside show the way, past the checkout counters, through the automatic door, and out, out, *out*—!

Into the night.

It's cool. The breeze—the breeze is cool, and strange on his body, and Daniel feels his legs slowing . . . his body stopping . . . but his heart pounds, and he knows they're still there, still too close. So he pushes on, his feet charging against the ground, dashing out of the parking lot and to the right, to the sidewalk, so fast they'll never catch him, so far away they'll never find him again. On his forehead, his sweat is ice, but his body, free, stretches and expands as he soars down the sidewalk, his loud, flat steps shouting their retorts from building to abandoned building.

His body soars.

His fists pump.

His legs cramp.

Stumbling to a stop, Daniel finds himself staring down the first corridor of the maze, streetlights as glowing walls, their bright yellow faces staring Daniel's way but providing no direction. The problem is they're all the same—identical twins, triplets, septuplets, more, and Daniel hasn't been acquainted with any of them long enough to distinguish them from their brothers. Maybe, a few days in, he could have remembered, and reversed, all the rights and lefts and this ways and thats that took them from his apartment at 512 Rentwood, but however long it's been—more than a few days for sure—have rendered the directions a dizzying muddle, illuminated entirely the wrong way by the shiny happy lampposts.

Daniel breathes. He coughs. Then he reaches into his pocket, pulls out his surgical mask, and puts it on. Then he steps forward. The tap of his step resounds—it meets no competition. He steps forward again. Forward is as good a direction as any. Checking over his shoulder to make sure he's not being followed—he's not—Daniel walks, the light wind tickling the tiny strands of hair on his arms. As he walks, he tries to imagine what his mom would tell him. "Stay close to Katie," she'd say. And if Katie wasn't there? "Stay where there's people."

And if there were no people?

If it was nighttime?

If the air was poison?

If there was no way out?

In his head, Daniel sees his mom fold her arms and ponder this, her lips pursed, as if she thinks Daniel might be lying, but can't . . . quite . . . put her finger on it. She opens her mouth to speak.

"Hey!"

The voice echoes. Daniel stops instantly, frozen mid-stride, and as the light breeze whistles by, freezing the sweat dropping off his head, Daniel turns around very, very slowly. From out the nearest alley, a scrawny, bearded, shadowy figure grips the brick wall.

"You got any spare change?" The voice is scratchy, as if there's a cough dwelling in the back of the man's throat, carried to term but in no rush to leave. With a shuffling footstep, like a piece of paper brushed hard against a chalkboard, the man steps out of the alley's shadow and into the spotlight, where the bright yellow light shines down upon his face.

Daniel's first instinct is to vomit. He heaves as if he's about to, but like the man's cough, deep acid takes refuge in the back of Daniel's throat, so rough and hot he has to swallow it, hard, back down.

Enormous red boils burst forth from the man's face, the right side mostly, bending up and almost over a glassy, dripping eye, and masking half of what looks like a grin, except part of the mouth is in entirely the wrong place. One boil—the fourth maybe—is popped like a pimple rubbed to excess, a whitish liquid dripping down over it, landing with a tiny hint of a splash on the sidewalk below. The man snorts like a pig. He steps forward, stretching a red finger, jagged in ways fingers aren't supposed to be. Daniel imagines a current of blood just below the skin, and he has to swallow hard again.

"Just a dollar . . ." says the man.

"No!" says Daniel, stepping back. "No, I'm, um—"

"All I want is a fucking *dollar*!" Something in the man's piercing red eyes goes dark.

The sidewalk scrapes beneath Daniel's feet as he stumbles backward. "I don't—I don't have anything—!"

With an animalistic roar, that man, that thing, tears forward in a mad, staggering charge, hands outstretched, and Daniel cowers and tries to shut his eyes, but they stay open, electric.

And a shot rings out.

The man spins off to the side. He falls to the ground.

Standing behind him in the street, smoking gun raised, is Derek.

"Are you okay?" Derek says.

But Daniel doesn't say a word. He shakes, eyes glued to that thing that used to be a person, on the ground just a yard or two away. A quiet stream of blood trickles into the crack of the sidewalk.

Slipping his gun into his pants, Derek steps over and wraps his arm around Daniel. "Come on," he says, "it's okay, it's okay."

"I—I just—he, and I—"

"It's okay. He's gone." For a whole minute, maybe, Derek keeps his hand on Daniel's shoulder and, eventually, Daniel finds himself leaning into it. His heart starts to beat quieter, slower, softer, until finally Derek pats him lightly on the shoulder and starts them both forward. As they step across the next road and toward the parking lot, Derek, his eyes gazing out to the supermarket, says, "That's what happens to them."

Daniel says nothing.

"It starts with a boil, just one, and then it tears them apart," says Derek. "Body and mind."

Then there's nothing but silence between the both of them as they head back home.

Returning to the basement alcove is awkward, even if most of the Listeners never knew Daniel was gone. The sentries to the left and right of the double doors are well enough hidden that Daniel can't see a reaction, but the man who was guarding the door is far easier to read, his eyes narrow and skeptical. But Derek, without a word, leads Daniel past him, down the steps again, and into the chamber, where the Listeners, evidently undisturbed, still slumber.

As Daniel starts back toward his bed, he feels Derek's hand on his shoulder. Turning, he finds Derek's finger move from his lips—shh!—to a blank spot of cold gray wall near the doorway. Their shoes clacking lightly, but obviously, against the floor in the otherwise silent house, Daniel and Derek take a seat on the floor. For a moment, neither says anything, their breathing intertwining with the scattered snores and sounds of the sleeping Listeners. But while Daniel stares aimlessly at the floor, Derek, eyes forward, is intense. He always looks intense.

And eventually—in a hushed voice, in an almost-whisper—he says, "I know how you feel." Daniel glances at him. "This is a disorienting place, Daniel, because on first glance, things don't quite add up. One ear, one voice, but you hear a lot of voices and don't know what to make of any of them. A new world for us, our own rule, but right now, this world's just a cramped basement. It doesn't make sense."

Nodding a little, Daniel glances toward the sleeping Listeners. Zeke, a fresh bandage where his right ear used to be, sleeps on his left, rolling onto that side every time the new wound hits too near the bed. His light, breathless cry carries through the bunker.

"This place was a lot emptier when I joined, but just as strange," says Derek. He stares ahead and into the door, as if it contains hieroglyphics only he can read. "The life I had before, it wasn't one I could have anymore—not because of the plague. Just because. I don't think I really got it until I realized what I was a part of."

"I know," says Daniel. "We're thrown off by the voices we hear, and the lies we hear, and we need to—"

"You know, but you don't know," says Derek. "Look, Daniel, see Loren over there?" Derek points into the basement, and even with just the faintest illumination of emergency lights, Daniel can see Loren, scratching his beard in his sleep.

"Yeah," says Daniel.

"He's your brother. See Brian over there, green shirt?" The tall man who stood guard the first day Daniel arrived snores loudly a couple beds down from Zeke.

"Yeah."

"He's your brother." Derek points into the basement, again and again and again. "He's your brother, he's your brother, he's your brother," says Derek, "and me? I'm your brother, too."

Daniel pauses. "Okay," he says.

"It's not just a word," says Derek. "These guys are your brothers because every single one of them would give up their life to save yours. Terry and I could have been killed just going out into the open and bringing you here, but any one of us would do it again. Like I just did."

In a flash, Daniel sees the grizzled, decrepit thing-of-a-man, the venom in his eyes, the flash of a gun and the splattering of blood, and Derek, pistol raised, bringing Daniel back.

"This place is cramped," says Derek, "it's scary, but Daniel, listen." Placing his hand on Daniel's shoulder, Derek turns from the door and looks him right in the eyes, a penetrating, breathtakingly honest gaze. When he speaks, he speaks as if the world turns on his words. "It's cramped because we're all here *together*," says Derek.

"Family isn't something that happens, it's something that's *made*. We're family here. All us brothers . . ." Without turning, Derek points behind him, and Daniel finds his eyes drawn to Adam's office. ". . . and our father."

For a moment longer, Daniel stares at Adam's door. Then his gaze falls back to the collected Listeners, and then to Derek himself. Daniel's hands press against the concrete wall, his skinny fingers taking it all in, rough and cold and impenetrable. His hands linger.

The Dream

Beams of sunlight run parallel to the window, but it's too midday for anything to shine through. Most of the light, the real light, comes not from outside, but from the birthday cake Katie's dad made, which is lopsided and chocolate and, frankly, probably tastes awful, but the chocolate stains on his apron show he tried. And the candles are nice.

The candles glow like torches. They flicker like fireflies. They cast a glow around them—Daniel and his mom, Katie and her parents, gathered here in Katie's apartment for what Katie calls "The Super-Spectacular Danny's Eleventh Birthday Spectacular!!!"

She wrote it on a sign. Exclamation points and all.

Daniel's mom claps. Katie's dad bows. Her mom says to make a wish. (Wish, wish, which is this?) So Daniel takes a step forward and blows against the candles, but though they flicker and dodge, they don't go out.

"You're the worst blower ever to blow," says Katie.

Daniel shoves his shoulder against Katie, who giggles and jumps back. He looks around—smiles everywhere, even brighter than the candles. They all gather close, almost in a circle, almost holding hands, almost a ring around the rosie. They are there, they arranged this, they arranged this for him and he will he will he will blow out the candles. So he breathes in, and releases—in, and releases—in . . . and he blows as hard as he can.

The candles flicker. The light dims.

His breath is endless. The air keeps coming. He's a fan on high, but the candles don't go out. The room grows darker, though the candles are still alight, and he blows more—darker—more—darker—MORE, until, finally, his lungs are empty, and somehow, on that lopsided mess of a would-be ought-to-be birthday cake, the candlelight remains.

But he's blown out the sun.

Suddenly it's nighttime. And the lights in the room are off—did he blow them out, too? In the candlelight, which is far too dim, he looks around the birthday cake, but he sees nothing. He hears nothing.

"Katie?" he says. "Mom?"

The candles cast a red glow, but they illuminate nothing but the melting cake beneath them. He takes a step back and spins around, but the door is gone and he can barely make out the table, and with the blinds up, he should be able to see some streetlights outside, but he can't. He holds his breath and keeps so quiet he could hear a pin drop, but no one drops a pin.

"Hello?" he says. "Hey! Hello?!"

Suddenly, the lights flip on. The room is filled with Listeners. It's Derek who flipped the switch, as Zeke eats some nachos and Quentin cuts himself a slice of cake. Adam relaxes on the couch.

"Surprise," says Derek.

"Happy birthday!" they cry.

Daniel reaches for his right ear and finds he doesn't have one.

᠕ᢥᢢᢥ᠕

When Daniel wakes up, he's surprised to learn he's been asleep. Most of the others are already up and about. One of the kids—Greg maybe—is reading Daniel's *Daredevil*. Daniel's eyes blink without sleepiness. When he climbs to his feet, his muscles don't ache.

And he doesn't feel alone.

Parallel Lines

In the mirror, Daniel looks weak—scrawny, even, his shoulders slumping from his neck like roller coaster tracks, slowing slightly before plunging the length of his bony arms. The arms especially peek out of the white undershirt Derek got him a couple days ago. They're skinny, and freckled, and as a silver blade drifts through his mind, they become prickly, too, goose bumps popping up where arm hair should be, but isn't.

He looks like a kid. He *is* a kid. As his arms drop to the floor parallel to one another, he feels his heart pumping all the way to his throat, where it squeezes the breath right out of him. A long, slow exhale follows, falling from his lips in inconsistent bursts, the plaything of his heartbeats. His breath fogs up the mirror just below his chin, and Daniel reaches forward to clear the view. The mirror squeaks as he wipes off the condensation, and then Daniel, now unobstructed, reaches his left hand up to the side of his head, covering his left ear. Mirror-Daniel covers his right. Breathing in, Daniel tries to stand up a little straighter, a little taller, the slopes of his shoulders transforming into ninety-degree angles.

"You nervous?"

Derek appears in the mirror. He's tall, so the mirror cuts off the top of his head, but Daniel knows it's him.

"A little," says Daniel. He looks into his own eyes.

Placing a hand on Daniel's right shoulder (mirror-Daniel's left), Derek says, "You don't have to do this now."

"I want to," Daniel says quickly. Then he turns away from the mirror, looking over his shoulder at Derek, who always stands tall and powerful, without even trying. "I'm ready."

Derek's hand squeezes.

ᴧᴧᴧᴧᴧᴧ

Four days earlier, Derek and Terry led Daniel and Zeke upstairs at 11 a.m. exactly. It had to be eleven—this was something they'd tested in considerable detail. At eleven, the back of the supermarket was at its most invisible, the sun causing nothing but glare on the outside, localizing the inside light to the back aisle alone. At eleven, sickos or cops could be standing right outside the Food Garden and never have a clue anyone was inside, even if they pressed their faces right up against the glass.

The morning-shift sentries took a break as the four lined up toward the end of the aisle: Derek and Daniel on one side of an invisible line, Terry and Zeke on the other. In Derek's big hand was a small, soft football, ragged on the outside, the orange foam exposed. The aisle was only about fifteen feet wide, and the food display in the middle (with chicken and turkey mostly) left little room to maneuver, but that, Derek had insisted, was part of the fun.

"Down!" said Derek, touching the nose of the football to the plastic floor. He said it emphatically, but not too loud. Although his voice wasn't likely to carry through the entire supermarket and outside, it was always possible. Daniel moved to a crouching position, staring forward intently, right at Zeke.

"Set!" said Derek. Dropping his right hand to the floor, which was much warmer than the floor in the basement, Daniel prepared to charge.

"Hike!"

As Derek dropped back, Daniel cut right, slipping past Zeke, who followed alongside him. Terry's hands went up for the block. Daniel's legs, cooped up for weeks, felt lethargic, but the moves came back to him—not football moves, but soccer moves—along with the required speed when matched against a good defender, and the agility to change direction with the Beckenbauer. Almost as if he had a ball between his feet, Daniel stopped short and jolted left, and with the open space, he turned back, watching the football sail up over Terry's hands and, arching perfectly, down into his own. The light ball bobbled in his hands as Zeke lunged for the tag, but somehow, even as his fleet feet tangled, even as his weakened knees buckled, Daniel secured the ball in his grasp. Ball and boy alike fell to the ground, squealing across the floor.

"Ow," said Daniel.

"Oh, *yes!*" said Derek from somewhere behind Daniel, clapping.

"No way, man," says Terry.

As Daniel rolled over and pushed himself upright, he saw Derek jogging over, Zeke laughing, Terry shaking his head. "You okay, Daniel?" said Derek.

"Ow," said Daniel.

"You okay?"

"Fell," said Daniel. Glancing down at his knee, Daniel found a scrape and just a tiny bit of blood.

"Held onto it, though," said Derek. "You held onto it." He reached his hand down and grabbed onto Daniel's, pulling him up to his feet with a forceful tug. "That was great. Seriously. The way you broke coverage? You guys see that?"

"Man, Daniel, you are *fast*," said Zeke.

"What the fuck?" said Terry. "Fuck's sake, he bobbled it the whole way down. Incomplete."

Derek punched him in the shoulder. Daniel laughed.

So did Terry. In fact, he smirked, shook his head, said, "Yeah, whatever," and lined up on the new line of scrimmage. The catch had taken them just about to midfield, right by the double doors and the glowing red exit sign. "You got him this time?"

Grinning, Zeke said, "No way he gets open again."

Daniel felt slightly winded and a little hurt. But the smile on Derek's face, on Zeke's face—and even, when he didn't think anyone was looking, on Terry's—were undeniably contagious. If everything going on outside that bright glass window could be set aside, if everything that happened could be forgotten for just a little while, then maybe this . . . maybe this could be *fun*.

"Try and stop me," Daniel said.

Later, out of breath and sipping from a couple of bottled waters, Daniel and Zeke stepped into the alcove, where the rest of the uninitiated gathered around the PSP, except for Ivan, the chubby one, who had his nose in a book, the title of which Daniel couldn't make out. As they passed by the mirror, Daniel caught both of their reflections, his and Zeke's, parallel figures side to side, with one key difference leaping out of the glass. Zeke's bandage covered the hole where his right ear used to be.

It stuck out like a healthy man out on the borough's

streets—weirdly content, somehow impossible, in entirely the wrong place. Maybe less than two weeks ago, Zeke had his ear cut off, and a few minutes ago he was laughing and playing football. Daniel's mom was gone, he had no way to get in touch with Katie, people were sick and dying in the streets, and he was having fun playing football in the back aisle of the Food Garden.

He choked on his water.

"You okay?" said Zeke.

Coughing, Daniel cleared his throat and wiped some droplets from his face. "What's it like?" he said.

Zeke took a sip. "You mean the ear?"

"Yeah."

He shrugged. Glancing at his reflection, Zeke said, "It's strange at first. Everything's gone mono, you know? And there's this ringing for a few days after." He nodded. "But then . . . man, when it kicks in, when you learn to *hear* with it . . . everything's so *clear.*"

Zeke plopped down on Daniel's bed. The *Daredevil* comic rustled underneath the pillow. "Everything that's confusing out there isn't, because if you listen right, you know what's going on." Smiling, he shook his head. "Man."

Softly, Daniel brushed the tiny bristly hairs of his earlobe and considered the parallels.

With a deep breath, Daniel steps past Derek and heads into the main chamber, where the Listeners gather tight around the initiation table. Illumination from a hanging lamp descends upon it like a stage spotlight. The Listeners murmur, but they part for him, and also for Derek, who follows close behind. As Daniel passes, a hand reaches out and touches his shoulder. He turns. It's Zeke.

"Congrats," he says.

The Listeners peel back for Daniel until they're the walls of a hallway, every bit as solid and straight. As he reaches the table, Derek helps him up, and Daniel lays back, the light shining down so brightly on his eyes he can barely see a thing beyond it, though it's not for lack of trying. He pushes his chin to his chest and tries to spot Loren, Terry, Quentin, the uninitiated, and especially Adam, but all he sees is light and shadow in sharp contrast. Once he's settled, the murmuring goes quiet, and soon he can't hear, either. But he will. Even now, he's getting better—shoes scratch against the floor. Two lines are formed. Footsteps pass through, and the lines re-converge.

Derek squeezes Daniel's left hand. Glancing his way, Daniel smiles and squeezes back.

Then, suddenly, someone else touches his right hand. When Daniel turns, he finds Adam beside him, the sheath in his other hand. As Daniel glances at the sheath, he realizes that the crowd, in reverence, has gone completely silent. In a warm whisper, Adam says, "Are you ready, Daniel?"

Daniel nods.

And then, Adam removes the silver knife from its sheath. Holding the tool in the air, he lets the blade fly like some kind of bird. He swings it down at this perfect angle, like he's done a thousand times before, but from down here, from directly beneath it, it looks far different, the knife sharper, bigger, and more beautiful. When he swings it upward again, the light from the lamp reflects perfectly into Daniel's eyes, and he blinks, but only for a second.

"In a world that grows darker, always darker, louder, deafer," Adam booms, the blade cutting through the air, "we need to know, always to know, whom to trust, whom to believe in, to whom to listen." Although Daniel can barely see his face, he sees his blade, and he knows the other Listeners are there around him, watching him, proud of him. On Derek's face, the only one he *can* see, he sees the pride. In Adam's voice, he hears it. "We are misguided, distracted, destroyed by the inconsequential, contradictory sounds of parents, of television and internet, of organized religion and the media," says Adam, "and so we lose sight of the *truth.*"

When Adam spins the knife through the air, he's like a circus ringmaster, but Derek is stoic, his hand solid, the sole ladder rung Daniel can grip if he needs to get out. He knows, even now, that Derek would let him back out. The others might be angry, but Derek would protect him, like any big brother would. He would save him a third or a fourth time, if need be, again and again and again. So when Derek's big eyes stare down into Daniel's, Daniel doesn't feel trapped—he feels released. He once ran from this place, but now he gets it. He could have left anytime he wanted. But he doesn't want to.

See? Already it's starting to come together.

"Always, we must listen for the truth," says Adam. "We must break away from the outside world, tear ourselves apart from the corrupting influence of those who would seek to disunite us." As he raises the knife straight up, as straight as his own body, his voice soars with pride and sinks with gravity, all at once. "Tonight!" he cries. "Tonight, we give the gift of freedom to yet another of our children. We close our eyes and open our ears."

Daniel shuts his eyes tight.

Two days ago, Adam stood before them all and spoke of good and bad, of right and wrong, of Listeners and cops and the Trent Street Incident. Daniel still thought of it the next day, as he tightly gripped his M-1911 and fired three shots into the target at the end of the range. The sound echoed in his ears, and as Loren always said, "It's the one sound you can always trust. It always tells the truth."

In that way, it's a lot like Adam.

"You would not have heard the details of the Trent Street Incident on the news," Adam said—and it was true. Daniel hadn't. Trapped inside his apartment, there wasn't much to do besides turn on the television and wait, but he'd heard nothing of the events Adam claimed happened at the Trent Street Hospital. A sicko the doctors were studying broke free, he said, killed two nurses, then freed another sicko. Four doctors, six nurses, and two security officers were killed, Adam said, and yet there wasn't a word about it on the news.

That was a complicated thing to understand, and that's where Adam and the gunfire differed—the gunfire was simple and uncomplicated. Even if everything Daniel had learned from the Listeners was true, and it had become clearer and clearer that it was, there was nothing uncomplicated about it. The cops were dangerous, out to secure their own power, but Katie's dad is a cop, and Daniel knew for a fact that he was a good man. He always was. He was like Daniel's uncle. And Derek called the Listeners his family, and every individual Listener his brother, but Daniel *had* a family—a mother he loved, a best friend who was like a sister, and her parents as surrogate relatives. It was as if there were two simultaneous truths, like parallel lines, and one thing Daniel remembered from math class is that parallel lines never touched, even if they stretched on until infinity. But Adam said there was only one truth.

That truth certainly wasn't in the newspaper. Before the gathered Listeners, Adam held up a copy of the *Tribune*, one of the last issues brought in before the doctors left, and showed them all everything that had been reported on the Trent Street Incident. Daniel saw the headline himself. It read, "False alarm at Trent Street Hospital," and the story was all of four inches.

"This is how I know what really happened," Adam said, holding up a pure black walkie-talkie. "The truth cops tell only to other cops, straight from their own mouths. They lied to the press, and the press conspired in those lies, because the cops didn't want us to know how they, and the doctors, failed. The *truth*"—and here he waved the walkie-talkie in the air like a lighter—"is that the Trent Street Incident is the *reason* the doctors left. The Trent Street Incident is the *reason* they climbed aboard those helicopters and *left us here.* But the cops would have us believe nothing happened!"

It sounded so simple. Good and bad. Right and wrong. Listeners and cops. And as Daniel stood at the firing range, he imagined parallel lines, and it didn't make any sense at all. Parallel lines never touched, but Adam said there was one true voice, and Zeke said everything became clear. Daniel, his fingers wrapped around the handle of a weapon he'd never touched before the quarantine went up, a weapon he'd promised never to touch to a man the Listeners called an enemy—a man who'd baked him a cake on his birthday even though he didn't have a clue how to do it—wanted so very much for it all to be clear.

When Daniel fired, two shots hit the chest. A third hit the right side of the forehead. A fourth went wide right, just past the head, but the next hit dead-on, and the sixth was another chest shot.

Six bullets, two lines of three, tilting ever so slightly toward one another.

Later in the evening, Daniel told Derek he was ready, and Derek agreed.

Leaning his head back against the dull red plastic of the cere-monial table, Daniel stares straight up into the light and lets it blind him just a little. When he can't see, all he can do is hear, as Adam says, powerfully, "One ear, so that we may hear only the voices of our brothers." As electric sparks dance around Daniel's irises, he turns left, where Derek, his big eyes nervous in the way a mother is nervous on her daughter's opening night, smiles. Daniel smiles back.

Adam presses his free left hand gently against Daniel's chest. The resistance forces Daniel to breathe a little less heavily, and he feels his heartbeat slowing with his lungs. "One ear," said Adam, "so that the lies of the world may be drowned out by the truths of our brethren."

The moment Adam removes his hand, Derek places a bright silver cup against Daniel's lips. Daniel remembers it as part of the ceremony, though he never asked what was in it. It doesn't matter now: As Derek tips the cup back, Daniel feels the liquid drop into his dry throat, and he swallows it down. It tastes like bitter grapes, and Daniel wonders, momentarily, if it's wine. He's never drunk wine before.

"Daniel Raymond," says Adam, dragging Daniel back into the moment. Adam's face, directly beneath the spotlight, is nearly in sil-houette, only the outlines of his face and hair illuminated in bright yellow. "Do you now choose to dispose of the lies of your past and embrace the singular truth of your future?"

With the word "singular" bouncing back and forth in his skull like a pinball, Daniel shuts his eyes, breathes, and says, "Yes."

"Do you accept the responsibilities set forth by this family, to follow your brothers wherever they need you, to lead those who hear too much?"

"Yes."

Something tugs against his shirt. Opening his eyes again, Daniel sees Derek above him, holding a thick cylindrical rod above his mouth. Daniel opens his mouth, and Derek slips in the wooden rod so Daniel can bite down on it. The strange taste of wood in his mouth keeps his eyes open as Adam, the shadow-image of a father, turns back toward the invisible crowd.

"The pain is great, but the reward is greater," says Adam. "This is the path you have chosen—the correct path. The one true path. One ear." He raises the powerful blade, then draws it down slowly, perfectly parallel to Daniel's head, until it's almost—but not quite—touching his right ear.

Eyes see the blade. Heart gets the message. But the knife is there. If he moves, he hits it. Because there's no turning back now anyway, Daniel stares up into the light and imagines it as a million individual beams, drawing together.

"Welcome to the Listeners," says Adam.

With a million rays of light pouring into his wide-open eyes, Daniel sees nothing but brightness and hears nothing but silence, until the very instant his ear explodes in heat and cold, and the light shines bright and bright and white and white, and the sound is loud and raw and *him*, but the light is oh so *white* and *bright* and *hot* and *cold* and *whitebrighthotcoldwhitebrighthotcold*

free

The Helicopters

To a lot of people, the most horrible images from the plague weren't of the infected themselves, although those were the ones banned from television.

Of all the horrific images, the one replayed the most was shot by a cameraman aboard one of the twenty-six helicopters employed in the evacuation of healthcare workers from the quarantined borough. The workers stood on rooftops, conspicuous in their brightly colored biohazard gear, climbing up the ladders the helicopters dropped down. The helicopters couldn't land, of course, because every resident of the borough, infected or not, was desperate to get out.

In the shot, taken above Carver Street, a young man, possibly a teenager, and healthy from the looks of it, breaks past the police barricade atop a rooftop. A woman follows close behind, the man pushes a healthcare worker out of the way, and both charge for the ladder. The man climbs up no more than three rungs before machine gun fire, from the helicopter, strikes him down, but the woman doesn't stop—she ignores the man, whom she might have known, and climbs the ladder herself. She makes it up four rungs before she, too, is fired upon, her dead body landing directly atop the man's.

This is the image they played again and again over the next two months. Some viewers complained, but not enough to banish it from the airwaves. The footage was viewed over dinner as families thanked the lord Jesus Christ that they didn't have to escape from that place.

Pointing Fingers

When Flower ducks under the bar, she's usually going for her shotgun, or at least pretending to, and when Roy sees Paul in the back of the crowd, he hopes to God Flower's doing it again. But this time she emerges with a box full of blue masks, like the kind the doctors wear on *ER*. She ought to keep her finger by the trigger, but she doesn't.

"Come on, take a bunch, pass 'em down," she says, nudging the box toward the end of the bar. "Ain't safe walking around without 'em."

"Ain't safe walking around, period," says Roy, slumped over at the corner of the bar—usual seat, unusual posture. "Just plain ain't safe."

"Ah, c'mon, it'll pass," says Flower. She slings the band of the mask across her chubby index finger and pulls, like she's going to launch it at the cap of Roy's bowed head, but instead she hands it off to Paul—Paul, of all people, who's managed to work his way up to the bar through the crowd of regulars.

They call her Flower because she's not. She's a big woman, an operatic fat lady but a hell of a lot tougher, and she runs her bar with an iron fist and an authority no one would dare question, or want to. She's the den mother, and under her watchful eye, Herman Road is a family. It's dangerous to step foot outside, with all the folks running around crazy and sick, but everyone important's here, and safe. Save two.

"Can I get a drink?" says Roy, glancing up a little bit, just enough to see Paul—just enough to know he's there.

"Ain't serving tonight, Roy. *Think*. We're here to figure things out.

Can't figure nothin' out when you can't even stand on your own two feet." Flower laughs and offers him a surgical mask. Roy points to the one already hanging around his neck.

"For your wife," says Flower.

"She ain't going nowhere," says Roy, turning his eyes back down to the hardwood of the bar.

Roy's dad was a regular before Roy was, back when Flower ran the place with her own old man. Coming to the Pub is an old family tradition, like getting loaded here, and passing out here, and having the neighborhood boys you grew up with and went to school with and got jobs with carry you home to the girl next door you wound up marrying. But taking care of your own, and protecting the family you care about, extended and otherwise, is tradition, too, and it's out of tradition as much as necessity Roy stays. You gotta protect what's close to you.

Paul leans against the bar and keeps his eyes down like he's got something to feel guilty about.

"Everyone take a seat now? C'mon, take a seat," says Flower, banging a mug against the bar like a judge's gavel, calling her court to order. It's the same way she did it the day she announced Isaac's little girl got into Bryn Mawr, or even just for old Willy's eighty-ninth birthday.

The scattered lines of random conversations die down, and the smiling faces turn harder, like in a town hall meeting of the most severe sort. Old stools and chairs scrape against the ancient floor and echo along the wooden walls, and soon there's only low coughs and whispers.

Roy watches Paul take a seat by his wife, Ani, up in the front, at the other end of the bar. He keeps them in his line of sight—keeps them nice and trapped before they get a chance to even think about escaping.

"I wanna thank all you for coming," says Flower, hand still clutching the mug. "Big risk just walking down the street, I know, but lemme tell ya, things get tough, bigger risk in not sticking together."

"Amen!" shouts a voice from the back.

"You be quiet," says Flower, gesturing towards the speaker with the mug, like she's giving a toast. The crowded hall fills with the light laughter of a reunion. "This is a family," says Flower, "and this here's a family place, see, and family takes care of each other. Now, this place used to house my brothers and my dad and me, and I still got a lotta extra room, so anyone wants to stick it out here, that's fine by me. This is your home 'smuch as mine."

"Can't stick it out," mutters Roy. A family can't stick it out when they treat the bad guy like an adopted son.

The man sitting next to him stares for a moment, then turns back toward Flower and shouts out, "What about food?"

"Damn good question, and we're tryin' to figure that out," says Flower. "We got a lotta leftover dinners the Corps and the Cross left behind. We're storin' 'em down at Steve's Market for now, and that's where we're gonna go for food. Short walk from here, and we'll bring the food down, eat together. Should be all right for a couple weeks till the government brings more."

This seems not to be good enough, and a bunch of muddled voices start to raise a ruckus until Flower beats it back down with her mug. "Hey! Hey!" she says. "We ain't alone in this. Phones work. We'll keep makin' calls till we get what we need. Chances are always better 'slong as we stick together. We don't know what caused this—"

"Like hell we don't," says Roy, and this time everyone listens.

"Roy?" says Flower.

"Guys wanna know why we're stuck in here? Why we can't go more than a block without worrying about who's gonna get sick and go goddamn nuts on us?" He points toward Paul. "Take a look at Osama over there."

A hundred eyes follow Roy's finger to Paul, and to Paul's gently middle-eastern features. Paul looks around a little bit, like he's trying to find out who Roy's pointing to, before he realizes everyone's focused on him. "Excuse me?" he says.

"This disease—it ain't natural. Sure as hell ain't natural," says Roy. He slams his hands onto the smooth, aged wood of the bar counter. "This ain't something happened. It's something done to us, and there's the guy what did it."

"Hey!" says Paul, standing up and kicking the barstool away. "Shut the hell up. I'm as scared as any of us—"

"Like fuck you are," says Roy. "Probably think this lands you in heaven with a buncha virgins or something . . ."

And that's when Paul tears towards Roy, but the crowd's too

thick, and arms reach out under Paul's shoulders and pull him up off the ground. He fights against them, has the balls to call Roy a bigot, tries to slam his head back into the chin of the big man right behind him, but he's got no leverage.

"Paul!" yells Ani, and that seems to calm him down a little— enough that the big man loosens his grip—but his gaze is as focused on Roy as Roy's was on Paul before this whole thing got started.

"Hey, hey, hey!" says Flower. She stomps over toward Roy and crashes her mug down right in front of his face. "What the hell you think you're doing, Roy, huh? Last thing we need right now's to be fighting with each oth—"

"He ain't one of us. Last thing we need right now," says Roy, calmly, "is to be blind when someone's spittin' in our eyes."

One last time, Flower smashes the mug to the counter, and with her other hand, she points to the door. "Out of my bar," she says. "Out of my bar. Ain't even drunk, and you're stirring up shit like this. Out."

And no one argues with Flower when she gets that way, so Roy nods, flashes a look at Paul, who's still being restrained but not really fighting anymore—one last look to let the guy know he's on to him. Then Roy forces his way through the crowd of friends and family toward the door he's passed through nearly every day of his life.

〜〜〜〜

"Throw me out," Roy mumbles as he pushes open the squeaky door to his apartment. "Can get drunk at home." He walks to the refrigerator and grabs himself a Coors, and as he's taking his first sip, he finds his eyes wandering up to the top of that lime green monster of a fridge, where Trina keeps the bananas in a basket, and sitting up there is the bear—the tiny, furry toy in a white T-shirt with a heart on it. Clutching the drink in his left hand, Roy reaches up and grabs it, and stares down at it.

He puts it back.

Roy takes another sip and walks into the bedroom, where Trina, bald as a newborn, lies on the bed with Becca, eight years old and out like a light. Teresa's nowhere to be found, of course, but still he half-expects to see her there. It's dark outside, but the light's on, and Trina, half-asleep herself, turns to Roy as he walks in.

"Hey," she says, rolling over flat onto her back.

Roy responds with a slurp. He looks down at his sleeping little girl, then out the window.

"How'd it go?" asks Trina.

Sip.

"Fine," says Roy. "Went fine." He sits down on the right side of the bed, by Becca, and straightens her hair along her back. "Everything's fine."

"Is she coming back?"

Sip. Roy looks out the window, but it's too bright inside to see through the dark out there, and besides, there's nothing to see. "Doubt it," says Roy. "Flower don't seem to think so, and she talked to them last, probably."

Trina rolls back onto her side. "Oh," she says. Her hands rub against the thick covers like she's petting some mutt. "There a plan?"

"I don't know, Trina . . . didn't stay the whole thing."

"Roy!"

"Didn't much see the point—"

"Roy, we gotta know what's going on . . . and we need things, 'sides. You ask about—"

"Didn't get the chance," says Roy. She looks at him like he forgot to bring home a paycheck, so he adds, "I'll ask tomorrow, when it ain't so crowded. It'll be fine." He takes a sip of his beer—the last sip. "This'll pass."

Won't, though. Roy bends the can a little and heads back out into the kitchen, telling himself there's some things a man can't take care of. You can't control what other people do and what other people do to you. That raghead bastard from the bar pops into his mind as he crushes the can in his hand and tosses it into the open trashcan, stuffed nearly to overflowing. The can bounces off some paper ball and lands on the tiled floor, spilling drops of booze around like little polka dots.

The Pub's emptier when the next day comes round—empty even for a Thursday at noon. It's not that people are always drinking this time of day. This is the neighborhood place to go, hang out, shoot a few, and kick back, and there's usually a couple guys in the back playing pool and a lunch-break poker game going on in the corner. A lot less people are willing to come, though, when even getting here's a risk, and there's a lot less people who need a break when they can't, or won't, leave their homes. But this here's the norm, this place is tradition, and as long as Roy can stop by here, the same old world's still around.

When Roy walks through the door, it's just Flower there, and a couple cops—a man in his thirties, a woman in her forties—having some words with her. The cops stand right in front of Roy's stool, so he eyes another one more toward the middle.

"Yo, Roy, you hear this?" says Flower, all of yesterday's anger gone for a regular. That's the thing about Flower: She'll get mad, she'll toss you out, she'll think nothing of it, but at the end of the day, or the start of the next one, she knows this is still a community she's leading and she's pretty forgiving, unless someone's there just to stir up shit. That she won't abide, and that's why the cops don't have to come around here too often.

"What?" says Roy. He takes the stool.

"Think they can take away my shotgun," says Flower. She talks about it like it's the old family pet. Unasked, she reaches down below the bar and pulls out a mug, then starts to fill it with Coors.

"It's for your own protection, ma'am," says the male cop, looking around awkwardly, like he expects the regular crowd to charge in and clobber him any second, which they may just do if he isn't fair to Flower. His name tag says "Weathers." The woman's says "Ballinger."

"Really? 'My own protection?'" says Flower, dropping the mug in front of Roy. "Seems to me 'my own protection's' the reason I got the gun in the first place."

"Lady, listen," says Ballinger, "just two blocks down we've got people out in the streets, out in the *streets*, so fucking panicked they're trying to blast their way out of the quarantine. We've got all kinds of people so sick out of their tiny little minds they can't do nothing else but pick up the nearest weapon and shoot whatever the hell they think is out to get them. We've got enough trouble without having to worry about every private citizen with a gun."

"You hearing this, Roy?" says Flower.

Roy is, and while it doesn't make sense all the way, at least they're trying to do something about the problem and make this place a little safer. Be even better if they cracked down on the ragheads and beat the cure out of them, or at least the disease, so government scientists could study the toxin or whatever and come up with some way to turn it around or stop it.

"All them things," says Flower, "is exactly why I gotta have this gun of mine. What if some diseased whack-job tries to get into my bar? What then? We're a community here. Gotta keep each other safe."

"Don't give up the gun," says Ballinger, "and you don't get food. That's the deal."

"Anne . . ." says Weathers.

"That's the deal," she says, staring Weathers down.

Flower pauses, and the pause takes Roy off-guard because he's here every day and he's never seen her speechless before. "You can't do that," says Flower.

"Way it's gotta be," says Ballinger. "We got our orders. Only way to keep things under control."

Another pause. Flower actually takes a step back, closer to the shotgun, like she's going to reach down and pet it before saying goodbye. "I'll think about it," she says, almost in a whisper.

Ballinger nods, and Weathers looks like a thief caught in the act. They turn to leave, and Roy realizes, it does make sense, the deal they're offering. You can't go outside to get the things you need, especially when they're things you can't buy at Steve's, and if everyone's armed, guns aren't much protection anymore, so you need the help.

"Wait," says Roy, and they stop as the bar door swings open. "I got a pistol . . . old gun, my old man's, down the street, 1209, room 403," he says. "My wife, she needs . . ."

And that's when Roy sees who's just walked in: Paul, all calm and casual, right past the cops like he knows they can't do anything to stop him. He could have a knife behind his back or a bomb strapped to his chest and all they'd do is look the other way because they're supposed to be all fair and PC and all that crap. "That's the guy," says Roy.

Ballinger and Weathers turn to Paul, who looks past them right at Roy. Flower, meanwhile, takes a deep breath and says to them,

"That's Paul. He's fine. One of the regulars."

Sure, everyone's a regular once they cheat their way in. Roy remembers Paul a year or so back, new kid out of Cleveland, college degree, a little bit down after some mishaps he wouldn't talk about, stuck working with Roy and the gang at Walton Paper. The first couple months, nothing changed Roy's mind about the guy: kind of snobby, standoffish, and real weird, working through breaks and even through lunch, back turned away and nose turned up at the guys who grew up around here and earned their jobs.

"Nerve of him," Kyle had said, "after all his people done to us. Oughtta spend every day saying how sorry he is—that's what he oughtta do."

Roy saw the guy as just another jackass, though, until Paul wound up assistant plant manager, even though Roy'd been petitioning for the job for months, and even though every other guy in the plant wanted Roy to get it. The boss explained about the business degree and how that kind of qualification matters, but experience counts for something, too, and when Roy approached Paul to tell him that, Paul just turned, grinned—the only time he'd smiled the whole time he'd worked there—and said, "Get back to work."

There are all kinds of things that take a guy from point A to point B, but when Roy looks back, this is what stands out—this Muslim bastard taking the job and the money that were his—and that's what lead him to this, to now, to him and his family trapped in some disease-ridden hellhole, with hope and health and even Teresa taken away from them. And Paul's people, people like Paul— they've got to be behind it, and that's the biggest injustice of all.

So Roy wants to protest when Flower stands up for the guy, but he can't get thrown out of the place again—he likes it here and, besides, he needs a beer. Not much beer left anywhere else. So Ballinger takes a look at Paul first, then Roy, and says, "We'll be by later." To talk about Paul? To talk about the gun? Good either way.

So the cops leave, but Paul stays. He takes a seat two stools down from Roy, asks Flower for a beer, and begins tapping his fingers on the bar in some kind of intricate rhythm Roy can't make out. When Flower puts the beer down, Paul stops and takes a sip. He doesn't pay, because Flower stopped charging once the plague began and money stopped being a consideration, and the community's been nice enough not to take advantage of that. "Running low?" Paul asks.

"So far, so good," says Flower, helping Roy out with a refill. "No means for more supplies, but not so many customers, so I ain't losing product fast as you'd think."

"Losing profit, though," says Roy.

"Well, yeah."

"What's your wife need, Roy?" says Paul. He takes a sip, then turns to Roy, whose eyes are focused on the copper-tinted wood at the bottom of the foamed-over beer.

"Shut up," says Roy.

Paul swirls the beer around in his mug like it's champagne. "That's what you said to the cops, right? Wife needs something?" Then he adds, almost under his breath, "I can think of a few things."

Roy looks up, glares at him, clutching the handle of the mug like he's about to break it against the bar.

"Paul!" says Flower, like an overworked mother at her son's birthday party.

"Just a guess," Paul says.

He's about to take another sip when Flower puts her pudgy hand atop the mug, holding it steadily on the counter, where a little liquid ring forms along the wood. "Yesterday's yesterday," she says. "Let it go."

"Like hell it's yesterday," says Paul, his voice breaking a little bit, his hand squeezing against his drink. "Guy just tells the cops to come after me. Like hell it's yesterday."

Roy stands up and pushes the stool into the bar. Paul instinctively scoots his own stool back just a little. "This thing's fucked up all our lives," Roy says, "and you got a better idea where it came from?" He's looking at Flower, like if he stares at her hard enough, he can push some mental block out of her mind and she'll see what's really going on here. "You got a better idea? It's this guy screwed up my life, him and his fucking Muslim frien—"

"Goddamn it, I'm not even Muslim!" shouts Paul, rising to his feet. "I'm an *atheist*, you racist—"

"Hey! Shut up! Both of you!" yells Flower, leaning over the counter and filling the space between them. "Three people in this bar and two gonna start a fight over some fool notion and a thin skin."

Paul gestures like he's about to say something, then doesn't, slumping into his seat like a petulant child. Still on his feet, Roy glares down at the enemy.

"Ain't his fault, Roy," says Flower, intercepting the gaze.

Roy turns and looks at her for a second. Then, he sits down, slowly, clutches his drink, and takes a long sip. He wipes some drops of beer off his mouth.

"It's *somebody's* fault," Roy says.

When Ballinger and Weathers come by again, it's the middle of the next day, and this time Roy hasn't bothered to go outside. No point, really, not if the only other guy out there is that bastard Paul, and not if the cops are right and the freaks are armed. Gun or no gun, he's got to be there to protect his family from the blistered whack-jobs wandering around outside, and from the real-life monsters who must have made them.

"It's not their fault," says Weathers, as he takes the old revolver from Roy's hands and opens the chamber, checking for bullets. "The virus—it starts at the skin and drills its way up into their brains. Messes them up inside. I doubt they've got any control there, in the end." He drops the bullets into his palm and pockets them. "Not their fault."

Maybe not, but it's somebody's fault. The world isn't one big domino effect, things piling up against you and yours. Families don't just find themselves locked away from the world that made them. Families don't just fall apart.

"Medicine, you said?" says Weathers.

"Um, yeah," says Roy, rubbing his nose. "For my wife. Cancer stuff . . . I have a list . . ." He reaches into his pocket and pulls out a crumpled piece of paper.

"Won't be easy," says Ballinger. "Everyone else is just food and supplies."

Before Roy can respond, Weathers says, "We can figure out something, though. The hospitals are gonna be pretty tapped, but give that here. We'll see what we can do."

Roy hands over the paper, and Weathers puts it in his other pocket.

Ballinger, undermined, says, "Gavin—"

"We'll see what we can do," Weathers repeats, to Ballinger this time.

They turn to leave, again, and again Roy stops them. "What about Paul?" he asks.

"Sorry?" says Ballinger.

"Paul," Roy says. "The other guy in the bar. He's got something to do with this— I'm sure of it."

Weathers and Ballinger share a look Roy can't really make out. "We'll look into it," says Weathers, and that's how Roy knows they won't.

The police leave, and Roy shuts the door behind them. He reaches down into his pocket and out comes the bear. It's tiny, and it fits cleanly in the palm of his creviced hand.

When Teresa had to evacuate with the rest of the health care workers some two weeks into the quarantine, she couldn't leave much in the way of medicine or supplies, because she didn't have any left, and she hadn't had enough notice to arrange anything. She'd come by for them every day for two weeks, covered head to toe in that crumpled plastic biohazard gear, face obscured by the plastic plate covering her face, like this was the moon and she was an astronaut.

But Roy could make out her eyes. She had friendly eyes, good eyes.

What she did leave, the only thing she could leave, was the bear, which she called, with a half-grin, a "priceless family heirloom." Good luck charm, something like that. Something to remember her by.

But the only thing it reminds him of is the fact that someone was there, someone who dropped into the borough to deal with the virus and stuck around to help with the cancer, someone who can't be there anymore because things got so much worse that no one could stick around no matter how much they wanted to. It's one thing to lose the things you count on—the girl you grew up with, married, made a life with; the bar where you bonded with your friends over beers; the borough you could count on being a good place to raise your little girl in. It's one thing to lose them all to something random like cancer, but something real different to have them, and their whole wide world, taken away from you.

Roy clutches the bear in his right hand and walks down the hall, into Becca's room. She's punching the buttons on a 3DS, which is running on the very last of the batteries. She doesn't notice him come in, but she'll notice all the time when her mom's not around anymore, and when her dad's the only person she can ever see or talk to and maybe the only person she'll ever see again. He thinks of his life, sneaking into the Market after-hours with the gang just to see if they could do it (not stealing anything more than a Hershey's bar as proof); first dates in junior high, more on a dare than on a whim; just hanging out on the streets and around the bar and having a life outside a home that can't be a home anymore when the most important part of it can't be around.

This house and this neighborhood are tradition, yeah, but tradition only goes so far. There was supposed to be more than this. Would have been, too, if not for Paul. There was a good amount of money to be made as assistant manager, a nice raise Roy'd earned, a nice raise he'd needed. When he'd come from work that day, he'd walked into the kitchen and sat down across from Trina, who was nursing a cup of orange juice, which was the strongest stuff she ever drank. She had a full head of hair then, but wouldn't for much longer. And Roy had to sit across from her and tell her, the extra money ain't coming. We'll have to pay for this another way. And we'll have to stay here, in this little apartment, in this little neighborhood, because without that extra income, with the cancer, there's no way we'll have the money to find a new place. A better place.

Outside the borough.

Roy'd been at the Pub one night with Kyle and the gang, and somehow the conversation got around to Muslims, and all the terrorist things guys like that do to take out good, American lives. And once Paul, who'd been sitting in the corner staring into his Kindle, walked out, Kyle turned the talk to him. "Guy like Paul," he says, "walks in here, total stranger, and takes work away from guys like us. Guys like Roy here. Kills off the lives we coulda had. Ain't that terrorism, in its own way?"

Roy looks at Becca now, lying on her too small, too worn, too dirty bed, and thinks it could have been different. Matter of fact, it should be different—even now. There are all kinds of things that take a man from point A to point B, but it all comes back to Paul, and the raise and promotion Roy never got, the move that never happened. Paul's responsible for all of this, one way or another.

Roy won't bother Becca now—he goes instead to his room, where Trina's asleep. She's asleep a lot, tired a lot, and if she was to get better and stronger, it'd only be for a little while, until whatever is killing people out there makes its way in here. The reason people in this city keep guns is because, if something they've got is being stolen, you don't want to give it up without a fight.

Roy squeezes the bear tight and leaves the apartment, though not before grabbing the last of the beers from the refrigerator.

∿∿∿∿

When Roy was first dating Trina, he'd knock on the door, then squeeze right up against the door, toward the left, so she couldn't see him through the eyehole and wouldn't know it was him. He does the same now against an obnoxiously bright blue door, and he waits.

The door clicks and opens inward, and Roy rolls in after it, pushing Paul back. Paul can't say a word before Roy punches him, hard, across the jaw, knocking him flat down onto the mint green carpet. Roy grabs him by the collar of the shirt and says, "Where is it?"

"Get *off* me!" says Paul as he throws his own fist against the crown of Roy's head, drawing a little trickle of blood. Roy reels back, and Paul stumbles to his feet, catching hold of himself on the dark brown table. "Get the hell out of my house," he coughs out.

"Give it back!" says Roy, charging, and Paul, still supported on the table, can do nothing more than watch the bull coming before finding himself bowled over and back on the floor. The back of Paul's head smacks down on the hardwood floor just where the rug ends, and he doesn't struggle much at all when Roy, still on top, launches his fist across Paul's jaw, again, again.

"Stop!" a voice cries, Ani's, and Roy turns to find himself looking down the barrel of a revolver that looks a lot like his own, and that feels completely wrong but there's nothing he can do about it. The woman, dark features more pronounced than her husband's, has tears falling from her eyes, and Roy, straddled atop Paul, just stares at the weapon for a moment.

"There's no bullets," he mutters. He wipes a bit of blood from the small cut on his forehead.

Ani opens her mouth, but what comes out is a choke, so she just nods.

"The cops . . ." says Roy.

"Haven't . . . come yet," mutters Paul, blinking hard and fast.

Roy puts his hands up and pushes himself off.

ᴧᴧᴧᴧᴧ

Ani lets the police officers in when they come. Paul, now seated on the easy chair, holds the gun on Roy, who's plopped down onto the couch, the bear bouncing around between his hands. When Weathers and Ballinger walk in, the first thing Roy does is turn to them and say, "You gave them my gun."

"What?" says Weathers. He notices what Paul's holding, and says, "It's not the same gun."

Ballinger walks, almost stomps, over to Paul and pulls the weapon from his hand. Paul looks up in protest, but Ballinger just turns away, punches the butt of the gun into her open palm, and shouts, "Goddammit!"

"Hey, Anne?" says Weathers.

"There are people," says Ballinger, "screwed up, sick-in-the-head used-to-be people, minds more fucked up than any drug could do, killing themselves and killing each other and spreading this thing around, and we gotta waste our time and waste our resources helping people like you? Damn it! And you wonder why we're confiscating the guns!"

Ballinger takes up the room the way Flower always does. Weathers shrinks away into a corner like a scolded child, and Roy just stares. Then Ballinger turns to Roy and pulls out her gun and aims it, right at him, and Roy hardly reacts, passing the bear from right hand to left hand, left to right. "We go out of our way to help you, and you waste our time. What if right now, one of these infected psychos breaks his way into your house and kills your wife and we couldn't stop it because you were . . ."

She breaks off, then walks over to Roy, reaches down, and pulls the bear from his hands.

"Hey!" says Roy.

"Get out of here," says Ballinger. "Go home."

Roy stands up and tries to stare her down. "Give it back!" he says.

She steadies the gun with both her hands, the bear poking out through her fingers. She looks at the gun and the bear, then looks at Weathers, who raises his hands in a calm-down kind of gesture, and Ballinger nods. "Take it," she says, flipping the bear back to Roy. "Take it and get the fuck out."

Roy pushes himself up off the couch, clutching the little bear tightly. As he heads for the door, Weathers mutters, "Blame doesn't matter." And he's wrong—it matters a lot—but Roy takes one last look around the apartment, no bigger than his own, at Paul's bloodied face and Ani's panicked eyes, and the cops who make the whole place seem way too crowded, and he thinks, maybe it's not enough.

"What's that?" asks Becca as Roy tugs the old black bag into his room. Becca and Trina are on the crumpled bed, in the middle of Go Fish, when Roy reaches down, picks up the cards, and starts piling them up.

"Suitcase," says Roy. "Fill it up. Only what you need."

"Dad?" says Becca, but he ignores her, instead opening up the drawers and throwing in the things he needs: some clothes, his jeans, underwear, socks—the basics. Just enough in case the border is more than a day's trip away.

"Roy, we can't—" says Trina.

"Flower can't keep this place together," says Roy. "Cops can't keep this place together. Ain't her fault. Ain't their fault."

"It's nobody's *fault*, Roy, it's—"

"It's somebody's fault," says Roy. "But we're getting through this, the three of us. We ain't defeated. If we stay here and wait for this thing, this plague, to find us and do us in . . ."

"Roy?"

". . . the fault's mine."

The Conversation

The plan had been to divide and conquer. And nothing's changed. Daniel shuts the door to Katie's room and locks it, and as he stares at the purple door, fingers running along the contours of the two vertically stacked panels, he keeps his mind on what Derek had said and why they're here, even if *here* isn't where he ever thought it would be.

"Danny," says Katie.

Did he lock the door? He locks it again. He locks it again because that way, if the cop (who he knows!) comes, there are two choices, and it's three against two from both sides just in case—

"Danny!"

"What?" says Daniel. He turns around now, his back to the door, toward Katie, who sits on her purple bed near the radio in the corner and across from the wildly disorganized bookshelf on the left wall. It's Katie's room. He knows it by heart. During sleepovers, he'd use the pull-out bed under hers and they'd read comic books by the Mickey Mouse nightlight she used as a kid and never threw away.

"What's going on?" says Katie. She's shaking. Oh no, she's shaking. "How could you—how could you *do* this? How could—"

"Are you okay?" says Daniel.

"Am I okay? Am I *okay*? How the hell do you *think* I am, Danny?"

With a shaky, broken exhale, Daniel leans back against the door. It rattles. He slides back against it, slumping into a seated position on the sky blue carpet, the wood cracking against the hinge as he pushes his head back.

"I'm sorry," he says.

"You don't have to do this," says Katie.

Daniel stares at the M-1911. He taps the barrel against the palm of his hand. It makes a light smacking sound. He does it again, and again, and again. "That's not what I meant," he finally says.

"You don't have to do this." Her jeans scraping against the tucked-in purple covers, Katie scoots to the edge of the bed and, sitting cross-legged, leans forward. "You can get me out of here," she says. "You can get them to leave—"

"That's not what I meant, Katie," he says, catching the cylinder as it hits his palm.

"You're not like this," she says. Daniel feels her eyes on him, but his own are reflected only in the silver gun.

"You don't—"

"You're not one of them."

Releasing the gun, Daniel looks up and touches the head of the pistol against the white bandage covering the spot where his right ear used to be. "Yes," he says, "I am."

"You're not," Katie says, but it's more a question than anything else, and Daniel has already given the answer. He is a Listener. He laid down on that table and stared into the light while Adam chopped off his ear, and he did it by choice, because it was the only way to make sense of everything that had happened, and now they're here and everything would make sense if only

(if only if only if only if only)

it wasn't Katie.

"What did they do to you?" she says.

Daniel doesn't answer. She wouldn't understand.

"Fine," she says. "Fine." As she shakes her head, Daniel looks into the corner of the room, where her black mp3 player is stuffed right between the bookshelf and the wall. She has five Hall & Oates albums on it and made him promise not to tell anyone.

"You know what they're doing to her in there, right?" Katie says. A tear drips from one of her reddened eyes. Daniel doesn't want to see it, but he does. Katie cried once when a bowling ball fell on her foot, and she said Daniel was her cheerer-upper—

"Don't cry," says Daniel.

"Stop them!" she says.

"She's fine," says Daniel. "They wouldn't hurt—"

"She's not goddamn *fine*. What the hell do you think they're doing to her in there? What do you think you're supposed to be doing in here?"

"Wha—"

"'Girl's all yours.' You got any idea what that means?" she says. "You're not stupid, Danny." She shuts her eyes and shakes her head, and when the tears come, Daniel knows she's not afraid, but angry. But she's also wrong about them, the same way she was wrong when she told Daniel about the Listeners in the first place in school that day. She got her information from the cops—her dad, the cop, Mr. MacDonald. She doesn't understand. She doesn't understand there's a civil war going on outside, and she doesn't know how she got on the wrong side.

"You don't know them," Daniel says.

"*You* don't know them!" she yells, and the force of it turns Daniel back toward the door, as if someone's on the outside eavesdropping. "They kill people, Danny! These guys are a bunch of psychos"— but they're not, they're all about truth and making things better for everyone—"and they killed some of my dad's friends"—and Daniel knows they have, of course they have; his friends are the bad guys— "and I don't know how they got you into this, but, God, Danny, *listen* to me, they're—"

"You don't know them!" Daniel says. "I can't listen to you because you're wrong, and I only listen to what's right."

"What?"

"'One ear, so that we may hear only the voices of our brothers.'"

"What are you *talking* about?"

"They took me in, Katie," Daniel says. "When I needed help, they were there. When Mom left and I was alone, I—"

"Your mom?" says Katie. "What happened to your mom?"

When Daniel opens his mouth to answer, no answer comes out. He remembers his mom's room, dark and empty, and thinks maybe she got back the day after he left, but he knows she didn't. She'd never have seen the note even if he'd found the pen to write one. He sees the look on the cop's face, the twisted smirk that said—he never wanted to admit it, but he knows what it said—*Kid, you're fucking screwed.* And there would never be more toilet paper. Never.

Leaning his head back against the door, Daniel says, "It doesn't matter anymore."

Katie climbs further back into her bed and picks up a

pillow—such a light purple it's almost pink. For a moment—a fleeting, passing, fluttering-away moment—Daniel imagines she's going to hit him with it. But instead, she pulls it close and hugs it tight.

Cops and Soldiers

The ringing passes—not instantly, of course. The day after, Derek had tried to tell him he looked good, but Daniel couldn't hear him over the ringing, which is like the squeal of a fluorescent bulb about to burn out. It's not loud, or at least it's too high-pitched to be loud, but it's nonstop until you wake up one morning and realize, not only is the ringing gone, but everything sounds okay. Everything sounds right. The footsteps mean most of the Listeners are out of bed. Some of them are talking about the cops. The sounds, floating and fluttering through the air like butterflies, no longer have to choose between two ears; instead, they pick one, and emerging unified and clear.

Of course, that doesn't mean everything there is to hear is pleasant. Adam speaks the one truth, but no one ever said that truth was *nice*. More and more over the next few days, in-between initiation ceremonies and training sessions, Adam speaks of cops and robbers, and calls them one and the same.

"I used to believe what you all were raised to believe," says Adam, pacing before the assembled Listeners. Maybe a week after Daniel's ceremony, Adam is the only one left with both his ears—the only one able to hear the lies, with all the burden and responsibility that entails. "That the cops protected us. That they enforced the laws that kept us safe. I believed that many years ago, before I learned to listen."

Daniel sits cross-legged on the floor and practices the new talent given him. He scratches the bandage over the spot where his right ear used to be—the skin there sometimes itches—and tilts his left ear forward, targeted so perfectly he can't possibly miss a single word.

"But here, dear Listeners, is what I realized," says Adam. "Militias take up arms out of necessity, to protect their people from oppressors. Armies in wartime are made to serve the greater good. But *cops*—police officers—*choose* the blue . . . and the badge . . . and the gun. They don't *need* to. No one forces them. They're not *given* power. They *seek* it. They *seize* it." He says the words with disgust. "In any other world, in any other context, what do we call men who seek power? Those who believe it's theirs to claim? We call them *tyrants*."

In the cavern of Daniel's mind, the cave of his single ear, the word "tyrant" echoes, cold and hard and true.

"Those on the outside will never *know* the plague has gone," says Adam. "They will never set us free. So what should we do? Live the rest of our lives under the iron thumb of tyrants? Or break their grasp and retake our lives—and our borough—for ourselves?"

The Listeners cheer. All of them.

A light drizzle, tip-tapping off the surgical mask, sprays and dampens Daniel's hair. Before him, in the misty gray, the expansive parking lot is dreary, but also warm and humid. Somewhere, he hears his mother saying how she *told* him he should bring a jacket.

Daniel hasn't been outside since the time he misheard the Listeners. The time before that, they were saving him. And the time before *that*, the quarantine had just begun. Staring out at an abandoned world left to rust and dust and die, Daniel can't believe he's been outside only three times since the quarantine began, and that three times is probably far more than anyone else in the borough, wherever they might be.

Beside him, Derek stares ahead, his eyes always alert, the water bouncing off his bald head and rolling down his face like tears. He wears an empty backpack, which hangs crumpled and weightless on his shoulders. Quentin flanks Daniel on the other side, his chubby cheeks poking out from underneath the mask.

"What do you think?" says Derek.

The shopping carts have been scattered, some lying on their sides. Daniel wonders if the wind blew them that way, or if the sickos were here in this very parking lot, a month or a week or a day before.

It's hard to imagine *anyone* having been here. Everything looks so dead. And didn't the doctors leave because it was too dangerous to stay with all the sickos wandering around, especially after the Trent Street Incident? It's so desolate in this parking lot. Where did they all go?

"It's weird," says Daniel. He holds out his hand, and tiny droplets of water pool in his palm. "Rain."

"When all this passes," says Derek, "we'll be able to go outside all the time. Run around in the rain and everything." He turns toward the sky, shutting his eyes as the water splashes onto his face. Though Daniel can't see it, he knows Derek is smiling. "Without masks. Without . . . cops."

"What a world that will be," says Quentin. "Fresh air, freedom . . . oh, man, and they'll be grateful. Daniel, hands."

Daniel gets it. Hand on the gun at all times when outside, just like Loren instructed. "No matter how short the trip," he'd said, "no matter how safe it looks, be ready. They're everywhere, even when they don't seem to be *anywhere*." What Daniel had never thought to ask is whether he was talking about sickos or cops or both.

The rain picks up a little. It actually feels kind of nice. The rain tickles.

"All these people locked inside their homes?" says Quentin. "You know? They'll be grateful. The girls will be grateful. They'll thank us, right, Derek? They'll thank the hell out of us."

Derek smirks.

"You know what I mean? Yeah?" says Quentin. He glances at Daniel, who understands but doesn't want to admit he understands. "You'll get it." He walks on, taking the lead out of the parking lot, Daniel following behind and stepping over every yellow line. This, Derek has explained, is a trial run—a book run, actually, because some of the Listeners are bored, and the Food Garden's reading supply, unsurprisingly, is sparse. Besides, part of being ready is being able to handle yourself in the outside world, and one-eared Daniel, a Listener now and forever, is ready to rise to the challenge.

(And if he can pick up some more comics so he doesn't have to read the same one over and over again, all the better.)

The raindrops play a symphony from high on the rooftops all the way down to the broken pavement, and altogether it quiets their footsteps, allowing them to move with relative stealth. Not that they have all that far to go. The bookstore, Derek had said, is at the end of the block. As they reach the end of the parking lot, though, Daniel gazes at the movie theater just off to the left, which claims to be showing an action movie Daniel saw advertised on TV in the days before he left his apartment. *Countdown to Chaos*, it was called. They advertised it even after the quarantine went up.

Someday, when the sickos are gone and the cops aren't in charge, someday when they can walk the streets again like Derek says, they'll all go to that theater, figure out how the projector works, and watch *Countdown to Chaos*. They'll go to every theater in the borough and find every film they can. They'll have a movie marathon. With all the healthy people safe, Katie will be able to join Daniel's new family, and everything will be normal again.

Beyond the movie theater is a restaurant, Bill on the Grill, and as Daniel, following beyond Quentin, looks ahead toward it, he can see its glass windows are shattered. The head of a chair pokes out through the sharp, broken glass, and Daniel feels a faint pounding, or the memory of pounding, in his hand. But he presses onward, until Quentin holds up his gun, drawing the group to a stop.

Quentin gestures left with two fingers, and the three of them circle in a wide arc, away from the window of the restaurant. Their footsteps are slow, pushing through the damp air and the light rain, until Daniel can see very clearly through the broken glass into the inside of the restaurant. Drawing them all to a stop again, Quentin keeps his gun on the sharp, jagged hole, while Daniel fingers his and stares at the two sickos seated at what once would have been a very nice table.

The sickos sit across from one another. One of them, who used to be a woman, doesn't look as bad as some of the other sickos, a big red wart poking out of her chin the only major disfigurement on her face. But something yellowish runs from her eyes, and again and again, she reaches over her shoulder to scratch what looks to be a hump on her back.

The second sicko is much worse off, with two or three big red lumps covering the entire right side of its face, so it's impossible to see if it's a man or a woman. Its head bobs right to left, as if moving along to a melody only it can hear.

The really weird part, though, is that they're both eating—or at least, they both seem to think they're eating. Like mimes, they reach and grab nonexistent food from a nonexistent plate, pull it up to their mouths, and pretend to bite, and chew, and swallow. As if on a date, they stare only at one another, oblivious, apparently, to the fact that they're being watched, and that Quentin and Derek have their guns trained on them.

"What are they doing?" says Daniel.

"They're not always violent," says Derek. "Sometimes they're just messed up."

"Check it out." Quentin gestures toward the unidentifiable sicko on the left. "He's a cop." Sure enough, there's a silver badge clipped to its shirt—a blue, button-down shirt Daniel wouldn't identify as a cop's. "A sicko *and* a cop," says Quentin. Then he squeezes the trigger. Blood spurts out the far side of the sicko's head, and it slumps over into its nonexistent lunch.

For a moment, the other sicko, the woman-sicko, pauses, staring ahead at the cop lying facedown on the red and black checkerboard tabletop. Then, she grabs hold of her invisible sandwich and takes another pretend bite, just before Derek fires another single shot and the woman falls right off her chair.

"It only gets worse from there," Derek says quietly.

They push on toward the bookstore.

∿∿∿∿

Awed and wide-eyed, happy laughter forcing its way out of his mouth, Daniel stares at the *Daredevil* trade paperback clutched in his hands.

"Ah-hah!" says Derek from over the shelf behind him. "Looks like you hit the mother lode." He hangs the slightly less empty backpack over the shelf, and Daniel drops the trade inside. The backpack shakes from the weight. Daniel turns back quickly, grabs five more trades, and drops them in behind it.

"You think this is okay?" Daniel says as Derek pulls the backpack back over the shelf. "I mean, we're only supposed to listen to the truth."

With a smile, Derek replies, "Adam says only fiction is truly honest." He picks a novel at random off the shelf and throws it into the backpack. "Besides, men like us are not easily misled."

Daniel's fingers dance along the spines of a few more trades. "Are the cops?" he says. "I mean, maybe they're not the way they are on purpose. Maybe they just bought into the lie, same as everyone else."

"Nah. They know. They know," says Derek, hoisting the now far heavier backpack onto his back. He grunts very slightly. "Try spending six months in state prison for something you didn't do because the officer on the scene hated your guts in high school." Adjusting the straps, Derek picks up a Vonnegut novel, flips through most of it, and stops momentarily on a crude black sketch.

"That happened?" says Daniel.

"The funny thing is," says Derek, "you can't get your job back when they let you off the hook for murder, because once your name and face is in the papers, you just try and convince anyone you didn't do it." He chuckles darkly. "So while you sit and rot in a cold damp cell—and I will tell you that where we're stuck now is *nothing* compared to that—Ramirez, voted Most Likely to Fuck Up Some Guy's Life, draws his paycheck and carries his gun and walks the streets you grew up on like he owns them, because that's *exactly* what he does."

Shoving the Vonnegut book back onto the shelf, Derek paces around the science-fiction section as the rain, picking up, beats an off-kilter 7/8 outside. Quentin stands in the doorway, hand tightly gripped on his gun, shifting from foot to antsy foot. And Daniel, leaning against a shelf-full of graphic novels, remembers what Derek once said in the basement, what seems like forever ago and yesterday all at the same time: *The life I had before, it wasn't one I could have anymore—not because of the plague. Just because. I don't think I really got it until I realized what I was a part of.*

In other words, what the cops stole away, the Listeners returned.

The walk back is colder than the walk to the bookstore—wetter, too. What was once a drizzle plunges down in huge wet droplets, soaking Daniel's hair and Derek's backpack, which, Daniel hopes, is waterproof. Quentin keeps an eye out for sickos and finds none. Derek scans the horizon for cops, but the streets are no place for them now, a rain-slick day in a plague-gripped city. When they slink past their familiar plastic aisles, stomp back down those stairs, and pass the books around that crowded concrete basement, Daniel tries to imagine what Derek must feel every time he steps into this place, and how furious this man, his brother, must feel toward the people who took his life not once, but twice.

List

This is a list of things the Listeners know about the cops:

1) Within twenty-four hours of the borough's abandonment by military and medical personnel, the borough, with military endorsement, declared a brand of martial law for its three quarantined police precincts (forty-first, forty-second, forty-third), ostensibly to keep the peace.

2) A major tool in the enforcement of martial law was a program called "The Give and Take," in which healthy quarantined residents were strongly encouraged to trade in their firearms for food, water, and supplies. Residents who refused to surrender their guns, or who were suspected of concealing guns, would not receive supplies.

3) In many cases, borough residents were also forced to surrender whatever valuables they had, or whatever else cops requested. It is believed this was done to maintain a state of fear and resultant police control. Those who violated orders were left to die or, in some cases, were killed.

4) According to intercepted police communications, abuses of the Give and Take program originated with the cops in the borough's forty-first precinct.

5) *They have no idea we're coming.*

The Drums

ow: The night is only silent to those who don't know how to listen, but those who do are privileged and few. In the shadows, there's movement, light scrapes of sneakers against cracked black pavement, and up ahead, a set of twin lampposts illuminate the granite stairway leading to the house the tyrants built.

In groups of three they travel, walking silhouettes, specters at best, dodging the haloed beams of streetlights, ducking into alleys and behind tipped-over trashcans, creeping toward the cars, blue and white in the day but as colorless as everything else at night. If they speak, it's in whispers, but they don't speak. A pistol catches the very slightest hint of light and oh, oh, how it shines.

then: "This is not our home," says Adam. "Our home is what they've taken from us."

Many times before, Adam has spoken before the assembled Listeners, his body tense and excited, his voice commanding and massive, but this is no sermon. There are no lessons to be taught tonight. School's out for the summer. Toss your hats into the air and *carpe diem.* This time, when Adam paces, he paces with Loren on his left side and Terry on his right, both with their weapons in hand, Terry's Walther P99 marked with a piece of tape that reads, in big red letters, "Property of Terry—Keep the Fuck Off."

"They've taken the borough, turned it mute, but still we hear it . . . calling for us, to us." He takes a breath, and in the silence that follows, Daniel, on his knees right by Zeke, truly can hear it calling, in floating whispers and desperate pleas. When Adam speaks again, he speaks the words Daniel has already heard: "'Take me back. Take me back.'"

Somewhere there's a *drumbeat, drumbeat, drumbeat,* the

revolutionary's call to arms, the steady *pound, pound, pound* of feet marching toward inevitability. It's an object in motion. It's an irresistible force. Let the drumbeat *drum beat beat drum drum.*

"And we listen!" cries Adam in perfect quarter-time. "We listen to the cries of the helpless, which are silenced by the lies of the cops."

Fists pump into the drums of war, scattered voices sing the song, and the band goes marching, marching, marching . . .

Now: As the shadows float on quiet air toward the granite citadel of the forty-first precinct, they divide like paramecium, the dark, ambiguous masses swimming in different directions. They split into sets of threes, two groups moving toward the dark alley on the left, where they're to stake out the windows and move, in time, as one. Quickly, the windows in front are covered, the back exits shrouded in shadow, and the final group of three, the three that were once individuals, once Loren, once Derek, once Daniel, float and flit right toward the front door.

Here, too, the drum beats, and it drives the heart, which drives the body; it's dominoes on a drumbeat drumbeat scale. Daniel feels it in his bones and his blood, pushed by the shadow and one with the silhouette, the memories of mothers and albums and broken windows, abandonment and left-to-die, flowing and shifting and swimming through his head, and through all their heads. Drum beats, heart pounds, and for a passing moment, the latter falls off-rhythm. The drum says go on, the heart says go back, but Daniel is not one but of a whole, and the drum beats on *drum drum.*

Loren cocks his Berretta.

Derek says, "Stay low. Stay close."

As Loren breaks ahead and charges for the door, the drum beats, drum beats, drum beats . . .

Then: The cries they make could be called cheers in another place and time, if their faces weren't so grim when the sound came out, and if the undercurrent to their voices was joy and not rage. Call it a roar. Call it a chant. Call it a drum.

It's loud, whatever it is, a chorus in crescendo, and the only sound that overtakes it is Adam's voice; Adam, as he says, "We listen to the pleas of the city, broken by the gibberish of its captors!"

In Daniel's lap is his M-1911 pistol, and he pounds it, pounds it, pounds it against his open hand, pounds it to the instinctive rhythm that overtakes the chamber, the rhythm so insistent it even lacks a contradictory echo. The first beat is for Katie; the second, his mother; the third for Derek, whom the cops destroyed; the fourth for Adam and all the Listeners, for Zeke (*drum*) and for Terry (*drum*) and for Loren (*drum*) and for Brian and Stone and Ivan and Quentin and *drum* and *drum* and *DRUM* and *DRUM* and—

"Who are we?!" says Adam.

"Listeners!" cry the Listeners.

"Who are we?!"

"Listeners!" yells Daniel at the top of his lungs.

"Who are we?!" Adam screams, and as drumbeats reach a fevered pitch with the powerful rhythm of a heart attack, they cry, the children, Loren and Terry and Derek and Quentin and Zeke and Daniel, they cry, the drum beats, and they cry . . .

NOW: When Loren kicks the double doors open, the sound echoes through the concrete, kills the drumbeat, and brings the shadowy specters to solid life. Glass shatters, everywhere glass shatters, and Loren turns left and fires, instantly, at the two cops standing in the hallway. Both go down and red blood drains to the floor.

For all the consistency and insistency of the drumbeat, the gunshots are random and chaotic, and they don't echo as they do in the shooting range, or mush into the mattress. Things break, people fall and scream and fire back, and as a woman with a crew cut takes a hit in the shoulder and lunges under her desk, as some of the cops grab or try to grab their guns, as Zeke and Brian and maybe Pip climb in through the broken windows, Derek fires a couple shots and leads Daniel through a nearby door and up into a stairwell.

Daniel holds his gun and aims but doesn't fire. "Stay low!" yells Derek as he fires up the stairs, where Terry and a bunch of the others, it's hard to say who, are already pushing ahead. A gunshot makes it down the stairwell, passing just a foot away from Daniel and digging into the door behind him. Several cops lie on the stairs. There's red and it's dripping. Most of the bodies don't move, but one twitches a little, and Daniel holds the gun—holds it, but doesn't fire. The gunshots ring and echo and everything happens everywhere—

Firing a couple rounds at an officer near the top, Derek ducks back behind the stairs and reloads. Daniel ducks with him, and he hears another couple shots and something hitting the stairs. "Yee-hah!" cries Terry somewhere up above. "Stay down! *Stay* the fuck down!"

The gunshots crescendo behind Daniel and in front of him and all around him and it all goes into his one ear, and he can't hear it's so loud—can't hear can't *hear* and . . . and . . .

As the shots fade away in the downstairs, only a couple scattered pops sliding under the door, things start to become clear. The gunfire is still heavy upstairs, descending down the stairway like a hundred Slinkies, and Derek pulls out from under the stairwell and starts his way up the steps. As Daniel follows, his fully loaded gun heavy in his hands, Derek motions for him to be quiet, but that's when the door behind them opens and Brian steps through, a little blood on his shirt.

"We're clear," says Brian. Sparks of light and sound, firecrackers dangerously enclosed, pop through the open door upstairs.

"You okay?" says Derek.

Brian brushes the blood away with his index finger. "Not mine," he says.

"Fatalities?"

"Ari. Stone. Maybe—"

"Clear up here!" says Terry, peeking his head through the open door. Sure enough, the gunfire has stopped, replaced now by the buzzing drone of the fluorescent lights, casting hazy illumination over the lumpy sky-blue bricks in the cold, silent, red-stained stairwell. (That same cop twitches again.)

Stepping over the bodies, giving the brown-haired twitching cop one last little kick, Derek climbs the rest of the way up, Daniel and Brian right behind, and as Daniel climbs, he tries not to look, and he holds his gun like he's going to use it, but every one of them every one of them could be him, and Katie Katie would—

Oh, and upstairs is worse—oh oh worse. The bodies in blue are everywhere, on chairs, many on their side; on the desks, solid and brown but wet now; in the offices. Some wear suits and ties, and are just as dead in them. Some are dying, but they're all disarmed, or at least they all seem to be. Daniel looks up at the ceiling because that's the only place the cops of the forty-first precinct are not.

"Spread out!" says Derek.

"Come out and plaaaaaaay," says Terry, sneaking around the long office, past a square support beam in the middle of the room.

There's a cop leaning against it, a brown-haired woman with her hat off and her neck leaning at entirely the wrong angle, her eyes wide open but completely empty in a way wide-open eyes shouldn't be. The drumbeat is strange and random, and so deep it pushes at Daniel's guts, and with dead eyes, the woman looks up at him and says, "It's just for toilet paper. I'll be right back," and Daniel doubles over and pulls off his mask and vomits in her lap.

"Shit, kid," says Terry.

Derek leans down next to Daniel. "Are you okay?"

"We . . . we just . . ."

"I know."

"They were just . . ." says Daniel.

"No. No," says Derek. "These are the people who went through your house and stole your things and would have let you starve to death. They're not—listen, they're not what you were taught in school."

"They—"

"They're not. Okay? Daniel? Are you with me?"

Daniel coughs. Just a little more vomit comes out. Still crouched over, eyes closed, Daniel nods, and Derek pats him on the shoulder.

Just then, a couple more shots, loud and jarring, cut through the air from somewhere on the other side of the office. Derek lifts his gun, but in an instant, Terry's voice calls out, "Got one!" Derek sighs.

Daniel closes his eyes and listens to the *drumbeat, drumbeat*, fading away into nothing but footsteps in a place as cold and dead as the one outside.

then: The basement buzzes. Fifty voices speak at once. They pull on their shoes and grab their guns and ascend the stairs as a unit for the first time. And Daniel, sitting on his bed in an alcove where not a single uninitiated kid remains, stares at the gun in his hand, his heart racing from the drumbeat, from Adam's words, from the Listeners' proud, unified cry. Daniel has shot a gun but never a person. He knew a good cop once, but he wants to be free, in a real world, not a basement world, and the drum beats, drum beats.

Footsteps echo up the stairs. Derek gives Daniel a look—it's time to go. When Daniel grabs his gun and follows, he knows, as the drum drives his legs and *all* their legs, that at this moment he is one of them, *of* them, the silhouettes in the shadows, the specters in the night, a Listener now and forever.

thiяD яEspitE

Martial Law

[*This transcribed recording was discovered in the office of Captain Ferdinand Ruiz in the police station of the borough's forty-first precinct. The speakers have been identified as Lieutenant Max Powell and Sergeant Gavin Weathers.*]

LT. POWELL: Listen. This is how it's going to work.
SGT. WEATHERS: You're recording this.
LT. POWELL: This is how it's going to work.
SGT. WEATHERS: Can't believe you're recording this.
LT. POWELL: I'm going to ask you questions. You answer them. You can't take the Fifth, because the Fifth doesn't really apply. None of the other twenty-seven either. I ask, you answer.
SGT. WEATHERS: Daubman too, right? Like hell—
LT. POWELL: Not finished. Listen. You have a question, too. About Anne. And I'll answer it. That's what you get in return.
SGT. WEATHERS: . . . You'll tell me why Anne—
LT. POWELL: Yeah. Also, I might not kill you.
SGT. WEATHERS: You're sick.
LT. POWELL: I'm sick, *sir*.
SGT. WEATHERS: You're sick, *Max*.

[*Few additional records were recovered from the forty-first precinct, but central processing has some basics. Weathers was thirty-six years old, a fourteen-year veteran of the police force, with a fairly nondescript record—no reprimands found, but no real accolades, either. He was considered a good officer, but apparently nothing more. Powell, forty-seven, has served for twenty-three years, and in that time*] *has gained considerable notice for his theories on interrogation tech-niques, first published in a 1996 issue of* Police *magazine. In his article, Powell describes interrogation as "a power struggle, which the ques-tioning officer has to be winning, obviously, at all times."*

The reason for this particular interrogation tape is a puzzle.]

. . .

SGT. WEATHERS: What I remember her saying, the thing I remem-ber, is, "The risks" . . . I'm talking. You don't need to keep that on me.

LT. POWELL: Talk.

SGT. WEATHERS: She said, "The risks of continuing our efforts inside the quarantine outweigh the benefits." Which you know. Because you were there. And I don't know what you made of that, but the gist of it was, they weren't getting anywhere on killing this thing, we're all exposed, goodbye and thanks and screw you.

LT. POWELL: You sound angry.

SGT. WEATHERS: Yeah, hey, odd thing, right?

LT. POWELL: What did you do?

SGT. WEATHERS: What did any of us *do*? Look, fact is, after Trent, we all saw it coming. And I bet there wasn't a one of us who didn't want to say, "Evacuate me, too, I'm fine, I'm healthy, I don't want to be stuck in this cemetery," but it was . . . it was procedure. I get pro-cedure, when there's a reason behind it. I get it. It sucks, but I get it. And we were all scared.

LT. POWELL: Are you scared now?

SGT. WEATHERS: Isn't there supposed to be a good cop with you when you play bad cop?

LT. POWELL: I—

SGT. WEATHERS: Or does that not matter when you're not playing?

LT. POWELL: But you were scared then.

SGT. WEATHERS: What?

LT. POWELL: When the doctors left. You were scared then.

SGT. WEATHERS: Yeah.

LT. POWELL: Scared you were going to die?

SGT. WEATHERS: Scared I was going to die, painfully, yeah. But mostly scared I'd get it and spread it. You know, there's only so many places to go here. Between the 9 Ball, which is where me and Anne first heard about the plague, and the docks, it's not all that far. It's claustrophobic, real easy to get sick, real easy to get someone else sick.

LT. POWELL: Like Anne.

SGT. WEATHERS: . . . Yeah, like Anne.

LT. POWELL: Or me.

SGT. WEATHERS: Hah, right. If I get sick, Max, I'm gonna give you a great big hug.

[Anne, referenced throughout the recording, is believed to be Sergeant Anne Ballinger, forty-three, a twenty-two year veteran of the forty-first precinct and Weathers's partner for the eight years prior to the quarantine.]

SGT. WEATHERS: In a way, you know, I think Anne was made for this? I mean, not that she enjoyed being out there. None of us liked being out there once the military left, because the second that happened, everything was chaos. People got sick, people got guns, people walked outside and started shooting them. Healthy people went to get some food, got shot or got sick. It was endless, and it felt endless, and I'm just talking about the first three *days*.

LT. POWELL: But Anne was made for it?

SGT. WEATHERS: Heh . . . you know Anne. Tougher things got, tougher *she* got, and that's the thing that always kept me strong. I remember this hostage situation a few years back. This guy is on the fourth floor, fifth floor, with a gun to this girl's head, and procedure is always—stay calm. Make him stay calm. But Anne takes the phone and says, "If you don't come down, if that girl gets hurt, I will come up there, throw you out that window, drag you back up, and throw you out again."

LT. POWELL: As I recall, she got a reprimand for that.

SGT. WEATHERS (laughing): But it worked! The guy came down, because when Anne's like that, you listen. You can't not. A lot of the time, I felt like I was just along for the ride, and that was fine by me. Anne—I mean, cop good as her, she could have moved up the ranks easily. But she always stuck it out with me, stuck to the streets, and that's the thing about Anne. That's her. You know.

LT. POWELL: Do you love her? . . . Do you love her?

SGT. WEATHERS: Get it off me.

LT. POWELL: Made for this how?

SGT. WEATHERS: Get off the trigger and get it off me.

LT. POWELL: No.

SGT. WEATHERS: She could reel them in. She could get people to stay inside. When the street was crawling with the sick, she could hit them before they hit anyone else.

LT. POWELL: How—

SGT. WEATHERS: She was made for this because she was needed every second of every day, because she was in control every second of every day, and that's what we needed when everything went to hell. That's what it was like for three days. We wore those surgical masks and hoped it'd keep us from getting sick, and Anne took care of everything.

LT. POWELL: And then what happened?

SGT. WEATHERS: Then . . .

LT. POWELL: What happened?

SGT. WEATHERS: Then what happened? Ah . . . damn. You know. You were there.

LT. POWELL: What happened?

SGT. WEATHERS: You killed the captain. That's what happened.

LT. POWELL: . . . The captain was killed.

SGT. WEATHERS: Oh, right. By "Listeners." Some fringe cult suddenly decides their brand-new goal in life is to off the captain, right. And, hey, if it works out as a promotion for Lieutenant Max Powell, all the better.

[~~There have been references in numerous other sources to a group called the Listeners, and it is believed there was a breakdown in communication between the military and the police officers in all quarantined precincts. Vague police records exist from before the quarantine began of a one-eared cult, but their presence has been poorly documented, except for occasional witness testimony and various references, as in a poem discovered~~

THERE ARE NO LISTENERS.]

. . .

SGT. WEATHERS: You know my record, Max. You know me. Do

my job, no less, no more, so I kept my mouth shut, even when the Give and Take became less about giving than taking. First Daubman and Abrams take some comics, and Anne says it's just comics, but it's not a domino effect after that. It's an explosion.

LT. POWERS: Abuse of power, would you say?

SGT. WEATHERS: Hah! You would know.

LT. POWERS: I didn't steal anything.

SGT. WEATHERS: No, sir, *Captain* Weathers.

LT. POWERS: And where was Anne during all this?

SGT. WEATHERS: Anne's my backbone. You know that. She didn't think it was a big deal, so I didn't do anything about it, and the only thing I can figure there is that she was too focused on fixing this place that she didn't see we were the ones screwing it up.

LT. POWERS: So what happened?

SGT. WEATHERS: We were on Herman, right? We'd just convinced the owner of the neighborhood bar over there to give up her gun, in exchange for supplies for the neighborhood, which we were gonna bring by the next day. See, the Give and Take worked, Max. It worked when that was all it was about. It worked when we brought that old woman a carrot cake after she told us her neighbor had a pistol. The sick weren't armed, the healthy weren't armed. It actually *worked*.

LT. POWERS: What happened?

SGT. WEATHERS: We were walking up Herman—

LT. POWERS: When was this?

SGT. WEATHERS: I don't know, ten days after the evacuation? Eleven? Anyway, we were walking up Herman, and we got a message on the two-way, situation on Rochester, a couple blocks up. Shots fired, sounded pretty bad, and Anne and I were close enough to respond on foot. Halfway there, there's another message, situation under control. Abrams's voice, but there's some kind of yelling in the background, and it doesn't sound right. We were already most of the way there. So I'm thinking about Trent, all the shit that's gone down since the quarantine went up, and . . . and I felt like I had to check it out.

LT. POWERS: You and Anne?

SGT. WEATHERS: . . . No. Anne thought I was being paranoid.

LT. POWERS: But—

SGT. WEATHERS: And usually, that'd be enough for me to believe it. It's like I said, Anne's my backbone. She leads, I'm along for the ride, but . . . I think it was because I was so on edge here, with all this going on, that I had to check it out. So I did. I went on my own.

LT. POWERS: And what did you find? . . . Gavin?

SGT. WEATHERS: This guy was on the ground. God knows what he did, if anything, but he was on the ground, and Abrams and Denton, they were just . . . kicking him. Again, and again, and again. And this girl—had to be his wife from the look on her face—she was handcuffed to the radiator, and they were just making her watch. I don't know what led up to it, I don't know, but . . .

LT. POWERS: So what did you do?

SGT. WEATHERS: . . . This . . . this is what I mean, about Anne . . . If she was there, and I've seen it a hundred times, she'd have kicked her way into the room, thrown Abrams off of that poor guy, stuck a gun in Denton's face, and told him to back the fuck off. She's my backbone. Me? I'm the little kid on the playground who wants the right thing to be done but doesn't have the guts to be the guy to do it. What did I do? I told a teacher.

LT. POWERS: Me.

SGT. WEATHERS: You. Captain Powers. I went back to the station, brushed off Anne, and went into your office. Your office. And you told me, that seems unlikely. You told me, forget about it. And that is when I knew, for sure, there was something wrong. I didn't know what just yet, I didn't have the whole picture, but . . . but whatever this was, wherever this abuse of authority was coming from, you were a part of—

LT. POWERS: Did you ever fuck Anne?

SGT. WEATHERS: . . . Excuse me?

LT. POWERS: Did you ever fuck her?

SGT. WEATHERS: What the hell—

LT. POWERS: Screw, ride, hammer, nail, pound, bang—

SGT. WEATHERS: You shut the fuck up—

LT. POWERS: Do *not* forget who's holding the cards here!

SGT. WEATHERS: . . . Is that what they call it?

LT. POWERS: Don't forget.

SGT. WEATHERS (laughing)

LT. POWERS: What? Something's funny?

SGT. WEATHERS: You're not after information. So what *are* you after?

LT. POWERS: You haven't answered the question.

SGT. WEATHERS: And you don't care that I haven't.

[Excerpt from Powers's article on interrogation techniques, "Balance of Power," Police 1996: "From a person-to-person standpoint, the information is secondary. The information is what he has and you don't, and as long as you make that your top priority, the power is in the hands of the interrogated, not the interrogator. You need to change the balance. Verbal abuse works. Humiliation works better. The interrogated needs to believe you are in control, and that you are better than him. Then he will tell you everything, because he believes you deserve to know."]

SGT. WEATHERS: You don't have a leg to stand on. Sooner or later, you know, they'll—

LT. POWERS: What did you do?

SGT. WEATHERS: I told Anne! Of course I told Anne. Who do I always talk to? I talk to Anne. I led her down to one of the police cars sitting outside the station, so no one else could listen in. I told her what happened, I told her how you reacted, and she was stunned, appalled, angry. And that's how I know you did something, or told her something, and you'd better tell me what you did because—

LT. POWERS: What next?

SGT. WEATHERS: You're screwed up, Lieutenant.

LT. POWERS: What next?

SGT. WEATHERS: I knew we needed help. The whole story. And don't even ask me who I went to because I'm not telling you, but the important thing I found out is that this was going on a little bit everywhere, but nowhere near as bad as here. Because the rest of the precincts aren't run by a two-bit thug in a high-rank uniform.

LT. POWERS: You shut—

SGT. WEATHERS: Fine, shoot me, prove I'm right. I found out about the other precincts and I found out that the Give and Take didn't even start with you. Just the level of abuse. And that's how two other precincts keep their captains and ours gets overthrown by—

LT. POWERS: Watch it.

SGT. WEATHERS: God, man, I'm not the world's best cop, but I'm no coward. You've got me at gunpoint in a little room and you're the one . . .

LT. POWERS: Shut up.

SGT. WEATHERS: . . . shaking in your boots. Your throne is on a damn house of cards. And I should have known it the second I broke into your office.

LT. POWERS: . . . What?

SGT. WEATHERS: Well, finally, we've stumbled upon something you didn't know. Guess you learn something with these little interviews after all, huh?

LT. POWERS: And what did you find?

SGT. WEATHERS: What do you think I found? I found the tapes. One for Red Wayne—you know, the guy Anne and I arrested for those convenience store robberies a few days before the quarantine. All kinds of stuff that should have been in an evidence locker. But the best one, the best one . . . was Daubman's.

LT. POWERS: You listened?

SGT. WEATHERS: Daubman, who didn't show up for work the next day.

LT. POWERS: You listened?

SGT. WEATHERS: Care to explain that?

[The Daubman tape was also recovered from the forty-first precinct. However, the tape was damaged, and thus far analysis has failed. The tape's very existence, though, raises serious questions regarding the accusations Weathers raises in this recording.

It's detrimental to any investigation that Weathers has not been found.]

LT. POWERS: . . . Then what?

SGT. WEATHERS: I go home. I sleep. Anne picks me up to go to work the next day. Today. This morning. I tell her what I found, I tell her I'm going to fight this, fight you. And I'm not the tough cop, Max. You know that. I'm not the guy who walks into a room and takes out the bad guy, but I do believe in this, and with the rest of the world screwed up, I was going to fight this. So we . . . so we go to the office and . . .

LT. POWERS: Heh. Hm. And things don't go as planned.

SGT. WEATHERS: How did you do it?

LT. POWERS: You're mixed-up, Gavin. You got it backwards.

SGT. WEATHERS: I—

LT. POWERS: This is not about what I need from you. This is about what you need from—

SGT. WEATHERS: How did you get my partner to stick a gun to my back and shove me in here? What do you have on her?

LT. POWERS: You need to know. It kills you that you don't.

SGT. WEATHERS: . . . Fine. Yeah. I put up with your shit and now—

LT. POWERS: The streets are quiet, Gavin. They're quiet because the people out there are dependent and afraid, and that—

SGT. WEATHERS: You—

LT. POWERS: And that is why we need to do things the way we have. That is why—

SGT. WEATHERS: What about Anne?

LT. POWERS: That's why—

SGT. WEATHERS: *What about Anne?!*

LT. POWERS: Anne agrees. You self-righteous piece of shit. Anne agrees.

SGT. WEATHERS: That's bullshit, that's—

LT. POWERS: You said it yourself. She was made for this, because it gave her the chance to be in control. And you get control . . .

SGT. WEATHERS: No.

LT. POWERS: . . . when you mix dependence and fear. Anne understands that.

SGT. WEATHERS (inaudible)

LT. POWERS: What?

SGT. WEATHERS: That's bullshit.

LT. POWERS: We're done here.

SGT. WEATHERS: That's bullshit.

LT. POWERS: Come with me.

[Chairs squeak. There are footsteps, then the sound of a door opening.]

WOMAN: Gavin, I'm—

[The recording cuts off here.]

One Ear

For a long time, Katie studies Daniel, cross-legged on the floor, and for a long time, Daniel looks away, ostensibly trying to listen for anything or anyone else in the apartment, but of course he hears nothing. The thing that kills him is that he wanted so badly to find her—find her safe and okay and take her the hell *away* from this place. He ran away once and almost died trying to get to her, and now, here she is, and she won't listen and he won't talk and he has to close his eyes and pretend she's still not here.

"Did it hurt?" she finally asks.

It takes a moment before Daniel realizes she's talking about the ear. He absentmindedly scratches the bandage with the barrel of the pistol. "Yeah," he says, "but it feels better once it's done."

Cautiously, Katie pushes herself forward to the end of the bed, then slips off. She crouches down in front of Daniel, dropping the pillow to her left. Then, she reaches forward with her left hand and brushes the bandage, which scrapes underneath her fingers. Tingles, like pins and needles, sparkle along the side of Daniel's head and down to his cheek. "Why do you do it?" Katie asks softly.

"'One ear, so that we may hear only the voices of our brothers,'" Daniel recites. There's a crack in his voice when he quotes Adam. It doesn't sound right out of his mouth. "'One voice, so that the lies of the world may be drowned out by the truths of our brethren.'"

He looks at Katie, and Katie looks at him. Her eyes are red, and damp, and she suddenly looks a few years older than she really is. Daniel feels her hand on his bandage, and it shakes. After a long breath, she wipes her eyes with her right hand and says, "That is such bullshit, Danny."

"We—we can help you," says Daniel, and from there the words

start to pour out, like a dam filled to capacity just now begun to crack. "We just want to help," he says, "and when the plague is gone, Katie, we can go outside and we can play soccer and we won't even have to leave. I thought we would, but it'll be a nice place, when the plague is gone, and they'll never lift the quarantine because *they'll* never know for sure but *we'll* know, and we can keep you safe. Me and Derek and the Listeners—we'll keep you safe, Katie, I promise." Bobbing back and forth, he smiles at a world twenty feet and only months or years away.

"Danny—"

"It's just because of the things *they* did, see. That's why we have to do what we do, because we can't . . . because no one should be oppressed, and the cops, Katie, they were going to take over but we *stopped* them! We stopped them so everyone could be free and equal in this place . . ."

"Danny—"

". . . and if you listen hard enough, you can hear that it's true, and, Katie, I just, I missed you so much," his voice breaks here, "and I wanted to find you and save you but I couldn't do it on my own, and now I can because they helped me, and I'll tell them your dad's okay, and once you learn to listen you'll see how—"

"Shut up!" Katie shrieks.

Daniel does.

"Just shut up, Danny," says Katie, softer now, picking up her pillow and sitting back on her purple sheets again. "Can't you hear yourself?" she says.

What a strange question. Daniel cocks his head and stares at her. "I hear everything, Katie," he says. "I hear everything."

Dirty Work

They always talk about "the calm before the storm," but that calm doesn't compare to the one after. It's like the end of a fireworks display, after that grand finale of lights and explosions, when the black smoke drifts across the gray clouds, the final rumblings of thunder roll over the trees, and everything seems empty and unfinished. You wait for the other shoe to drop, but you're waiting forever.

As Daniel descends the stairwell, feeling queasy and holding tight to the handrail, he tries to avoid the bodies but can't help but step on a flaccid hand, the same way you can't help but cough when someone tells you to be absolutely quiet. It's the same one that was twitching before, but it doesn't twitch now. Bones roll underneath Daniel's shoes, and the lack of any cry of pain or protest is unsettling. "I'm sorry," Daniel feels compelled to whisper.

From the step on which the hand rests, a tiny stream of blood rolls down, ending in the puddle below. Daniel takes care to avoid that, too.

At the bottom of the stairs, Daniel pushes open the door and heads into the main lobby, where the bulk of the Listeners mill about, some in pairs carrying dead cops outside, others pulling tarps and body bags over the bodies of the three or four fallen Listeners. They watch their step, of course. The floor is littered, and the cleanup is in its earliest stages.

"We hit the jackpot here," says Loren, standing by one of several desks, talking with Derek and Terry. "I mean, walking distance from the market? Adam was right on the money. This is the headquarters. Look." He flips through a rolodex, which sits in the corner of the desk by a dingy can filled only with an unsharpened, gnawed-on pencil. "Name, age, address of every single cop in the borough. All three precincts. We can go house to house, finish the job."

"What about weapons, ammo?" says Derek.

But Daniel doesn't hear Loren's response. Instead, he steps past the group, toward the back of the room, where a heavy-looking steel door stands incongruously beside a light brown desk and a white plastic phone. There's a small window in the door, revealing some illuminated space beyond. Daniel tries the knob. It doesn't turn, but only rattles.

Somewhere behind him, scattered voices talk strategy. Someone trips over a body and laughs about it. The knob rattles again. Glancing to his right, Daniel spots, on that same brown desk, a set of keys peeking out from underneath a disorganized stack of papers, right above some pink form only and always half filled-out. He grabs the keys, which jingle in his hands, and tries them, one by one, in the tight key slot in the doorknob. The first one fails, the second goes in most of the way but won't turn, but the third one is the charm and the steel door, not quite as heavy as it looked, pushes open.

As the voices of the Listeners fade into the background, Daniel steps into the narrow hallway, surrounded on both sides by empty holding cells, six total. The buzzing of the fluorescent lights is almost deafening, and that's all Daniel hears until the steel door swings shut, the boom echoing through the chamber. His feet tapping loudly against the concrete floor—it's strangely like the supermarket bunker in that way—Daniel walks over to the first cell, his eyes landing on some chiseled graffiti on the far wall. "SO VERY VERY NEAR" is what it says, and *all* it says.

"Who's there?" someone says.

Daniel jumps at the voice, his feet scraping as he spins around toward the back of the holding cells. He remains still, completely still, his breathing drowned out by the fluorescent lights.

"Someone's there," says the voice. It's a man's voice, strong but piercing and nervous, like the sound of an isolated flute in an unrehearsed solo.

Very slowly, Daniel wraps his fingers around the barrel of his gun, tugs it from his pants, and takes a step forward. "I have a gun," he says.

"I don't," says the man.

With the echo, it's difficult to tell what side of the hallway the voice is coming from, so Daniel stays in the middle, his footsteps tapping along the concrete now, the *tips* and the *taps* bouncing like basketballs. The third and fourth cells are empty, that's certain, but soon, in the cell on the right and at the very end, the man appears. He's a tall man, maybe in his mid-thirties, sitting on a skinny little bed and rubbing his fingers along the cross hanging from his neck.

When he turns to Daniel, the man blinks and squeezes the cross harder. "Who are you?" he says.

For a moment, Daniel studies the man. He's dressed in worn jeans and a torn, dirty, short-sleeve collared shirt. Tall though he is, the man shrinks under Daniel's stare, and Daniel pushes his M-1911 back into his pocket. "I'm Daniel," says Daniel. "Who are you?"

The man sighs. "Tyrone? I guess? Hah." He chuckles nervously. "It stopped mattering once the quarantine went up, you know. It's a different . . . context. Or something."

The buzzing lights fill the silence as Daniel takes a step closer to the cell. "What did you do?" he asks.

Clasping the cross in both hands, Tyrone shuts his eyes and drops his arms to his thighs and his head to his hands. Tears squeeze through his eyes like blood through a pinprick wound. When his voice emerges again, it's a laugh, dark and bitter and so heavy it plunges right to the floor. "*Do?*" says Tyrone. "What did I *do*? I did . . . nothing."

He laughs again as his eyes shoot open. "I let them die." He sniffs. "I let them die."

∿∿∿∿

A few minutes later, back in the lobby of the police station, Daniel finds Derek with his surgical mask on, leaning by the body of a fallen cop, an Asian guy with a small nose. When Derek looks up, he says, "Daniel. Get the legs?"

But when Daniel looks down at the body, he winces, his eyes darting back to Derek. It'd be easier, maybe, if this was the scarred man, or the fat one with the bulldog cheeks, but this man is someone Daniel never knew, and he's never even *seen* dead people until today, and now they're all . . . all of them. Every one.

Derek sighs. "Please," he says.

Hesitating for a moment, Daniel keeps his eyes off the dead man's face and reaches for his own pocket, from which he tugs his crumpled-up surgical mask. Daniel stretches the straps behind his head and ties them in a knot, then crouches down and, grunting heavily, lifts the cop's legs, Derek supporting the rest of the body and the bulk of the weight. As they carry the cop toward the double doors at the front of the station, Derek says, "The things we do to survive, right?" A couple other Listeners hold the doors open for them, and on the way down the steps into the humid night, they pass Zeke and Quentin, on their way back. Zeke looks at Daniel wide-eyed, an almost brotherly glance Daniel dodges as Zeke steps back into the police station. "The things we do," repeats Derek. Walking backwards, he guides Daniel to the right, where a couple of Listeners emerge from around a corner.

On the other side of the steps, Daniel spots Terry scanning the street ahead of them, keeping guard for sickos. It has to be the sickos. It can't be the cops, now, can it? "I know they were . . ." starts Daniel. "I know—"

"You know we had to do this, but you wish we didn't," says Derek.

With a sigh, Daniel says, "Yeah."

"Me, too," says Derek, readjusting the load. "Believe me . . . believe me, me, too." He chuckles, glancing over his shoulder. "I'm not a violent man. You know that, right?" Daniel nods. "Of course you know that. You're my brother. You're the little brother I never had."

Derek exhales deeply as they turn the corner into the alley bordering the police station. At the end of the alley is a rusted green dumpster, marred with deep red spray paint. A couple Listeners by the dumpster push a cop's body in, but one leg catches on the edge, a limp knee curving over. One of the Listeners reaches up and, with a grunt, nudges the rest of the leg over and in. The body lands with a muffled thud. The Listeners start to head back.

"I believe . . . I really believe that, when the quarantine went up, this borough became . . . independent. Separate," says Derek. "If not then, then when the doctors left. This is where we live. This is life." He shakes his head, lifting the cop's body up to his shoulder. "Can you imagine spending the rest of your life in that basement, forced to stay there by people who lie, and steal, and kill, and rule this place like tyrants?"

Tyrants. Enemies. Trying not to look toward the dumpster, Daniel remembers what they did to Derek. "It's a war," Daniel says, as his footsteps echo down the alley.

"It's a *rebellion*," says Derek. "I've seen first-hand what they do. It scares me. And if they ever find out, on the outside, what happened here . . . it'll start again. Because they won't understand. But today . . ." He smiles. "We stopped them, Daniel. We stopped them. We're heroes. Do you believe me when I say we're heroes?"

"Yes."

"Do you believe me?"

"Yes."

As Derek pulls to a stop next to the dumpster, he glances up, then takes a step back. Daniel does the same. "Okay," he says, pulling the body away from the dumpster, "now, one . . . two . . ." They swing the body back and forth, away and toward, and on the third effort they toss the weight into the dumpster, where some part of it hits against the back and a light tinny sound emerges. Derek cracks his knuckles and stares up at the dumpster.

Back down the alley where they came from, Daniel sees Brian holding onto the dead hands of another cop. Greg carries the legs. Daniel hears them struggling.

"I know . . . I know you feel a certain way about cops," says Derek. "Because your friend Katie's father, on Applewood Street—"

"Rochester Avenue," says Daniel.

"Right. Because her dad is a cop," says Derek, "and you guys were close, right?"

"Yeah," says Daniel. "Yeah."

"You want to think the best of him . . . and all of them, *because* of him," says Derek. "Because of what you were told once." He looks down toward Daniel. "But, Daniel, you're a Listener now. What do you hear?"

With a ragged sound, Brian and Greg shove their cop into the dumpster, though a bit less efficiently. Greg tosses the cop's arm, which hangs over the edge, the rest of the way in. Daniel glances up at the dumpster, where the cop's body is no longer visible—none of them is—and then back toward the police station, the side windows shattered by the Listeners' advance. He remembers the two in his apartment, and imagines the one who locked Derek away.

"He's one of them," says Daniel, almost absently. He stares at the broken windows, a jagged outline all that's left of the glass inside the frames. Even as someone on the inside forces a plank of wood onto the hole to close it up, Daniel sees one of the sharp points tinted red, and it glows as the light from the station pushes through into the alley. "He's . . . bad."

"He's bad," says Derek. He pats Daniel on the shoulder. "Let's head back."

"Only five more," says Brian. He slaps his hand against the dumpster twice, and the metal vibrates like thunder. "Packed."

As the four of them start back toward the front of the police station, Daniel takes one more passing glance at the broken window and the bit of blood pooling on the tip, like a water droplet on a shower faucet that refuses to drop.

"How about our guys?" says Derek.

"Adam'll probably want a memorial service when he gets here," says Brian. The alley grows lighter as they head toward the streetlight, and a light breeze blows through the surprisingly cool summer air. It's a cloudless night. It's peaceful and, for the moment, silent as well. Slightly pulling on the gun in his pocket, Brian says, "Did you see how I—"

A fist catches Brian's jaw the moment he steps out of the alley, and the crack resounds through the city streets as Brian tumbles hard onto the concrete. Daniel jumps back, but the others hold their ground, and in an instant the man, in a trench coat, is on Brian, pummeling him savagely with fists red, lumpy, and sick.

"You killed them! You killed them!" cries the sicko, spitting out its rage. The fists come fast, and the impact severs a boil, spilling a whitish pus onto Brian's bloody face. Brian's mask slips off his mouth.

"Get the fuck off!" yells Brian.

Derek reaches for his gun, but before he can draw it, a shot rings out and the sicko rolls off of Brian, blood gushing from the top of its shoulder. As Brian scrambles to his feet and coughs heavily, Terry steps forward from the left, gun targeted on the sicko, who lies on his side. "It wasn't me!" the sicko says.

The second shot comes from Derek, dead-center in the chest, and the sicko falls over onto his back. "Pretty night," it says.

"Stay down! Stay down!" says Brian, drawing his own gun and aiming low to the ground. "Asshole!" Tugging his mask back on, Brian coughs again. "Shit! Shit! That was close, right? Holy shit!" The sicko gasps, breathing only very slightly as it stares up toward the stars. "That's right, punk," Brian mutters.

The mutter turns into a quiet little chuckle, but it fades in an instant when Brian turns back toward Daniel, Derek, and Greg. Off to the side, Terry stands a safe distance away, his gun still drawn. "What?" says Brian. They don't answer, and his eyes go wide. "Come on, he barely touched me, I . . ." Brian shakes his head, then reaches up and wipes some blood off his temple.

"I'm sorry," says Derek. Daniel looks from Brian to Derek and back again.

"Fine," says Brian, nodding. "That's okay. I'll be back in a week. You'll see." With that, he turns around and walks back out into the street, arms outstretched, the breeze blowing back against his face. "Healthier than ever!" he says. As "ever" echoes building to building, he aims his pistol up higher and fires into the air. The shots resound like distant cannon fire. "Come and get me, you assholes!" he cries. "I'm a fucking Listener!"

Derek clasps his hand onto Daniel's shoulder. "Let's go inside, yeah?"

"I'm a *Listener*!" cries Brian.

"Let's go inside."

As Derek leads them all back toward the building, Daniel watches the tall but tiny figure of Brian, walking into the distance, growing smaller and smaller and smaller until the endless night envelops his body and he's gone.

The Voices of Martyrs

When Adam arrives, the Listeners collect themselves upstairs, Derek and Terry in opposite corners and Zeke on one knee not far from Daniel. The entire floor has been cleared out of all but the right bodies, covered in tarps someone found in a closet. These bodies—of Ari, of Stone, of Pip, but not of Brian—have been laid on desks. Daniel hasn't asked what will be done with them after, but Adam will know.

As Adam speaks, his children mourn, some standing so close they're nearly arm-in-arm, others simply closing their eyes and remembering. There are thirty-some Listeners in the room, and Daniel didn't know very well the ones who died, or even Brian really, but he feels drawn toward them, and weighed down by them. "They died for *us*," Adam says. "They died for each and every one of you." The brotherhood is unified by its martyrs.

Derek bows his head and shuts his eyes. His lips move, but no words come out. Daniel, meanwhile, flashes back to the gunshots and drumbeats of the battle itself, and thinks of the cops who fired at him and tried to kill him, and of the scarred and dog-faced ones who brought him down to desolation, and, finally, of his best friend's father, the cop he knew, the demon in disguise. "He was bad," Derek had said, and if it was cops who killed his fellow Listeners, murdered them and left the rest of them mourning, and if it was cops who locked up Derek, and cops who tried to kill Daniel, and cops who kept everyone in this place locked up, then how could he possibly be *good*?

Though Daniel never knew Ari or Stone, and only knew Pip a little from the times all the uninitiated kids would play cards or video games, he hears their voices now. They plead—they beg—for what anyone would beg for. "They want their lives to mean something," says Adam. "They want their brothers to continue on in their honor."

Even Brian, forced to walk away, had proclaimed proudly that he was, before anything else, a Listener. He had walked away to save his brothers from any possible infection. That was what Listeners *did*. The other three lie still on the desks, cold and growing colder, and if before today Daniel had never seen a person dead, he'd also never seen someone die for him.

"We are one," says Adam. "We listen as one. And in their names, we still have work to do."

⋀⋀⋀⋀⋀⋀

The Listeners spend the rest of the night in the police station, which is too important to abandon now. They can't return to the Food Garden and let the station be recaptured, so this night, the Listeners sleep sprawled out on the floor—uncomfortable, but necessary, a time of solidarity in both triumph and mourning. The next day, Listeners bring breakfast from the Food Garden (killing, they claim, three sickos along the way), and for the first and only time that Daniel has been one of them, they all eat together. Still, by instinct, the large group filters into smaller ones, and Daniel finds himself against the back wall, with Zeke and Greg, both chewing on granola bars.

"Three," Zeke says, his mouth full. "I fired a lot but I think I hit three."

"You did not," says Greg. "By the time you came in through the window, they were already on the ground. Don't lie—"

"I am not lying, man, three, one-two-three, and they were scared, too, like, cowering in the corner when I climbed in—"

"Bullshit!"

"Hey—"

"Bull! Shit!" Greg cracks up, bouncing his spine against the bluish wall, while Daniel chews his honey wheat granola bar thoughtfully. He takes a sip of orange juice.

"What about you, Daniel?" says Zeke.

Both Zeke and Greg turn Daniel's way, and Daniel, swallowing the juice, shrugs. It's not that hard a question, though. It doesn't matter how many bullets are flying or how many cops go down—if you never pull the trigger, you never hit anyone.

Daniel says nothing, but Zeke seems to get it. "No worries, man," he says. "If you guys coming in through the door weren't drawing the fire, we'd have been blown out those windows." He raises an open left hand chest-level, and Daniel swings his right hand in Zeke's direction. Zeke catches Daniel's high-five.

There's still work to do, so a few hours later, after a few other groups have already set out, Daniel follows Derek and Loren down the sidewalk on a pleasant, slightly damp morning. A bird flies overhead, cawing loudly, and Daniel wonders if birds can get sick. Although he's been outside twice in recent days, this is the first real trip. They will travel the borough. They will catch the cops where they live. Reaching into his pocket, Daniel pulls out a bottle of water and takes a sip.

The borough looks strange in the daytime. It always looks strange, but on a nice day especially, instinct tells you there ought to be people walking the streets, yelling into cell phones, holding hands, and clutching the leash tight so the dog doesn't run into the road. There should be cars struggling through a busy intersection and motorcycles weaving their way in-between them. There simply aren't. To the right is an antiques store, with a sign out front that says, "Sorry, we're closed." Daniel almost smiles at that. It's so *redundant*. But then he catches the eyes of someone in the fourth floor of a nearby building, and his near-smile fades in an instant. He remembers that the borough looks abandoned, but it isn't *really* abandoned. A lot of people are probably still alive, and even still healthy, if they have enough food. They're just trapped.

Dodging the cracks on the sidewalk, Daniel glances behind him, toward Derek. "We should let them know," he says. "We should let them know it's safe now."

"It's not," says Derek, quietly. "Even if we protect them, it's not safe till the sickness is—" He breaks off suddenly, aiming his gun forward, past Daniel. "See it?"

Looking ahead, Daniel does: an old woman, boils down her neck, walking around in a circle. Loren pauses, training his gun on her. Then he glances back over his shoulder. "Daniel, you want this one?" he says.

Does Loren know he didn't fire a shot in the station? Does he know Daniel didn't do a thing to help? Daniel starts to draw his gun from his pants, but before he can get it out, Derek's gun fires, and the woman slumps to the ground.

"Hey, Derek!" says Loren.

"Keep going," says Derek.

As Derek takes a sip of water, Daniel turns back his way. "How much further?" says Daniel.

"Just a couple blocks," says Derek. "Down on Rochester Avenue."

The sidewalk turns to quicksand, Daniel's feet turn to clay, and his legs to mud; he wobbles, but not forward. Even as the world spins and the bird caws and the sicko woman lies splayed across the pavement—the pavement he knows, now that he looks at it, and he remembers what it was like to know parts of this place by heart—Loren steps on ahead, but Daniel doesn't move because he knows he *knows* what it means and

and Derek's arm is around Daniel's left shoulder, and his hand squeezes his right, and he says, calmly, "You can do this," with confidence, always and every time with confidence.

"Yeah," says Daniel. He shuts his eyes and his legs start to move. The quicksand yields. "Yeah." But his heart sets a new pace and his feet step on the cracks in the sidewalk and they move him ahead step by directed step.

When they turn onto Rochester Avenue, with Legends, the comic book store, on the left and that broken yellow fire hydrant they never bothered to fix on the right, Daniel sees her running toward her building, winning but only because she got a head start while he was tying his shoes (which is *totally* cheating), and closer to the streetlight, he's showing her his favorite panels from a *Daredevil* trade, and over there she's shaking up his Mr. Pibb and spraying it on his face, and this is this is this is *home* is this is this is this?

The other voice, the one voice, says, if she's there, she *needs him.* If he's there, he's *one of them.* And she needs him like they all need them and the cops will lose their stranglehold and the Listeners will make things safe for everyone, for *everyone,* so, Daniel, do what you need to do, do what's right to do, do what you were trained to do and free her, free her mom, free them all. The one voice screams, but there's static in the message, and Daniel suddenly feels his right ear so strongly that he reaches up to grab it, clutching only air, fingers brushing against the rough, dirty bandage.

The apartment building is five stories tall and green with deep red trim. Loren is already there at the door. He holds the door open for Daniel. But Daniel stares up at the building, with the one window that has a jack-o'-lantern grinning outward every day of the year, and the other one with blinds that, when closed, flash a smiley face to the world. He stares up at the building where he spent every waking moment outside his own house and school.

Maybe she's not there, maybe she is, maybe she's both or neither. "Let's go someplace else," he says.

"Daniel—" says Loren.

"There's something else we can—"

"Hey, Daniel, Daniel," says Derek. Again: the hand on his shoulder. Again: the eye contact, bright and piercing. "You can do this. Okay?"

"No," says Daniel.

"They're the bad guys. All of them."

"You don't understand—"

"As long as they're alive, we're all at risk," says Derek. At that, Daniel blinks, and he knows, he *knows*, but . . . "I need your help, Daniel," says Derek. "I need you to help me."

The heart pounds. The breathing doesn't do a thing to stop it. But Daniel shuts his eyes, nods, then steps through the door into Katie's building. The climb up the staircase is terrifying, footsteps rattling on the red metal steps. On the second floor, a small boy, maybe seven years old, tosses a tennis ball up and down, up and down, up and down. When the Listeners train their guns on him, he doesn't react, but he doesn't look sick, so they move on. The fluorescent lights hum, and the Listeners' footsteps rattle in an atonal symphony, and every one of their steps brings them closer to it, every one, until they're on that third floor, and outside 306. Everything has a sound, and they're all so different through one ear. It's quiet, and it's loud, and Daniel feels the pinpricks on his skin from a static electrical field prodding him, begging him, to be anywhere else. So Daniel, eyes wide, looks at Derek one more time, but Derek instead turns to Loren and nods, and Loren, in response, knocks on the door.

Maybe they're not home. Maybe they are. Everything crisscrosses and doubles back. Daniel wants to walk away and pretend they were never here, and also walk in and save her and tell her about her dad, and also never bring it up. Maybe maybe, please God, maybe she's not home.

"Who's there?" The voice is muffled. It's Katie's mom. She'll *see* him.

"Police," says Loren.

There's a pause on the other side, and maybe she was never there, maybe they all just imagined it or only Daniel heard it or maybe they *were* there and aren't anymore, having escaped through a secret passage—it *could* happen, it *could*.

"I don't believe you," says imaginary (*please*) Katie's mom.

Then Loren turns to Derek, and Derek nods, and before Daniel can figure out what *that* means or what's happening or if maybe he imagined the whole thing, Loren charges forward and knocks Katie's door off its hinges in one powerful kick, and the breeze blows in behind him.

Sisters and Brothers

What seemed so slow in the present is so fast in retrospect, but broken, too. It's a series of stills that wouldn't turn into a movie no matter how hard you flipped them. It's like a comic book. Katie's mom is on the ground, furious and subjugated. Katie sees Daniel and is scared or mad at *him*. Derek and Loren are forcing Katie's mom to the other room. Daniel and Katie are in Katie's room. Katie is hugging the pillow. She's yelling at him. He's trying to make her understand, but she only yells more.

And now they sit in silence, Daniel against the door and Katie back up on the bed again. Katie is *here*. They're *together*. Some days he was sure they'd be together again, but other days he doubted it completely, and even if the Listeners took care of him forever, his mom wouldn't be there and Katie wouldn't either, and he wonders if he'd really be okay, forever, without them both.

"They let you take your comics?" asks Katie. Even as she holds her fuzzy pillow close to her, squeezing all the stuffing into the top half, her eyes drilling into Daniel, who sits against the door and scratches his bandage.

"What?" he says.

"Your comics. They let you take them, wherever it is you hide out?"

"I didn't bring anything," says Daniel. "I got new comics."

"Remember who got you the first ones?"

Though he knows there's a trail she's trying to lead him down, he doesn't want to follow, and he especially doesn't want to remember that he knows the way. Hers is not the voice he should be listening to. But it's the voice he's *always* listened to, and he feels it squeezing through a tiny gap in his sticky bandage, weaving between lines of tape, forcing its way into the hole where his right ear used to be. He feels the start of a tear, single lines breaking into parallels like a Kit-Kat Bar, and then he says, "Was it your mom?"

"Yeah," says Katie. "Remember? We were at the mall?"

The mall was outside the borough. It was always special when they went. It was three stories high and made of white and marble, and from the top floor you could see heads and baseball hats and Abercrombie and Fitch sweatshirt hoods, but what you really wanted to do was drop a penny and see who would notice, or if you could nail anyone on the head. Katie's mom would insist, if you're going to drop a penny, drop it in the *fountain*—as if that's any better, with the older kids always fishing the money out, as if it was some giant, wet take-a-penny leave-a-penny tray.

They'd gone to the mall after lunch. Daniel was in a bad mood. They'd given him cheese on his burger when he'd specifically said no cheese and, instead of a refill of Mr. Pibb, they gave him a pickle. But on the third floor, past the boring clothing store where all the older girls liked to go for some reason (and Katie made fun of it too before she started going herself), there, in the bookstore, behind the display window between some biography and *Harry Potter*, were the trade paperbacks, the words and art that would take him in and spin him around until he was so dizzy he could never leave.

Katie stood at the display on his left. She reached behind him and tapped his right shoulder. He turned right, turned left, smiled, and nudged his shoulder into hers. And just a moment later, when Katie's mom came back from the bathroom, and they were supposed to stay *right* on the bench and how *dare* they scare her like that, she saw him staring, positively entranced, the possibilities in his mind already exponential.

"Your mom," says Daniel, now.

"My mom," says Katie. As Katie leans forward, Daniel studies the gun in his hand and tries to push the lines together, because two lives and two Daniels are too many. "You're breaking us up, you know," says Katie.

Daniel jerks to attention. "What?"

"My family," says Katie. "My mom, my dad, and they have *always* been there. For you."

All Daniel can think about is what it was like when they were younger—how they'd get into these pillow fights, the fate of the world at stake, and Katie would nail him, absolutely nail him, by getting a shot in from nowhere. She'd be sitting perfectly still, like she is now, clutching a pillow tight behind her back, and in an instant she'd whip it around before he could possibly react. This time feels a lot like those. And he never thought he'd see her again, but she's *here* and she's talking and he hears.

"We'll take care of you—we will," says Katie, pushing herself further forward, all the way to the end of the bed now. "I mean, God, if we'd known something had happened to your mom, we'd've done everything we could to get over there and bring you here with us. Danny, are you listening? Danny?" He looks up. He's listening. "You're not—you're not *alone* here, Danny," says Katie. "You don't need these guys—you don't. We'll be your family." She smiles and leans forward. "We *are* your family."

The oxygen goes out of the room. Daniel drops against the door.

"You're my best friend," says Katie.

Daniel sees a flickering flame—a candlelight on a birthday cake, one of twelve (eleven plus one for good luck). The cake is a muddled mushy mess, but the messy apron on Mr. MacDonald is an appropriate "Kiss the 'Chef.'" This isn't the dream, but the real thing, Katie's apartment in better times, the kitchen a plastic-paneled place splattered with chocolate discards as the red icing makes a last-minute appearance. "Almost done, Daniel," says Katie's dad.

Friendly hands land on Daniel's shoulders. "Over here," says Daniel's mother, guiding him from the little kitchen into the living room, where the door is secure on its hinges and the fuzzy egg-white carpet pushes up in-between the toes of Daniel's bare feet. In the corner of the room, near the couch, they're both there, the way they're always there—Daniel's mom and Katie—standing by a big potted plant, and a group of multicolored presents, one spaced prominently from the others.

"What is it?" says Daniel. Sun shines through the window.

"It's a Daniel Bush!" proclaims Katie, happy and sprightly. She jumps and throws her hands toward it. "Ta-da!"

She makes him laugh. She *always* makes him laugh. And as his mom applauds, Daniel drops to his knees and reaches for the first present, the one in the blue and silver wrapping paper. "Can I open it?" says Daniel.

"You better," says Katie.

He tears off the shell loudly, inconsistent scraps of paper littering the floor, revealing, underneath, comics—two trade paperbacks, and a whole stack of individual books. Jumping right back to his feet, Daniel stares down at his gift, glancing back at Katie, who shrugs.

"There must be, like . . ."

"A lot," says Katie.

"So many! Look at it, Katie!" says Daniel.

"I see!"

Daniel creeps backwards, toward the couch. "Look closer!" he says.

"I'm looking!"

As she steps a little closer, Daniel reaches back behind him, grabs a velvet pillow from the sofa, and finally gets in the first good shot, right into her shoulder. Spinning around, giggling, Katie side-steps and says, "Oh, you're dead. You're dead!"

The words echo through Katie's room, from the purple door to the CDs in the corner to the bookshelf full of fantasy and Roman mythology. They bounce into Daniel's ear from every angle. Again and again he hears them. He hears everything.

"I didn't . . ." Daniel looks up at Katie. "I didn't know it was your place we were coming to."

"You know now," says Katie. Tears in her eyes, she smiles. It's been so long since Daniel has seen her smile. "We're your family," she says.

The echo stops suddenly, like a light switch has flipped it off. From out of somewhere, two rooms or two miles or two months away, a strong, confident voice, speaking in a near-whisper, says, "Look, Daniel, see Loren over there?"

In an instant, Daniel is back in the supermarket basement, his breathing raspy and broken, an image running through his head of a red-marked monstrosity, reaching for him with disconnected fingers, screaming at him with a ragged, furious voice, nearly killing him before Derek shoots him down. He sees Derek point out Loren, asleep in his bed. "Yeah," says Daniel.

"He's your brother," says Derek. "See Brian over there, green shirt?"

"Yeah."

"He's your brother."

As Daniel thinks of football with Zeke and Terry in the back of the supermarket, scraping his knee as he dives for the reception, Derek says, "He's your brother." As Loren tells him to aim a little bit more to the left and Greg gives him a comic book to read, Derek says, "He's your brother." And as three fallen soldiers lie on desks in a police station, their lives sacrificed to save their family, Derek says, "He's your brother. He's your brother. He's your brother."

And as Adam stands beside Daniel, clutching the knife and holding it in the spotlight, the light wrapped around Adam's head like a halo while the other Listeners cheer him on in silhouette, Derek says, "And our father."

When the knife comes down, Daniel shuts his eyes, and when he opens them again, he's in Katie's room, where Katie, clutching her pillow tightly, sits on the end of her bed. The air is still and cool. The apartment is silent. Daniel turns to Katie and looks her right in the eyes.

"I have a family," says Daniel.

Shivering, Katie turns away, her eyes red and glassy, and Daniel looks away, too. He hears Katie sniff, her breathing broken and somehow far away. The bedsprings creak as she pushes herself back.

And then, through the door, something else creaks, too. Immediately, Daniel presses his ear to the door.

"Danny—"

"Shhh," says Daniel. He can't see but he can hear—he was reborn to hear—and what he hears are footsteps, light and muffled against the white carpet. He imagines it like a cop show on TV, sneaking into the apartment as quietly as possible, gun held tightly in both hands just the way Terry taught Daniel. Footsteps hit the carpet— Daniel hears them through the door and down the hall, and there's a slightly louder step as the tip of his toe (it has to be him) hits against the plastic of the kitchen. Shutting his eyes, Daniel puts it all on his left ear: *step, step, step . . . step.*

Then nothing. Daniel opens his eyes.

Suddenly, there's a crash of splintering wood. "Fr—" yells a voice, but that's all it says before it's cut off by an ear-shattering gunshot, and another, and another. Katie shrieks and Daniel turns her way as the gunshots blast somewhere else and the first drowns out the second and the second the first, and two more shots blast and Katie just keeps screaming, and that's all Daniel hears, like that same show with just the audio, entirely out of context.

"Oh my God!" yells Katie. "Oh my God!"

It's all much too loud, so Daniel presses his ear to the door as hard as he can and listens for anything, but all he hears is Katie, and he's supposed to threaten her or tell her to be quiet, but he can't, and the sounds are scattered and they don't make sense and Daniel, Daniel, he's gone selectively deaf, so he pushes his right ear even further into the purple door, as far as it will go.

And that's when the door flies open, cracking brutally against Daniel's ear. Nearly losing the grip on his gun, Daniel falls back onto the floor, rolling and bleeding, the red blood staining the sky blue carpet into the same purple as everything else. The air swirls in a tinny mush like the audio on a bad video camera. He rolls over onto his back and finds himself staring into the eyes of Katie's dad, his surrogate uncle, covered in blue and badge and blood. His gun is trained on Daniel, but it's frozen, as if it knows where to point but not what to do. His lips are moving but Daniel can't make out the words.

The red on his uniform doesn't make sense, and Daniel wants to wonder where Derek and Loren are, but his ear pounds and he can't *think* or *hear* or *move*, so he looks up into Mr. MacDonald's face and sees wide, shocked eyes, and lips that make no sounds, and the strangest thing, right under his chin, at the top of his mouth, is the tiniest red boil.

Daniel's down on the ground and backed in the corner and his brothers may be (can't be) may be gone, but he's paused, Katie's dad, he's talking and not acting and not listening and Daniel may not be able to hear, but he sees his opening. He sees that dot, that little red dot, and he sees the red mark on the black target outlines on the firing range and he knows, he *knows*, that the dot will grow and more will follow and Katie's dad will fall apart and lose his mind and strike and claw and kill and threaten everyone, even Katie, and he knows what he has to do to save her and he has to do it now, and *fast*. So he points his gun and he fires, *fires*, just as he did on the target range, and the bullet hits the chest dead-on and Mr. MacDonald loses his balance and stumbles and flies back. Daniel feels his legs return and he stands up, slowly, the sound all tinny and fuzzy like a black and white TV screen in a little broken room with a broken man outside shooting randomly, but the sound is all screams and echo, a loud metal slap that echoes through all the walls and halls in the apartment that once that once that once was another home.

Katie leaps off the bed and grabs her dad, the cop, the killer, the uncle, the amateur cake-baker. For a moment, Daniel stands there, frozen, and tries to add this to the list of things to explain to her. He was sick, Daniel wants to say, it was only a matter of time, and you have to get away from him before it gets you, too, but she's clutched to him like the world's strongest magnet and things have played out the way they're going to play out and the room has stretched long and she's too too far away, no matter how far he reaches.

He's out of the picture. Irrelevant. Katie has her one voice and it isn't his. So Daniel slips out the door, the once straightforward hall a funhouse maze, and into the living room, where silence has returned but the carpet is still bloody, and the door is cracked open like a broken window, but Daniel has to check, not out but in, down the next hall, over the kitchen where chocolate might stain the floor yet, down to Katie's parents' room.

The red is contagious. It spreads. It's spread everywhere in their room, covering the bed, the floor, the people, the (bodies) *people* on the floor, and the door makes no sound and Katie makes no sound and her mom makes no sound and her dad makes no sound and Derek and Loren make no sound and the only sound is the sticky red blood pushing out his heart and through his veins, *ba-BUM, ba-BUM, ba-BUM.*

There's nothing left to do here, so Daniel checks out. His body does the rest. It closes the door, it heads back into the room where the Daniel Bush once stood, the room where the most epic of pillow fights once took place, and his body doesn't remember anything. There's nothing to remember except the way back to the only home that's left.

Blood drips from his ear down onto the carpet.

Daniel leaves his mark.

Hear it?

End of First Part

Cinderblock

Retreating from the light outside like a mole, I back away from my mangled scratching post, and I listen—listen hard and carefully and well. I hear the city talk, yes, but mostly it's for him I listen—tormentor, captor, and brother, robber of light, bringer of blood and boils. Yes, the boils are his and so is the illness, all made up, a prison of lies turned a prison of dark. I had a tunnel and he closed it off, I had a rope pulling me out and he cut it, painted the red on my skin and called me infected.

Crawl now. Crawl on rough fuzzy carpet carpet, hard to see, smells like me, urine and feces, animalistic. But this animal thinks. Lay the trap. Lie in wait. Strike.

⁓⌁⌁⌁⁓

"We've got food for fifteen?" said the first policeman, crusty nose scrunched up like a warthog's. "Big group."

"Small church," said Anton. "Where's McDaniel?"

Anton stood tall in the large double-doorway to the church, Tyrone's church, where he'd insisted they stay for the duration. "A community's got to stick together," he'd said, and though Tyrone had never been forceful—he'd fall in a second if pushed, not hard like a ton of bricks but soft like rain—he could sometimes guilt Anton into doing something he didn't want to do. And sometimes Anton took at face value the wisdom of a brother eight years his senior, which, in this case, had certainly been the wrong decision. But the church was, fortunately, inside McDaniel's patrol range.

"McDaniel," said the policeman, leaning against a large cart of tightly-packed food outside the church. "Aah . . ."

"Shot," said his partner, a pimply man with a voice too high for his size. "Shootout with some infected guy. Ugly. Don't know if he's gonna pull through."

Anton blinked a little and scratched his fingernail down his nose. "And Owens?"

"Sticking by his partner," said the second policeman.

"Good man," said the first.

"Right," said Anton. He was never clear on whether or not that was true of Owens—McDaniel, who was always so vocal with opinions about his fellow officers, maybe even unprofessionally so, never said anything more than "he's all right"—but it was undeniably true of Stanton McDaniel.

"Hey, one purse," McDaniel had said the first time the two met, at the tail end of Anton's sentence, when the neglected city streets were calling softly to their favorite son. "One purse. One bet. Six months." Anton could taste the beautifully stale city air on the tip of his tongue, and was so overwhelmed by it that he could hardly hear his new parole officer until the man tapped on his shoulder. "Hello? Listening?" McDaniel said. "Six months, one crime, but you're a kid, practically. There is so much you can do as long as you don't go back."

To prison, he meant. Anton, already robbed of half of his twenty-third year, glanced out through the bars of his cell and said, "I'm not going back."

"Good, good," said McDaniel. He was casual. He wore his hat tilted a couple inches to the right though it was strictly against regulations. "They don't get to tell me how to wear my hat," he said. He was casual, and he was supportive, and Anton was inclined to call him the big brother he never had, but for the fact he already had a big brother.

Tyrone was here now, taken away from his game of poker, thanking these new guys, blessing them in the name of God, acting as if it was normal, and acceptable, when they asked for something in return.

"Um, well," said Tyrone, "we, um, we haven't much to give, of course, but if there's anything you need—"

Tyrone gave in too easily. He was too dependent, and in a big way, that's why they were here. Anton took a step forward, puffed out his chest, and looked the second officer in the eyes. The second officer pulled back and dragged his arms up to his chest. "McDaniel never asked us for anything," said Anton. "Not a thing."

"This isn't a charity," said the first policeman.

"It's protection," said Anton.

"Protection isn't cheap," said the second.

"McDaniel—"

"Any valuables?" said the first. "Money? Necklaces? Donations, I guess. It's a church, right?"

"It's a church," confirmed the second.

Tyrone behind him, Anton took another step forward, close enough that the second officer stepped back out onto the empty street. "Are you insane?" Anton asked.

"Hey, hey," said the second. "No money—"

"No food," said Tyrone. "Come on, Ant, we'll scrounge up something . . ."

"No fucking way," said Anton, stepping forward into the second policeman, who was knocked further onto the road.

Both officers stepped back, and the first, air noisily snorting out his warthog nostrils, dropped his hand on his sidearm, the black leather holster shining in the midday summer sun. He tapped his fingers against it, precariously. "Kid," he said, "watch it."

"Ant—"

"Come on, Tyrone, they're—"

"I know," said Tyrone.

"We can't just—" He started to take another step forward but found himself stopped by his brother's skinny arms, barely wrapping around his shoulders. It was a grip easy to break, but it was always enough to hold Anton back.

"We need food," said Tyrone.

Anton, released, folded his arms, dropped them, then folded them again. With a shake of his head, a glare from his piercing eyes, he retreated into the church to find some form of currency.

What neither the police officers nor Tyrone noticed was that he did so with the second officer's walkie-talkie tucked neatly into his pocket.

The church had been transformed into a hostel. Pews were filled with suitcases and toys, and sleeping bags slumped off the edges of the benches, dropping onto the rough floor. One little girl slept in her sleeping bag, her head on the thigh of her worn mother, her legs, obscured by the sky-blue bag, nestled into the legs of her half-asleep father. In the right aisle, a group of young men, Tyrone and his friend Zeb included, played a game of Texas Hold'em, while a teenage boy and girl crept through an unlocked door into an unoc-cupied hallway.

Sitting on the second stair leading up to the pulpit, Anton fid-dled with the black walkie-talkie. It was not, of course, a radio, not in the classic sense; there was no music, there were no words, and for the most part there was no communication, perhaps because there wasn't much to communicate, and partly because Anton didn't know what channel to tune to.

Mostly there was quiet static, long-forgotten white noise it was suddenly easy to feel nostalgic for. They had lived here in this unfamiliar church since the quarantine began, around three weeks now, reasoning that they all had a better chance for sustenance and blessed morale if they would stick together and become the community under God that had always been more preached than practiced.

But Anton was not a part of that community, and hadn't been since he was sixteen, and old enough, his mother reasoned (mere months before she passed away), to decide his spirituality for him-self. In his mind, there was no God—something that had come up in conversation with McDaniel—so McDaniel was considerably amused by the fact that this is where Anton had settled in for the duration of the quarantine. "Found religion, huh?" he'd said.

"Found Ty," Anton had responded. "Religion's just something to put up with."

"Got it, Brother Anton."

This was another of the many ways Tyrone was different. Anton remembered a time when he was five, sick, wrapped in the thick covers his mother always used to sweat the sickness out of him. Seated on a chair next to the bed, thirteen-year-old Tyrone read Bible stories—Anton couldn't recall now which ones—but he did remember the reason: to inspire him back to health. When Tyrone insisted they stay in the church, he'd said it was for community, for safety in numbers, but Anton was sure it had something to do with being close to God, and being able to pray to God should one of them fall ill. The "community" line was just the one Anton was more likely to believe. And he'd fallen for it. He was here.

It was a church, and so there was no television, save for the small black and white portable some young churchgoer had thought was essential, and there was a radio, but it had lousy reception and could pick up only a few local stations. Anton, in fact, preferred to pay attention to neither. He missed them both, television and radio—of course he did. All his time not wandering the city streets had been spent instead in front of Tyrone's silver big-screen, or with headphones squeezed into his ears and plugged into the world. But all TV and radio talked about now was the plague, how little they knew, what it meant, if a cure could be found. And Anton didn't need any help remembering what the world had become. It had become a claustrophobic dungeon, and the sixth months he'd already spent in one of those were six too many.

The walkie-talkie, police-band radio, was different. It was the one live broadcast from inside the quarantine, with up-to-the-minute news from the only people making it. Anton fiddled with the dial, experimenting with the frequencies, trying, and failing, to remember what channel McDaniel had it on when he received those tinny, muted messages—most likely the same frequency it had been on originally, but by now Anton had fiddled with the machine enough he no longer remembered where it was, or precisely what he was looking for. So he continued to mess around with it, pointing its stiff antennae in various directions to see if it made any difference.

Suddenly, Anton became aware of a body standing over him, and from the sound of the sigh, he knew whose body it was. He looked up into his older brother's eyes, which were disapproving in a passive sort of way. It was the same kind of disapproving look Anton had seen when Tyrone visited him in prison—the first to visit, the first to condemn.

"Is that the officer's?" Tyrone asked. It obviously was, but Tyrone didn't make assumptions.

"He dropped it," said Anton.

"You shouldn't have taken it."

"Fair trade." Anton switched to another frequency, raised the walkie-talkie up toward the roof, and tapped it with the knuckles of his right hand.

Tyrone sighed and put his hands in his pockets. "We got the food," he said. "That was the trade."

"Food was free," said Anton. "This was worth one engagement ring."

"Anton . . ."

"I'm sorry, I should have said 'please.'"

"Anton."

"Please, Mr. Officer, may I borrow your radio . . ."

"That's not—"

". . . while you're robbing us blind?"

Tyrone took a seat on the step right above Anton, his knees in line with Anton's head. "McDaniel wouldn't approve," he said.

Anton looked down the pews, fourth row, at Ms. Knightley, thirty or so years old, staring at her naked ring finger. "No," he said, "he wouldn't."

". . . report . . ." was the first word that squeaked through when Anton stumbled, finally, upon a channel that appeared to be in use. He was flipping through very quickly, a frequency a second, so he'd already changed to the next channel by the time he'd heard the one word—besides static, and clicks, the only noise he'd heard in hours.

In the nighttime, when the community slept, there were very few options for a restless refugee like Anton, but his hours had never matched those of his fellow captives. Church lights went out at ten-thirty, a compromise made for the benefit of the young children in the group, and silence at that point was a matter of simple consideration, but Anton was a man of the night. The streets outside were his streets, the city was his city, and he missed it. Sometimes, he felt as if the plague was the latest in a long line of disasters designed to rob him of his connections to the outside world—the heat and the pavement, the extinguished nightlife.

In theory, late hours could be spent outside, without interrupting his sleeping companions, but the outside was dangerous, especially at night, and especially for a man with no means of self-defense listening hard to a precious piece of pilfered property. So his only options to listen privately were the office and the supply cabinet, and the office at least had a chair, so there he sat in a small cube nearly as small as his prison cell. The light hummed above his head and the static hissed below it, until that one word broke through the monotony: ". . . report . . ." *Report.*

He switched the channel back.

". . . travel safely?" a voice finished. It was thick and scratchy. Anton could imagine the face, fat and scruffy, with cheeks like flaps of useless skin slapping against the sides of the speaker's jaw.

"It's secured," another voice responded, this one clear and authoritative. Buzz cut. Thin moustache, like in a 1950s film. "Expect little difficulty. Straight line down." Crisp and to the point, although Anton couldn't tell what it all meant.

"Sir, the risk . . ." the first voice started. The second, the calm one, began something before the first resumed: "It really isn't necessary."

"I want to see," the second voice said.

There was a pause, and Anton imagined the first man smacking his flaps of cheek skin against his chin, creating some strange sloppy sound. "Yes, sir," the first voice said.

"Forty-third," said the second voice. "Two-hundred."

"Yes, sir."

There were no voices after that. The dialogue was replaced again with the hiss of empty airspace, and the light, in restlessness, made itself known with a suddenly louder hum. Anton looked at the walkie-talkie as if there was an indecipherable message hidden inside the black plastic. But it wasn't indecipherable to him.

He knew, at least, what "forty-third" meant. McDaniel, delving into police officer gossip when not bent on being the parole officer he was supposed to be, used numbers like that, so Anton knew "forty-third" was a precinct, and he knew, in fact, where it was: about a mile's walk from the church, and not more than ten blocks away from the outer perimeter of the actual quarantine. He also knew what "two-hundred" meant, or thought he did. Military terminology for two o'clock in the morning.

Anton tapped the walkie-talkie on the scratchy old desk, just lightly enough so it wouldn't wake someone up. He chewed a little on his available thumbnail and glanced up at the closed door in front of him. As he always did at this stage—before doing something possibly ill-advised—he thought about what Tyrone might say if he was in the office, if he'd heard the message.

"It could mean anything," Tyrone would say.

"It could be important," Anton would reply.

"None of our business," would be Tyrone's second argument, to which Anton would reply that it was now. It was a meaningless comment, but it always felt significant.

"You could die," Tyrone would say.

And that was the tricky one. Anton loved the pound of footsteps on a dark and quiet city street at an unreasonable morning hour, especially in the summer, when it was dark and warm and humid, and the city was your temperate playground, but he hadn't gone beyond the church steps in three weeks, because he was sure that if he went too far—took a wrong turn down a sick alley—he'd run across some random infected person, or, worse, some diseased variation of someone he knew, close enough to infect him without even touching him. He had, he'd always thought, an intrinsic knowledge of this borough—where it was safe to go at any time of night, even the maximum he could do—but prison had made him just a little gun shy and the plague had terrified him. This wasn't his city anymore.

Sometimes, though, he wondered if there was a way out of here, if there was an escape route no one had found or even thought to look for, something only he, first-hand knowledge of the city's intricacies at his fingertips, could hope to find. And then, too afraid to wander outside and test his theory, he wondered if the plague wasn't designed to make him scared. He even wondered if there was no disease and no quarantine, and people weren't getting sick, and this was all some conspiracy. That was, he knew, absurd, but still . . . he missed the city. He wanted to be there. He wanted to see. He could die, but still he wanted to see.

Tyrone would respond to that with a resigned sigh. Sometimes that was enough to make him feel guilty, but most of the time, the sigh was Tyrone's surrender. That's why Anton had usually done the things he wanted to do.

When the schoolroom-style clock in that cinderblock cell of an office turned to one in the morning, both too late and too early, Anton put the radio squarely on the desk, exited the office, and crept quietly through the snoring pews and out into the welcoming city air.

Tippy-tap tippy-tap-tap on the tip-tap tiles between the congregated crowd of captors and the hidden hidden hall. Tap-tap-tap just a little, for the hall is short and the prey is near. But creak and swing, another door is opened, tippy-tap stomp stomp, creak, creak, slam.

You see with your ears when your eyes are blinded by no-light, but you think with your mind and your instinct. Tippy-taps through the hidden hall to torment me with nearness minus closeness, tippy-taps that say, maybe the door will open, maybe they'll set me free, into the night, into the cool and quiet city, clunk-clunk on the pavement, scramble-slide down the sewer and free.

I can plan and plot and I do, and that's how I know what they've done to me. My hole in the door, like the hole in the floor, is growing growing, but my friendly fingers need a rest, and so I listen, ear to the door, suction, for the sounds of tippy-taps and the sigh of the traitor-brother, trapped in the crypt where he keeps me.

Creak creak, stomp, stomp, tippy-tap, tippy-tap, stop. Tap: skinny fingers, sibling fingers, rested on the door, pushing in because I'm too strong and too smart and might escape. Brother-breathing.

"Hey, Ant," *brother-breather says.*

I feel the felt of floor and crawl in a circle and listen for the brother-breaths.

"You all right?" *the brother says.*

"Let me out," *I say, in words he understands, victim to victimizer, prisoner to guard, tippy-tippy-tap.*

"I can't do that, Ant," *says Tyrone. I'm an ant, like a trapped bug in an ant farm, digging holes but going nowhere, knowing the one way out's the carpety carpet I can't dig through. Dig dig.*

He made it all up. "You made it all up." *No danger out there. Danger in here. I went out there, clump clump of sneakers on pavement, cool and dark and free.*

"Zeb's coming back with a bulb," *says Tyrone.*

"Light?" *I say.*

"Real soon," *he says.*

Tyrone sends Zeb. Zeb brings light. Zeb is free. What of me?

It could be a long walk to the forty-third, but Anton had no intention of walking. Outside of the church, perched on the sidewalk immediately by the curb, he scanned the darkened sky, speckled with piercing white stars extended by tiny beams of light and, closer, glowing streetlights glazing the brick walls of the beckoning buildings. He took a deep breath, inhaling the smell of early morning, the smell of concrete and pavement, open air, freedom.

He slumped and grinned and let out a low chuckle. Then he looked to his left, and his right, because anyone else out this time of night was probably sick, but the road ahead was unimpeded, and he rubbed his cooped-up thighs and took off into the night.

At night, when the other sounds are gone, every footstep is larger than life, its prominence magnified by every little echo off every big building. The city is a captive audience, there for you, reflecting only you, and Anton, jogging through this place, the summer wind flowing over his face, couldn't help it. "Yeah!" he cried, and the city cried back, *Yeah! Welcome back, Anton. Welcome back.*

He ran, sweat and tears dripping down his face, and the water was like tension pouring out of his body. He called to the borough, asked for its input, and it told him where to go, through just the right shortcuts, the perfect paths—Anton a mouse who already knows where the cheese is. The buildings, the sentinels, stood tall and protected him as they guided him on his way.

And if there were infected people out here, he didn't see them, and they didn't see him. The dangers and disease took the night off so the borough's favorite son could have one more adventure on the damp pavement, one more morning dashing through the maze uncontested, one more run to the forty-third.

Anton's watch read 1:56 when he got there, in front of the building, a contemporary brick outcropping framed by almost Romanesque pillars. It was part of his borough, one of the hundred-thousand parts that made up the whole, and this particular one was his goal for the night. *Stay quiet*, the city told him, *and I'll keep you safe, and you'll see what you want to see.*

He rested his back against a cool brick wall, just below a spray-painted "SK"—red, apparently, although it was hard to tell at this time of night. Anton, breathing heavily and happily, did not know what he was waiting for, what would happen at "two-hundred," but as he recaptured his breath and looked out into the open, uncharacteristically unpolluted city air, he thought, it doesn't matter. It's worth it.

The barest movement of an arm caught Anton's eye and he noticed, where he hadn't before, a lithe figure in a surgical mask backed against the bare wall of the precinct house, looking, as was Anton, at the front of the building. Anton hadn't noticed the man before—and it was a man, around Tyrone's age, a tall man, but skinny like an anorexic—but he must have been there as long as Anton had, probably longer. Someone else who'd heard the message? Another addict of the city streets?

At about the same time Anton noticed the man, the man noticed Anton, and turned toward him. It was at this point that Anton noticed his fellow observer was missing his right ear, or at the very least it was obscured in such a way that it didn't seem to be there. In its place was some sort of flat bandage. Before the quarantine began, there had been rumors of people called Listeners, some sort of one-eared gang, but Anton had never seen one of them.

For a few moments, Anton and the Listener were trapped in a staring contest, but then footsteps, loud and clicking, echoed from building to building and drew away their mutual attentions. What Anton saw, when he returned his attention to the front of the station, was a police officer, also in a surgical mask, stepping out onto the street. The man looked right and left, almost directly at Anton, but protected by shadows and hidden by stillness, Anton remained unnoticed. A buzz and a voice emitted from the officer's walkie-talkie, but Anton couldn't make out what the voice said. The officer stepped forward into the middle of the street, then kneeled down by a dull gray manhole cover.

With an audible grunt, the officer (who was not fat, and whose cheeks were not long and flappy) pulled the heavy metal ring up and onto cracked pavement, causing a loud, thick clang. Wiping sweat from his face, the officer reached down into the open hole and emerged holding onto someone else's hand.

From out of the sewer, climbing up what must have been a ladder, came a broad man wearing military green. With the officer's help, he pulled himself out of the sewer and, once on the surface, climbed up to his feet. The officer offered a salute, and Anton was sure he heard a "sir." The military man (who did, in fact, have a moustache, but any possible buzz cut was covered by his hat) carried what looked to be a newspaper, rolled up and sticking out awkwardly from his pocket. He and the officer kneeled down and capped the manhole again with the checkerboard metal cover, and then walked into the precinct house.

Anton blinked. He crossed his arms, uncrossed them, and crossed them again. He glanced over toward the side of the forty-third where the Listener had been standing, but now he was gone. So Anton was alone in the city with a secret no one else knew. Smiling, rubbing the bridge of his nose, Anton turned around and began to jog back to the church. The city showed him the way.

ᴧᴧᴧᴧᴧᴧ

"Tomorrow night," said Anton, seated, again, on the hollow steps below the pulpit. "I can lead everyone there. I know the way."

Tyrone was seated on the altar this time, his hands clasped onto the altar-rail behind him, his body stretched out horizontally across the top of the stairs. "It's too dangerous," he said.

"No. Tyrone . . . here. *Here* is too dangerous." He gestured toward the churchgoers and churchstayers, distributed amongst the oak pews, sprawled along the crowded halls, the dust and dirt of borough refugees floating through the open air. "Here we're living like animals, Tyrone, like . . . and the cops—they'll only keep us alive as long as we have what they want . . ."

"Ant . . ."

". . . and this isn't living. This isn't living. Out there . . ." He trailed off.

Tyrone sighed, sat up, and put his open palm on his brother's shoulder. "You shouldn't have gone out there," he said.

"I like it out there," said Anton. "And there's—there's a way *out*, out there. We don't have to . . ."

"What . . ."

". . . *live* like this. There's no reason to be stuck inside a quarantine we got no reason to be . . ."

". . . move your head a little . . ."

". . . stuck inside, and we can save everyone, you and me . . ."

". . . oh no . . ."

". . . can . . . what?"

Tyrone stumbled to his feet and backed away, and Anton, confused, turned around and looked him in the eye. "What is it?" he asked. Then he reached back, brushed his neck with his rough hand, and found the path interrupted by a small lump, smooth like plastic, bulging from the base of his neck.

〜〜〜〜〜

"It's only for a little while," Anton heard Tyrone say through the thick, padlocked door. "Only a matter of time, Ant—just a matter of time until they figure out how to cure this thing . . ."

Anton sighed and tried to find a comfortable spot under a shelf filled to near-capacity with hymnals and worn Bibles. "No one's coming," he said.

"Well . . . something—"

"No one."

There was a light scratch at the door—Tyrone was leaning against it, moving as close to Anton as he would allow himself to be. "Someone hears," Tyrone said. "Someone's listening."

Anton, after a while, pushed himself to his feet, batted the thin metal chain for the humming little bulb out of his way, and walked to the back of the closet, where he found a thin children's popup book about Noah's Ark. He could have been Noah, he thought. He could have led them all to a sewer safely from out of an invisible flood.

"I can't even see it," Anton said, as he felt back toward the bump on his neck. "How can it be there if I can't even see it?"

Tyrone didn't answer.

"Have you even . . . have you even seen someone who's sick, man? Have you? I mean . . . how do you know . . . how do we . . . maybe it's just a pimple—just some . . ."

Still no answer.

"I want to be out there," he said.

"We need to keep you safe," said Tyrone, finally.

"You need to keep *you* safe," Anton said. Then, he smirked and slammed shut the book, with its bright and happy pictures of Disney-style animals escaping the onrushing water sure to kill their families and destroy everything they ever loved. "Quarantine within a quarantine," said Anton. "Plague within a plague." McDaniel had warned him not to go back.

There was a sniff on the other side of the door.

"Let me out, huh?" said Anton, approaching the door. "Just for a little while."

But again there was no answer.

ᴡᴡᴡᴡ

Tippy-tap tippy-tap-tap. Brother T, brother comes back. Knock-knock on the door. The warden speaks: "Ant, Zeb's back. We got some light for you."

"Light," *I say, sneaky-sneaky. If you listen, the city talks to you and tells you the way home. It tells me, it says to Ant,* Crawl home, wait and crawl and bite and find your way home.

Crawl and bite, crawl and bite, fight fight fight.

"We're gonna open the door and throw it in to you, okay?" *Other voice, Zeb. Let there be light.*

"I'm ready to come out now," *I say.*

"You're sick," *says brother. He pretends I'm sick so he can take care of me again. Pretend pretend. Five years old, wrapped in a blanket, brother reading Bible stories. Pretend pretend.*

"I'm feeling better now," *I say. I crawl by the door and crouch on invisible hands, hide in my corner, coiled up.* Get ready, *says the city.*

"I'm throwing it in," *says Zeb-voice. Tippy-tap, tippy-tap, click.*

Cinderblock cell says stop even when it's time to go. Plague is a lie meant to keep you inside. Brother's the predator now turned prey. Creak creak creak, the door opens, I coil and wait and I see with my ears and my hands.

Open just a little, and then I jump and push and roar and say, "Let me out!" *I'm fast and strong and there's light and I see, pushy-push, through the crack, down the sewer. I push and I'm free.*

The short man is Zeb and he screams and I punch him, punch punch punch. Arms try to hold me back but not hard enough and I shrug them off and step forward and punch and punch and punch.

Then brother comes and pushes Zeb-voice away, and he looks strange and I see only part of him—there's a fat thing blocking my leftest eye like a fat floppy cheek, but it's still and it's hard. I don't need both eyes because I can see with my ears, the sighs of a brother, captor, liar, brother.

"Don't do this," says brother. "You're sick."

There's pain and there's poison all over my body, I glance at my fingernails with my right eye and most are bent and broken from clawing-clawing. He leads me to church with his hand on my shoulder. He's the first one to visit when I'm locked in that cell. Tyrone is my brother.

He stands and he breathes and through the door to the sanctuary, week old and week gone, I see the others, Others, creaky-creak, tippytap. My brother has gathered an army to stop me. The city is calling, Tyrone wants me deaf.

Brother dearest. My arms fold and unfold, then I go for his throat.

SECOND PART

The Playground

The rain beats down on the gymnasium ceiling. There are no windows, just brick walls and basketball nets, but still it feels wet, as if the wave bearing down on the school ceiling is soaking right through the brick and mortar and onto the smooth wooden floor, where basketballs dribble and soccer balls pass from kid to kid.

Off the walls, laughter echoes—those strange, hollow echoes that always dominate a giant room designed for games and not acoustics. You can't have recess outside when it's raining, but Daniel can't make himself get up off the bleachers to go for that soccer ball. He looks to the left and to the right, and he recognizes all the kids from his fourth-grade class—all the happy, laughing little kids who never talked to him even once.

When the bell rang, he asked Mrs. Callis where Katie was. She said Katie's sick today.

But as the rain pours down so hard any cats or dogs would drown in half a second, he finds his eyes on the double-doors leading outside, where the rain is always loudest, where if you push your head to the crack between the doors, you can maybe feel the spray from the mist bouncing up from the concrete sidewalk right outside. Something in the deluge calls to him in Morse code. When he closes his eyes, the drumbeats form into words, and he thinks he gets the message.

Mrs. Callis is watching the other kids. No one ever watches Daniel. So while a lumpy orange basketball bounces loudly off the rim of a low-hanging basket, while a red, white, and blue soccer ball ricochets off the tiny yellow paint splotch on the wall, he slides down the bleachers, further, further, further, until he's right next to the double-doors, and right below the bright red "EXIT" sign. He knows that if he pushes down the bar and shoves the doors open, the fire alarm will go off, but the raindrops call and he doesn't care.

He pushes down the bar. He shoves the doors open.

The fire alarm doesn't go off.

In an instant, Daniel is drenched so completely it's as if he's jumped into a pool with his clothes on. The sky is almost black, the wind is freezing cold, and all he's wearing are jeans and a bright yellow short-sleeve shirt, now dulled like a room with a burned-out bulb. Thunder sounds and resounds, and past the grass, along the road, street signs bend and sway in the wind, streetlights waving back and forth. The only cars in sight are parked along the curb.

Between Daniel and the street is the playground, cold and wet and abandoned, mist rising from the slide. The sandbox has turned a dark muddy brown. Wiping a steady stream of water from his face, Daniel sees the one refuge under the tree, the one where Daniel always hid before Katie met him and gave him her juice and pulled him out toward the sandbox. And now, under the tree—not up in the branches where she used to be, but sitting against the bark—is a dark figure in near silhouette, hands wrapped around her legs, her long red hair drenched into a copper brown.

As Daniel walks toward her, his shoes squish through the muddy ground, water seeping through the holes in the toes into his socks, soaking the fabric and chilling his feet. A gust of wind knocks him left and he nearly stumbles, the rain charging at his side like a battering ram, but he pushes back against it and soldiers on, muddy and shivering and cold. Soon, he sees the side of her face and he knows for sure it's her, hugging her legs and crying in-between her knees.

"Katie!" Daniel calls, but the words are carried away on a gust of wind, swirling like a dust devil in the distance. "Katie!" he shouts even louder, but if she hears him, she gives no sign. By now, though, he's almost there, his feet turned to ice and his hair cold and matted.

He reaches the tree, pushes his hand against the cold bark, and crouches down beside her. "Katie?" he says. "What are you doing out here?"

For a moment, it looks as if she's going to turn, but then she scoots left along the bark, facing toward the playground. The dirt around the *tree is nearly mud and her khaki pants are soaked. She sobs, or seems to, though it's hard to tell through the driving rain. Even the leaves in the tree offer no shelter. "Katie?" he says.*

Then she climbs to her feet, the mud having left the back of her pants a dark brown. As thunder breaks the air, Katie walks onto the playground, a fresh wave of rain battering her head, her shoes kicking the soaked wood chips. Her arms folded, Katie stares out toward the traffic light above the street, which waves back and forth, back and forth.

Finally, she speaks. "I'm mad at you," she says.

Daniel stands up and follows her out toward the playground. His feet feel numb. "Why?" he says.

Her arms still folded, she glances back toward him. He sees her chest heaving as she breathes hard, and harder, and harder, and suddenly she's not nine but fourteen, taller and angrier, and she unfolds her arms and steps toward Daniel with a long finger and yells, "You killed me!"

She's fourteen and he's nine and there's nowhere to go because the tree's useless and the gym's too far away. "I didn't!" he says.

"You killed my dad and my mom and you killed me!" she screams, and as she says it, red lumps start popping through her skin, splitting into two and growing, covering her face and pushing through her soaked hair. The water slips over the lumps as if sliding down a malformed waterslide. "I'll kill you back!"

Daniel's right foot slips into a mud puddle and he falls over backwards, ice water soaking into his back as a bolt of lightning blasts from the sky and explodes the tree, splitting it in two so thoroughly that even the ants would have nowhere left to go. Katie stomps forward, mud splashing in her wake.

"Oh, you're dead," she says, her every footstep a splash. He's stuck in the muddy quicksand, which seeps over his arms and legs, stomach and chest and throat. "You're dead!"

Katie lunges.

When his eyes shoot open, Daniel doesn't know where he is. The bones below his back are bruised, and they ache, and as he pulls his head back into the wall, he pulls it all together—the desks, the chairs, the abandoned guns, and the paperwork. It's the top floor of the police station, and though Daniel shuts his eyes and tries his best to sift through his mind, he can't for the life of him remember how he got back here. All he remembers is being led, by someone, up the stairs to an office, where Adam had taken residence.

Adam must have asked what happened. Daniel must have told him. Then Adam said something Daniel couldn't make out through the endless ringing in his left ear.

"What?" Daniel had said, eyes on his gun.

"Derek and Loren didn't die in vain," Adam said, his voice strangely distant. "They are martyrs to the cause." The incessant ringing almost drowned out his next words. "And you're a hero," said Adam.

"I guess," said Daniel. He stared at his gun. He couldn't remember how many shots he'd fired. Maybe it was none. As he reached for the doorknob, he said, "Um, Adam."

"Yes?" Adam tapped his fingers against a walkie-talkie on his desk.

Daniel looked back at Adam. "Why aren't there any girls in the Listeners?" he asked.

Chuckling, almost like Derek had, but really not like that at all, Adam leaned into the desk Daniel supposed was his. "Daniel, Daniel, Daniel . . ." said Adam. "Women are our hope. Our salvation. Our future. We could never put them in harm's way."

Daniel nodded. "Okay."

"And they're fragile, too, Daniel," said Adam. "They may not be willing to do what has to be done . . . so that we may survive."

After that, Daniel was dismissed, more or less, back out into the police station, where those Listeners left guarding the place waited for the other teams to return. Daniel wondered how many of them would. Then, he found an empty corner, leaned back, and drifted off to a distant playground where he could hear the only voice that really spoke the truth.

Moving Day

When the Listeners first left the supermarket, they left in shadows, silhouettes riding along the breeze. But when they return, it's in broad daylight—probably more people on the streets at one time than at any point since the quarantine began. And why not? One of the greatest hubs of cop activity has been captured and emptied, and yesterday's mission to hunt down the police stragglers went very well—fifteen more enemy voices silenced, at the cost of only three Listeners. It's a veritable bargain.

The best marksmen walk the borders of the gathered group, Terry in the lead with pistols in both hands, Quentin in the back. As for Derek and Loren, they walk, as all martyrs do, on clouds, watching down upon them all and keeping them safe, their angelic eyes aimed especially at Daniel, who keeps to the middle of the crowd, bumped along like an empty raft over rapids. Surrounded, he can see neither left nor right, and so he has no choice but to assume there's nothing on either side but Listeners.

Someone fires. Someone falls.

That's how it goes.

∿∿∿∿∿

They travel through the center aisle where Daniel once shopped with Derek, but they do so this time without Derek. They open the door Brian once guarded, but they do so without Brian. And in the cold basement, they no longer wait and bide their time, lifting, in pairs, the beds that once belonged to Stone, Ari, Loren, Ivan, and whoever else bought the farm this time. As Daniel holds his

Daredevil trade paperback in his lap, his fingertips brush against his cheeks and ear, and the one true voice whispers an alternate point of view, but it's drowned out by the ringing of a television with no channels. He looks into the corner and sees, in the mirror, Katie, sitting behind him on a bed Quentin and one of the others have just started to lift. Katie waves.

"Did you hear?" someone who's not Katie says.

Daniel turns toward Zeke, who piles the PSP and some chips into a backpack. Behind him, two of the other recently initiated carry a bed from the alcove and, grunting, start up the steps.

"Hear what?" says Daniel.

"There's this cassette, right?" says Zeke. "In the police station. Some cop talking down his own guy."

Daniel says nothing. He glances in the mirror again, but Katie isn't there, and neither is the bed. They must have carried her upstairs. She can grab some salt and vinegar potato chips and they'll be set.

"And, listen, Daniel, they totally admit it!" Zeke says. "All the stuff Adam and the guys said the cops were doing—all the abuse of power shit and lying, stealing, hurting people . . . it's all there, man." He smiles. "I wonder if the guy in the cell is a cop—like, the only good cop who they locked up for not being bad enough. Oh, I'll take that." He grabs Daniel's trade paperback and drops it into the backpack.

When Zeke moves on, Daniel doesn't know what to do—probably move a bed or something. Instead, he sits on his and tries to listen to the creaking bedsprings. He brushes his hand along his pillow, which is cold from not having been used the last couple days. Absently, he swings the pillow forward, but misses by a mile.

"Kid."

Daniel glances up. It's Terry.

"Adam says I'm doing the whole mentor thing, you know," says Terry, "with Derek dead and all." He shrugs. "So, you know, stand straight and fly right or some shit like that."

As Terry steps away, flipping his gun into the air and catching it, Daniel's eyes drift toward a floor that feels suddenly unfamiliar all over again. Fair enough—they *are* leaving, after all. So Daniel gets up off the bed and grabs one end of it, Greg stumbling over to grab the other end. Their hands will be occupied once they get outside, should a sicko attack, or worse, apparently, a cop, but with so many brothers around, Daniel is sure to be safe from anyone who would do him harm.

It takes the entire group about three trips to move the contents of the Food Garden basement into the police station. "We will not spend another minute trapped *anywhere*," says Adam that night to the approval of the gathered crowd. It's his explanation for why they're giving up such easy access to food. It doesn't matter— there's more space in the forty-first precinct, there are *windows* with *sun*, and now, throughout the lower floor, there are beds, the desks having been pushed aside.

"Take that, you dead fuckers," Terry mutters.

That night, after they've all eaten what provisions they brought, after Zeke has safely returned Daniel's comics and after the Listeners have all rejoiced in the return of honest-to-God plumbing—Shit Creek no more!—they gather upstairs, where they memorialized Ari, Stone, and Pip that first night, which seems forever ago. Adam again takes center stage, lighting the room not with electricity but by candle, and with his children at his back, he proclaims their freedom from underneath the thumbs of the cops. "They're still out there—some of them. They know what we've done and they're hiding, but we will find them. And when we do," he says, "we need only wait until the plague clears to be truly free."

Crouching near the back, Daniel glances toward Zeke, the candlelight reflected in his glassy eyes. Zeke is entranced. They all are— even Katie, sitting in the opposite corner, turning Daniel's way on occasion to make a funny face. Daniel's pistol weighs heavily on his thigh, and he adjusts it as Adam continues.

"Our major steps these past few days have come at a cost," he says. His voice cracks. "Ari. Ivan. Stone. Pip. Jason. Wesley. Loren. Derek."

Daniel winces. He rubs his thumb and index finger into his eyes, hard, and when he opens them, he's not in the police station, but in Katie's apartment, creeping silently into Katie's parents' room, that dead red place where three bodies lie scattered and sprawled.

Derek's eyes are as wide as ever but no longer intense—the light's gone out, and what were they doing in there?

"You're not stupid, Danny," says Katie.

Then Loren—dead Loren—props himself up on his elbow and says, "Girl's all yours."

When Daniel's eyes jerk open, Adam is going on about how Derek and Loren heard the truth—how they died so that others might hear. But Daniel scoots back, stands up, and slips away, into the staircase, down the steps, and to the bottom floor, the bedroom of the now. The lights are off and he doesn't bother to turn them on. Night after night in the supermarket basement has taught him how to see in the dark, but now he maneuvers through the bedroom not by instinct, but by the dim light emerging from the holding cells.

He passes between the beds, stubbing his foot slightly on the leg of one but ignoring it. On the desk by the door are papers, cast a slight yellow by the square of light through the door. The keys are there no more, but Daniel knows where to look. Reaching into a drawer, he pulls them out and uses them, stepping out of the darkness and into the heavy fluorescent light, the hum melding with the ringing in his ears to create a discordant two-part harmony. The moment the door slams shut behind him, the heavy bang rattling all six sets of bars, Tyrone's nervous voice calls out, "Hello? Who's there?"

Daniel doesn't answer, but he walks down the hall with purpose. At the end of the hall, someone has brought in and left a chair. Zeke had said that maybe the guy in the cell used to be a cop, and maybe that's what Adam or someone had wanted to know. But the man there, the man Daniel spoke with before, didn't seem like a cop to him, holding his cross and speaking in riddles. Daniel's tip-tapping footsteps bounce off the hums and ricochet against the ringing, providing an off-time rhythm to the screwed-up symphony, right up until the moment he stops before the cell bars, where Tyrone sits on the bench on the right of the cell. He has a black eye.

"Oh," says Tyrone. "It's you."

Nodding, Daniel looks off to the side. He listens for Adam's sermon, but no sound from the outside makes it into these cells. "Why are you here?" Daniel says.

"It's better here," says Tyrone. "Nothing can get me." He smiles a little. "I used to think you people were just a myth, you know," he says. "Listeners. But my brother saw one of you once." Then, the smile fading, Tyrone points a naturally trembling finger toward Daniel's bandage. "Why do you do it?"

His own hand cold and unsteady, Daniel reaches up and brushes the tape where his right ear used to be. The entire side of his face tingles, the sparks floating through his face until he blinks and scratches the bandage. "So we can hear only the truth," Daniel says.

"Does it work?"

Daniel shrugs. Then he rolls the chair toward him and slumps down into it, the wheels squeaking against the concrete floor.

"Do you believe in God, Daniel?" says Tyrone. Again, Daniel gives no real answer, but he does look up at Tyrone, who's strangely jittery, nearly electrical, rocking back and forth on the bench. "I do," says Tyrone. "I used to think God and I were on pretty good terms, too. When the doctors came in, in those biohazard suits, I thought He was going to save us. Even when the helicopters came and took them away, I thought He still had a plan. Heh."

Then, placing his hands on a bench that looks to be rough and cold, Tyrone pushes himself closer to the bars. There are scrapes on his forearms, Daniel notices, and another bruise underneath his jaw. But Tyrone doesn't seem to react to any of that. Instead, he turns to face Daniel, and says, "When you listen . . . do you hear God?"

Sitting up in his chair a little, the wheels squeaking, Daniel sniffs. "No," he says.

"Me, neither," says Tyrone.

"I can't hear very well anymore," says Daniel.

"I tried to." Tyrone smiles and nods, and the movement is so constant it's almost as if someone else is inside him trying to break out of his skin. Daniel wonders how long Tyrone's been here, but he doesn't have the opportunity to ask before Tyrone starts again. "You see, when that quarantine went up," he says, "I told myself . . . I told myself, we had to wait, and listen, and survive. So I led us somewhere we'd *hear* God . . . no matter how quietly he spoke."

From there, Tyrone speaks nonstop, the words flowing like water from a collapsed dam. Some of his thoughts are random, some tangents, but mostly he tells a story—a story of a man named Tyrone and a little brother named Anton, a story of a church full of survivors who got into trouble when the cops stopped bringing food for free, a story of the day Anton stole a police-band radio.

"He listened day and night to that thing," says Tyrone, "as hard as I listened for God. And one night, it paid off." He looks up at Daniel. "He found a way out."

Daniel jerks his head up to stare at Tyrone. *"What?"* he says.

Nothing Tyrone says from there—not the things the cops demanded, not the sickness Anton suffered, not the way Tyrone had to lock him up—registers compared to what he tells Daniel about the military man who emerged from the sewer near the forty-third precinct, observed not only by Anton, but by a Listener. A military man summoned, apparently, from *outside* the quarantine. "He wanted to save us," says Tyrone. "He said he wanted to be like Moses—move us from the borough to the promised land. But I wouldn't have it, and he was in no position to do it."

"Because he was sick," says Daniel.

"He escaped," says Tyrone. "And I ran. I ran here. I asked the police to lock me up . . . so I'd be safe. And the others . . ." Just like that, the flow of words starts to fade into a steady trickle as he shrugs and sniffs. "I just wanted to survive," he says.

"Yeah," says Daniel.

Tyrone squints. "What is He doing to us?" he says. Then, opening his eyes again and clutching his cross, he looks up toward the ceiling. "What is He trying to say?"

Later, Daniel sits alone on his bed, the Listeners still gathered upstairs. If they've noticed his absence, they haven't come looking for him. Maybe they wouldn't look if he left this place tonight and found the forty-third precinct. Maybe they wouldn't care. Or maybe they would, maybe they'd miss him, maybe they'd follow him. They knew where it was, after all. Or one Listener knew where it was, which meant Adam knew where it was, even though he hadn't told the rest of them. But maybe they'd track him down, like Derek did a million years ago, and say, *Daniel, don't go. We need you. We love you. You're our brother.*

And maybe the whole thing is bullshit. Maybe Tyrone has lost his mind. Maybe his brother was already sick when he thought he saw what he thought he saw. Maybe the forty-third precinct sewer was used once and sealed up, and almost definitely, no matter what a half-crazed man in a prison cell says, there is no way out.

Daniel sits on a bed that has moved several blocks today. The bed supports a boy who has moved much, much further and nowhere at all. Derek would make sense of it all if he was here, but he's not, and Katie would give him a viable alternative if she could, but the rest of them are still here, and didn't Brian and Loren and all the rest die for him? Didn't they? *Didn't they, you selfish bastard?*

The invisible weight that replaced his right ear weighs him down, and as the rumbling of footsteps starts down the stairwell—the only true footsteps—he feels locked in. *Where you are is where you're supposed to be.* Isn't that something someone said once? It makes sense in a sensical sort of way, a cyclical sort of way, and Katie screams at the circularity of it all, and her scream is so loud, Derek dies again. Besides, there's nothing for him out there, or in here for that matter. A flutter of movement in the corner could be a rat, or it could be Katie, and Daniel absently wonders what the barrel of his gun tastes like.

The Locusts and the Seagull

More skirmishes follow over the next few days, or weeks, or whatever. Daniel isn't really keeping track. Groups of Listeners, armed to the teeth with weapons picked up from the forty-first precinct artillery, find themselves stacked against the cops, now a sort of underground militia comprised of stragglers from the forty-first combined with the bulk of the forty-third, but Adam seems to have a sixth sense about where the cops are going to be, so the Listeners come out on top again and again. "He's a prophet," Derek once said. God works in mysterious ways.

In the course of the fights, which take place on otherwise abandoned streets and sometimes include a few sickos thrown into the mix, just for shits and giggles, it comes out that the plague drove its way through the forty-second early on, and the bulk of the cops there either got sick or went home. All the better for the Listeners—with a listing of their addresses, they strike at the cops' homes, keeping the police militia so scared for their families they pretty much have to disband. It's hilarious, really. Quentin laughs his ass off.

And, hey, once the tide turns, it's easy to pick up some orphaned kids who want to be on the winning team. Who doesn't want to be a winner? So Adam gets out his knife, the Listeners gather in the forty-first, and they get rid of those unsightly right ears. The Listeners, in short, take control. Katie's dad would be pissed off, if he wasn't dead.

In front of the forty-first precinct, Terry lies back underneath the driver's seat of a police car he's forced open—the only one there, it turns out, with any gas left—and works with the wires below the steering wheel (because finding the right keys would take forever) while Daniel scans the horizon for any sickos or cops who want to upset the newfound order of things.

"It's all the government, you know," says Terry, grunting as he reaches into the car. "It's always the fucking government." The motor whirs, a long-forgotten sound pushing out from the hood of the car. Making some more adjustments, Terry pushes himself out a little as the car hums louder, and then, finally, starts up. "Hell, yes! Hah-hah!" says Terry, as the motor runs strong and red dust filters off the vibrating hood. "Ladies and gentlemen, we are *mobile!*"

Sweeping the horizon one last time for hostiles of any kind, Daniel heads back to the sidewalk as Terry reaches over the passenger seat and opens the right front door. For the first time since the start of the quarantine, Daniel actually sits in a car, feeling the rush of air conditioning blowing against his face before Terry shuts the mechanism off. "Air comes from outside," he says. His surgical mask is still on. "Letting it hit you like that is just *asking* for trouble." Terry shuts his door, Daniel buckles his seatbelt but Terry does not, and in seconds they're on the road.

If the emptiness of the borough has gradually become less strange, it's bizarre all over again to be not only the only car on the road, but the only car to have been on the road the whole time. The dark buildings fly past, and Terry gleefully ignores all traffic lights, sailing through intersections and swerving past trash cans, shopping carts, and whatever else happens to be littering the street. As the buildings give way to a park, faded green with rusted monkey bars, Terry starts to speak.

"Think about it," he says. "The government sends in these doctors, right? And they make a big show of it with the Peace Corps, and . . . you know, they were all wearing those biohazard suits, right, all orange and . . . shit. Remember?"

"Yeah," says Daniel. One of them gave a talk to the residents of his building during the first week. Daniel doesn't remember what he said, but he knows he heard it, standing right next to his mom.

"Remember?" says Terry. "And they're gone in two weeks. The helicopters came back and whisked 'em right up—shot anyone tried to come along." Shaking his head, he scoffs, and swerves around a body in the road. At the speed he's going, it's impossible to tell if it's man or woman, sick or alive or dead. "What the fuck's the point of that?" says Terry. "Just a show, man. This is all a . . . test or something."

For a moment, they keep driving, the buildings growing shorter out here as they head closer to the waterfront. Daniel leans his head against the side window and focuses on the cracks in the sidewalk (*step on a crack, break your mother's back*) until, finally, he turns back toward Terry and says, "That doesn't make any sense."

"What?"

"Why would the government poison us," says Daniel, "and spend the money to keep up a quarantine, and—"

"You're not thinking like the government," says Terry. "Jesus fucking Christ, you're a stupid kid."

Pushing his head back against the glass, Daniel watches the borough pass by outside, until the buildings, stouter and fewer, give way to a relatively open expanse, in the middle of which is a school—P.S. 128. Daniel doesn't have to look at a sign to know that, because this is *his* school, or was, until the quarantine began. There are two school buses, faded orange and abandoned, in the loop out front. As Daniel stares, figures start to emerge, growing from the grass and the sidewalk, manifesting in the buses—boys and girls, teenagers, the way it was before, pushing and shoving and picking up books and skateboarding toward the orangish double doors in the front of the building.

Along the sidewalk, heading toward a set of concrete steps with red spray paint graffiti covering the handrail, Daniel, that is to say before-Daniel, walks with his head down, kicking a little pebble along the sidewalk as the other kids pass by. Katie walks alongside him, of course, and this is before-Katie, as she grins and clutches a red and white marble composition book. With a mighty cry of "Bop!" Katie clocks Daniel in the head with the book, and before he can even start to turn, she's already scampered off to the left, and the chase is on. Watching it all through a smudged glass window, now-Daniel, today-Daniel, Listener-Daniel shuts his eyes and tries to make the vision go away.

~~~~~~~~

The sidewalk by the street sign is cracked, but it's always been like that, the jagged line jutting in and out, sometimes both, before filtering into the crack by the sidewalk tile, like tributaries feeding a river. As for the sign itself, it watches over the street like a tree—like a green tree hoisted on a metal pole with big white letters that read "Herman Road." As Terry brings the police car to a halt along the curb, across from the street sign, Daniel stares down a road he actually does know, or did know. It's like identifying a body in a morgue. "Yes, that's him," but it is and it isn't. The body's here but the soul is *gone.*

A pound against the window he's leaning against startles Daniel, and he turns to find Terry already outside. "Knock knock, kid," says Terry. "Wakey wakey."

Rubbing his eyes, Daniel pushes the door open—Terry steps aside—and heads out onto the gravel of Herman Street for the first time in months. The street is set on a downward slope, the bottom relatively near the docks, and as if in confirmation, a breeze with the distinct smell of sea salt howls through the stout apartment buildings and neighborhood shops. "What does Adam want us to do?" says Daniel.

"Patrol," says Terry. "You know, keep the peace, let people know who we are . . . slice a few ears off, if you know what I mean."

As Terry chops at the air with his gun, Daniel glances over the police car and up the road a little, where a little pizza shop, Leo's, sits with a "Sorry, We're Closed" sign hanging in the window. Someone's scrawled beneath it, in red marker, "FOREVER." The door is very slightly open, and every now and again, the slight wind tickles the bell in the window and it rings. "We used to come here," says Daniel absently.

"What?"

"After school." Leo's is a straight shot from P.S. 128, and during his first year of high school, it also intersected with Katie's dad's patrol. So sometimes after school, they'd walk down here, past the red and yellow fire hydrant and around the candle store Katie thought smelled absolutely horrible (and why would anyone even go in there?) and all the way to Leo's, where they'd hang around and wait for Katie's dad to come and take them home. Sometimes, he'd be a little late, and she'd find him in the Pub down the street—not drinking (never did that on the job), but chatting it up with the regulars.

Maybe he's still there. It's right down the road, only a few blocks away. Maybe Katie went down to get him, she'll be back in a second, and he'll take them home. "Maybe," the breeze whispers.

With a snort, Terry spins and glances down the road. "Listen," he says, "you take the street here on down, I'll take the rest. Meet me back in four hours."

"What?" says Daniel, jolted, again, into the city sidewalk's cracked-up reality.

"Shit, kid, I got better things to do than change your diaper and hold your fucking hand," says Terry. Shaking his head, Terry starts the hike up the hill of Herman Road, muttering, "Just don't throw up again. Shit's disgusting." He *tsk-tsks* as he walks, and in a moment Daniel is alone by the police car, the breeze blowing on him and him alone.

The bell in Leo's chimes as if there's a customer.

There isn't.

The next hours are spent in the footsteps of the cops. That's clear almost instantly, at the first apartment building Daniel visits. It's a tall, narrow, dull green tenement with a splotch of brown on the wall near the door. Once he walks in—no easy task, his eyes jerking back behind him at every breeze, every rattling pebble, every no sound at all—he finds the halls quiet and empty, and the first apartment deserted. Or at least, there's no answer when he knocks.

But at the second apartment (as Daniel's eyes flit back constantly, as he tries to listen—could he even hear them coming anymore?) there's a small voice behind the door—a man, or maybe even a kid. "Who's there?" the person says.

"Daniel," says Daniel. That's the wrong answer, though. "I'm a Listener," he adds.

"Where's Sergeant Ballinger?" says the person, his voice through the door muffled and high.

The hallway groans. Daniel spins around and aims his M-1911 toward the front door, but pulls it back down when nothing moves or sounds. It was his own feet, probably. Or maybe Katie's in the corner, keeping him company. Turning back to the door, Daniel clears his throat and says, "He's not coming."

After a pause on the other end, the voice says, "Please go away."

"Do you . . . do you need food?" says Daniel. His voice cracks, and the hazy sun casts a foggy afternoon glow through the empty hall-way. Maybe somewhere, a bell chimes. But definitely, now, no voice answers, and Daniel moves on.

That's how the first hour goes, more or less. Half the time Daniel has to ask the people on the other side to repeat their answers, and half those people don't bother. If the goal of the cops was what Adam said it was, to keep the borough scared and trapped inside, it seems to have worked, but as Daniel takes every corner slowly, as he jumps at every sound without Derek or Loren or even Terry to watch his back, he can't say the people—and maybe half the apart-ments he finds are occupied—have the wrong idea. He wonders if any cops lived here—if, maybe, another group of three busted into one of these apartments and left a room of red and a dead uncle and a broken best friend. He wonders if the cops here were actually bringing people food, and he wonders if Adam has any intention of having the Listeners do the same.

In the next building, it's more of the same. No one opens their doors to Daniel. Maybe if he kicked one down they'd let him in, and maybe Loren would walk in, tap Daniel on the shoulder, and say, "Girl's all yours." There are maybes everywhere, flying in the breeze like locusts, and they swarm over Daniel's hair and over his eyes and into his mouth and especially into his ear, and they buzz louder than a thousand fluorescent lights, and they say, "*Maybe maybe maybe* the girl is dead, *maybe maybe maybe* it's your fault, maybe there's no one here, maybe there's a sicko right behind me, and *maybe maybe maybe* you have it coming—"

"Hello?" A door cracks open. A woman's eyes peek out.

Running his hand through his hair, Daniel looks into the crack. "Hi," he says. "I'm . . ." He trails off. *Maybe maybe.* "I'm here to help," he finally says.

"Where's the police?" says the woman.

"They're . . ." *Maybe maybe maybe.* "They're not coming anymore."

As always, the door shuts. As always, the sound echoes through the abandoned hallways, where people, their homes their whole worlds now, have no place to go. But this time, a chain rattles behind the door, and then the door glides open, warm air filtering out. The woman stands unprotected before him.

She's a tall woman, with long red hair, and she stands in the doorway one heel behind the other, and for all the time she must have been stuck here, she doesn't look like she's starving or dying. In fact, she's beautiful, and she looks Daniel in his eyes—Daniel who has no right ear and a defective left ear and holds a gun. She stares at him and she's beautiful and Daniel feels very very fourteen, but this is the sort of thing he tries not to think about, except for what Quentin had said one time, that once the cops were gone and everyone in the borough was free, the girls were going to be very grateful, *if you know what I mean*, and Daniel acted like he didn't but he did.

"Is there anything I can do for you?" she says.

Maybe maybe maybe, say the locusts. *Maybe maybe maybe*, you Listener, you earned this. You saved everyone, didn't you? Didn't Adam say you're a hero? Didn't Adam say Derek's a martyr? Wasn't Katie's mom *grateful*, and wouldn't Katie have been *grateful* if only she'd—

"No," says Daniel. "No."

Maybe maybe no.

∿∿∿∿

Tiny little voices scream in Daniel's head, but there are so many, their gabbing jaws chew at his pink fleshy brain. One of them is Katie, and one of them is Derek, and the rest of them insist that none of them is Katie or Derek, and now, outside, wandering aimlessly on Herman Road, how can you how can you how can you get some fresh air when the air is tainted, and how can you clear your head when all the holes are plugged? He breathes hard and fast. Come on, the woman would have, come *on*, what the hell what the hell is this place?

The nails of his left hand dig just below his palm and his right hand squeezes the handle of his gun like tinfoil and a bell rings and an angel sings and a knife slices down down down cuts ear cuts Katie cuts aunt and uncle and mom and get it together get it together "You can do this" says Derek-voice and "Derek is dead" says another voice and "I'll kill you kill you kill you back" she—

A heavy cry breaks through the air—not Daniel, but something above Daniel. Looking upward, he sees a seagull flying overhead, moving fast from the left side of Herman Road. The bird lands atop another apartment building on the other side of the road, and then it caws and caws again, its curved little beak pointing right down at Daniel. When it takes to the air again, it does so more slowly, gliding gently along the breeze back to the left again, above the alley between a couple tenements. The seagull caws, and eventually, Daniel follows it into the alley, his eyes glued to the gray and white bird.

The alley opens into another street, and the bird flies to another alley, and that alley opens to *another* street, and as the bird speeds up, Daniel moves into a run, salty air blowing against his face, powerful footsteps ricocheting off the buildings. He runs faster and faster, faster than any bug or voice can follow, breaking through the wind and out the last alley all the way to a body of water, wide and endless. The sun glistens off the waves as a rowboat, nearby, hits again and again into the wall beneath a short set of docks.

The bird caws, loud and proud, before going into a tailspin and diving into the water. A tiny, insignificant splash follows, and Daniel waits for the bird to emerge with a fish, then land on the dock in front of Daniel, swallow the fish, and go on its way, or give some kind of clue, but the waves and the water are still, and the bird does not re-emerge.

Daniel looks out into the water and he sees the boats. He'd only heard about it before, on the news and from Derek in passing, but at regular intervals all along the water are green military boats anchored and floating, with people in biohazard outfits looking right back at the borough, and surely right at Daniel. The breeze blows, the water waves, the seagull makes no sound, and the military boats remain stoic, as if daring Daniel to jump into the rowboat and try to make it through. *There is nothing this way. There is nothing any way. Maybe maybe.*

Everything's back in an instant—the voices, the locusts, the cops and sickos and the woman—and Daniel kneels down and shuts his eyes and thinks of Katie, just Katie, Katie in front of P.S. 128, Katie walking up ahead carrying her notebook, Katie's red hair and back and down to—Daniel shakes his head, but the synapses won't fire right. He tries to think of her *right*, but again, not her face, further down. The woman in the apartment looked kind of like . . .

"Stop it," Daniel says. His fists are clenched. His left hand bleeds. Then he shuts his eyes even harder, and now he sees her face, bright and smiling.

"What?" says Katie.

"Stop it!" cries Daniel, slamming his fist into the wood of the dock. In the silence that follows, the waves smack against the wall, the mist sizzles, and the rowboat smacks again and again into the concrete, as if it's going to fall apart. Daniel shuts his eyes and shakes and trembles and almost doesn't hear when a step sounds on the pavement behind him.

He hears the second step, though. Moving fast to his feet, holding onto his gun, Daniel spins around to find, already outside the alley and drawing closer, a pair of sickos (people), an old man and an old woman (people), marked with red boils but not horribly so, their faces still recognizable as human, their legs stiff. They limp closer, but uncertainly, and their eyes flicker about, occasionally finding Daniel but focusing erratically.

"Is this the market?" says the old woman in a voice both warm and raspy.

"Where's the market?" says the old man.

Daniel's gun moves from one to the other.

"What happened to all the boats?" says the old woman.

"Where's the market?" says the old man.

The sickos lurch forward, and Daniel steps back, pointing higher, grabbing his gun in both his hands. Maybes buzz in his ear. The sea breeze whispers and the military boats on the horizon watch like voyeurs.

"I had a granddaughter once," says the old woman, stepping nearer.

"I'm . . . um . . . I'm," says the old man.

"Stay back!" says Daniel, but they don't, instead stepping closer. The old man's left leg hits a stray pebble on the gravel, and the pebble rolls unevenly to the ledge, landing in the water with a tiny plop.

"He seems like a nice young man," says the old woman.

"Um," says the old man.

Taking one final step back, Daniel pushes his gun ahead and fires, twice at the old woman and once at the old man. They both fall back instantly, collapsing upon the ground as the old rowboat hits against the wall again and again and again. Lying on the pavement, the old man coughs. So does Daniel, as their bodies bleed and the million observers in Daniel's head provide a standing ovation.

ᴧᴧᴧᴧᴧᴧ

Later that evening, as the clouds slowly devour the sun and savor it, the police car's headlights cut through the growing darkness the way no headlights have in the borough's short-term memory. Fading light reflects off the flagpole near P.S. 128, and Daniel, in the passenger seat, leans against the window.

"So I'm stranded in the desert, right?" says Terry, hands pressed against the wheel. "And I see this towelhead . . ." He's incessant. He gives the voices in Daniel's head a serious run for their money. But still the locusts swarm over Daniel's face, and Daniel asks them, mentally, because they can read his thoughts, to swallow him up and eat the whole brain out so he doesn't have to think about it anymore, and the locusts say, not yet.

Something moves outside the window. Daniel sits up some and looks ahead, where a girl—in the fading light he can just barely make her out—walks along the sidewalk. She's probably sick but he can't tell for sure, and as he stares, her hair turns long and red, and she turns around and becomes Katie, waving and laughing.

"Hello!" says Terry. Rolling down his window, Terry draws his gun from his hand, extends it out the window, and fires, nailing the girl in the back of the head. Daniel sees the hint of red in a nearby streetlight before the girl goes down, and in the next instant, they drive on past.

Terry cackles. "Holy fuck!" he says. "Did you see that? Did you see that?" He laughs again, but Daniel just shuts his eyes and beats his head lightly against the window. Glancing in Daniel's direction, Terry snorts. "Damn, you're a quiet kid," he says. "Say something." But Daniel doesn't. Terry drums on the wheel. "What's your report?" he says. "What did you find, huh?"

Seagulls and strangers, old men and women, boats and water and locusts and maybes. Somewhere, another Daniel stands by an ocean and waits for a bird to come up for air. But there is no air in the water and, let's face it, the water is everywhere. What used to be the borough has drowned—that's the only way this could be, right? And Daniel thinks, if everything has drowned, surely he can drown, too.

And the maybes answer again: Not yet.

"Nothing," Daniel mutters, which is as near to the truth as anything else.

"Heh," says Terry. "You weren't *listening*. But I was. Wanna know what I found?" He grins, leaning into the steering wheel. "I found doctors."

Surviving

"**O**uch," says the doctor, his hollow voice filtered through the plastic mask of the biohazard gear. Derek said something about a doctor once, but Daniel can't remember what. As the doctor's gloved fingers tug and brush across Daniel's ear, Daniel flinches, the plastic strangely cold. Sitting on a chair in the second floor of the precinct, which has been deemed, for the next few hours at least, the doctor's office, Daniel glances at the doctor out of the corner of his eyes, the bright, heavy uniform sticking out like a radioactive thumb. He feels his ear slip out of the doctor's fingers two, maybe three times before he gets a good grip, and then the doctor's other hand moves in with an otoscope.

"Okay, the good news is, the cut isn't that bad," says the doctor. "It's healing okay. The bad news is . . ." He tugs the ear back and forth, and Daniel's head goes with it. ". . . I don't . . . know . . . much about ears." When he shrugs, the plastic crinkles, and a nervous laugh forces its way through the plastic. "You know, honest truth, I'm not even really a doctor?" Snorting, he pokes the otoscope further into Daniel's ear.

Doctor or not, Terry found him in the Trent Street Hospital on the first day of their pseudo-patrol. A hike up the hill of Herman Road had taken him to Trent Street, and from there, he headed back inland until he found the hospital. The way Terry told it, all he'd been after were some supplies for the injured Listeners, but he found a couple doctors still inside.

When Terry brought one of them back to the precinct a couple days later, he sat the guy down in front of everyone—a bunch of one-eared men staring at a doctor just like the ones who had abandoned all of them, bright and colorful like a piñata surrounded by particularly vicious gun-wielding children. The doctor, who said his name was Carson (but who now said he was not in fact a doctor), looked nervous, to the extent his face could be seen at all beneath the plastic, but he managed to tell the Listeners how he came to be here—how the sickos (though he didn't call them that) had broken free of their bonds, how they'd killed doctors and nurses and security guards, and how they'd managed to break through his biohazard gear before the whole episode was done. It all happened just the way Adam said it had.

"The rule—the rule was, inside the quarantine, we were to remain . . . covered at all times," Carson had said. "And once I wasn't . . . they couldn't fly me out. They couldn't take the chance. So . . ." He opened his arms. The plastic crinkled. "Here I am."

And now, Daniel feels the cold black plastic pull out of his ear, and instinctively, he replaces it with his finger and pushes away the earwax. Carson the non-doctor drops the otoscope into a bag of tools. "Wish I could help a little more," he says, "but . . . I mean, I'm a nurse. This isn't quite my . . ." He shakes his head. "You'll probably hear fine—is I guess what I'm saying. Maybe. You could."

Cupping his ear, Daniel listens, not to the ocean, but to the piercing sonar cry cutting through it, the endless ring, the high-frequency voices and the headache pounding like a dentist's drill into his skull. When he exhales, it hurts a little less, so he lets the exhale grow into a sigh, and *that*'ll teach it. The floorboards shifting underneath him, Daniel climbs to his feet. "Thanks," he says. He starts toward the stairwell, but then turns back around. "Do you . . . do you need food?" says Daniel. "At the hospital?"

"We're good on food," says Carson. "Left behind a ton when they flew off."

"Okay," says Daniel, glancing down at his feet. The overhead lights buzz downward. The stairwell beckons, its door shut tight but its lights still louder, and halfway down, the ghost of a corpse twitches. Shutting his eyes, Daniel says, "What do you *do* there?"

After a pause, and a little smile, Carson says, "I live with her."

"Katie?" says Daniel.

"What?"

Daniel blinks. "Nothing," he says, heading for the door.

As Zeke riffles through unlocked doors in the evidence locker, Daniel stares into a copper badge someone left behind. In the shiny metal, Daniel's reflection is strange and distorted, his nose jutting out in a long and warty mix, the right side of his face twice the size of his left and his ear a quarter as big as it really is. In just the right light, at just the right angle, Daniel swears he looks sick.

After the checkup, Daniel hadn't felt much like congregating with the mass of Listeners waiting their turn on the bottom floor, or with anyone, so he'd exited the stairwell, passed by the beds, and slipped away to the right, entering a hall where, eventually, he found a door he knew had been locked. It was unlocked now, and when he pushed it open, he found Zeke with a set of keys in his left hand, going through drawers.

"Oh, cool!" says Zeke. When Daniel turns, he finds Zeke brandishing a six-inch knife, not entirely unlike the one Adam uses, albeit shorter. "Think this'll help me if they get up close?" Zeke steps back, takes on a wide-legged stance, and slices the knife through the air. The overhead light reflects off the shiny blade and casts multiple reflections around the room.

Without answering, Daniel stares, again, at himself in the copper badge. The bandage where his right ear used to be is massive. When he tilts the badge slightly right, Daniel can see Zeke, black-haired and scrawny, though a bit less so than he used to be. In the dull reflection, Zeke is somehow undistorted into a little kid playing pretend, maybe Peter Pan slashing at invisible pirates in the hour between dinner and bedtime. There's a smile on his face, a toothy grin below eyes that have already left the room.

"I saw my school the other day," says Daniel, turning around from the evidence locker. Zeke lunges toward the other corner and stabs at nothing, grunting with every strike. "It was weird, you know, to see it like that. I don't even know how long it's been." With a backhand motion, Zeke slices somebody's throat. Very slightly, Daniel smiles, leaning back into a set of eggshell-white lockers. "And I could see myself, maybe in the window, you know? Second period history, with Mrs. Jordan, and . . . and I'd spent like an hour at Katie's house doing homework—"

"Homework sucked. Forget about it," says Zeke.

"It was, like, this paper on Archduke Ferdinand and World War—"

"I said *forget* about it, man!" says Zeke, the tip of his knife nearly hitting the keyhole beneath a tall, skinny chest of drawers.

Clutching the badge some cop used to wear, Daniel studies Zeke, whose movements are a little more ferocious now—as if he decided to stop playing Peter Pan and start *being* him, and do to Captain Hook what Pan should have done a long time ago. The tendons in Zeke's arm strain, and when he lunges forward in a full slash, Daniel sees his arm shake like a hummingbird's wings.

"Zeke, did anyone you know get sick?" says Daniel.

Mid-stab, Zeke pauses. "Brian, I guess," he says. "They say Brian got sick."

"I mean before the Listeners," says Daniel.

"Doesn't matter." Then Zeke pulls his arm back and stabs again. "Take that!" he shouts. "And *that*!"

"What about your parents?" says Daniel.

Stopping again, Zeke shakes the knife a little. "Adam's my dad," he says.

"Zeke—"

"Adam's my dad, Daniel!" says Zeke, spinning around and looking at him for the first time. "And he'll listen and keep us from danger."

"I—"

Raising his knife triumphantly, Zeke cries, "One ear, so that we may hear only the voice of our brothers!"

Daniel pushes himself back into the lockers. "Zeke—"

"One ear, so that the lies of the world may be drowned out by the truths of our brethren!" With that, he pulls the knife back down and stabs it through the air again and again and again, in short, frantic jabs, as if his life depended on it.

The Asylum

One by one,

        drum by drum,

                they come

                        they come.

The borough, no matter how empty and dead it might be, is never quiet, not for Daniel. All morning, stepping along the downward slope of Herman Road, he's heard the drums and their echoes, the underlying whispers, the footsteps, the heartbeats. If he listens close enough, they seem to chant a song, but he doesn't know the words. The sky has a gray cast, a monotonous cover that may as well be an impenetrable shell, and the drumbeats echo like a slammed door in a small room.

Though footsteps scrape along the pavement, on and on, scrape by scrape, beat by beat, Herman Road remains largely unexplored, partly because there were more cops here than there are Listeners now (although Adam has mentioned recruiting plans), and partly because Daniel, jumping at corners and pushing through whispers and drums, doesn't know exactly what his job is and, whatever it is, isn't doing it. Some of the time, he spends in the apartment buildings, looking for little and finding less. The rest of the time, he sits on the docks and wonders how far he could get in that rowboat—if he could slip past the boats or if they'd shoot him down.

From the air descends a rain so light it's just barely more than a mist, floating like snowflakes. (This place would be hell in the winter, if it wasn't hell already.) It cools the air, but Daniel has found himself a jacket—a light olive green number swiped from an abandoned sporting goods store, where the display window was already broken and half the merchandise looted, by whom Daniel neither knows nor cares. Daniel takes a sip from his water bottle. The water pounds, pounds, pounds down his throat.

Down the abandoned streets of Herman Road, past the rotting corpse of the sicko woman Daniel had to shoot yesterday, he finds himself outside a wide, red-brick building with a heavy-looking wooden door, and big wide windows letting in the sun on better days. A sign hanging from a pole reads "The Pub" in simple red calligraphy. It has to be the place he and Katie would go to find her dad whenever he was late picking them up from Leo's. Although the window on the right is hazy, fogged up in the humid air, Daniel can make out the vague outline of a bar, and, very quickly, the pink hint of movement.

Redoubling his grip on his gun, Daniel stands before the door, then glances back over his shoulder to make sure the road is otherwise clear. Then, sucking in a deep breath through his surgical mask, he shoves the door open with his left leg and rushes in, gun arcing left to right and landing squarely on the fat woman standing behind the bar, who rubs a dishcloth along the inside of a mug.

The woman, in her forties maybe, looks slightly haggard, mostly in the face. But even with a gun on her, she doesn't flinch, or even react with surprise. Instead, she leans forward and says, in an almost accusatory way, "Who are you?"

"I'm . . ." The door behind him was unlocked—he didn't break it down, and probably couldn't have. Any of *them* could step through that door at any time, *one by one*, but still the woman stands here, alone and, by all appearances, healthy. The bar itself is dark, the bulbs either unused or burned out long ago, but the pool table in the back, only three balls left on the table and the eight ball very near the far left corner pocket, looks as if it's just been played on. The walls are lined with portraits, but Daniel can't tell of whom. There's a jukebox, near the bathrooms, but it isn't playing.

Air—the non-sound broken only by the heartbeat drumbeats

—swirls through the bar. Pulling the gun down some, Daniel says, "I'm Daniel."

"Daniel, huh?" says the woman. With a shrug, she places her mug down and raps her knuckles against the counter, *rap rap rap*, drum by drum. "Have a seat, Daniel."

They're still exposed, with that door rattling on its hinges, a *rattle rattle* cymbal, but Daniel steps forward over the solid wooden floorboards, pulls out a deep red stool with a slight tear near the middle, and sits down near a small bowl of sharp tan toothpicks, still clutching his pistol tightly. With a light groan, the stool settles into the floor, and the woman, stepping across from Daniel, extends her hand. "Name's Flower," she says in a loud voice. "Welcome to the Pub."

As mist creeps along the vague window like long, skinny, methodical fingers, Daniel switches the gun from his right hand—it clacks as it hits his left—and shakes her hand. Though Flower certainly seems to have noticed the gun, mostly she focuses on Daniel. When she speaks, she speaks with a drumbeat, but Daniel doesn't catch it.

"What?"

"Drink?" Flower repeats.

"I'm underage," says Daniel.

At this, Flower laughs, but the laugh is absorbed into the floorboards. Reaching into his pocket, Daniel removes his water bottle and takes another sip, and when he pushes it back onto the bar, it hits hard, like a drum—of course, like a drum. There are bottles of wine and scotch behind Flower, though most appear empty, and in the upper right, there's a television affixed to the wall, its screen a dusty blank. "Does that work?" says Daniel, pointing to the screen.

Flower grabs a slim remote control from underneath the bar and clicks it at the television. Although the television comes to life, the only image it receives is as black as the screen itself, a high-pitched whine filtering out the small speakers beneath the screen. The shining blackness casts a strange almost-glow to the bar, a faded half-light that gives Daniel a bigger headache than the one he already had. When Flower changes the channel, again and again, nothing changes but the bright green number in the bottom left corner.

One by one, drum by drum, the static whispers, *they come they come.*

"No signal for some time now," says Flower.

But that doesn't make any sense. The high whine washes down in waves. "I was just . . . I was just watching," says Daniel.

"When?"

"I . . ." It was yesterday, or forever ago, in an old room with a broken window, soggy Cheerios floating like dead goldfish in a bowl of water on the counter. Beneath the distortion were pictures, a military man, a vague promise unfulfilled, and then reality ripped apart in static tears and the heavy drums of thunder, a prayer for toilet paper at 7:10 giving way to cold and concrete, a gray as never-ending as the gray outside, whispers and drumbeats and drumbeats and whispers.

When Daniel's voice emerges, it emerges as a choke. "How . . . how long has it been?" he says.

"Almost five months," says Flower. She presses the remote and the television dies like an uncle.

Daniel tries to conceive how it's even possible. The dark wooden swirls on the bar offer no answers. In the echo of a drumbeat, five months become twenty weeks; in the next, twenty weeks become one hundred and forty days; and in the third, one hundred and forty days takes everyone to October, the summer ended without ever having begun. In the hazy dead television screen, Daniel sees himself hunched over a desk, sketching superheroes on notebook dividers when he's supposed to be taking notes on federalism. No problem—Katie has him covered, one pen on paper and the other above the ear, blue jeans stained a light brown and nose a little stuffy, like it always gets when fall's coming. *One by one, drum by drum, they come they come*: Waking up to a military march at 7:10, meeting Katie at 8 and starting school at 8:45, feeling dead twelve hours later but having time still for a DVD, even if it does have to be *Harry Potter*, Katie's choice. In a month, the Daniel Bush will re-emerge with, lesson learned, a store-bought cake, and then it will be winter, and spring, and summer all over again. "It's the best summer vacation *ever*," whispers a voice that sounds like Katie's but isn't. The clack of a mug against another accentuates the point.

Knock knock. Daniel's there but no one's home, because no one can be nowhere—it's math or something. His fingers, autonomous, tap-dance along the bar, faster and faster into something strange and nonexistent, like a waltz in quarter-time. His left pinky nudges the bowl of toothpicks, and then his hand reaches in and draws a bunch of them out.

Flower asks if he's all right. Flowers die.

Daniel snaps the first toothpick, not in two but just so it bends. He snaps it twice more, once on each side of the first break, and manipulates the thin piece of wood into half a circle. The next toothpick is its mirror image, and the third, its own smaller circle. Four more toothpicks form arms and legs, and just as Daniel's hand seeks out some more, a small cry emerges from behind the bar, and Daniel pulls back the chain and undoes the latch and opens the door, *rattle click creak, drum drum drum.*

But no, the cry—it's a baby's cry, like the one that used to come down through the ceiling in Daniel's apartment before it didn't anymore. It stopped a week and a half into the quarantine. When Flower glances down toward her feet, it means the sound is real, and Daniel pushes himself up. "Is that . . ." he says. He can't get a good angle on anything below the level of the bar. "Is there . . .?"

There is. Flower crouches down, and when she stands up again, she holds a large picnic basket lined with faded blue towels, and in the basket lies a baby—skinny, of course, but not too skinny. She— it's a girl, congratulations—grabs for air and emerges with nothing, and maybe that's why she cries.

"Your daughter?" says Daniel.

"Shh," says Flower to the baby, smiling sweetly. "Shh. It's okay." She places the basket softly on the bar, then lifts the baby from her cradle, rocking the girl back and forth, back and forth, until the girl is lulled not to sleep but to silence. "She ain't mine," says Flower to Daniel. "Homeless man came by 'bout a month ago carryin' her . . . Said her mother'd passed on." She smiles at the baby. "Said she was good luck, too, so I took her in." Tickling the baby's tummy— the baby smiles but doesn't laugh—Flower looks down at the bar. "What is it?"

"What's her name?" says Daniel. He cups his hand over the toothpicks, touching them only slightly.

"Don't know what her mother called her," says Flower. "I call her Posey."

"What?" says Daniel.

"*Posey.*" Flower sighs. "You don't hear too good, do you?"

Daniel shakes his head, but the fact of the matter is, he hears beautifully. He hears the drums when they're silent to everyone else. He hears the whispers when no one even knows what to say. And he hears them coming, hears them coming, drumbeat drumbeat drum. But Posey—maybe she's the one who truly hears *nothing*. She's oblivious—maybe even happy. When Daniel reaches for her hand, she grabs his finger. "Hey, Posey," he says very quietly. And as Posey squeezes his finger, as tightly as the little girl can manage, Daniel tries to imagine growing up in a cemetery. He tries to imagine the last time anyone held his hand.

As he stares at the baby girl, his finger in her clutches, the drummer takes a break and time fades into the ambiguous thing it's been ever since the clock stopped running. Posey studies the bar—the toothpicks Daniel has left on the counter, and the dusty reflection on the television screen—and Daniel silently watches her do it, the only sounds Posey's gurgles and cries. Finally, in the novelty of a genuine moment of silence in the eye of the storm, Flower lays Posey back atop the blue towels, and Posey gurgles some more and seems to smile as her head taps the wooden weave.

"She'll grow up here," says Daniel quietly. The door, he knows, is still unlocked, but he doesn't quite grasp why he keeps looking at it. Doesn't he know he's already been told the answer? "She can't grow up here," he says. When Flower doesn't react, Daniel leans over the bar and says, louder, "Why are you here?"

"It's my place," says Flower.

"No, I mean . . . they're out there." He points back toward the door. "They could walk in, just like I did, and—"

"They do."

Hear now, Daniel? Hear it? "What?" he says.

"They still come," says Flower, "like they always came. They just want a drink." She smiles. "They bring friends."

In an instant, Daniel is on his feet, the pistol in his hand but the water bottle rocking back and forth on the bar, the barstool wobbling but, ultimately, settling back down on the floor. From a couple feet back, he stares at Flower, whose face is the same bizarre calm it was when Daniel came through the door and pointed a gun at her. He feels his heart jabbing against his ribs like a dying prisoner. It's the drumbeat all over again, but now, maybe now, he gets it.

One by one, drum by drum, they come they come.

"But they—" Daniel starts.

"They don't try to hurt me," says Flower. "Not since Posey came along." The heartbeat drumbeat *pounds, pounds, pounds,* as Flower beams at her surrogate daughter oh so warmly. "Isn't that right?" she says in a high voice. "Isn't that right?"

Drum. Drum, louder. Drum, louder still. *Hear* it, Daniel? *Hear* it, Listener? Do you hear the whisper over the drums? "But they—"

At the moment he says it, the swinging door, the unlocked door, the door left unlocked for any of the creeps and cops out there, whines as it opens, a gust of wind and a steady drumbeat muting the footsteps of the fat man, thing, *sicko,* stepping into the bar. He's the first, but the drums accelerate, and Daniel pulls his gun on the thing but he doesn't fire. The drum beats but he doesn't fire, not with the baby, not while she's so close, but Flower—Flower is calm, she doesn't flinch or run or hide, but instead she lifts Posey from her basket, drops the basket to the ground, and cradles the baby as she smiles at the sicko and waves a three-fingered hello. "What'll it be?" she says.

"Bud," says the sicko, its voice a throaty growl.

"Sure thing," says Flower. Shifting Posey into her left arm, Flower grabs a mug—it clinks with the drumming, clinks in time—and fills it, one-handed, with beer, dropping it onto the bar just as the sicko takes his seat, right next to the stool Daniel occupied a moment ago. The thing, boils covering so much of the top of its face it's amazing it can see, absently brushes Daniel's toothpicks onto the floor and takes a huge sip.

Still, Daniel doesn't fire, even as he steps back from the bar, even as the shot is clear. Like a master alcoholic, the sicko stares into its drink, and it doesn't seem to know Daniel is here, or that its absurd excuse for a life could be cut down in a second, but Daniel doesn't shoot it in the back and he tries not to cough or cry or even breathe as the door opens again, and a second sicko steps through.

This one has lost most of its hair, and all that remains juts out from atop each of the uneven red lumps which form a crown above its head. Some are so white at their borders that they must be on the verge of bursting. As soon as it walks in, it seems confused by the Pub, but it doesn't notice Daniel, either. It just takes a seat at the bar, and the stool scrapes against the wood right on the beat: drum, drum, *scrape*, drum.

One by one, drum by drum, they come they come, short and tall, fat and thin, a few women but mostly men, the pounding drums, a kid, a girl, one by one, drum by drum.

Despite Daniel's best efforts, his pistol goes off-target, his right arm shaking too much to hit anything, so he tries to steady it with his equally shaky left arm. Through the crowd, the bartender tends bar with one arm full, nudging the lever and letting beer fall into the mug her right hand holds. She provides service with a smile to the rotting clientele, and the sickos stay in their seats, red, infected arms on the table, pulling back whenever Flower drops a mug on the counter. No, no, in fact, they pull back whenever Posey is near, and so the sickos surround Flower and Posey in a ring, solid as a halo.

One by one, drum by drum, they come they come. Though they talk, the words they speak are gibberish; the barstools creak, and on rhythm, two sickos collide, a boil explodes, the pus inside drips down onto the hardwood floor. On drumbeats, more push through that door.

Every step back Daniel takes is another step away from the door, but the door is full as the sickos filter in, twenty and counting, and there's no way out that way. The pistol rattles so heavily Daniel is terrified he'll pull the trigger by accident, maybe shoot Flower or Posey. Either way, he'd let them all know he's here, and that he hears. And still they come, endlessly. How can there even *be* that many? A boy steps through, no older than ten. A woman follows the boy. Could she be her mother? And she's, oh God, she's pregnant? Like this?

Flower serves them all, and they push back whenever she draws near with her little bundle of joy. Murmurs fill the room and Daniel can't make out any of them, stepping further back from the open door, the exposed door, and now even the air has to be poison. Their tapping footsteps are off rhythm, but no less constant, and as they push Daniel back, and he hits a loose floorboard, the squeal is louder than it has any right to be, and several of them turn.

"Who's that?" says a sicko.

"Who's that?" says another.

Flower says, "He's—"

"He did it!" someone shouts.

One by one, drum by drum, they come they come. In unison, the sickos rise, a one-eared boy trapped in their eyes. "Who's that?" says one, and through the room, "Who's that?" becomes the call, and soon they stand together and cry for all they fail to understand. One falls, two trip, some stumble. Just the same, most lurch toward the one they blame. One by one, drum by drum—the space breaks down, they come, they come.

Daniel's breaths come hard and fast as he veers his gun left and right but sees them all in a blur. "No, no," he says without even knowing he's doing it, and he tries to let instinct take over, tries to look and aim, tries to fire, *does*. The gun fires like a staccato drum, and a sicko falls to the ground; he fires again, and one collides into the pool table.

"Help!" says the sicko.

Moving further back into the only space he's got, Daniel fires again, again, *again*, and a couple more fall, another tripping over the fallen. "He's crazy!" someone says as Daniel reaches into his pocket for another magazine and reloads.

Smoke fills the air and the bullet could go wrong and she's all there is but they're coming closer, not one by one but two or three by four or more, and the blood pounds behind Daniel's ear as he fires, again and again and again, the bodies falling before him, some crawling along the floor and some still standing, drawing nearer, fury beneath the boils. They fall: a man. The pregnant woman. As the leaders of the pack go down, two more step forward like hydra, and the girl, the teenage girl, steps to the front.

Her boils start at her cheek and plunge in a line down her neck.

Her jeans are faded, stained brown with mud and dirt.

Her long red hair falls halfway down her back.

"Katie . . . ?" says Daniel.

Katie cocks her head to the side. Her steps are somewhat sideways, a strange, shambling shuffle. Her eyes are above the boils, and they are unmistakably hers, just that shade of blue, but with the lights flipped off like an extinguished birthday candle. Staring askance, Katie shuffles a little closer, and the pack, behind her, stays still. But then those eyes, those dull blue eyes, go cold, as Katie leans forward and charges toward Daniel. Spinning around, Daniel drives for the back of the Pub.

"The bathroom!" yells Flower from the bar. "There's a window in—"

But by then Daniel is already there, pushing open the bathroom door, kicking Katie back just enough to slow her down and rushing inside. Turning around again, Daniel pushes the door, but he can't get it all the way closed as one of them, maybe Katie and maybe not, pushes into the door, and the too-wide crack gives voice to all their moans and cries and accusations. Shoving his shoulder against the door, Daniel looks behind him at the bathroom, which is tiny, with dingy white tiles on the floor, a couple stalls and a urinal, and a half-window just above the sink so skinny even he probably can't squeeze through. But another pound at the door makes it clear he's not going to get the time to try.

"Let me in!" yells Katie. There's a rasp in her voice but it's undeniably her. With another powerful shove, Daniel forces the door the rest of the way shut, the sounds of the sickos going quiet immediately. But the door rumbles still, hands knocking on the wood again and again, and they scratch and push and Daniel pushes back, and the window is far away as another shove on the other side forces the door open again.

"Let me in!" cries Katie, and with her voice come the voices of all the others, as loud as ever. As the crack widens, Katie peeks her face through, the boils on her face mere inches from Daniel, who struggles and strains and pushes back. When Katie opens her mouth, what comes out isn't a word, but an animalistic roar.

"Katie!" says Daniel, but Katie's eyes are cold and she doesn't respond. "Katie! It's me!" he yells. "It's Danny!"

But Katie doesn't seem to hear. With a piercing shriek, she smacks against the door, then tries to force her arms through the narrow opening, but she doesn't have the right angle. Daniel strains, his body shakes, his pistol dangles precariously from his right hand, but still he pushes as hard as he can and, staring into Katie's eyes, shouts, "It's me! It's me!"

And then the pressure lessens. The pushing stops. And even as the cries continue behind her, Katie goes silent, her eyes blinking, quickly at first and then slowly. The drumbeats fade into the background, maybe out the window, as Katie stares through the crack in the door and says, "Danny?"

His face soaked in sweat and tears, Daniel smiles, and Katie smiles back. Pushing back from the door just a little, Daniel lets his burning muscles relax, but that's the moment when Katie's eyes go cold once more. Whatever was once there floats away, now and forever, as she roars and pounds at the door all over again. With an agonized groan, Daniel pushes back against the door and struggles to hold her back, but the force is too strong, and his sneakers are pushed back along the sleek bathroom tiles.

Shaking now, muscles and body alike, Daniel slowly moves his right hand over toward his left, and as he shoves his knees and his head against the hard wooden door, he drops his gun into his left hand, where it points now toward the ceiling, just inches away from the feral Katie, pushing at the door. He wraps his hand right around the gun and finds the trigger with his index finger, and then he moves his hand further left, toward the crack in the door—toward Katie.

Another powerful shove hits the door, and Daniel falls back some more, just enough for Katie's hands to get through. There's no more time, Daniel knows, and so he aims the gun at Katie, at her face—at Katie, his best friend—and his arm shakes and his body shakes and the drumbeat *pounds* and *pounds* and *pounds* and he aims the gun at Katie, who roars, and pushes, and screams and yells and pushes and Daniel swings his arm around and shoots the glass of the window above the sink, shattering it. He swings his arm right back to the door and holds it for another second, two, three, before he pushes himself away from it and leaps up onto the sink.

Behind him, Katie falls to the bathroom floor, but the others step past her and over her—*her*—and Daniel pushes through the window, grasping and clawing for the black pavement outside. The shards of glass stab at his body, through his jacket and his shirt and into his back, jagged lines of blood cutting along his arms and his stomach, but still he tries to crawl through the gap. Outside: abandoned buildings, a bird flying past a restaurant, no people and no sickos, so he struggles and strains, and just as he manages to push his torso through, one of the sickos grabs his ankle. With a frustrated cry, Daniel pulls, kicking at the hand, again and again and again, until it lets go just long enough for Daniel to pull himself the rest of the way through and struggle to his feet.

His hands are bleeding, and the glass has cut through his ankle as well, but he doesn't pause, even for a second, instead tearing away from the window of the Pub, charging through the abandoned street as drums pound in his ear and bile clutches at his throat. He runs faster than they can move. Daniel runs and he doesn't turn, choking on the tainted air of the borough, the whispers pushing through his ear and the hole where the other one used to be— through his ears, *one by one, drum by drum*.

First Day

He seriously thinks he's going to die. With his throat on fire, depleting what little breath he has left, his tendons screaming and his stride breaking into a limp, his heart squirming and squishing its way through his ribs *again* and *again* and *again*, he honestly thinks he's going to die, so when he slows, it's not to catch his breath or to get his bearings or even because he just can't run anymore, but to welcome the inevitable.

The world, unfocused, shifts back and forth, even as Daniel stops by a pothole in the pavement, and red bricks and white bricks and green grass and trees dance around a flagpole as if it's Mayday. His headache pounds and the world is as dizzy as Daniel, and it's only when the spinning continues, when the breathing still hurts and the legs still burn, that he knows he's still in this world, still a kid with one ear and a surgical mask, stumbling on the street with glass in half his body.

And it's only when the spinning stops that he realizes where he is.

On the other side of the street stands P.S. 128, almost like a fortress, with its flag flying proudly, the grass and vandalized concrete stairs its moat. If he should be anywhere, he should be inside here, staring out the window at himself, wondering why that kid has one ear before figuring out the answer to number four. That's where he should be, unless today's a weekend, and even if he knows it's been five months, he doesn't know that one way or the other. The orange double doors, their handlebars slick in the almost-mist, sit out front, and Daniel limps toward them, his left leg dragging. As he walks, he picks the shards of glass from his arms and back, reaching down to pull one from his ankle. Streaks of blood taint his skin, but the bleeding has mostly stopped.

Footsteps echo backwards as he climbs the steps. The graffiti on the stairs reads "P.L. and T.R. 4ever." It's funny when you think about it. The ache in Daniel's lungs starts to fade a little as he spits onto the sidewalk and heads for the door, pushing it open with a rattle and, somewhere very far away, a bell.

The hallways inside the school are dark, but then again, they always were. The lights never seemed to do the trick, and Daniel doesn't bother to turn them on now. (Besides, he's not even sure where the switches are.) Dark brown tiles continue left to right along the wide hallway floor, all the way to the brown walls, the olive green lockers, and the old tan bulletin board outside the front office, where someone posted a notice for her lost dog Rembrandt at least a year ago. Further down the hall, there's a display case where they keep the trophy for a perfect season in soccer last year. It's dark up ahead and Daniel can't see it, but he knows it's there. He knows this place. And as he walks down the halls, the *click* and the *clack* of his feet along the tiles breaks the heavy silence.

His throat rattling, Daniel walks to the bulletin board, his finger landing on a long stretch of white paper, or rather several pieces bound together, pinned up with a green tack. When his finger scrolls down the names on the paper, the Honor Roll, his whole hand shakes, and though he tries to steady it, it still leaps back and forth like a wave on a Richter scale. But he forces his finger down the list, all the way down to the Rs, where it lands, finally, on "Daniel Raymond." For a moment, the finger lingers—Daniel pushes it hard into the paper so it can't leap about no matter how it tries. And then, just when the red of his fingertip starts to turn a bright white, he lets it go and pushes it up, the shaking slowing now, little by little, until it lands in the Ms, right atop "Katie MacDonald."

Then his arm jerks so hard his fingernail rips through the paper, and the noise of the tear carries through the hall. With a small, stuffed sniffle, Daniel studies the tear when, from the hallway, he hears another loud step—one that very much isn't his. Spinning left, Daniel spots a woman in a purple- and blue-striped suit, walking toward him quickly.

"Do you have a pass, young man?" says the woman.

Daniel recognizes her. Her name is Mrs. Beckel, and probably he would have been in her creative writing class, maybe at this very moment. He would have written a story about superheroes, and she would have given him a bad grade for it, because she made it clear in the note she sent home back in May that she would *not* accept genre stories in her class, and Katie would have stood up and defended it because it was very well-written and creative, and isn't that what creative writing is really all about? Daniel recognizes her, and he also recognizes the red boil encompassing her nose and right ear, so he draws up his pistol and shoots her in the head.

Behind him, the office door creaks open, and a man Daniel doesn't recognize at all, a hunched-over bald sicko with confusion expressed in its half-shut eyes, lurches out into the hallway, and Daniel shoots this one, too. Exhaling hard, coughing with the effort, Daniel wipes the sweat out of his eyes with his cut right hand and reloads the gun, and just as he finishes that, someone says, "Excuse me."

Down the hall, just near enough that Daniel can see it, is another sicko. But this sicko isn't a sicko. This sicko is a little girl—a little girl, who can't be more than eight years old, her brown hair in pigtails behind a yellow headband that sits askew on her head thanks to the bulging red thing popping up from her scalp. She leans back and forth, heel to toe, heel to toe. "Where is everyone?" she says.

The moment she takes a step forward, Daniel pulls his gun up and aims it right at her, but if she notices, it doesn't show. Unlike Mrs. Beckel, she walks forward slowly and curiously, little footsteps dancing wall to wall. She's so completely oblivious to the red pocks dancing down her face. Slowly, he pulls his gun down, though his arms shake as he does so. Moving his finger away from the trigger just to be safe, Daniel says, "They're in the auditorium . . . down the hall." With his gun, he points down the hall just ahead to his left. "They're waiting for you."

"Oh," says the girl. She stops, as if she's thinking, before turning right and skipping down the hall. The moment she's out of sight, Daniel stares at the pistol in his hand, then takes an unsteady step forward, nearly tripping onto the tiles. His bones ache. He needs water, but when he reaches for the bottle in his pocket, he realizes he lost it somewhere along the way, maybe back in the Pub or maybe after.

But it doesn't matter—not in the slightest. Pulling himself

forward with whatever little energy he's got, Daniel finds the door to room 103 on the right, a classroom with black construction paper taped to the little window, and pushes it open. The air is instantly colder in the room, the floor a red carpet, the chalkboard filled with geometry problems in purple chalk. Out the window is a small field of untended brown grass, which cuts suddenly into the abandoned borough streets and useless stop signs. His joints screaming, his whole body shaking so hard he nearly drops his pistol, Daniel collapses into a desk in the back left corner, the metal rattling beneath him, the legs of his chair groaning against the carpet.

When he breathes in, only half the air makes it, as if he's carrying a cup of soda he's filled too close to the rim. When he breathes out, it's in tiny little bursts, muted machine-gun fire. And when he stares down into the desk, he runs his finger, as best he can, over the front corner of the desk—and sees the initials "D.R.," scrawled in black pen on a day he ran out of paper to sketch on. Sniffling again, Daniel looks out to the right, near the window again, at the desk on the other side of the room where Katie used to sit. He now sees her as she was months ago, scrawling on a piece of paper, pushing her hair from her face, staring up at the chalkboard. When Katie-then sees Daniel looking, she turns, wiggles her fingers, and sticks out her tongue.

Dropping his pistol onto his desk with a heavy thud, Daniel slams his fist into the wood so hard one of the two might break. He falls into the wood, into his folded arms, and cries, his shoulders shaking. Five months of pent-up tears crash through the dam and fall onto Daniel's own initials. The desk shakes, the loose metal groaning against the wood, and the saltwater tears burn the cuts on his arm. That only makes him cry more.

"Hey," she says. "Don't cry." As Daniel's red, hazy eyes peer over his shoulder, he sees Katie, her pen flat on her desk, her body turned sideways toward him. She leans forward, her hands squeezing one another the way they always did when she was worried and didn't have anything to hug. "Don't cry, Danny," says Katie.

"I'm sorry," says Daniel.

"Danny—"

"I didn't—"

"Danny—"

"I'm sorry," says Daniel. Snorting loudly, he wipes his nose with the sleeve of his jacket. His arm shakes against the desk, and the sitting pistol rattles in place. His chest burns, and it heaves, and that makes it very hard to talk, but Katie, always and forever patient, looks his way and waits. "I screwed it all up," says Daniel, finally, the words croaked out past the frog in his throat. "I screwed it all up."

"I know," says Katie. The chair beneath her grunts as she climbs to her feet. Her hip hits against the desk, knocking her pen off it and down onto the floor. "Oops," she says, as she crouches down to pick it up, places it back atop her notebook, and steadies it. "Now you stay there," she says quietly, before walking away from her desk and taking a seat again in the one next to Daniel. Turning his way just a little, she says, "Everybody screwed up, I think."

"I did what I—" Daniel's words break off as another cry erupts. He fights it back, but not well. "They said I was supposed to—"

"Shh, shh," says Katie. She nudges her chair a little closer and places her hand against his back, rubbing it as he cries into his arms. "Shhhh."

"They told me you were wrong, and he was bad," says Daniel, "and I, and Derek said—"

"I know."

"I tried to listen, I tried to listen, I tried . . ." With a loud sniffle, Daniel turns back toward Katie, who nudges her chair closer. "I'm tired of listening," he says.

Katie responds with a very small smile. "Then don't," she says.

And then Katie is gone. Daniel cries for a long time, his broken breathing filling the classroom wall to wall and ceiling to floor, but in time, his heart begins to slow, the breaths come more easily and go more steadily, and the tears stop. After that, Daniel remains alone in room 103, staring sometimes at the chalkboard and the numbers he can't make out anymore, sometimes at the initials on his desk. And sometimes—sometimes, he holds his breath, and when he holds his breath, and shuts his eyes, he listens as hard as he can. He doesn't make a sound. Neither does anyone else.

When Daniel holds his breath and shuts his eyes, all that's left is silence.

At last, silence.

A Pocketful of Posies

irst snapshot: Surgical mastermind Dr. Bowdin, his ridiculous flapping moustache visible even through the jumpsuit, as he races through the door of Room 125. The camera clicks when he's halfway through, his skillful hands, despite his legendary calm, outstretched and bent in ways neither should be. Careful analysis shows his jaw dropped inside the biohazard mask, and if a snapshot could have an audio track, the sound would be a scream—one of those horror movie screams that never happens in real life because you never encounter anything to be all that scared of. But a scream would be window-dressing. The silence is the story.

Some surgeons and some nurses, when they head home at the end of the day ("day" being a relative term in a job that includes eighteen-hour shifts), think of the blood on their gloves and on their patients—the people, dead on their table.

I think of Tanya. (*Thought* of Tanya.)

I saw her first during my tour of Thomas General. Some doctor, Xavier or whatnot, gave me a lay of the land before I started work officially the next day. I spotted Tanya at the counter in the lobby, taking filled-out paperwork from a harried patient, flashing her bright smile, big enough to fit as much of a good thing as you can possibly have without it being too much, but how could there ever be too much of that? That enormous smile should be on all the time—that's the ideal. Tanya's smile is a torch: It guides you. And then you feel like the guide, an honest-to-God hero, when you're the guy who caused it. That first time—the first of many times I saw her—I hoped she'd talk to me. She pulled back her hair, black, weightless, and tucked it behind her smooth, outstretched ears.

"What's with the ear?" she says, now, today. Beneath the face-plate of her biohazard suit, her voice is muffled, but she can still project it: It's powerful, like a piece of straw propelled by a hurricane and speared through a tree. Tanya and I sit side by side, huddled together, on the neatly made but far from fresh hospital bed, staring up at the skinny man without a right ear who's training his gun on the two of us, but mostly on me.

If he fires, the bullet will shatter my faceplate or tear my suit, and if the bullet doesn't kill me, the plague probably will. Like a surgeon with a knife, all he has to do to end me is move his index finger less than an inch in the wrong direction. I think escape routes, I think excuses, I think of ways to talk my way out of the quarantine if I survive, but Tanya? She has the presence of mind, the calmness, the assuredness, to say, "What's with the ear?"

God. She's amazing.

"I'm a Listener," he says, roughly, proudly, like a patriot would say, "I'm an American," as if "Listener" is some kind of nation, but it's ridiculous, it's insane, because I don't even know what it means. I don't know what a Listener is and how this person is here, and unin-fected, and pointing a *gun* at me.

"What do you want?" says Tanya.

I wonder if he's ever shot a gun before. I wonder if he'd kill me just to see what it's like. I wonder how Tanya can be so brave that she isn't thinking any of this.

Finally, the man lifts the gun, takes me out of the bulls-eye, and, with the barrel, scratches the bandage where his ear should be. "Medicine," he says. "Supplies."

"We," I say. It's the first thing I've said, so maybe that's why I repeat it: "We-we-we—"

"We don't have much," says Tanya. "The doctors took most of it when they left."

"Why didn't *you* leave?" says the man, the Listener.

With the gun no longer pointed at me, I wonder if I could take this guy out, fast, before he could shoot me. Fast, like some kind of ninja nurse. Or maybe I could grab a needle from the cabinet behind him, force it up to his neck, and tell him there's poison in it—lethal, worse-than-the-plague poison, and I'll inject it in him unless he lets us go. He'll be terrified, and I'll hold him hostage, lead him up to the office, grab the tranq gun, and take him down—a hero, a superhero, saving our lives from this man, this *armed* man, all by myself. I wonder if Tanya would love me if I did that. I'll bet she'd at least smile.

Tanya sighs. "We were studying the plague," she says. "The patients broke free. One took off Carson's glove. Another ripped my suit, so . . ."

"Trent Street Incident," says the Listener. So that's what they're calling it. "They left you here?" he says.

"Thought we might be infected," says Tanya.

"Fucking fuck," says the Listener.

Now's the time to strike, when he's imagining the incident, and his gun is down by his hip. I could lunge, the way the patient lunged, the way I should have the first time—if only, if only—but they moved so fast, and he has a gun, and if he fires, the bullet goes where the plague, I pray to God, can't.

The Listener looks Tanya over, only Tanya, and grins. I can't believe someone would grin, stuck in here. "You look pretty healthy to me," says the Listener. "Really healthy. Heh." He laughs, then tosses the gun into the air—I hold my breath, because how can you be that careless with something that could actually *kill* people?—and catches it. It lands the right way, or right enough that it doesn't misfire and something doesn't break or shatter, and someone doesn't die. But, wait, forget that, forget—

"And I *have* been feeling a little sick," the Listener says. He steps forward, but not toward me, and he reaches and clutches her wrist. "You can help me out, right, Doc?"

She tugs away, or at least tries to, her left hand grasping the bed for support, but the Listener's grip is strong and she struggles. "Get the fuck off," she says, and he laughs.

I think gun and ear and drugs and nurse and Tanya and try to put the words together into some coherent image, some playing-card pyramid that won't collapse with the slightest touch, but then maybe the words are the touch, and I see a hand, and her wrist, and her eyes through the mask, and the grin of the Listener, and I get a clear enough image, a puzzle with most of the pieces in pretty much the right order. He's going to—what is he going to do?

I want to be a hero. I want to make her smile. At me.

"Let . . . let her go," I say.

The Listener smirks. But he doesn't listen.

"I'm serious," I say, not gaining confidence but figuring out how to fake it. "Let her go."

Then the Listener lifts his other arm and aims the gun, directly, seriously, at me, but that's a distraction, and I need, I need, I need *logic*. I'm a smart, confident guy. I'm logical and I take charge. See, Tanya, see?

"You can kill me, and you can take the medicine you find," I say, blinking, then shutting my eyes, "but the only people who know how to use it are me and Tanya. I'll be dead, and, and she sure won't tell you, not if you . . ." I don't want to say it. That wouldn't make her happy. I open my eyes to see if she's smiling.

She isn't, but I see the gun isn't trained on me anymore, and the Listener, grimacing, drops Tanya's wrist. "Here's the deal," he says, "shithead. You're our doctor. Keep us happy, we leave you guys alone. Fair trade?"

If I nod, he might see me trembling, so I don't. "Yeah. Sure." And what does he mean by *our* doctor?

He extends his hand. I take it. We have a deal. I'm a smart, logical, confident, take-charge guy.

And Tanya, head down, smiles.

Second snapshot: Dr. Bowdin and his trademark moustache aren't visible in this one, because his head is facing up while his neck is being snapped. This one shows what he was running from: The thing, the misshapen, distorted thing, boils overtaking its face, thrusts its arms, skin dripping off (the shot actually shows a small piece of it partway down to the floor), onto Bowdin's body, onto his neck, twisting it entirely the wrong way. There's a rage in its eyes—his eyes. That's the thing that's hard to forget. If there was a snapshot of the interior of room 125, it would refer to a patient named Vlad something—human, male. But there are no pictures of that. Those images, the everyday images, fade far more easily. This one shows Vlad, an "it" now, snapping its doctor's neck, only a half second after chasing him out the door.

Inside the quarantined borough, the night after the Listener came and left and promised to come again, Tanya sat on top of me and kissed me and let me love her. The quarantine is dark at night. There are some lights on in the city, but not many, and when it's time for bed in our uninfected fourth-floor alcove, our lights are off as well. The dark is total, the silence almost as much so, although sometimes there are gunshots, and the sound of her breathing.

Tonight she breathes on me, and she smiles at me after I kiss her, and then after everything, and it is bright, it's guiding, and I caused it, I am her savior, and she mine. This is an escape, this is a way out: a field trip, outside the bounds of the quarantine, and as long as we're back by morning, we can leave again anytime we like. It's not so bad in here, not with Tanya beside me. I knew it wouldn't be.

Things are different the next morning. The next morning we're closer. We talk over breakfast, one of our thousands of leftover frozen dinners. (I have chicken fried steak, she has turkey.) We wonder who he was. We try to fit the pieces together. We, we, we—I say it again, and again. I can't survive in this place, but we, we, we can. *We* can and *we* will.

The hard part, I think, was separating the old life from the new. When that thing, that once-human thing, attacked me and tore my glove off, part of me, probably most of me, knew what it meant, that I wouldn't be on my way home anytime soon, but still a small voice said, *They won't leave me! They wouldn't!*

Thank God, thank Tanya, they didn't leave me *alone*.

It *was* quiet those first couple months, and it *was* alone, because Tanya was quiet and sad and distant, and she, like me, was hoping for a way out. We hadn't been infected. We were fine, and surely after a few weeks stuck here in this Trent Street Hospital, constructed in a rush for the borough's lowest classes and used the same way for its dead and diseased, they'd come to their senses, realize they'd abandoned two of their own, two healthy, useful, wonderful nurses, and they'd send a helicopter back to pick us up.

"You know we can't do that, Car," said Owen, the hospital director, the first time I called. "We don't know how this thing works. Sometimes infection is instantaneous, sometimes it's not. What if you're infected, but it's developing slowly? What if you're immune, but still contaminated, and you and Tanya carry it into the city? We can't take that chance."

"But we're both fine," I'd reply. I wanted to be the one to convince him that, yes, there are risks, but screw the risks! Get her out of here! Yes, and then Tanya would know I'd brought the helicopter here just for her, and thanks to me she'd be able to see her sister Teresa and her parents and her little nephew Peter, and she'd eat at McDonalds and drink Dr. Pepper and go swimming at the YMCA on the weekends, and I'd have saved her and she'd love me for it.

"How do you *know*?" Owen would say. How do I know I'm fine, or Tanya's fine?

If I was being honest, I'd say, *I don't know. I don't give a damn. Just get me home, get her home, and let us live a normal life together. I don't want to die here. I don't want her to die here.* Instead, I said, "I *know*. Trust me."

About six weeks in, Tanya and I having lived well past the life expectancy of anyone infected, Owen finally said, "Call me in a week. If you're both okay after a week, I'll see what I can do."

I was ecstatic, but I couldn't make Tanya smile. She was skeptical. There was no reason, medically, it could be safe for us to return, until the disease was eradicated . . . and how could we ever know if that was the case? Could we live long enough to see that happen?

I couldn't make her smile.

I called in a week and the phone just kept ringing, ringing, ringing. Turns out my boss, my friend, just wanted to mollify me, and now he wasn't going to answer my calls. Our last connection to the real world was cut, ties severed, etc. etc., but I still had Tanya, and Tanya still had me, even if she didn't want me all the way yet.

But now she does. We are we. After breakfast, and a little more screwing around—Tanya! With me!—we head down to examine the patients. It was Tanya's idea, after about a month of sitting around and waiting, playing cards, eating frozen dinners, reading and re-reading the tiny selection of magazines in the hospital library, and watching the infected through the fourth-floor window, that we may as well continue the work we'd been sent here to do. If we were stuck here until we found a cure, then by all means, let's find a cure.

She's a hero, I swear to God. I don't know how she does it. That's why she wouldn't love me until I proved I was a hero, too.

The patients live on the second floor. There's a large room there—oak-plated floors, tall, wide windows, air in a constant state of must and dust. What it was for, I don't know—maybe this building, a big, tall building in a decrepit, dirty, broken-down little neighborhood, doubled as a community center. Maybe this was an auditorium, or a cafeteria, or something. In any case, when the plague broke out, the doctors moved emergency beds in here and strapped the infected people down, and we do the same today.

The cries begin as soon as I push open the double-doors. "Lemme go!" cries one, who used to be a young woman—probably a pretty young woman, but not half as pretty as Tanya. I wonder if the woman still thinks of herself that way—if, in her mind, she sees herself as beautiful. Does she realize there's a boil on her forehead that extends as far out as her nose? Does she know another one covers half her mouth, so when she cries out, the words are slurred and confusing?

Does she know she's as good as dead, and does she understand why we have to strap her down, tie her up, and cut open her decomposing skin?

There are a total of six of them now. The woman is my patient. Tanya heads to an old man near the back—he's only just become sick, and he's sure he's going to pull through. He doesn't understand why we won't let him go home. Tanya's so brave to ignore his cries, but I know it hurts her, and now that she's opened up to me, and become one with me, I can finally help her. I can make her feel better.

"We slept together last night," I tell the woman, who sometimes says her name is Julia, as I stand over her, peering down through the plate that protects my face.

"Please lemme go," Julia slurs. "I wanna see my kids."

"It was wonderful," I say. I reach into a tray of medical instruments below her bed and remove a scalpel, sanitized as best we can manage, which isn't very well. I run my orange-clad fingers up and down the blade, trying to get a feel for it. When you lose your sense of touch, surgery is astoundingly difficult, and all the more so given that I'm not, in fact, a surgeon.

"Now, this is going to hurt a lot," I say, gripping the scalpel tightly.

The old man cries out in pain. Tanya doesn't even wince. I won't either, so she'll love me still.

Things are okay now.

I cut into the boil on Julia's forehead.

Third snapshot: This one is head-on. The photographer must have been very brave, or too scared to move. Its eyes dark and furious, boils bursting through its forehead like asymmetrical horns, it/Vlad leaps forward, its bare left foot hardly touching the ground, its right foot well above. Its fingers are red and bloody, and they curl at odd angles, claw-like, reaching. At the bottom right of the frame, you can see the hand, the gloved hand, of the photographer, not nearly far enough away from that thing's outstretched left hand. What you can't see, because the frame's too small, is that the photographer is walking backwards (although maybe you can guess from the angle of the photo), that it/Vlad has slightly miscalculated its leap, and that an extra few inches of distance will be meaningless when the glove is tugged off. But there's no shot of that. Maybe he wasn't looking when it happened. Maybe his eyes were closed.

The borough is different than it used to be. It's weird—the streetlights especially. When you pass through the intersections, you pass through red as easily as green or yellow, and you find your-self looking both right and left, just waiting for the oncoming cars to hit you, based on everything you've learned since you were a kid, since the first time you took your mother's hand and strolled across the street. But no cars come. And the light clicks—you almost never hear the click, or you never used to—and the light turns yellow, and then it clicks again and it's red, but there's nothing to stop and noth-ing to go except us.

You can't see a traffic light from Trent Street Hospital—not clearly anyway. But just two days after he found us, the Listener, whose name is Terry, takes me with him in a car, a police car, the only moving car I've seen or heard in months, through the near-deserted streets to the place where his people—the Listeners (do they all look like him, with the one ear? Is it some sort of ritual?)—live. I don't want to leave Tanya alone, and I'm not sure if I can be brave if she's not with me, but she's beautiful and strong, and she tells me to go ahead. The fact that Terry seems perfectly happy to use that gun doesn't help.

So for the first time since the quarantine went up, I move through the streets, protected by one-eared Terry, his pistol, and the metal doors of the police car, myself armed with only my tranqs. The streetlights click for a tiny audience that isn't paying attention, and the car motor echoes along the silent buildings. I clutch my medical supplies close to me, as if someone's going to reach out and snatch them. Which is silly—not just because I'm in a car, but because if something reaches out and grabs me, losing my supplies will be the least of my concerns.

I wish Tanya was here.

"You know what I heard the other day?" says Terry, disturbingly calm in the middle of the deserted borough. "I was walking by this school, right? And this kid sicko, this little girl, like, seven or ten or something, she's just walking around in a circle, singing 'Ring Around the Rosies.' You know that one?" He sings, "Ring around the rosies, a pocketful of posies."

"Yeah," I say, eyes darting right and left.

"So I tell Adam about it, right? And Adam says that song's about the plague, in England or whatever. I fucking swear to God."

"It's not really," I say. "It's just a—"

"It's a lie. It's a miracle cure." Terry shakes his head and smirks. "The pocketful of posies, I mean. Doctors, scientists, whatever, wanna feel better about themselves, so they spread the word of a cure that don't work, won't work, and everyone buys it so they can feel better about *them*selves for just a little while, till the plague screws 'em all up." He chuckles. "And how's the rest of it go? Ashes, ashes . . ."

"They all fall down," I say.

"Exactly!" says Terry, leaning back and clapping. "Ex-fucking-actly! Doctor lies to protect. Doctor's lies bring the whole thing down. That's you, Carson. Professional liar."

I pause and panic for a second, because I think he's figured it out. But then he just laughs and pats me on my biohazard-protected shoulder. "Fuck, you're uptight, man. Lighten up!" Turning the wheel, he shakes my shoulder, and I laugh a little.

He's right in one way, because I am a liar, but wrong in another, because my cure works, for me at least. What's the pocketful of posies in a boroughful of sickness? It's the light that allows you to see that the world isn't dark all the time. It's the feeling that even if there's almost no one left outside the door, it doesn't matter because you're not alone inside, because someone—not just someone, but the perfect someone, the most perfect someone there's ever been—is there with you.

A gunshot crashes through the borough, and it's a second before I realize it came from Terry, shooting right through the rolled-down window. It takes me another second before I realize it was *my* rolled-down window, which he must have rolled down when I was laughing. He shot someone, something, practically beside me— one of them, I see when I look back over my shoulder, malformed but not as badly as the ones in the room back at Trent Street. It's forty yards away now, and counting. Woman, mid-thirties maybe. For a moment, I think how I'd have never seen her. What if I was driving, and the car broke down? I'd have never reached my tranqs in time. I'm on *their* turf in *their* home and it would have reached me and grabbed me and doomed me all over again, because I couldn't get back to Tanya. I couldn't go back. I'd maybe get sick and she could get sick and I love her and I could never go back.

But then again, she'd never know.

She'd never know if Terry didn't tell her.

"Hey, wake up," says Terry. He raps my skull and I come to. "Just some chick. Snap the fuck out of it."

"Yeah," I say.

I expect Terry to lead me to some underground lair, a fortified bunker for this war against the cops he'd mentioned, but he actually takes me to a police station, a precinct house, which he says, with a grin on his face, they cleared out.

"The war's *over*, man," Terry says. "It's *long* over. Cops tried to keep us down, we fought back, like Adam always said we'd have to. Mowed 'em down, cleared 'em out, moved above ground. This is *our* territory now. We *own* it."

But I feel like we're in a prison and he's a visitor, talking to me through one of those short-distance phones, behind a soundproof see-through plastic screen. This world, this borough, is another world—a different borough from the one me and Tanya occupy. So I'm the prisoner, and he's the guy on the outside, telling me about his kids and wife and how little Billy won the soccer game and Fred is going to college, and none of it clicks, none of it's real, because it's happening in a world I don't see. They may be half-deaf but I'm all the way blind to their everyday life. There's a world before the lockdown, and a world after, and things are different, but the in-between didn't happen—never happened—because I wasn't there. It's just a story someone tells.

My world is behind the plastic screen. Tanya's my cellmate. It's less complicated. I'm happy.

"This is Carson," Terry says as he pushes open the door, exposing me to that other world, where Listeners bide their time. "He's our M.D. Heh."

Their faces are like the doctors' faces, back in the hospital—grim, the way you have to be when you've got lives in your hands and a solid half of them slip through your fingers, slowly, like maple syrup. I wonder if Owen had that look on his face when he told me he couldn't help us. I'll bet I did when I told the lie, and it's all worked out for the better. But my face and his face aren't like theirs in one important way—we don't have just one ear, but every last one of them, except a curly-haired man who seems to be their leader, does.

I spend the next several hours treating the Listeners as best I can with the tools I've got. Terry's no doctor, but he described the situation as best he could, and I brought everything I thought I'd need—antiseptics and bandages for the cuts, antibiotics for what sounds like a tough little flu, and expertise, for the diagnosis of bruised and broken limbs the tougher ones have ignored.

Some are young—kids even. I wonder how the Listeners found them. I help some kid named Daniel with his ear, and I wonder how he can hear at all with one ear gone and the other damaged. He's none too happy with me, but he didn't seem happy in the first place.

When I'm out of patients and supplies, which happens at more or less the same time, Terry reloads his pistol and drives me home. While we're traveling, he glances over at me like he's expecting some commentary, some reaction. I don't care. I don't want to leave the hospital again.

"It's a war, man," says Terry. "Shit. First it's the fuckers, then it's the fucked-up." He glances back at the police station. "Some of us ain't gonna make it. Some already didn't, but hell, they went out with a little dignity at least—not like the rest of these shits." Then he gestures outward with his pistol—the infected people everywhere, he means.

"Animals have dignity," he says. "I was in the Gulf, right? Iraq.

Special Forces. Got trapped out in the desert, which is what happens when your transport dies and your team is ambushed and you're the only one who makes it the fuck out." He chuckles. "I'm going through the desert, and I see this sheik shithole on a camel. I'm hungry, probably gonna starve to death, so I shoot the camel. Bam!"

And he punctuates our non-conversation with an actual shot through the window, which is loud even through my facemask. First, I think he's just making a point, but then I see what he did—a kid, maybe twelve or so, and sick (I hope), now lying on the sidewalk. Terry is alert—he's ridiculously alert. If I'd tried to stop him that day we first met, I'd be dead.

"Anyway, the rider wasn't too happy about that," says Terry, "and turns out he's armed, but no one's faster than me, so, bam. Shoot him dead, too. And now we've got a case study, right? Animal versus human. And the human, that towelhead, is staring up at me and begging me, *begging* me, to save him—me, the same guy he'd just tried to kill. Camel just looks away and accepts it. Don't need anyone's help, you know? Do what has to be done, accept it when it's over. Fuck, you're quiet."

I'm quiet, but he's loud. He always talks, but this is the most he's ever said to me.

"There's not gonna *be* a rescue," Terry says. "There's no fucking miracle cure. We are where we are. This is life. Accept it. That's what the guys back there do. That's what the fucked-up freaks gotta learn."

For a while, we're both quiet. Outside the window, a light breeze tip-taps a tin can along gravel, and I wonder if it's been blowing around this whole time or if some surviving person, sick or otherwise, tossed it out the window just today.

This is where we are. This is life. But they're very different places—the hospital and the police station. The refuge and the borough. There were no women in that group. No love. No hope.

"I've got a miracle cure," I muse. I don't even realize I said it out loud until Terry says something.

"The girl?" he says.

"Yeah."

He smirks. "Guess that makes you her plague."

Fourth snapshot: This one, let's face it, sucks. The composition is lousy. It's off-center. All that it shows, really, is a hand—a naked hand— pulling away so fast it blurs as the plastic surrounding it stretches and tears. At the right edge of the photo, nearly outside the frame, just the barest hint of a red hand can be seen grabbing at the glove, but other than that, the photographer completely missed the feral aggressor, and the victim, too. But the victim, to be fair, hasn't been in any of the shots. He hides behind the frame like the photographer does. Maybe he's someone who wishes to see everything and control, completely, the world within the frame, revealing all there is to know about everyone but himself.

Also, in the very back of the photo, near the green wall, you can make out the upper body of what looks to be a woman, but like everything else in this shot, she's horribly out of focus.

I don't know how it happened. I can go over it a million times and I won't know how it happened.

Things were wonderful when I returned to the Trent Street Hospital, because Tanya knew exactly what I'd done—risked my life going out into the borough, just to save her. When she smiled, I knew Terry was as wrong as he could ever be, because if I was her plague, she could never be this happy. I knew she missed Teresa and Peter and her parents, but if she was with them, she'd never be with me, and I know the friends and family she used to have could never make her smile this bright, this luminescent. They could never make her light a whole borough. That's how I knew she'd forgive me.

Everything about the next hour was wonderful. Making love was wonderful—in the bed by the window, then on the couch by the window, where any Listeners or sick people could see how safe and happy we were. Lunch was wonderful—I had the turkey she had had the day before, and she had the pepperoni pizza. And as we took the elevator down to the second floor, we smiled and laughed in our biohazard suits, and nothing in the world was more beautiful than Tanya when she laughed.

But when we opened the door to the patients' room, the woman who used to be Julia wasn't lying in her bed, but standing on the other side of the room over someone else. Her arms—and at least one of them was dislocated—were working around the straps of some other infected person, and the others started making noises as soon as we entered the room, and I knew something was very wrong. One thing that was wrong is that we'd brought only one tranq gun and I was holding it, and another thing that was wrong is that, when Julia charged, I didn't shoot her.

Julia tore through the room faster than she ever should have in the condition her legs were in. And even though I'd been her doctor, it was Tanya she pushed against the wall. Maybe she couldn't tell who was who under our biohazard suits, but Tanya yelled and fell back and Julia was all blisters and broken skin as she screamed and yelled and searched for flesh, and I had the tranq gun and I wanted to be the hero and make Tanya smile, but Julia should have been in her bed. It's not my fault she wasn't. I thought escape routes, I thought excuses, and I froze because I was confused. That's why I froze, but I froze and Julia knocked Tanya to the ground and Tanya yelled.

When I think about what happened, it doesn't come as a moving memory. I don't recall it the way it really went down. All I can remember now, when I try to think about it, are still photographs.

The first one is Tanya on the hospital auditorium floorboards, her face turned toward me, nearly invisible with the angle and the way the sun filters in through the windows. It's like an unfinished portrait, a body with no face, and it's disconcerting because Tanya's face is the most amazing part of her. Julia is in the shot, too, but her back is turned, and with the boils running down her back, she's more a thing than a person, but she'd been more a thing than a person for a long time now.

The second photograph is from the same angle. But this one, though an action shot, is surprisingly still. Tanya's right leg is extended, looking huge in the crinkled plastic of the uniform, and the thing that was once named Julia is flying backwards, suspended in mid-air, its arms reaching forward and grabbing nothing. It's like a panel from a comic book. Tanya is like a superhero. She is amazing, but I really wish the camera angle would change.

In the third photograph, Tanya is halfway to her feet, reaching toward me, her face clear thanks to a synchronicity of lighting and angle. But the world isn't bright because Tanya isn't smiling, and Julia is moving to her feet in the back left corner of the frame. The intensity of Tanya's movement is clear, even though, as in all the photographs, she doesn't, in fact, move at all.

And in the last still photograph, the angle is different, turned further into the auditorium, as if the camera is being pulled backwards. The new shot reveals twenty patients strapped to their beds, and at least three others somehow not. One of them, near the back, is touching his feet to the floor like a baby attempting its first steps, and another steps right down the middle of the composition. But this image has been overexposed—the images are so bright they've almost faded away, and the body of light surrounding the sick doesn't make any sense. No wonder I don't fire the tranq gun. Why fire if nobody's even moving?

I don't know how it happened. I still don't know. But now, sitting on the couch in the refuge of the office, the quarantined borough's oasis, I feel more alone than I have for months, because Tanya won't talk to me. I think she pulled me from the patients' room, and I think the patients are still loose down there. I think they might find their way up here if they get enough brain cells together, but I know Tanya isn't talking to me because I didn't help her. As she stares blankly out the window at the evening sky, I feel exposed. I tried to be brave for her, I tried to do everything that would make her happy, and all I ever wanted was for us to be together, but now she knows I'm *not* a hero, I'm *not* a warrior, I'm just a *me*, and I'll never be as brave and wonderful as she is.

But she can still love me. I know she can. We can be *we* again. And as she moves away from the window, opens one of the freezers, and pulls out a frozen dinner I can't quite see because she hasn't turned the lights on and I haven't stood up to do it myself, I think I know how I can make her love me again. I tried to convince her I was her hero, I tried to *be* her hero, but now she's mad because it was a lie. So I will tell her the truth. I should always have told her the truth. That's what you do when you're in love.

"Tanya," I say, but she doesn't respond. Her perfect black hair hangs down over her shoulders as she opens the microwave and pushes the dinner inside. She doesn't smile. That's why it's so dark in here. "I'm sorry I didn't shoot."

She doesn't answer. She sets the timer, and the microwave hums to life. Still photographs flash through my head, and I wish they were only of her. I need to tell her. I need to make myself tell her.

"They didn't break your uniform," I finally say, sitting up and baring my soul. "That day, when they broke free. *I* did. When everyone was distracted." She glares at me, her eyes cold, but still she doesn't speak. "I didn't want to be alone here," I say. "I knew we'd be happy together."

Tanya doesn't say a word, and doesn't break her glare. And she doesn't smile.

Eventually, the microwave beeps.

The Chain

It's not until Herman Road is finally in sight, with the corner of Leo's Pizza visible past the small brick building on the right and Terry almost certainly the figure circling in front of it, that the sun finally breaks through the mist, and the rain, such that it ever was, dissipates. Daniel, at this point, is on his second wind, his feet chugging against the pavement less out of rejuvenation than out of numbness, but he charges forward just the same, hearing nothing but the sounds of his own feet and his own thoughts in his own head.

But those thoughts are no quieter for being his own. And they tell him, more clearly than anyone or anything else in this godforsaken place, where to go.

The sun beats down and, little by little, the distant figure of Terry becomes clearer, his feet pacing back, his gun turning everywhere his eyes do, one merely an extension of the other. Both eyes and gun land on Daniel for only a split-second before breaking away; Terry's seen him, knows he's not a sicko, and is pissed as hell. And Daniel thinks, *Let him be pissed. Let him be whatever he wants.* If the voices of his brothers won't provide the answers, they might as well be irrelevant.

As soon as Daniel is close enough to hear him, Terry shouts out, "Shit! Fucking shit. Where the fuck have you been, huh?"

Daniel doesn't answer, but he tucks his pistol into his pants as he reaches Herman Road, crossing to the closed-forever pizza place where Terry spins around in a rage. His bandage is comically white against his skin. "I wait a fucking hour," Terry says. "A fuck-fucking hour!"

"I'm here," says Daniel.

"Hour late, you're here."

"I'm here. Let's go." The police car is parked by a yellow fire hydrant, bits of copper rust poking through around its screws, and Daniel starts toward it, kicking a few scattered pebbles of gravel at the front tire. But as he walks, Terry looks him over.

"What the hell happened to you?" he says.

Although he doesn't turn around, Daniel knows exactly what he means. The scratches still run down the skin on both his arms, and his right sock is damp with deep red blood from where the last shard of glass cut into his ankle. There are still holes in his jacket. The damage of the day covers his body. And as he feels Terry's eyes boring through the back of his skull, Daniel says, "Nothing."

"Kid," says Terry.

Daniel turns around. "They attacked," he says. "I got away."

Immediately, Terry's eyes jolt left, then right, and then to Leo's Pizza right behind them both. "In here. Come on," he says, pulling Daniel by his damaged arm onto the sidewalk, then shoving him toward the restaurant.

"Hey!"

With a heavy kick from Terry, the glass door flies open, and the bell in the window jingles loudly, fair warning for any chefs still waiting in the kitchen. He pulls Daniel in behind him, nearly hurling him through the door like a discus. Inside, the place is still strangely orderly, the tables where they should be, chairs upright, although that doesn't last for long as Terry, still gripping his pistol, tosses the chair nearest the door over the counter and into the kitchen, where it rattles onto the red-tiled floor by the dull silver oven.

"They attack you? They attack you?" says Terry.

"Yeah."

Fists clenched, Terry breathes out in a near hiss through clenched teeth, staring at a painting of Venice on the wall. Daniel looks on from behind, watching his arms shake with built-up tension until, suddenly, Terry spins around and clocks Daniel across the jaw, sending him spiraling backwards over a chair and into the edge of a table. The table shifts left, the chair falls back, and Daniel hits the floor, landing on his butt as his head crashes into the wall so hard the plaster cracks.

Before Daniel even has a chance to look up, the pistol is on him,

Terry's fingers squeezing the metal so firmly they're as bright white as the masking-tape label identifying the gun as his. Daniel pushes himself into the wall so hard he might just pass right through it, and he'd better, because Terry has Daniel in his crosshairs, and there's a rage in his glassy eyes as he steps forward.

"Only a matter of time, you know," says Terry.

"Wait, Terry—"

"You fucking coward. You're just like them," says Terry. "Accept it."

Forcing himself as far back into the wall as he can go, Daniel stares into the barrel of the gun, and then anywhere but. When he feels his heart racing again, he gasps for the breath he no longer has after the last couple hours, when he almost died, then lived, then found, for the first time in this hellhole, a real reason to go on living. But Terry's finger is on the trigger, and *Terry doesn't miss*—

"What, you gonna throw up again?" Terry says, glancing up at the dead rectangular light above him. "Shit. Go out with some dignity."

Derek's words, and Loren's words—all the words that maybe could have helped Daniel—vanish into nothing, and the only words he can think of come from a sad man in a sad cell, clutching his cross and swearing to God there's a way out of here. But Terry aims the gun, and then there are no words at all but his. "Sure as shit not gonna get me sick," he says. "Sure as shit."

Shutting his eyes, clenching his fists, Daniel rolls his head back into the wall again and braces himself.

Terry pulls the trigger.

The gun clicks.

"Fuck a duck," says Terry.

Tugging his gun fast from his pants just the way Terry taught him, Daniel forces it forward and *fires, fires, fires*, the hard metal bullets plunging into Terry's chest and knocking him backwards onto a red-padded chair, which snaps under his weight and sends him sprawling onto the pizzeria floor. Red blood pools through and over his yellow shirt, dripping down onto, and blending into, the stained square tiles.

As Terry heaves, his breathing strained and throaty, Daniel pushes himself back onto his feet, nearly stumbling back down but catching himself on a chair. Stepping across the floor, rubbing his left hand against the back of his head, Daniel looks down at Terry, who stares up at him with scared eyes, stretched so wide they almost look like Derek's, and that's why Daniel has to look away when he fires the last shot straight into Terry's head.

He keeps his eyes shut, and the gun clenched tight in his hand, until the last of the cannon-fire echo slips out the open door, jingling the bell as it leaves. When there is nothing—truly, honestly nothing, not even a sniff from Terry's nose—Daniel opens his eyes again and studies his handiwork. Maybe the hole in Terry's head makes up for something. Maybe Brian had been wrong just to walk away.

Crouching down, trying not to notice the blankness in those eyes, Daniel pulls the gun out of Terry's still warm hand. Though it says "Property of Terry," Daniel doesn't keep the fuck off, putting it, instead, into the left side of his pants. In Terry's pockets, he finds five more cartridges of ammo, and moves them to his own right pocket; he also finds a water bottle, which he takes a big drink from immediately. Then he sees Terry's silver watch, and takes that, too, slipping it around his own wrist. The metal chafes against his skin, but he doesn't remove it. It's 2:48, the watch says. It's been months since Daniel has known the time.

Daniel pushes himself back up to his feet, his worn legs bearing the extra weight nobly. Taking another sip, he stuffs the water bottle into his left pocket and pushes himself out the pizzeria door, the bell signaling his exit. Terry remains in Leo's, and that's where he'll stay, unless the rest of them want to come by and get him. He was killed by sickos. Or maybe he got sick himself. And maybe retrieving the body would be opening the rest of them up to infection. They'd have to believe Daniel about that. They always listen to their brothers.

Back on Herman Street, the road is empty on both sides. Daniel slips past the fire hydrant and up to the blue and white police car, its door ajar. He kneels down and studies the dangling wires beneath the steering wheel and, experimentally, touches two together, but nothing happens. He tries wrapping them tighter, and then combining another set, but it doesn't make a difference. The car is every bit as dead as Terry.

So Daniel's legs begin to move, one in front of the other. They accept the burden. They don't return to the carnival funhouse of P.S.

128, and they don't point to the forty-first precinct. When Daniel's legs start up Herman Road, they seem to move out of pure stubbornness, because it's certainly not out of strength. But in short order, their lurching, unfocused steps grow stronger, pushing against the pavement as Daniel draws both his guns and takes control.

The Borough

Once upon a time, a lonely boy named Daniel imagined the world beyond his apartment, and beyond his room, and beyond even the lonely traffic light, flashing its signals, minute in and minute out, to no one at all. He imagined the plague as the dull red ashes of some distant volcano, blowing in the breeze, sitting like copper coating the buildings, the streets, the motionless cars and motorcycles, the deconstructing people. He imagined it that way because red ashes, however microscopic, were something you could see, and if you could see them, you could hide from them. But the plague is bigger than ashes, lying along the ground, bearing footsteps as Daniel tromps through it. It's something so big it's everywhere at once: on the quiet carpet of an apartment even before the window is shattered, in the deep gray cement of a supermarket basement, behind the impenetrable walls of a police-precinct fortress, and everywhere outside, from the abandoned docks and their military guard, all the way to whatever was really keeping this borough isolated from the rest of the world.

As the afternoon sun begins its descent, the mist of the morning all but a memory, Daniel walks the borough's streets, both scarred and scared but moving all the same. The plague surrounds him on all sides, but he tightens the surgical mask around his mouth as best he can, and if that doesn't do the trick, if their closeness in the Pub, and their grip around his ankle, dug deeper than he imagined, at least he'll have seen the whole quarantine, every inch of it, and known what all the Listeners and all the voices, singular or otherwise, could never tell him. And maybe—just maybe—there's another world beyond this back-breaking place, one not completely unlike the one he knew, and if he isn't going to be there with Katie, and her parents, and his mom, and if he'll never again be a fourteen-year-old kid who reads *Daredevil* comics and lives in his own world so he doesn't have to face the real one, at the very least, he can be somewhere, anywhere, please God anywhere else.

As Herman Road moves further and further away from the docks, the buildings grow taller, and three-story tenements become five- and six- on one side of the street, while on the other are a series of storefronts to keep all those people occupied. The shattered glass in front of a place called SafeKey makes Daniel wonder who needed a new set of keys so badly during all of this. A bank is similarly damaged, but there's no way whoever took what was inside—velvet ribbons lie across the floor like dead snakes—ever had a chance to use it. There are a couple of bodies on the floor of the bank, but Daniel keeps walking.

More bodies show up on a construction site, a wide-open expanse save for the silvery metal pillars rising from the ground, and for the brownish yellow crane, unused so long it might as well be frozen. These people appear to have been sick, and they're so far gone their faces are nothing *but* red boils. Flies feast on their remains. It does no good for Daniel to look, much less dwell on the sight. Instead, his legs strain and yell and pound against the pavement, maneuvering around the cracks and potholes that make up the dead veins of the borough.

Some of the tenements have shops of their own on the bottom floor. Some double as office buildings. In one, Daniel sees a series of dentists, but right across the road is, of all things, a candy shop—Pete's Treats—and it isn't empty. Stepping up to the window, Daniel sees a ten-year-old boy standing over a pot of gummi worms, shoveling them into his mouth, piece by gummy piece. The red boil poking out from underneath the boy's shirt tells only part of the story. Although Daniel raises his gun, the boy doesn't turn; moreover, the boy looks strangely content as red, yellow, and green gummi worms miss his mouth entirely and fall onto the floor. Daniel leaves the sicko be.

Time seems to pass, inasmuch as it matters here; at the very least, the sun looks to be somewhere different in the sky, and it's hotter than it was when Daniel started. The sweat pours down his face, and the cuts along his back start to ache again, but Daniel keeps charging ahead, turning off Herman Road onto Heartland, which consists more of individual townhouses aligned side to side. Someone glances out the attic from one of the top windows, but turns away the moment Daniel looks, leaving only curtains swaying in their wake. The whole place is so much like a cemetery sometimes, each home a family plot at best or a tomb at worst, but it's always hard to say how many are buried alive, how many are dead, and how many are somewhere in-between.

In a sense, it's the traffic lights that are most interesting. They show up with relative frequency, and while the occasional light is out, or at least flashing yellow, most of them are as stalwart as ever—as stalwart as the one outside Daniel's old room. When the traffic lights, like the one on Heartland, flash from green to yellow to red, and then, eventually, to green again—Daniel pauses at one point, takes a sip of water, and waits to watch it happen—he looks building to building, home to home, and wonders who exactly is watching. He wonders if the sickos who pass this way remember what traffic lights are and what they used to do. He wonders if, in fact, he only imagined what traffic lights used to do, and if, instead, this is all they ever were: light displays in an empty city, there for show or, at most, to let someone out there know that something is still alive in this corpse of a place.

And the gas stations, in their way, are just as strange as the traffic lights. One, covered by a yellow and red awning, still has a couple of cars parked by the pumps. The quarantine may have been sudden, but there was still time to drive back home, so Daniel wonders what the cars are doing there, stuck at pumps that must be long inactive, driver's side doors wide open. Maybe their owners were trying to get out, only to find a couple of sickos. Maybe they got sick themselves. Maybe this place is filled street to sky with too many questions than can ever be answered.

Turning left onto a more commercial street called Friendship, Daniel thinks of Katie. When he tugs down his mask slightly for another sip of water, a metal rumble sounds from a nearby alley. Daniel reaches for his gun immediately, and has it in his right hand and aimed by the time the sick woman steps out into the open.

"I'm thirsty, too," says the woman, blinking in the sunlight. Her gait is slow and uncertain, her eyes wide and hopeful, her left ear covered by a boil. The skin on her right hand appears to be dripping off.

For a moment, Daniel keeps his pistol trained on her, but then, tucking the water bottle back into his pants, he moves on, listening hard for the woman's footsteps behind her. "Aww," says the woman. As Daniel powers ahead down the middle of the road, he glances over his shoulder to see if the woman is pursuing. She isn't. "Water, water everywhere, and not a drop to drink," says the woman.

The borough, Daniel finds, isn't crawling with sickos, but they're not exactly scarce, either. This long into the quarantine, Daniel wonders how many there ever were—how many died, how many continue to get sick, and how many are holed up in places like the Pub, hiding until they believe they have someplace to be. As a crumpled-up newspaper dances along the road, an old man walks into the brick wall of a bait and tackle shop, again and again and again. Like a lot of them—most of them, even, no matter what Loren said—this man is too damaged to be dangerous. And then Daniel thinks, maybe there was another choice with Katie's dad. Maybe Katie will be peaceful soon, or maybe she'll just fall to pieces. And maybe everything, like the old sicko walking into the brick wall, is too far gone.

Once upon a time, there was a lonely boy named Daniel. The plague took from him anyone and everyone who could make him less lonely, but the little boy remained, just beneath the skin of the teenage Listener who tries so hard to reach the finish line. He tugs open the long wound on the Listener's left arm and pokes little boy fingers out into the air. He pushes his head through the gap and the red blood splashes to the ground like amniotic fluid. A harmless old man pounds into the wall and he might as well be Katie's dad, alive and, if not well, maybe not altogether miserable. And somewhere, Katie is a sicko, Katie is a sicko, *Katie*, of all people, is too far gone, and too far gone is too far gone *forever*.

Down the block is a comic book store. Daniel sees it near the top of the road, past the old man, and he's pulled toward it like a copper filing to a magnet, returning his gun to his pants along the way. As he draws near, the sun pushing down behind him like waves in the Dead Sea (the constant push of too-hot water, the accumulation of salt on wounds), he sees himself reflected in the comic store window, an empty storefront behind him. Stepping closer, Daniel reaches up with his right hand and covers the bandage over his right ear. He cups it broadly, the knuckles sticking out as if there's something more substantial there to cover—as if, by magic, he'll remove his hand to find, voilà, a flawless ear where once there was no ear.

A cloud passes over the sun, the reflection fades, and Daniel spots some *Daredevil* trades. They're on prominent display, the red-clad figure swinging through a dark city, and somehow they must have been stolen from his room, repackaged, and brought here to be found once again. Daniel stares at the books in the display window and, simultaneously, stares at the one in the mall bookstore. Little boy Daniel and even littler boy Daniel stand side by side and want. And while all then-Daniel had to do was wait for a surrogate aunt, destined to die very badly, to enter the store and plunk down her credit card, Daniel now only wants. He places his hands against the store window and pushes, and *wants* a birthday present. He wants a tap on the shoulder from a friend. He wants a chance to read those comics and lose himself in the only world left untainted.

He steps to the door and he tugs at it, but it's locked, which is so stupid. He tugs again, but it's still locked, the latch rattling, and Daniel wants to shoot the glass, he wants to tear the book from the plastic, he wants to forget about everything and sit down in a corner and play and build until he's sick or hungry or dead and then stay some more. But then the clouds push past the sun and Daniel sees his reflection again, and the old man is there right there, drawing fast behind him and clutching the barrel of a pistol, and Daniel spins around and grabs for his own gun and fumbles with it but pulls it up as the man draws closer and Daniel fires and the sound is loud and the glass shakes and the old man falls, falls, falls, its head bounding against the pavement not once but twice.

Little boy Daniel retreats. Oh God, how Daniel misses him.

A mile and a few roads later, Daniel passes by what looks to have been a club, a place called the 9 Ball with a big picture of its namesake at the pointed end of a pool cue. The sign is dirty and tinted brown, but it looks to be otherwise intact. Behind the glass door is nothing but blackness, but in front of it is a computer printout, a piece of paper taped to the glass. The message, in red letters, reads,

"With the quarantine line so very very near, it's hard to deny the apocalypse is here."

Daniel's legs ache, as if they've just now become aware of what they've been put through today. The sun is fairly low in the sky—it might be evening now, which seems hard to believe. And when Daniel rubs his hand against the back of his neck, he feels a bright red burn, on top of everything else that's wrong with him. But there's a sign on the door, a message, and it has to mean the journey's almost finished. So Daniel presses on down the road, where the buildings have grown shorter once again, and the birds cry out in the distance.

The street doesn't quite dead-end, but its only continuation is a narrow alley between two buildings, and down that way, Daniel can see the water. For a moment, he imagines he's lost his sense of direction—that he's walked all day, only to make it back to the docks at the very end of the quarantine, behind Herman Road. But no, this has to be the front of the borough—they passed by the water every time they left, to the mall or to camp or to that state carnival Katie really wanted to go to, every time they drove down that bridge, and it has to mean the borough is narrowing like a bottle cap, and the boundary of the quarantine is near.

However long ago it was, Daniel remembers the way Derek described the place. "Trapped in this borough by a fort and an ocean," he'd said. But out of all of them, everyone he knew—Derek or Adam or Terry or any of the Listeners, or even Katie and his mom—who had asked about it? Who had even tried to get out? The Listeners were content to rule this cemetery, as were the cops, and everyone else listened to whatever anyone else said. But the borough is a prison cell with no bars—you only hear about them in rumors and whispers, like the great and powerful Oz. And little by little, the walls close in and the paths shut down, and everyone here ends up scurrying around like a rat without a maze—that is, nowhere, within whatever confines whoever's telling you what to do provides. In the end, you're cornered, backed against every wall there is, until it's pressing down against you so hard and so relentlessly that there is nothing you want in the entire world, not survival and not comic books and not even Katie, more than *out*.

So now, as Daniel turns right into a narrow alley, he stays as far away from the walls as possible. A fly buzzes by his face, and then another one, but he swats them away and keeps his eyes focused ahead, on the road the alley empties into, the road a small street sign identifies as Crawford Road. His feet scrape against the alley, and the flies scatter, and his hand grips his gun, and the wind pushes the ashes away. Tired from the walk, tired from the borough, and tired of listening, Daniel stumbles from the alley into the road and turns left, to the end of the borough—its unexplored final outline.

Dead eyes look back at him.

The first body is about twenty feet away, sprawled on the ground, flies buzzing around it and something else wiggling in its ear. It is an "it"—it can't be identified as anything else. It's impossible to tell even if it was sick. But it's just the first, and past it is another body on the ground, this one clearly sick, and then another man, a woman, somehow a dog, and a couple children off to the right— more and more bodies as the road narrows and the buildings lean into it, threatening to collapse. The flies together are as loud as a lawnmower, and what Daniel sees, and can't stop seeing, what Daniel sees and can't stop seeing and thinks he might never ever be able to stop seeing, is what he could only imagine from pictures of genocides in third-world countries, in movies or on TV or in social studies books in school. As the road goes on, the bodies are piled one upon another, randomly, just the way they ended up whenever the next one collapsed. Some have prominent red boils, others less so, others not at all as far as Daniel can see. Just a little past the first body, there's a bald woman with a fine hole through the left side of her head, all the way through to the right. A little girl's foot, a shoe half-off, is in her hand, and the little girl's head lies against the thigh of a bearded man, whose whole body covers a baby. First there are fifty dead, then a hundred, then two and three and five and seven hundred—maybe even a thousand.

There are cars, too, parked in every direction along both sides of the road, some right in the middle, with more dead bodies piled upon other dead bodies. The windshields are largely shattered, and the shards of glass would surely cut the bodies they hit, if there were any blood left to spill. Near the front of the street is a bus, the kind that once traveled over the bridge to the mainland city, tipped over on its side with its headlights in pieces, and from where he stands,

Daniel can't see if there's anyone still in it. But if he had to guess, he'd guess a busload of people tried to get out before nearly anyone else, and didn't make it. Daniel recalls the sound of car motors in the borough streets, cars he heard but never saw, cars that went and never seemed to come back. Seven on one day at the most. They had to stop somewhere.

At the end of all of it, at the end of the street, there is no more bridge, not as far as Daniel can see. From end to end, building corner to building corner, is a massive structure, sleek and metal, a miracle of military construction. It stands at least thirty feet above the ground, and its rooftop is patrolled by three men in brightly colored biohazard suits, like the one the doctor who wasn't a doctor wore, and the long metal objects held in their orange hands probably aren't medical supplies. There's no hole past them, not a single crack or opening, and there's a sea of bodies in the way, a rotting pile of corpses, the stench unbearable, the flies buzzing louder and louder, as if they've bored their way into Daniel's skull, buzzing like locusts and maybes, buzzing and feasting and eating the dead and the bald woman has a hole in her skull and a fly picks around the hole and all these people, all these people, the borough a thousand less.

Stumbling, Daniel coughs, but he holds it together even if he isn't sure how. How could the Listeners not know? How could anyone not know? How did they keep this a secret—with all these people out in the open? Was it already like this when the Listeners took him in? Did this happen after? What was going on? What the *hell* . . . They must have been sickos—the thousand people in front of him. They had to have been. That's why they're not crawling through the borough all the time—they're all here, and they must all have been sick. That's why they're all dead.

But Daniel isn't sick. No, no, no, he's not. No matter how close it got back there, he isn't sick. He feels suddenly sure of that, even as the flies buzz around his head, and he coughs again, and he draws the other gun, Terry's gun, from his pants and, both of them in hand, steps forward. The road is clear at first, but his footsteps are completely mute—the flies are too loud, and the streets are too full, so the echo emerges stillborn. He tries to look above the bodies, to the top of the fortress before him, but his eyes are drawn downward, as if the flies are pushing his head from behind. So when he reaches the first dead thing, he looks right into the side of its head, which has a red boil on it, before stepping over onto the only piece of empty pavement between this thing that might have been a man and the next corpse. Their smell—rotting flesh in the early fall sun—fills his nostrils, and his eyes water.

"Attention!" The word echoes the way the footsteps couldn't, although the sound is tinny and distant. Daniel freezes instantly, staring left and right, trying to place the voice, which seems to come from everywhere and nowhere. "You are entering a forbidden area." It's a man's voice.

When Daniel looks up, he sees the people in the biohazard uniforms looking his way, and one of them—this he can just barely make out—appears to be lifting his headpiece, just a little, to speak through a megaphone. The voice says, "To maintain the health of the city's remaining populace, no one may pass beyond the quarantine." But Daniel cannot, will not, stay here, so he starts to step forward, but the moment he does, the voice says, "Anyone who attempts to do so will be shot."

On the ground near Daniel is the bald woman—the one with the hole through her head. Glancing down at her body, her face turned onto the pavement, Daniel sees no sign whatsoever of the plague. The girl next to her wasn't sick, either, but she *is* dead, and that has to mean they were like him—closed in, broken down, desperate to get the hell out of this place and shot down for trying to escape. Many of the thousand dead people here were sick, but Daniel tries to imagine what percent were not, and he nearly vomits right then and there.

"Turn back now," says the voice.

The request seems impossible. Daniel's legs, cut and stiff, have worked too hard, and come too far, and after getting so close, he can't, just can't, go back to the Listeners, who had to have known about the fortress and the bodies before but never mentioned them. He can't go back to that place and live—or die—there. But as the flies buzz around him, crawling on his ear, creep-creep-creeping up his legs, and as the fading sunlight glistens off the distant rifles pointed his way, Daniel raises both his hands, both clutching guns, and steps backwards over the first body. From there, he sidesteps away, his eyes attached to the guards atop the quarantine structure.

Without another option, without a single card to play, Daniel tucks Terry's gun back into his pants, turns away from the bloodshed laid out before him, and walks from the rain of flies to the inescapable rain of ashes, as the endless night falls again.

Boys and Girls

The onset of night is quickened by the return of clouds, gathering over what little sun is left. Daniel is on another road now, and he pretty much has to be, lest he look back over his shoulder and again see the thousand bodies littering the street. But he sees them anyway, every time he closes his eyes. He sees them every time he blinks. He tries to keep his mind where it right now has to be, on where he's going to sleep and what he's going to eat—he hasn't had a thing since the stale rolls at the precinct this morning—and there's no way he can make it back to the forty-first on what he has left, but every time he tries to focus on the problem at hand, all he sees are the flies and a carpet of fallen humanity, and the bug in the hole in that woman's head . . .

Suddenly, Daniel coughs, loudly and violently, catching himself on the empty street. His rough, ragged coughs echo through the concrete, but they're drowned out by the memory of the flies, and Daniel coughs again and goes for his water bottle, but the bottle is empty. He starts to his feet, but he's only partly there when another cough and a mighty heave bring him back down. There's nothing in his stomach left to expel as he crouches on the street, eyes closed again.

There was a fly in her skull. What was it doing there? It buzzed around her dead brain, across her empty eyes. She was dead and decomposing and she might as well have been Katie, and then the woman becomes Katie, not sick but dead just the same, and the fly creeps through Katie's brain and Daniel heaves again, nothing coming out but the slightest drop of spit. But it opens the door, and Daniel coughs, again and again and again, the force tearing away at his sandpaper throat, again and again and again, and the coughing echoes only until it encounters something stronger: a gunshot nearby, sharp and angry.

Suppressing the coughs, Daniel pushes himself, with some effort, back to his feet, his eyes scanning the windows in the buildings above for any sign of life. At this point, the gunshot is a mere receding echo, and without a clue where it came from, Daniel spins in the street, ready to give up when a voice shouts out, "No!"

The voice, a woman's, is close. In an apartment building up ahead, a few lights are on, and although it's at least four stories up, Daniel can make out the hints of a figure in the window, the slightest silhouette before it moves elsewhere. Another shout emerges from that direction, but Daniel can't make out the words.

When he tenses his muscles, fire rips through his veins and he feels so damn half-dead he can barely move, and why move anyway? This place is a maze where every path dead-ends—some sooner than later, but eventually every single one. You either run around in pointless circles or try to break down the walls and force your way through, and get shot down for trying.

They're all dead. All of them.

They're all dead, they're all dead, they're all dead, they're all dead—

The woman yells something again, and it sounds so much like Katie, holding her dad, the cop who could never have been a cop the way the Listeners said, crying out for something, anything, doomed the second she held him and kissed him as Daniel slinked away, like vermin into the sewers, Daniel the coward, Daniel the murderer, Daniel the Listener. Then Katie gets sick. Katie tries to kill him. And Daniel deserves it.

Another flash of movement breaks through the dim light in the apartment down the street, and Daniel, pushing back the pain in his legs through clenched teeth, breaks into the closest thing to a run that he can manage. His feet might as well be anvils for what they seem to weigh, but Daniel holds one gun tight and makes it to the door of the building, dull green and metal with ambiguous red graffiti strewn at a sharp angle top to right.

He turns the knob, and the door opens, but it's heavy and it tears at the overextended muscles in Daniel's arm. A bit of blood trickles through the stretched-open wound, the wound formed by the glass that cut through his arm this morning, although it couldn't possibly have been just this morning. Still, the door opens, and Daniel steps into the narrow building, apartment doors on the left and right and stairwell to the next level up ahead. The door on the far right cries softly as it opens, and eyes peek out from the darkness before the door slams shut again.

Another gunshot rings out—it's definitely from upstairs—and so Daniel charges up the stairway, footsteps pounding as the front door closes behind him. He runs up to the second floor, covered in an orange carpet stained a red so faded it's almost gray, and then onward to the third floor. On that floor, he pauses and glances around. Shutting his eyes, he holds his breath and listens, just listens: to the rocking of the door behind him, which means someone's pressed their own ear against the wood; to the moan of the floor settling beneath his feet; to the air itself, swirling through the building under the quiet hum of dying light bulbs.

"Off!" someone yells. Daniel cocks his head up, and immediately takes off for the fourth floor, which looks very much like the third. The apartment in the corner is the one that would face the road, the one that would have had its lights on, and it's toward that apartment Daniel creeps, his gun clutched in both hands, held at the ready, eyes and ear wide open and alert. He steps so softly the floorboards keep the secret.

The door he sneaks toward is open just a crack. Tightening his grip on his gun, Daniel starts into a silent run for the door, charging forward and kicking it open with a loud crack as he spins and aims the pistol toward the first person he sees—Quentin, one-eared Quentin, half-naked and crouched over an athletic woman with a crew-cut, her jeans off and underpants down.

"Daniel?" says Quentin.

"Didn't want to," says someone else. His eyes darting instantly right, Daniel finds Zeke huddled in the corner, both his arms and his jeans around his knees, clutching himself tightly. "Didn't want to," says Zeke. "Didn't want to."

"What are you doing here?" says Quentin.

But Daniel doesn't answer, instead glancing from Listener to Listener, brother to brother, his gun drooping toward the floor. As the woman grunts and takes the opportunity to pull herself out from under Quentin, Zeke says, again and again and again, "Didn't want to. Didn't want to."

Grabbing the woman's arm, Quentin grins Daniel's way and says, "Want some?" In an instant, Daniel raises his gun again, the barrel aimed directly at Quentin. "Whoa now!" says Quentin, and as he raises his arms in self-defense, the woman pulls away completely and scrambles back across the floor in a crabwalk.

Daniel aims. Quentin pushes his hands forward, calmly. The woman pulls up her jeans.

"Didn't want to," says Zeke.

In the split-second Daniel turns Zeke's way, Quentin darts his arm down toward his pants for his gun, and Daniel catches the motion and twists himself back around, pushing the gun Quentin's way and aiming, and by the time Quentin has his fingers wrapped around the pistol, by the time it starts to rise into the air, Daniel's gunfire cuts through the room, one shot into Quentin's shoulder, the next his stomach, the third his head, *bang bang bang.*

"No!" yells Zeke, leaping to his feet. His face is tomato red, his voice a ragged scream, his eyes a tearful squint. "Why would you do that?! Why would you do that?!"

"He—"

But before Daniel can react, Zeke has the drop on him, his own gun aimed squarely at Daniel's head. "We have to stay together!" Zeke cries. "We have to!"

When Daniel tries to respond, all that emerges is the hint of a choke, but it's not the gun to his head that catches his attention but the look on Zeke's face, like a kid who missed the tying free throw the last game of the season—or, no, like a kid whose dad has just walked out the door for the last time—or none of those. Like a kid, period. Daniel never asked how old Zeke was, but he can't be any older than Daniel. The Listener with an M-1911 to his skull is no older than Daniel.

"Zeke, don't," says Daniel, his voice higher than he means it to be.

"I didn't want to!" Zeke shouts. Stumbling, he scampers back a little, pulling his pants up a little with his right hand while the gun in his left stays on Daniel. He starts to say something else, but then, instead, spins around and dashes away, pulling his pants the rest of the way up as he tears out the open door.

From the floor, the woman, her face stony, a lot more pissed-off than scared, pushes herself up and stares at the open door. "Where ... where's he going?" she says. She pulls her pants the rest of the way up and buttons them.

Daniel looks at Quentin, bleeding all over the green carpet, and when his eyes shut, he sees a thousand Quentins, coated by flies and stench and death, sick and healthy and man and woman and child and all of them. And then he imagines Zeke, making his way back in a full-out sprint through the depleted borough streets.

After a cough, Daniel, too, looks to the open door, and says, quietly, "He's gonna *tell*."

The Sea of Blood

The water is red, and it glows in the moonlight, and that makes it strangely beautiful and compelling, like a magic mirror. In the silence, underneath the steady breeze that cools the night, the water splashes against the rocks bordering the beach, a spray of red mist, like tiny little ashes, floating up into the air. Standing on the beach on the red-stained sand, you marvel at the water and wonder how it got its color. You step closer. You dip your toes in. It's strangely warm.

So drawn are you to the deep beauty of the red liquid surrounding your toes that you fail to look up when it pulls away, fail to hear the roar of water against water, fail to move when the eight-foot wave crashes down upon your head, forcing you back into the dark sand and pulling you by your toes deep into the endless pool.

And when it gets into your mouth, when you start to be choked by it, that's when you know what it is.

⌁⌁⌁⌁⌁

The light in the olive refrigerator flickers out nearly as soon as it turns on, like something thick and liquid and red had worked its way in there and shorted the circuit. No matter, though; the woman, who's maybe in her forties, draws from the refrigerator's cool darkness a bottle of water and drops it upon the green-rimmed brown kitchen table, and Daniel guzzles it down even before he finishes swallowing the Ritz cracker in his mouth.

"How old are you?" says the woman. She goes back to the corner between dishwasher and counter and stares at Daniel, who gives no answer at all until the water bottle is half empty.

"Fourteen," says Daniel, wiping his mouth.

"Shit." She folds her arms. The suspended kitchen light shines through the water and hits off the table, casting an odd copper glow. "What's your name?"

"Daniel."

"You one of them, Daniel?" When she stares at him, Daniel knows she's staring at the ear. One ear so that he may hear only the voices of his brothers, like the one he killed in the next room. Brushing his hand against the bandage, covering it for just a moment, Daniel reaches back into the box of crackers.

"Not anymore, I don't think," says Daniel. Not when Zeke, who tried so hard to make him feel like part of the group, loaned him a comic, then put a gun to his head, makes it back to the police station. Hearing those footsteps in his mind, *stomp* by *stomp* by *stomp*, louder and louder like a dark tidal wave in the night, Daniel stuffs another couple of crackers into his mouth and chews loudly to drown the steps away. His stomach growls. He feels dizzy. He takes another sip of water.

"I'm Anne," says the woman. Her voice pushes through the wave like a current. Sniffing loudly, she looks off to the side and says, "Thanks."

"They'll come for me," says Daniel. The words come out at the end of an exhale, and now he has to gasp for breath. There are more than forty Listeners, and they know where he is, even if he doesn't; they know what he's done, they know he's armed and with what, and he knows they're armed with much, much more. He wonders how long it takes for a wave to form at the steps of a one-time police precinct and swell to the tsunami it will become by the time it makes it here, and he wonders, in fact, how far away they are now. They'll want to kill him. They'll actually be trying to kill him. Daniel chokes on the copper in his throat.

"Came for all of us," says Anne. "In the forty-first." She stands tall in the corner, tall like a cop, and Daniel suddenly feels pummeled from both sides, as if caught in a rip tide. "Were you there?"

Rubbing the dark, sticky liquid from his eyes, Daniel mutters a very quiet, "Yeah." He doesn't remember her there, but what does he remember anyway, besides the crash of gunfire, flashes of light and blood and bodies, and above it all the drums, the endless drums, the pounding drums in steady crescendo like the onset of footsteps and one-eared men and sounds, they travel (he remembers from school) so much faster in water, and, and-and "I didn't shoot anyone," says Daniel.

"Goody for you," says Anne. "I got shot." She points to her shoulder. "Got out the back."

It fills his lungs and up to his throat like his mouth is a funnel for everything and everywhere, tasting the bullets and the drums and the legs of a cop corpse tossed into a rusty green dumpster, and rust is just what it tastes like—dirty and strange like the scent of a penny. "This is where we live," Derek had said that night, the words floating up with the determination of bubbles. "This is life. Can you imagine spending the rest of your life in that basement, forced to stay there by people who lie, and steal, and kill, and rule this place like tyrants?"

The waves would part for Derek. Standing over the bodies of people they killed, Derek told him they were only doing what they *had* to do to survive, and Daniel believed him. He said they were heroes, and Daniel believed him. But to say this is the life they fought for, drowning in the blood of everything they and everyone else has done, trapped more surely and deeply than anyone in any cell, trading tyrant for tyrant and like for like—that's just sick. That's sick. That's sicker than the sickos, and unless he can break the surface. Daniel will choke on it, feel it in the back of his throat, dripping down his esophagus, filling his dying lungs as he chokes and blacks out and smells it on his soul, and he will never, ever be free of it.

"You were . . ." says Daniel. "You had to be a cop, right? You were . . . you're—"

"I *am* a cop," says Anne. She clears her throat. She's choking on it, same as him. Her face is covered in red—not *sick* red, just red—dripping off her chin and into the body of water below her. It swirls around them. They float to the ceiling, through it, above it, as high as the waters will go, which is, in fact, endless.

Daniel feels soaked. He wants to ask if she ever closes her eyes to forget about it, or drown in it for good, but whenever he opens his mouth, the red streams in and cuts him off, and he senses only the currents around them, pushing them all toward the middle, cop and Listener alike, refilling the bloodbath with every shot they fire, and as blood pours from everywhere like a million waterfalls, Daniel finally chokes out, "How did this happen?"

Glaring, Anne says, "You freaks killed my friends. That's how it happened."

It comes from everywhere. Like the ocean, it never ends, and never starts. "They stole my mom's necklace," says Daniel, quietly, wondering about the words as they escape out of his mouth and float around his head. "You kept everyone scared. You locked everyone away. You left them to—"

"Fuck you, huh?" says Anne. When she says it, she sounds strangely subdued, like she's talking to someone else—maybe herself—tired and ready to drop from treading water all this time. "Get out of my place. Get the fuck off my water." Daniel doesn't move, and suddenly, Anne springs to life, steps forward, and snatches the water from Daniel. She jerks her arm like she's going to throw it at him, once, then again, but in the end, she just holds the cup tight, which is all for the best anyway. It wouldn't go very far in the thick red sea.

"All we ever did," says Anne, "is what we had to do. We had to keep order." She squeezes the bottled water, and a few drops leak from the top. "We had to survive," she says. "We're *alone* out here. Do you have any idea how hard that is?"

The more adrift, the more alone. They are, all of them, choking on it. "I've got to get out of here," Daniel says.

"Where?" says Anne, her voice breaking.

"To the outside," says Daniel. To the shore. "They're coming for me."

Anne laughs, a whisper-laugh, into her hand, and the words "There's no way out" emerge in scattered gasps, floating but not rising.

"There is," says Daniel. He feels cold all of a sudden—the kind of cold you feel when, even after you've gotten used to the water, you've been in too long. Shivering, he clasps his hands, and says, "Through the sewer. That's how Anton found it."

"What?"

But that's how water moves, isn't it? That's what the sewers are for. Whatever's in them is in them to be taken one place to another, and if a military man can ride the stream to the middle of the ocean, then it should be possible—even if it's against the tide, it should be possible—to ride the same waters back, ocean to river to stream to solid land. Tyrone was sure of what his brother had found, and Daniel remembers what he said about Anton. "He said he wanted to be like Moses," Tyrone had said. Moses, who parted the waters of the Red Sea. Moses, who found dry land where there was none.

"I need a radio," says Daniel, climbing to his feet. "Walkie-talkie, like the police—"

"Police-band radio?" says Anne.

"Yeah," says Daniel.

"I've got one."

"You do?"

Again, Anne laughs, and chokes a little on the blood that creeps its way into her nose as the air slips out. "We needed the radios," she says. "That's how we were going to strike back."

The waters crash your head against the blood-stained stones and taunt you, with the beach so reachable, before you're pulled again deeper, still deeper, into its depth, to the point where neither rock nor beach is visible, especially not if the blood has stung your eyes, or if the rock has cracked your skull. If you're still awake, though, you feel it's not like normal water, sticking to the hairs on your skin as it slips through like syrup, filling your nose like a nosebleed in reverse, the stench of copper and the sight of blood twisting your stomach and sending it up out your throat until it lies still on your tongue. You can't breathe, but you can choke.

If your eyes are open, you find you're not alone down here, and as the floating bodies slip by, the water is no longer so beautiful, or so strange and mysterious, because you know exactly where it comes from: a thousand dead, two thousand eyes, four thousand limbs, though not all where they should be. The water crashes you into bodies; it pushes you into a rip tide of offal; the putrid meat of death and decay swallow your face, and you can swim for the surface all you want, but you're too far down to even know what that is.

Sunlight isn't there to help. You're the one who wanted to see the sea of blood at night. At night, it's everywhere. And as long as it's everywhere, it's night.

ᴧᴧᴧᴧᴧ

"Hello? Come in?" says Daniel. The words are like the oar of a whitewater (redwater) rafter, sticking up out of the water in the slim chance someone might see him and save him. As Daniel clutches the cool black plastic of the police-band radio, he hears the rushing wave of the Listeners approaching, louder and louder every second, pushing on to the levels of natural disaster.

The only answer is static. For fifteen minutes, the only answer has been static. Every time Daniel switches the station, every time he calls for help, he feels the water, he chokes on it, but he hasn't drowned yet, and he cannot, will not, be here when the tsunami hits. He insists on this, even as he feels the water tug away from underneath his feet, hears the roar down the alley, knows exactly where it's going.

As he searches, Anne passes the time telling him what happened after the Listeners took over the forty-first precinct. She couldn't fight back—this she repeats—because she couldn't shoot with a bullet in her shoulder, but she made it out the back window and joined the coordinated counterassault. But that, she says, fell apart like a dam in the maelstrom, the little bricks removed one by one, because the Listeners were aware, every time, where they would be, and when.

"Hello? Come in?" says Daniel.

Most of them were killed in their homes, the way Katie's dad had been. The cops had been prepared to defend the two other major stations in the borough, or at least the one that wasn't rife with plague, but not every single cop at every single apartment. Those who got the word in time went underground, and that's why Anne wasn't around the first time the Listeners came for her, but as they lost more cops with every attack, as they drowned in the blood of their own brothers and sisters, the cops found survival to trump dominance and went home. All for the best in the end—you can ride the waves all you want, but the tide always turns.

"Hello? Come in?" says Daniel.

"So I stuck it out here," says Anne, sitting at the kitchen table across from Daniel. "Until now, they never came here. Don't even think those two knew I was police. And that," she says, pointing to the walkie-talkie, "is a fucking waste of time."

"It's not," says Daniel. It's a life preserver. It's a beacon—it has to be. "Hello?" he says into it again. "Come in?"

"You're going down the same stations all over again," says Anne. "You've cycled the whole way through, kid. Almost twice now."

"Hello? Come in?" says Daniel.

"Even if it worked . . ." says Anne. She leans back in her chair, which scrapes across the kitchen tiles. "Even if it did work, once," says Anne, "even if that guy's brother was right, how long ago was that?"

"Hello? Come in?"

"One month? Two months?" Sniffing loudly, Anne gets up out of her chair. "You're right about one thing, though. We do have to get out of here."

"Hello? Come in?"

"Forty-first's about an hour and a half from here. If they move fast, they'll be here by eleven. We can't be here when they—"

"This the captain?" A woman's voice emerges from the police-band radio, silencing Anne and Daniel. In an instant, it's gone again, disappearing in the ensuing static so completely it's hard to believe and impossible to prove it was ever really there.

"Shit," says Anne.

Another moment of static follows before Daniel, his hand shaking, grips the walkie-talkie again, presses the button down, and says, "No, ma'am." He tries to sound older than he is, but the wear and tear at the back of his throat and the weight of the day do the trick pretty much on their own. Shutting his eyes, Daniel lets the lie float out of him. "The captain," he says, "was killed. By those Listeners." Anne stares. "I'm Officer Daniel Raymond," says Daniel.

After a pause on the other end, the voice comes back, "Captain's dead?"

"Yes, ma'am." Standing up and backing away from the table, Daniel begins to pace back and forth, clutching the walkie-talkie as tightly as an M-1911 pistol. "We need a visit," says Daniel, "at the forty-third precinct. We need a visit, um . . . to let the rest of us know we're . . . not alone out here." When there's no answer, Daniel stares into the walkie-talkie, picking up the pace before pressing the button and saying, again, "Hello? Come in?"

"Still here," says the voice. "We're talking it over."

The static returns, and neither Daniel nor Anne makes a sound. The hiss—the buzz—is like a deep red mist on the waves, and the way it seems to grow louder, more omnipresent, with every moment is like eighty footsteps on the borough streets, two thousand eyes hosting two million flies, the blood red wave growing a hundred feet high. The static invades Daniel's ear like a fly, or maybe a fish, and just as he moves his finger to push the button again, the voice on the other end comes back, "Can you assemble relevant officers at the forty-third by one hundred?"

"Forty-third precinct," says Anne. "One a.m."

"Forty-third. One hundred," says Daniel. Though Daniel anticipates a reply, a minute of static confirms none is coming. But what is coming, what has to be coming, is a parting of the water, a hole in the sea like the eye of a hurricane, or maybe a funnel spinning its way to what passes for dry land below. Blood stains and stings, offal burns the nose, and every time Daniel closes his eyes, the dead of the quarantine are there, on either side and every side. But when the waves crash, when the water falls, he will be somewhere, anywhere, else.

On a wave of blood, the Listeners come. For him.

Let them drown.

ᴬᴧᴧᴧᴧᴧ

As waves bash you left to right, as tides carry you through the bodies of those you loved and those you never knew, you start to wonder why it takes so long to die here, even when it's so easy to choke and drown. The bile rises and joins with the water, you gasp for air and feel the weight of every open part of your body filled with the desecration, but still you're alive enough to feel it.

It's only as the tides toss you down into the rocky sand once again that you get it. Your nose hits the floor and it cracks, and breaks, and bleeds, and as the blood joins the rest, you realize that even as the body chokes on blood, it thrives on it; blood powers your body even as it kills it. When you drown in blood, you drown forever. And when you realize that, when you realize you're lying at the bottom and know, finally for certain, where the surface has to be, you kick your way up and swim, faster and harder than you've ever swam before, pushing severed limbs and blistered faces out of the way, choking and spitting but pushing forward like a tidal force all your own.

And when you swim head-first into the floor all over again, you understand that there truly is no way out.

Poem

This was found in a basement in a little house on Pleasant Valley Avenue.

No one was inside.

The drizzle turns into a pour;
I hear it through the cellar door
but hear it's all we have the guts to do.
The footsteps carry from outside;
they've been so loud since Father died
and all that's left down here is me and you.
They say we're not allowed to leave
which makes the outside make-believe,
our memories the most the world allows.
The night has swallowed up the day,
the one-eared men are on their way,
the floorboards cry above us even now.

FINAL RESPITE

The Front Lines

amirez raps on the door at 3 p.m. sharp. He's like clockwork—he really is. They all are—they run this place like a machine. A generator at the heart of a cold and empty factory, a broken-down frame that once cradled a community.

Saturday, at three, he's knocked, every week for the past eight weeks or so. Sometimes it's hard to believe it's been more than two months since the start of the quarantine. Sometimes it's hard to believe that's all it's been.

As Ramirez pounds at the door, Esmeralda picks Josie up from her crib, holds her close, and hurries to the door. He's like clockwork, Ramirez, and he hates it when she isn't, and that only makes things worse. Not much worse, relatively, but even when your arm's being sawed off slowly, a poke in the eye still hurts like hell.

She turns the padlock, unhooks the latch, and unlocks the door. She doesn't open it—he does. "About fucking time," he mutters through a surgical mask. Crouching, he lifts the four grocery bags sitting next to him, then grunts as he carries them into Esmeralda's apartment and drops them down on the chrome counter. Esmeralda pets Josie's head and pulls her closer.

"Thank you," she says, softly.

"We got cereal," says Ramirez, pulling a box from the second bag, removing the mask. Lucky Charms this week. "We got milk—still got electricity?"

"Yes," says Esmeralda.

"Good. Lucky. Power's down on Moore and I don't think G.E.'s gonna do anything about it anytime soon, heh," he says. "We're trying to relocate some of 'em, but most are gonna have to just face the fucking music. Hell, half of 'em are sick anyway."

She doesn't want to know about that—not anymore. She wants to stay inside with the door locked and the TV on and Josie close to her, and see nothing out the window and hear nothing outside and know nothing about what's going on in the deadened streets. But her baby needs food. She needs food.

"We got Gerber's for the kid, we got crackers, toilet paper, couple of bottles of water, some fruit, some veggies, toothpaste, soap, diapers—lots of diapers—aaaaand that about does it." He turns toward her. His jacket flies up a little and she can see his pistol poking out his side holster, and the badge on the blue of his shirt. She takes a step back, involuntarily.

"Hard work, bringing this shit up three flights of stairs," he says, stepping a little closer. "Wouldn't do it for just anyone, you know." A step, another, and he's right in front of her. "So much work," he says. He runs his hand through her long black hair.

"Just a—second, just a second," Esmeralda says, stepping back, closing her eyes. "The . . . baby—I've got to put the baby down . . ." She walks into their room—hers and Josie's—and lays the little girl down in her crib. She pokes her in the belly. Josie giggles.

Ramirez waits in the living room. Esmeralda doesn't want Josie to see this, though she's much too young to understand. She gets her food. She lives another week. They both do. When you cut off goals and desires and meaning and religion and all the rationalizations, that's all that matters.

She leaves the bedroom to pay for her food.

ᴧᴧᴧᴧᴧ

At first, there were just rumors—whispers, really, like a stop sign in the middle of a one-way street. Nobody listened. It was like every other disease you hear about on the news—it's happening to another person in another place, and you can't see it or feel it, so you can't fear it. Over lunch, a friend tells you what her friend's friend told her, about someone down by Sheepshead near the docks who's got these giant blisters all over his body. And you say, "That's horrible." And you eat your salad.

Esmeralda never talked much to her neighbors, but she talked to her friend Steph, who once mentioned it over drinks in passing when Carrie the babysitter stayed with Josie. And it was part of a bad joke told to her by Kyle, trying to be genial, like he always did before asking how Josie was doing. But it was all intangible. It was like that West Nile Virus she'd heard about on TV all those summers ago—something people seemed to be worried about but no one actually got, something that couldn't hurt her or touch her baby, and she of all people knew how the print and TV media hype these things, so she ignored it.

Everyone did.

Some nights when Josie was asleep, when Esmeralda wasn't too tired, when there was a lull in *Tribune* assignments, or when she felt just a bit too lazy to work, she'd sit in front of the television, with the apartment lights off, falling half-asleep beneath the flashing beams of the screen. This night, two long and short months ago, she was watching some *Survivor* and trying (somewhat) to figure out how to get eight hundred words out of a damn magicians' strike when the show was interrupted for "a special news bulletin."

Hype. She focused on her article. *Look what they're pulling out of their hats now.*

The word "virus" brought her back again. Her heart pounded, just for a second, the way it does when you let yourself think you took the wrong train home. But her eyes opened. And she sat up. And she paid attention.

And they repeated it.

They described it as an "unknown virus" within the borough—localized near the waterfront, secured, no danger for the rest of the city some distance away. Roz and Jim traded off the information: contagious, spreading fast enough for some concern. Not considered a great risk for the bulk of the borough, but residents were advised to stay indoors for the time being, unless moving around was absolutely necessary. For just a little while. Just until "medical experts" can determine the nature of the illness and how it can best be treated.

"The way the skies are looking this weekend, you may want to stay inside anyway," segued Craig, before Esmeralda shut the TV off for the night. A perfect silence followed, the kind that seems like it's whispering, but you can't make out the words. Esmeralda sat up and gazed at the dark screen as if it was still on, but she could hardly see it in front of her.

And then, before too long, "advised" became "demanded." The blockade, the physical manifestation of the quarantine, went up fast, secured by helicopters, a number of blocks down the street, cutting off the roads to the rest of the city, rising like a brand new mountain in the concrete canyons. A five-block area on the other side was evacuated, because the plague was airborne now but it could only travel so far—far enough, though, because Carrie the babysitter knifed her roommate when the disease worked its way into her brain, or so she heard from a neighbor who took the time to look through Carrie's address book and call her friends. And the doctors and the volunteers and the healthcare people, once visible everywhere in their bright, bulky biohazard uniforms, retreated behind the quarantine, and the cops took over. And then the world turned on itself and the streets, as if they'd been set ablaze, became forever empty.

⌁⌁⌁⌁⌁

When Ramirez is done with her, Esmeralda usually wraps the covers around herself like body armor. Doing that before never worked. These aren't her covers, the ones she sleeps in; she uses the guest bedroom for this. Ramirez allows at least that much. He never says another word, because the sale is over. Transaction completed. Why waste time? He's got a job to do.

It must be nice to be king of a graveyard.

The first few times she watched him dress, in much the same way you watch a fly scamper across a light when there's nothing else to do. She watched him put his pants on in front of the mirror, taking his time, making sure they were the right height, hitched up just the right way, belt buckle through the right hole. But now she'd rather put the covers over her head and wait until he's gone. When she hears the door slam shut, she'll check to make sure Josie's okay—not that she wouldn't be. Ramirez wouldn't do anything to her. He's the law, after all.

And then she'll go into the kitchen and unpack the groceries. She'll put them in the cabinets, which are mostly empty, because

Ramirez only brings enough to last a week or two. Keeps her dependent. Keeps the service necessary. She'd go to another store but no one else is selling. And when you're cut off from the rest of the world, conventional currency means very little very fast.

And you've got to eat. You've got to live. Even when the world's stopped breathing.

Later, Esmeralda types away at her computer and tries to do what she's always done: lose herself in words. Disappear into a maze of black and white type, create something out of nothing when the rest of the world is being uncreated. The funny thing is, when you've got phones and TVs and e-mail, not even a five-block quarantine and an untreatable plague are enough to keep you completely cut off from the world. The wireless is down—she's not sure why—but the phone works fine and she can dial up and get her assignments.

Not that that does much good anymore. For the first few weeks, the *Tribune* was fascinated with the insider story of the quarantine—the real story only they could provide, because, thank God, they had their local news opinion columnist on the beat. But when you get past the first month, the story gets as boring for the reader as it does for the writer. When you can't go outside, nothing much happens. You can only go on for so many words on how unbelievably boring the end of the world is.

There are some things that would capture the public interest—she's a journalist, after all. She knows what sells. An exposé on the police department's abuse of power would be a fascinating story to read. But starvation would be a terrible way to die.

"You never realize how many diapers a spastic eight-month-old can go through," she writes, "when you can't go out to buy any more." Which isn't at all what she's thinking, but writing about raising a kid in what's left of the borough should make all the men and women who can't imagine what it's like and can't be bothered to do a damn thing about it very, very happy. She feels like shit exploiting her kid for a column, but she's run out of things to write about, and it'll be funny, she supposes, in a few years, if Josie's around to read it.

No—she will be. That's the one thing that's important. There's no money in writing anymore, and there sure isn't any joy in it, but if people are reading and listening and someone cares, then maybe, maybe, Josie will see her first or second or fifteenth or fifty-sixth birthday.

She spends about five minutes thinking about this. Then she tries to remember if *Tribune* format requires "eight-month-old" to have one or two or any hyphens and, if one, where it should be. That, at least, is one decision someone else can take care of. She keeps writing.

Sunday and Monday are uneventful, Tuesday and Wednesday even more so. Most days are uneventful. Esmeralda recalls hearing once that soldiers in the first World War spent most of their time in foxholes waiting for something to happen. Being a soldier in some bloody conflict could be as boring as sitting around your house on a Sunday afternoon with nothing to do. This, she supposes, is sort of like that, except that when something happens—even maintenance of the status quo—no good can come of it. It's like treading water—the kind of treading water in which you're almost, but not quite, choking on putrid salt.

On Thursday around half past twelve, Esmeralda, seated on a kitchen stool by the counter, holds Josie in her right arm, a spoonful of mushy baby food in her left. Carrot. Gerber's. The basics. "Here it comes," she says, flying the spoon through the air like a spaceship.

Josie watches it. She giggles. She's oblivious. Her life, Esmeralda realizes, hasn't changed that much: She was in the house almost all the time anyway, eating and sleeping, and the only real consequence of all this is that Mom's around a lot more. She's surely not the only baby stuck inside the quarantine, but Esmeralda considers this, and thinks, maybe—but she's special. Josie's happy here: The one bit of good in all the bad, and she's found it. Her skin glows. Her cheeks are red. She's beautiful.

Esmeralda sniffs and brings the spoon down, into her mouth. She eats the food and smiles. A little bit of the orange stuff gets on her face, and Esmeralda wipes it up with her hand. They can get through this.

There's a knock on the door—three knocks. It's a ticking clock in an empty room: louder than it really is. She jumps and jerks her head toward it. Josie coos. The knocking doesn't fit here and now, but it's familiar. *Knock, knock, knock.*

One reason people get seasick is that their minds have trouble grasping contradictions. (She used this metaphor in an article once.) You're in a small port with no windows. You feel movement, but you don't see it. Movement is familiar and understandable, but only when it can be visually confirmed. Esmeralda feels a bit sick, then, to hear consistent-as-clockwork Ramirez pounding at her apartment door at 12:30 p.m. on a Thursday.

She breathes. She stares at the door—green, wooden. Josie makes a sound, and it hardly registers to Esmeralda. She stares at the door, and it stares back, quiet, as if it's keeping a secret, as if it wants her to think she imagined it. But she trusts her senses. She heard it.

Knock, knock, knock. The door shakes. Esmeralda jumps. The baby looks at the door as if she'd never noticed it before. Then, muffled through the door, there's his voice: "Open the door." Esmeralda doesn't move. She can't, or doesn't want to.

"Open the fucking door," says Ramirez, "or . . ." *Or I'll break it down. And I'll force my way in. And I'll fuck you right in front of your baby and I'll leave and I'll never come back and you'll starve, and you'll watch her cry and wither and die right in front of you.*

Esmeralda, shaking, stands up and clutches Josie close to her. "It's," she croaks, but can't finish the sentence. She tries again. "It's Thursday," she gets out, but quietly, trapped inside the door like the rest of her.

"Let me in, you fucking bitch," says Ramirez. "Let me—"

"It's Thursday!" Esmeralda manages, loud enough. It's Thursday. It's Thursday, her day, her week, her respite in-between the times he comes, tears her life apart, and sustains it. The plague infects her once a week, and she can deal with that if that's what she has to do. But it's Thursday. God, it's Thursday.

"It is?" says Ramirez, clearly. He must be pressed right up against the door. Esmeralda hugs Josie. Josie starts to cry a little, and she pats him on the back. "Aw, shit," says Ramirez, "I forgot, but hey, got all this food for ya. Gotta let me in so you can get your food."

She says nothing. She kisses Josie's forehead and rocks her a little.

Slam! The door caves in a little toward the top. Esmeralda can see the brown wood splinters peeking out and takes an instinctive step back. "Better fucking let me in. Better let me in right now."

And she realizes: She has to. Like a patient in intensive care, she's helpless, useless, and entirely dependent. You can't make the rules. You just deal with the pain whenever the powers that be inflict it, or fail to prevent it. This isn't her house, this isn't her home. This is the place where Ramirez lets her stay and, clockwork or no, she's at his beck and call until the plague is gone and the quarantine is over.

"I'm coming," she says, loud enough so he can hear, and she lays Josie down on the couch. She pats her on the head. She'll be all right. She walks over to the bulging, splintered door, and puts her eye up to the peephole. On the other side she sees him, staring, distorted as in a funhouse mirror. She can make out his off-center hat, his shirt not buttoned quite right, no surgical mask at all, and huge red blotches, like bubble wrap, strewn across his rough face.

His eyes are wide. He grins like a deranged jackal. Pus oozes out the biggest of the crusty red sores, dripping down onto his cheek. He's sick.

"You're sick," she says, more quietly now, but she's close enough that he can hear her.

"Naw," he says, "just a little cold is all." He pulls his eye right up to the peephole and stares through it. "Better let me in."

"Go away."

"Let me in."

"Please go away."

"Let me the fuck in!" he roars, crashing his fist into the door. It budges just a little and the wood slams into Esmeralda's nose. She jumps back and retreats to the couch. She picks Josie up and holds her close, then keeps her eyes glued to the door as it's hit again, and buckles again.

"This ain't funny, Julia. This ain't funny," and Esmeralda has no idea what he's talking about, but he keeps pounding, pounding, and finally his black boot shatters the door into shards, poking a permanent hole into the last thing keeping her apart from the disease-infected landscape outside her refuge. The leg disappears from the hole, only to be replaced by his face, Ramirez's face, crouched down, staring in, beaming.

Up close, no longer mucked around by the lens of the peep-hole, the face is bright and distorted, so much more so than in the pictures on TV. There is a red crusty thing oozing out and over his left eye, like a gigantic pimple stretching at the edges, just about to pop. A tiny stream of white liquid drips down over his face and off his chin, like bile. The right side of his neck is torn, the fleshy fragments of a bulge that must have popped already hanging off the side of his face. It's cut open and bleeding. And this thing, this inhuman thing, has the gall to smile at her—not a cruel smile but a comfortable one. And then it looks confused, to the extent it can, its features and expressions thrown off-track by the growths. "Hey, what . . ." he says. "What the fuck you do to—"

Then, with the sound of a firecracker, the back of the head explodes, the face remaining disturbingly intact, frozen like a deer trying to figure out what those bright white things are. Esmeralda's mind flashes the cliché, *He never knew what hit him.* Josie cries, loudly, and Esmeralda hugs her.

The face—what's left of the head—is pulled away from the door, and then there's another sound, pop, explosion, and this time she recognizes it clearly as a gunshot. The door splinters around the doorknob, some broken splinters hit the ground, and the door creaks open. It's given a push.

There are two men standing there, young men, hard-eyed, armed. They're dressed more casually than anyone she's seen in two months: T-shirts and shorts, and, of course, surgical masks. One is white, one is black. Both are missing their right ear.

"Everything all right?" says the white one, glancing around the room, holding his pistol in both hands, as if he expects a terrorist to jump out at him.

Esmeralda pauses. She looks at Ramirez, lying flat on the ground behind the two men, perfectly still, as good as decapitated. Is everything all right?

"I . . ."

"Which one was that? That Ramirez?" says the black one.

The white one turns to him. "Don't matter. A cop is a cop." He turns back to Esmeralda. "We followed him here. We're taking care of all of them. Cops think they rule everything, but not anymore."

"Is there . . ." Esmeralda gulps. *Get it under control. Calm down. It's over. He's gone. It's over. Calm. You're a journalist.* "Is there food out there?"

"What?" says the black one.

"For my baby. For me and my baby. He said . . ."

"Ain't no food," he says. "You one of those, huh? Can't go outside, cops deliver your food?"

"Good deal, good deal," says the white one, "'cept I bet it ain't free. Bet you gotta pay for it somehow."

"You know, I bet you're right."

"We can get you your food, girl," says the white one. He takes a step toward her. "Gotta have food to live, right? We all wanna live. Here's the thing, though." Another step. Esmeralda is frozen. "We own this place now, see, and it ain't an easy place to run. We can get you your food, but . . ." He's right in front of her now. He brushes his hand through her hair. He doesn't seem to notice the bawling child. ". . . we're gonna have to charge you double."

Esmeralda breathes, hard, her eyes wide open. She pulls Josie to her chest as if they're trying to steal her away. She looks around, at the closed-in walls, and suddenly that broken door doesn't seem nearly as open as it did a moment ago. She pulls away, but there's nowhere to go.

"Can you . . ." she manages. "Can you . . . can you at least get rid of the body first?"

For some reason, she expects things to look different when she looks outside, even now, after almost three months. Part of her expects the plague to be a visible thing, covering the buildings outside in some sort of copper rust. But it's normal. It's a sunny day. A few pigeons fly by, soaring effortlessly, oblivious. The light shines through her window, into her apartment, and casts a beam of brightness all the way into the kitchen. She has to cover her eyes.

Ramirez rapped at the door at 3 p.m. sharp, every Saturday, like clockwork, and those were the times when things were, on some level, tolerable. Livable. A punch in the gut isn't nearly so bad if you brace yourself for it, but when it's random, you're on the defensive all the time. But there is no defense—not when your arms are tied behind your back and you're paralyzed below the waist.

"Out of milk," says Stork, finishing up the carton. Stork is the black one, and Esmeralda doesn't know or care why they call him that. She turns around as he wipes a milk moustache off his grinning face and tosses the empty carton onto the living room floor. "Guess we're gonna have to bring you some more."

She nods. Guess so. Quentin zips up his pants as he walks in from the guest bedroom, then rubs the flat bandage where his ear used to be. They call themselves the Listeners, but she hasn't bothered to ask why. She doesn't ask questions anymore.

"Aw, damn, she goes through that milk so fast," says Quentin.

They crack up, and Esmeralda stares at them, blankly. Quentin notices. He turns to her and opens his mouth, but the only sound is a rattle from outside, something metal like a trashcan. Stork and Quentin run to the window and look down. Esmeralda follows. There's a man there, an old man, hard to see, unremarkable except for the red splotches on his bald head. He stumbles randomly along the gravel.

". . . take care of this . . ." says Stork, and he and Quentin pull their masks from their pockets and head for the door. Quentin rubs the right side of his head. Stork cocks his gun. They exit through the fractured door, which can't be locked or even closed. Anytime they want, anytime anyone wants, they can come right in. There's no separation. It may not be a clear red dust, but there it is, outside her window, inside her house. No defense.

They have to leave, she and Josie, if Josie's going to live, if they're both going to live. This place is a prison—worse, a torture chamber. Esmeralda walks into her room, Josie's room, their room, and sees her sleeping soundly. She looks at her skin, pale and soft and beautiful, and imagines it bulging in bloody sores, oozing. She wonders what happens to a still-forming mind when a virus worms its way in and tears it apart. She wonders if she'll have time to feel guilt for getting her sick before the disease takes her own mind.

There's no choice. They'll understand. They'll let her through. They have to. Looking around like a kidnapper, she lifts her up out of the crib and hugs Josie to her. There's a bang from the outside. Josie gurgles and starts to wake up, but Esmeralda shushes her, softly.

Sleep. She'll be free soon.

She returns to the living room and looks out the window. Lying in a tiny pool of blood is the old man, shot down, crazed mind blown to bits. Quentin clasps Stork's shoulder. Esmeralda watches them turn around and walk away from the building, away from the man, away from her life, and she takes the chance to exit through the shattered door and down the stairs.

ᴧᴧᴧᴧᴧᴧ

The streets are surreal. This was a bustling place, a lively place, the sidewalks not so crowded you'd have to squeeze your way through them like it was the middle of the city, but crowded enough so you felt surrounded, protected. A part of something. A community. But now they're desolate, empty, for no visible reason, so Esmeralda feels seasick again. But she keeps walking.

Her footsteps echo into the alleyways and off the sides of buildings, the only sound on a bright white day in a once lively part of an American city. Keeping an eye out for other outside survivors, sick or otherwise, she heads towards a barrier she knows is a mere ten blocks or so ahead, down by Crawford, but too far away to see.

Josie is calm—in fact, transfixed. For Esmeralda, this is simply her first trip outside the apartment in three months. But three months makes up a great big part of Josie's life. Maybe Josie can't remember the last time she was outside. Maybe she's forgotten the sun, and the streets, and the buildings.

Esmeralda walks fast, and it's an easy walk, made easier by the lack of people and cars and traffic signs. Actually, there *are* traffic lights, and perversely, they still work, blinking from red to green for an audience of no one, guiding invisible cars through roads with no practical function anymore. The cars themselves, most of them anyway, are gathered along the sides of the road, nice and orderly, and Esmeralda walks down the middle of the road on a meaningless double yellow line.

The first time she sees a person, she freezes in her tracks, but only for a moment. She coughs and pulls Josie close, and tries to make sure she doesn't see, and more importantly, that the red, blotchy man in the alley doesn't see her. She hopes he's too far gone to hear them. After the disease peaks, all that's left is a mindless, shuffling dementia, physically harmless, unquestionably contagious—or at least that's what Ramirez said. This diseased thing stands in the open, empty, dark alley, staring at something in a brick wall only he can see. He never looks up. She keeps walking.

Many of the sick people are like that. Some look at her blankly and show no reaction. Some can't even see beyond the bulging sores cluttering their mangled faces. A couple do seem to notice her, do step forward, but then stop, as if point A to point B has become a lot more complicated than it has any right to be.

But then there are the ones still in the worst grip of the virus, their bulging faces vaguely recognizable as human, their steps sure and directed and deranged. One woman, walking out from an apartment lobby, spies Esmeralda and Josie as they hurry by, and starts to approach them. "Hey!" the woman cries, a boil on the left side of her neck bulging like a wart the size of a tennis ball. Esmeralda keeps walking, but she can hear the rapid footsteps behind her, coming closer, stepping nearer, then . . . stopping. Entirely. She turns around and finds the woman staring at them, but approaching no further. There's no time for questions and no sane minds to ask, so Esmeralda turns around and continues on her way. A number of the sick people are like that, too, halting just at the point of attack. Esmeralda finds herself feeling safer than she has any right to feel.

But most amazingly, not everyone she sees is sick. Through the window of a small, abandoned factory, fire-scarred wood hanging down loosely from an ill-supported ceiling, she sees an old, sad man, in a green wool cap and a large brown jacket—homeless, maybe, but somehow still alive and unaffected. He looks at her as she walks by, and Esmeralda cannot understand how there could be no surprise on his face, to see a woman and a child alone on these desolate streets. It's as if he knew they were coming. It's as if people pass through this place all the time.

And maybe they do. Just beyond the factory, one block down, the bright and the quiet reveal something no one told her about— a barricade of human flesh—as if the road was dirt, the skyscrapers huts, and the people massacred by some genocidal warlord. A couple hundred bodies lie on the streets the next few blocks. They lie on their backs, sometimes mostly intact, but just as often faceless or headless. Esmeralda slows as she nears the scene—she has to, she can do nothing else. They lie all along the street, in both lanes, and on the cars, and on the sidewalks. Most are marked by massive red splotches, but some are not. Flies—thousands of them—soar in circles above the remnants of these people, large, small, man, woman, child. There's a middle-aged man in a suit lying awkwardly on his umbrella; it must have been raining the day he approached. There's a large man holding the hand of a girl who must be his daughter and a bald woman who must be his wife.

The one closest to Esmeralda is a small black woman, and that's where she stops. She wasn't sick, or doesn't seem to have been. Her body is mostly intact, her skull cleanly penetrated by a small hole in the forehead, her face frozen in shock. Josie cries a little and Esmeralda pats her on the back.

Clutched in the woman's hand, frozen by rigor mortis, is, of all things, a copy of the *Tribune*. In the bottom left of the slightly curled paper, Esmeralda can actually see her byline from her column, but from how long ago? Paper delivery stopped when the quarantine went up, so it's got to be a few months old—a lifetime ago, a whole other world ago, when she could write and raise a kid and live. The paper is grayed, splotched with red. Up ahead, she can make out the barricade, the cement towers, maybe even people standing guard.

She kneels and tugs at the newspaper. It won't give; the woman's death-grip is tight. She pulls harder, and the paper finally comes out, tearing a little bit at the edge. There's a little bit of white still remaining in the woman's hand. Esmeralda glances down at the column—her column—and reads the words.

But it's wrong. They're her words but not the right words. It's an exciting little piece about how the first couple of days since the healthcare evacuation have been disorderly, and downright violent, but the police are taking over, and everything's under control. It's deluded and naïve, but that's not the problem. It feels like years and years have passed since she wrote it. It's an e-mailed submission, from when there was e-mail. It was delivered after the quarantine had gone up and after the borough had been abandoned to the ravages of the plague, some two and a half weeks in, after the Red Cross and the Peace Corps and the military were lifted away in helicopters for their own safety.

After.

This paper doesn't belong here, inside the quarantine. It shouldn't be here.

She feels sick again and stumbles; her foot lands uncomfortably on the woman's arm, and Esmeralda jumps away and backs into another corpse before steadying herself. But this one doesn't have a head, and Esmeralda vomits. Josie bawls, and Esmeralda, heaving, tries to wipe off the bits of vomit that landed on her.

"Attention," booms a tin voice, projected from some unseen megaphone. Esmeralda looks ahead, to the concrete quarantine, focusing on it for the first time: impassable towers, extending across the whole border between this and the other boroughs and, as she understands it, blocking the bridge, followed by another five blocks of No Man's Land. Atop the structure, she thinks, are multi-colored people, moving. She can barely make them out. It's bright and sunny, and she realizes: She's made it. Past the bodies, sick and otherwise, but to the exit—the escape. Right in front of her. There.

"You are entering a forbidden area," says the voice, authoritative, dramatic. "To maintain the health of the remaining populace of," something something something. She gets it: It's a quarantine. Sick people can't be allowed to cross, but she is *healthy*, and so is her baby, and she's walked all this way, away from Ramirez and the Listeners and through the sick people to here—to the way out, with her daughter.

". . . will be shot," says the voice. And Esmeralda knows how to respond to that: She picks up Josie, bawling, and holds her up in the air.

"We're not sick!" she calls out, and she hears the voice echoing from building to building, loud, confident, unafraid. "We're not sick!" She walks forward, holding Josie up in front of her, stepping over and around the bodies on the ground. Buzzing flies part in her wake.

"Turn back now," says the voice.

She walks forward, she raises Josie higher, and higher still. "We're—we're not—"

A sound echoes down along the buildings, louder than her voice and louder than his, whoever he was—a sound like a fire-cracker or an exploding head. Esmeralda stops abruptly and stares ahead, blankly. She kneels down on someone's chilly chest, then falls forward.

ᴧᴧᴧᴧᴧᴧᴧ

The baby lands safely on the street, in-between a blotchy young girl and a wrinkled old man. She leans against her mother and looks around, as if she's trying to take it all in.

Footsteps echo toward the quarantine structure, through the bodies. The homeless man deftly hops through and around the dead. He looks down toward the towers, the multicolored men, and he points at the baby. He gestures toward the kid, then reaches down to pick her up. He pulls her gently, as the baby tries to grasp her mother, but the grip is weak and the homeless man takes her up into the air. Holding the baby in his arms, he stares down at the child's mother, her heart stilled.

The man turns around and hugs the quiet child. "Sssshhh," he says, "sssshhh." The baby's cheeks are red. She's beautiful. The man holds her close and carries her away.

September

The main problem is that Katie forgot her key. It's something she does sometimes, the way her thoughts bounce around her brain and switch around at random, but it's not a problem when they head home with one of their parents. It is, though, when they take the bus. So Katie, keyless, slumps down on the curb outside her house, and Daniel sits down next to her. He glances at the knees of a man passing along the street in front of him, to his car. Another car, a sleek black one, roars a little too loudly down the road.

"I'm thinking of a number between one and twenty-six," says Katie.

"Seven," Daniel says.

"You are wrong."

"Your face is wrong."

"Oh," Katie says.

The sun shines off the window of the electronics store across the street and blinds Daniel. There's a piece of gum stuck to the curb, which has to mean someone has sat here before. It wasn't Daniel and Katie— he doesn't chew gum, and Katie doesn't when he's around because she knows he hates the smell.

"Thirteen and a half," Daniel says.

"Even wronger," says Katie. She leans over and nudges his shoulder with her head, but Daniel, his eyes catching a couple ants scuttling around a fallen french fry by the sewer drain, doesn't move.

"Nudge nudge," says Katie. Then, after a pause, "I think I like Vic. I think I should ask him out."

"Why?" Daniel says.

"You're a jerk." She sticks her tongue out at him. He responds in kind. "So what do I say?"

"You should say, 'Go out with me or I will stab you.'"

Snorting, Katie leans over again, pushes her head against Daniel's, and bites the flap of his right ear. "Hey!" Daniel says, pulling away, and Katie giggles, the sun casting an orange glow through her long red hair.

Another car passes by, a green one, and when he turns away from the exhaust, the sun catches his eyes again and he squints. Turning back toward Katie, he sees her smile is gone, and she stares straight ahead into the other side of the road, where a ten-year-old boy walks a pug dog over the surprisingly deep crack in the sidewalk.

"It would have been like this," says Katie.

"When?" he says.

"In September." She stares out at the dog, who yips and pulls the boy behind her. "The summer would have been boring. And fast. And kind of great." She shrugs. "Then, September, back to school."

A deep red car speeds down the road, and the moment it passes, he sees a man sitting on the steps across the street, legs spread, pistol clutched within his dark hands. His wide eyes stare at Daniel, and his grin spreads ear to no ear.

"Is it ten?" Daniel says.

"It's pretty messed up, huh?" says Katie. She waves across the street to Derek, and Derek waves back. "It's pretty messed up. And he would have said yes, too." Leaning right, she raps her knuckles against the bumper of a yellow car. "It's really, really messed up."

As a light breeze blows, the air grows colder, fall approaching like a whisper. Daniel glances down at the pavement, at the ants retreating into the drain, and when he looks up again, the street is empty, as is the sidewalk across the street. Suddenly, the sun has fallen behind the clouds, and the sky has become a dull gray. The wind blows still. It whistles.

Daniel stares ahead at nothing. "Is it twenty-four?" he says.

"It's not twenty-four," says Katie.

"Is it three?"

"It's not three."

"Is it nineteen?" he says.

"Goodbye, Danny," says Katie. The words float away in the wind. Daniel doesn't look right to see if she's still there. He doesn't have to.

All Fall Down

Ring around the rosies,
a pocketful of posies.
Ashes, ashes,
we
      all
            fall
                  down

               ᴧᴧᴧᴧᴧ

Thunder rolls across the sky like gunfire. After all this time, Daniel *has* learned the difference. As he opens his tired eyes, as he pushes himself out of Anne's easy chair, the walkie-talkie atop the arm rest, he listens to the rain beginning its staccato drumbeat on the pavement outside and tries to hold onto his dream just a little while longer—not forever, the way he was so desperate to when his alarm cried out to him at 7:10 that morning, but just for now, to see her maybe one more time. Just for a little while.

An hour. A minute.

A second.

Another crack of thunder cuts through the sky like shattered glass, and it's gone.

Daniel's legs ache under his weight, but they at least feel a little better. They have to—he has a long way to go yet. The clock on the wall says it's just past ten, and the Listeners will be approaching soon. Where Anne is exactly, Daniel doesn't know. The room right now is empty, but for the furniture—the chair, the olive green sofa with the pillows askew, the counter by the broken door with the unnecessary keys splayed in a shallow, chipped ceramic bowl.

And Quentin. Quentin's there, too, blank-eyed, staring up from his spot against the wall, his fingertips still touching the handle of his pistol. His face is frozen not in surprise, but in befuddlement, and as Daniel steps over and stares down at him, he remembers the first time he fired a pistol in the cold basement alcove of a long-neglected supermarket. He remembers missing—he remembers imagining the target bleeding and pulling away.

As for Quentin, the bleeding has long since stopped, the blood turning patches of the green carpet black and the blue wall purple. With his neck bent right up against the wall, the one ear on his tilted head points up to a hanged, framed photograph, one of three arranged in an upside-down pyramid. Daniel follows the line of Quentin's ear to the photo, a group of people arranged as in a school portrait, except the students are cops in uniform.

Tracing the photograph with his finger, Daniel finds Anne kneeling in the front just left of center, her lips almost curled into a smile. A kind-looking man to her right glances very slightly her way. The label below the photograph, in gold font, reads, "41st Precinct – 2009."

Maybe fifty officers sit on those bleachers. Most must have been there that night, nearly all of them anyway, ducking behind desks and firing back, lying on the stairwell twitching, but here in this picture, their faces are indistinguishable, eyes and noses and mouths with only the slightest variations, and Daniel wonders how many of them, if any, are still alive. Which one was the one Daniel and Derek threw into the dumpster? Whose legs needed that extra push to make it all the way?

Daniel's finger runs left to right, row by row, and the eyes, again and again, stare out every bit as blankly as Quentin's—and for all intents and purposes, every bit as dead. One, very tall, stares into the camera. His eyes are blue, like ice. The one next to him has a moustache, uneven, sunglasses clipped onto his collar. Beside him is a woman, slightly wrinkled, smiling broadly.

And then Daniel sees Adam.

Fourth row from the top. Seven over.

Curly hair spreading around the rim of a blue police officer cap. A tight smile. Confident eyes.

Adam.

And sitting right beside him, with eyes big and white, is Derek. He has two ears.

"It's time." Anne says the words but they barely register on Daniel. Adam and Derek sit shoulder to shoulder in a portrait of men and women the Listeners killed, gold badges pinned to the right side of their chests. Adam and Derek.

"Hey. Daniel."

That's when Daniel realizes that there are forces at work here he will never understand, not now inside the quarantine, not tomorrow when he's outside it, not for the rest of his life. Everything that's happened to him, everything that started the day the quarantine went up, from the moment Derek and Terry took him in through initiation, through Derek and Loren and Mr. MacDonald and Terry and Katie, is just one little thread in whatever's been unwoven here. Adam and Derek in uniforms of blue sit surrounded by cops, but that doesn't change anything.

They're still coming for him.

"Dan—"

"How far away is it?" Turning away from the picture, Daniel glances out the window, where lightning breaks open the sky and the rain begins to fall.

Anne folds her arms. "Thirty, thirty-five minutes, moving fast," she says. As Daniel kneels down by Quentin and grabs the pistol from his grasp, Anne says, "Is it true? What you said about the captain?"

It takes a moment for Daniel to realize what she's talking about. *The captain was killed*, he'd said. *By those Listeners.* So now, he turns to Anne and shrugs. "Probably," he says.

Nodding, Anne walks over to the counter by the door, opens the squeaky drawer beneath it, and pulls out a gun not unlike Daniel's, but slightly smaller and uniformly black. "I'll wait," she says.

"You're not coming?" says Daniel.

"I'll wait," Anne says again, pointing the gun slightly toward the door and stepping back toward the kitchen. She points left and right, and Daniel figures out she's plotting her position for when the

Listeners arrive. Her dark eyes are almost pure black when lit up by the lightning outside the window, and when the lightning fades, she turns his way. "What?" she says. "You gonna warn them?"

On the floor, dead-eyed Quentin looks Daniel's way, but when Daniel thinks of the Listeners, he always thinks of Derek first—big brother Derek, strong and protective. Derek, who saved him and took him in and saved him again. Derek, who persuaded him again and again that the cops were evil and the Listeners necessary. Derek, who spoke of Adam the prophet and the tyrants who ran the borough. Derek, who brought Daniel to Katie's house and shouted as he threw her mom to the floor and made Daniel bide his time with Katie until the other shoe fell and all their lives were over. Derek, who said he went to jail.

Derek, who was a cop.

Daniel shakes his head. He won't warn them.

Casting one last glance at the picture of the forty-first precinct circa 2009, Daniel hands Quentin's gun to Anne. But that won't be enough, so he reaches into his pants and pulls out Terry's *keep the fuck off* pistol, and hands that to her as well. Then he goes back to the easy chair and lifts the walkie-talkie, sticking it into his left pocket. As he heads for the door, he turns back to Anne and almost says something, but at this point, with guns in both hands, she is steel, leaning against the wall by the kitchen and waiting. Daniel leaves her there. The rain beats down.

ᴧᴧᴧᴧᴧ

The rains are torrential. It's a flood. Maybe, once upon a time, schools would be closed tomorrow. As it is, Daniel, dripping wet even after an hour out of the downpour, even underneath the hood of his jacket, paces along the marble underneath the balcony of the forty-third precinct building. Anne had told him how to get here, and it's a building Daniel recognizes—the pillars stood out, even riding in the backseat of his mom's Volvo. It's a weirdly archaic place. As the rain drives down against this rooftop, and all the other rooftops, sliding off and dripping down like a waterfall onto the marble steps, Daniel crouches down, pushes his hand through his damp hair, and stares at the sewer cover in the nearby pavement. Raindrops splash off it theatrically.

Around his wrist is Terry's watch, ticking away. Eleven o'clock was nearly two hours ago. Whatever happened then, Daniel doesn't know—sometime around then, he could have sworn he heard gunfire, but if it was ever there, it was drowned out instantly in a din of thunder and raindrops. If they came, they probably won. They'll still be looking for him, if not tonight, then tomorrow, and every day for the rest of his life until they find him and kill him. So Daniel looks left and looks right, then ahead at the sewer cover, and he checks Terry's watch, which says 12:55.

The sewer cover doesn't budge. The rain falls. Daniel sits down against the wall, but almost as soon as he does, something taps against the marble, and Daniel jumps up and spins left.

Out of nowhere, a figure slumps down against the wall of the precinct, wearing a ripped green shirt and glancing Daniel's way. It's a skin-and-bones thing, haggard and drenched, and very sick, two large boils extending from its cheek. As Daniel pulls his pistol from his pants and aims it toward the figure, it says, "Um, hi."

Daniel freezes. The voice is familiar, but it's the missing right ear that gives it away. "Brian?" Daniel says, pulling down his hood.

Disfigured, but still recognizable in a vague sort of way, Brian tries to smile. "Yeah, I, um," he says. "You know I . . . I saw a thing here once?" He looks out into the street, toward the sewer cover. "It was a thing . . . I . . . something. Um." Then, suddenly, he jerks his head forward and slams it back against the wall, so hard Daniel winces, and Brian cries out, "Shit!"

Tentatively, Daniel steps forward, his fingers still wrapped around his pistol. The minute-hand ticks forward on the watch, and thunder rolls across the sky. "Are you okay?" says Daniel. It's all he can think to say.

"It's like . . ." says Brian. "The thoughts . . . just to keep them there, I'm . . . is . . ." Raindrops splash off the sewer cover with a hollow thud, and Brian's eyes roll left. "It's raining," he says. "Rain is wet." A high-pitched cry escaping his throat, Brian slams his head into the wall again and yells, "Shit shit shit!"

The words cut through the rain and ricochet off the buildings, breaking through a lull in the thunder and filling the street. Daniel stares out into the darkness, and at the sewer cover, and back at

Brian, whose eyes shut so hard a white liquid squeezes out of the left one. "I, it . . ." he says. "It does this, to my . . . head." Brian sniffs loudly. "Am I a monster?" he croaks. "I don't feel like a monster."

Shaking just a little, Daniel kneels down to meet Brian at eye level.

And that's when a gunshot rings out and Brian's head explodes.

Tripping back over himself, stumbling onto the marble and pushing himself up immediately, Daniel waves his gun out into the darkness and tries to make out anything, but the street is dark even with the streetlight, and he sees the water bouncing off the sewer cover and rolling along the street, but there's no one else there but Daniel and Brian from the neck down.

But then Daniel sees him—a small figure, standing in the street well left of the sewer, the raindrops bouncing along his outline and streaming down his sleeves. Water splashing around his heavy footsteps, a furious, soaking-wet Zeke charges out of the storm, clutching his gun so hard his knuckles are almost as white as the lamppost's light.

"He was sick!" Zeke yells. "You saw!"

Backing away along the platform of the precinct building, holding his own pistol without aiming it, Daniel says, "Hey, Zeke, don't—"

"I heard," says Zeke. Reaching into his pocket, he pulls out a walkie-talkie and holds it up triumphantly. "They went back to the apartment, but I listened! I heard!" Cast directly in the light now, Zeke's eyes are bright and furious, as wide as they were in Anne's apartment and, simultaneously, distant and desperate. When he steps forward again, toward the precinct building steps, he points the slick wet barrel of the gun straight at Daniel. "He'll be proud of me," says Zeke.

"Zeke—"

"He'll be proud of me!" Zeke yells.

"That's not . . ." says Daniel. Sidestepping down the stairs and onto the right side of the street, still a good distance away from Zeke, Daniel holds his hands up high, while Zeke aims the gun but doesn't fire. Immediately, the rain covers Daniel as surely as if he'd leapt into a waterfall, and he doesn't even bother with his hood. He spits a small stream of water out his mouth as he keeps his eyes on Zeke. Zeke's broken, stuffed-nose breathing carries across the entire length of the road. "It's not worth it," says Daniel.

"What else is there?!" Zeke shrieks. "What else is there?!" His face is a mess of snot and tears, and his entire arm shakes as he extends it as far as it will stretch. The rain drives the snot down his face in a green mudslide. He steps closer to Daniel, the gun aimed securely, his footsteps rolling alongside the thunder, until Zeke's scattered breathing, his temper-tantrum face, are just feet from Daniel's. The gun is only inches away.

"They're my family," says Zeke.

Just then, Daniel's walkie-talkie squawks, "Officer Raymond? You there?"

Zeke looks down at the walkie-talkie in Daniel's pocket, and the moment he does, Daniel swings his fist through Zeke's jaw, the crack resounding through the street, Zeke spiraling to the gravel and landing with a splash. The gun flips from his fingers and hydroplanes along the gravel, coming to a stop shortly before the manhole cover.

As Daniel kicks the fallen Zeke, once, twice, Zeke reaches into his pocket and grabs hold of something, and when Daniel moves to kick him again, Zeke cries out and jabs his fist forward into Daniel's right calf.

Daniel screams as Zeke pulls the knife away, drops of blood flying backwards with the rain. Limping, stumbling, Daniel falls back, the left side of his head slamming against the rough asphalt, and in that instant the ringing is back, the locusts, the white noise so loud it drowns out the world as surely as the rain. As the water soaks through Daniel's pants, as his leg bleeds onto the street, Zeke stumbles to his feet, grabs his gun, and aims it, again, at Daniel.

"They're my *family*!" Zeke yells. Even through the piercing shriek in Daniel's eardrum, he can hear it.

"Come in," says the voice on the walkie-talkie.

And as Daniel tries to push away the sound, tilting his head sideways so the water can wash the noise away, he looks up at Zeke, whose face is red, whose eyes are wide and angry, and whose finger shakes against the trigger. If Daniel can't quite hear right, he can still see—he can see the kid who gave him *X-Men* to read and asked him to play cards, the kid who cheered Daniel on in supermarket football, the kid who is, in the end, just a kid, just a *kid*, just a kid just a kid just a kid in his apartment with the window shattered and (the locusts buzz and hiss and swarm) the door cracked and broken and knocked open (and Daniel forces them back, *back*), just a kid just a kid exposed and abandoned, a kid, a *kid*.

"My mom disappeared," says Daniel, eyes on Zeke's. "*Listen*," he says, though he can barely hear himself. "My mom disappeared. Before the Listeners." He leans against his hands, scratched on the pavement. The walkie-talkie squawks. Daniel can't make out the words.

"Shut up," says Zeke.

"She disappeared."

"Shut up!" The rain beats down against both their skulls, washing the blood along Daniel's legs and ear. Shaking, shivering, holding his pistol with both hands, Zeke shudders and moans just a little.

"They're not our family, Zeke," says Daniel, breathing hard, pressing his hand against his bleeding leg. Pointing out toward the streets, he says, "*He* is not your dad."

When Zeke exhales, it's a croaking, rattling sound in the back of his throat. Slowly, very slowly, he pulls the gun down, steps back, and sits in the street, in the rain, right across from Daniel.

The walkie-talkie says something. The buzzing fades a little. It fades enough.

"My dad got sick," says Zeke. "My mom killed him." He cries, his pistol slipping out of his hand and very lightly splashing onto the concrete. "I wanna go home," he says.

Pushing his wet hands against the rough concrete, Daniel forces himself to his feet, crying out as he puts weight on his injured right leg. Hopping on his left foot, Daniel pulls the walkie-talkie from his pocket, puts it to his mouth, and says, "I'm coming."

As soon as he says it, and limps toward the sewer cover, the cover itself starts to move, rising from its puzzle-piece hole in the ground and scraping, loudly, across the street. Daniel moves as fast as he can, gripping the end and pulling it out the rest of the way. The metal scrape is even louder than the thunder, louder than the rain, and as a bolt of lightning cuts through the sky and as the rain, dropping down the sewer, takes on a cavernous, hollow sound, Daniel again finds Zeke, sitting in the storm, oblivious.

"Zeke . . . Zeke!" says Daniel. But it's no use. Zeke stares down at the street between his legs, the water falling from his face equal parts rain and snot and tears. He's gone. He's checked out.

From the sewer, someone in heavy biohazard gear starts to climb out, but the second his head emerges, Daniel pushes it back, signaling downward. As soon as there's room to, Daniel looks down, drops his feet to a ladder descending from the opening, and climbs down behind him.

With his body most of the way in, Daniel looks out across the street at eye-level. The rain splashes up like water from a park fountain. It soaks the contours of Zeke's gun, and his knife, not far from one another. And it flows around Zeke, sobbing and broken.

Daniel's shirt is heavy with water. His pants are heavy, his legs are heavy, his head and his gun are heavy, and as the rain falls, at him and over him and down into the sewer, he feels overwhelmed, as if maybe it would be easier to walk over there and sit down beside Zeke, just for a while. But you drown in these waters—Daniel knows that. You drown forever. His right leg screaming at him, a roll of thunder tinny through his damaged ear, Daniel tugs the heavy metal cover back into the opening and disappears down into the sewer.

Tunnel

When the sewer cover closes again, the dark tunnel becomes an echo chamber, but Daniel doesn't know if the sounds are from the sewer or in his head. Something hums, loud and incessant, and with the quarantine flies buzzing through his mind, the sound is atonal and pounding-pounding-*pounding*, and Daniel's brain beats against his skull as scattered drops of rain squeeze through the holes in the sewer cover like Chinese water torture.

Favoring his left leg, Daniel climbs the entire length of the ladder, holding on tight until he can reach the surface of the shallow stream on the sewer floor with his toe. There at the bottom is the man—he sees now that it is in fact a man—in orange biohazard gear. He's barely illuminated by the dim emergency lights set alongside the tunnel, and Daniel sees, just past him, a wide gray moped with military tags. The moped hums. The hum empowers the buzz, which stabs at Daniel's brain.

The man says something. Daniel can't make it out.

What he can see is that this looks to be the end of the tunnel—that is, there's a way forward, but none back. Behind him may have once been another opening, but it's boarded up now with a round sheet of metal, maybe open at the bottom for the stream of water to pass through. The water sinks past his shoes and soaks his socks, but his socks were already wet from the downpour outside. His toes are freezing.

The man says something.

"What?" says Daniel.

The only answer is the buzzing, and more buzzing, his left ear now a useless ornament, and as the man speaks louder, or looks to be speaking louder through the faceplate, Daniel tries to make out words, but the flies just scream—scream and multiply—and the motor hums and the water splashes and the man yells and there's a way out and all Daniel wants to do is hear.

With a heavy grunt, Daniel pulls at the bandage covering the side of his face where his right ear used to be. The tape grasps his skin and tugs it hard, but still Daniel tears it away, gritting his teeth as the white, now dingy gray *thing* that's covered the side of his face for months drifts downward into the stream of water on the sewer floor. All that's left is a hole, a small round hole that was once surrounded by an ear, but it cuts the buzzing in half instantly, and in that instant, the man in the biohazard uniform has a voice.

"You're not a police officer," he says.

"Get me out of here," says Daniel.

"They'll never let you through," says the man. "They'll kill you."

"Take me there," says Daniel. The man only stares at him. "Please," says Daniel, but still the man won't budge. With a wince—he really doesn't want to do it this way—Daniel raises his gun and aims it at the man. "Take me there."

For a very long moment, the man stares at the gun. And then, finally, he says, "Get on the back."

The man climbs onto the moped. Tucking his gun back into his pants, Daniel sits up behind him, wincing as his right leg hits against the metal. But he ignores it, holds tight to the plastic biohazard gear, and stares at the sewer walls as the moped turns around slowly, then roars down the tunnel.

Water sprays behind the moped in a constant stream, but Daniel finds himself focused more on the sewer itself. Maybe the lights were always there, but at regular points throughout the tunnel, he spots video cameras, fastened to the ceiling and turning left to right or right to left as the moped roars ahead. At several points, the sewer breaks off into different tunnels, but half of them are blocked off by more metal plates, and the other half, the man just seems to know not to take. The entire path appears to have been fortified. As Daniel clings to the driver, feeling the air brush against his face, he wonders how often this tunnel has been used. He wonders how long it's been here. He wonders why there would be a path in and out of the quarantine, which only those on the outside can use.

But in the end, none of it matters—none of it. There's a plague.

The borough is dead. Adam and Derek were cops. None of it matters.

Not much farther down the tunnel, a bright light emerges, very nearly a spotlight, and the moped slows, first to half its speed, then to half of that, and then, finally, to a stop, the idling motor still echoing through the chamber. The man doesn't move, and Daniel stares at the light, blocking the intensity some with his right hand.

Then, footsteps suddenly splashing through the water, two guards in biohazard gear step out of the light, armed with what look to be rifles. Moving fast, Daniel draws his own gun, aims it at the head of his driver, and steps off the moped, hiding the lightning bolt of pain as his right leg hits the sewer floor. "Let me through," says Daniel, pulling the man off the moped.

The guard on the left says, "You can't—"

"Please!" says Daniel. He pushes the gun at the man's head.

"Drop it!" yells the guard on the right.

For a moment, they remain like that, Daniel's pistol unflinching and the guards' rifles just the same, and Daniel can't see through the light, but behind them *has* to be the way out. It has to be. They wouldn't be here otherwise. And after so many hours and days and months of swimming, after being stuck out in the borough so long, Daniel can't be turned back.

Then a tinny voice says, "Let him through."

At first, Daniel can't see where the voice comes from, but then he spots an intercom affixed neatly to the curve of the right wall.

"Sir?" says the first guard.

"Let him through," the tinny voice repeats. Then, instantly, the light dims, and as the guards hold up their rifles, Daniel sees beyond them, beneath the bright light, to a metal door at the end of the tunnel. A high-pitched beep sounds, and then the door slides open, metal scraping against metal somewhere beyond the walls. Still holding his gun on the man, Daniel pushes him forward and follows him through the suddenly open passageway, out of the sewer and out of the quarantine.

The room on the other side is almost oppressively pale green. It has an air of sterility about it, and as he scans the place, Daniel realizes he's actually in a room within a room—a glass chamber separated from the open area just beyond. As he glances toward a glass door to his left, which looks to lead to another chamber, the beep sounds again, the whirring resumes, and the metal door behind him shuts tight before Daniel can get there.

Daniel brushes his hand against the warm metal, but there's no opening, no button to press or knob to turn. The glass door is very much the same. And as he spins around in the cool air, searching hard for some opening above or beneath him, the voice from the intercom, no longer quite so tinny but echoing through the room just the same, says, "This is Decon."

Both Daniel and the biohazard man turn to find an older man in military green walking into the room on the other side of the glass. His hair is gray and close-cropped, and his eyes are very, very tired. He's a captain or a colonel or something, and he looks strangely familiar as he steps toward the glass, hands clasped behind his back. "Decontamination," says the maybe-colonel. "To make sure no one sick gets in here."

Daniel takes a step closer to the glass, and as the colonel moves closer as well, Daniel taps his fingers against it. The high-pitched *tak-tak* disappears without echo, but glass is glass. He's seen it a hundred times, shattering to pieces in an apartment window, or a police precinct, or a bathroom in a pub. Hesitating a moment, Daniel raises his gun to the glass, but the moment he does, the colonel shakes his head just slightly left to right. "Bulletproof," he says.

Lowering his gun, Daniel steps back as the colonel steps forward, nose nearly touching the glass. "Officer Raymond?" says the colonel.

Daniel stares into the colonel's eyes for a moment. They're half-closed, as if he's jet-lagged, and has been for a very long time. Then Daniel tucks his pistol into his pants and says, "Daniel Raymond."

"You're not sick," says the colonel, "are you, Daniel?"

Daniel remembers Brian, abandoned by the Listeners for coming too close to the sickos—Brian, who genuinely did get sick. He thinks of a bar full of sickos yesterday—*yesterday?*—twenty anonymous people and one Katie, roaring and clawing and closing in, grabbing at his ankle as blades of glass cut into his leg. He thinks of Tyrone's brother Anton, who got sick just from going out there, and he thinks of himself, trapped in the quarantine for four months and out in the street all day and most of the night.

Then he answers, with absolute confidence, "No."

The Shore

When the water comes, it comes like rain, only harder and colder, soaking Daniel's naked body. And all he can think is, it's been forever since he's had a shower. It's been forever since he's been naked. The water pummels his worn-down, beaten skin, pushing against wounds on his arms and back and especially his legs, which haven't even begun to heal. It's like the beach when the waves are high and strong, and you want to play in them, but they dictate the game—when you fall and when you rise, whether you live and breathe or die.

But the thing about waves is, they only really crash against the shore.

Daniel's wet hands squeal against the transparent wall in the room past the glass door. The water from the ceiling pushes down on his head, his body, and his buttocks, and he spreads the water over his body. He's freezing, the goose bumps poking through his skin, but still he washes himself, because water can also be cleansing, if that's the way it wants to be.

In the next room over, through the wall and into still another pale green room, Daniel dries himself off with a thin white towel, then reaches for a white shirt hanging above white pants. He hasn't worn a new pair of pants since the day he left his home behind, and he covers himself up with them just as the colonel steps back into the room. Pulling the shirt over his still-freezing body, Daniel looks like the cultist he's been, and as the next glass door opens, he steps into the room itself to face the colonel, who hands him a bandage. For a moment, Daniel thinks it's for his ear, but then he takes it and wraps it around the open wound in his calf. He winces.

"Nasty cut," says the colonel.

Daniel nods. He wraps the bandage tight.

"I've been stationed here since the crisis began," says the colonel. "Four months and twenty-five days ago."

Gasping a little, Daniel tests his leg, then climbs to his feet. The colonel walks through the open passageway, and Daniel follows him into what turns out to be another sterile-looking place, but this one is a hallway, painted a uniform chromatic gray. They move past a room, then another, and Daniel sees men and women at computers and monitors, talking over one another.

"Our job," says the colonel, "was to maintain the integrity of the largest quarantine in world history." In one room to the left, a man and a woman focus on a series of monitors that look to cover the sewer tunnel. Daniel can see the guards, and the man in the biohazard uniform, but only for a moment, because the colonel leads him past the screens. The next room has monitors, too, but these cover blank-looking city streets at night. It can't be the borough, but it looks like the borough.

"We were supposed to find out what caused the plague, too, but we haven't," says the colonel, glancing into a room on the right. There are more televisions in there, but these are tuned to various news networks, CNN and whatever the others are. Daniel can't make out the headlines. "It was too dangerous to keep the doctors on the inside," says the colonel, "so we took them away and focused entirely on defense."

"Why—why are you telling me this?" says Daniel.

Stopping just a few feet before a doorway, the colonel sighs, then turns around to face Daniel. When he frowns, the tips of his lips tug down on his entire face, like upside-down strings on a marionette puppet. Adjusting his hat, the colonel says, "Every day . . . every day, people come to this fort. Some are sick. Some are not. We tell them they can't come further. The sick rarely listen, and many of the people don't, either. They're Americans." He pauses. "There was this girl, beautiful girl, carrying a baby. We shot her. I gave the order, but I didn't need to. Standard procedure."

He clears his throat, and it's a rough, rumbling sound, like a wave. "It's the appearance we have to maintain."

"What?" says Daniel. But the colonel has already turned, typing numbers into a keypad by the door. "What?"

The door slides open, and Daniel follows him up a narrow stairwell. As the colonel walks, he silently reaches into his pocket and removes a surgical mask, and before Daniel has a chance to ask why, they're at the top of the steps and in another hallway like the one below, except with another metal door on the right, and another keypad. Typing in another series of numbers, the colonel slips the mask over his mouth and presses a button, and the door slips open.

The rain blows in immediately, but it's a light rain now, carried on a quiet breeze. The colonel steps through, and Daniel follows, finding himself just in front of the short bridge into the bulk of the city. Streetlights light the way on both sides, but as Daniel stares out ahead, then back at the colonel in his surgical mask (where did Daniel's go, and why would he need it?), he tries to see where the city should be and he tries to hear the city sounds, but he doesn't see or hear anything.

As his eyes adjust to the light, he can see the vague outlines of buildings, blocking out the clouds and the stars. But all the lights are off—every last one of them.

On the other side of the quarantine line, on the shore of the sea, finally away from that diseased corpse of a borough, every single light is off, and the colonel wears a surgical mask.

"It's night," says Daniel, very quietly, staring out ahead.

"No different in the day," says the colonel.

Then Daniel sees the first of the bodies, which is rolled up against the deep red of the suspension bridge just before it turns into the solid gravel of the borough. The body is curled sideways, and the streetlight a few yards away reflects against the dried blood around its head, which has tainted the dust-like pieces of gravel broken when this man's head hit the ground. He lies in a bed of red ashes.

A boil covers the bulk of his left ear.

Once Daniel sees it, the others become clearer—fallen men, women, and children cut down on their way to the wrong side of the quarantine fortress. It's not like the other side. There aren't nearly as many, but there are enough—women with no faces, teenage boys with no chance, scattered along a bridge that leads, damn it, that leads, god damn it, that leads directly into another sea of blood.

"It only took a month for the plague to spread beyond the

quarantine," says the colonel.

Daniel's left leg gives a little, and he cries out when he catches himself on his right.

"We still don't know how, but a diseased man showed up about a block past the bridge." He points down toward the city, but it's too dark there to see what he might be pointing to. "Spread from there."

"How?"

"We don't know."

"Why?" The word catches in Daniel's throat, turning into a deep, painful cough, and the cough itself ends in what sounds almost like a roar. He turns toward the fortress behind him, a tall metal structure squeezed perfectly between the edges of buildings on the right and left, patrolled up top by those biohazard soldiers with guns and megaphones and a propensity for using them.

"Once the disease spread," says the colonel, turning with Daniel to the structure, "we found ourselves with far more people to cure. It's spread so far now. I don't know how far it's spread." Then he glances, almost, but not quite, at Daniel. "We need to let it run its course," he says, the words slipping out just above a whisper. His lips smack audibly against each other. "See if anyone survives. See if anyone's immune."

Daniel stares. The colonel shrugs.

"Maybe there's someone in there who can't get sick," says the colonel. "Maybe there's someone the sick . . . instinctively avoid. I don't know." Turning out toward the bridge again, the colonel says, "Then we can return. Find that cure. Find—"

"You're just *waiting*?" says Daniel.

"We're—"

"You're just waiting till they all die?" says Daniel. Daniel steps back from the quarantine, then spins around out toward the city, his ragged, accelerating breath loud in the relative silence as the misty rain leaves drops, like bells, on the ends of his hair.

After a long, slow sigh, the colonel says, "Essentially."

"I . . ." says Daniel, glancing back to the fortress, then again out into the city. "You . . . my mom, Katie . . . Derek, I mean, he, they . . ." His fists hammer against nothing, and he stumbles sideways and forward and back on legs that no longer give a damn about the pain. His breathing becomes louder, ripping against his throat, and his eyes focus on nothing and everything as he bounces against walls that don't exist, until, finally, sniffling loudly, fists clenched tight, he weaves his way to the quarantine wall and leans his head against the cold, unforgiving metal.

And then, his skinny arm so tense his whole body shakes, he hurls his fist against the wall, sending a dull clang shuddering through the metal and back into himself. With a shattered grunt, he punches the wall again and again, and whether the cracking sound is his knuckles or his bones, he doesn't even care. Finally, pushing his head against the wall, he feels the tears come and drip onto the street, splashing into the wave that overtook the shore a long time ago.

When he finally turns around again, looking out over the bridge, past the dead he can see to the dead he can't, Daniel wonders if anyone's alive out there, the way there is inside the quarantine. He wonders if they ever ask why this borough is still separate from everywhere else. And he wonders how the people back inside the borough—Adam and Zeke and the Listeners, Anne and what cops are left, Tyrone in his cell, Flower in the Pub, and every other man and woman and kid holed up in their apartments and surviving on scraps and fear and getting sick one by one—would react if they knew their only purpose was to die. That they were all locked up specifically to die. They'd done a damn fine job so far. Daniel knew a lifetime of people who could attest to that.

Turning back to the fortress, Daniel tries to see Zeke through the metal, but fails. So instead, he imagines Zeke still sitting on the asphalt, searching out some way to hold onto the only thing he has. Maybe he knows it's doomed, but he doesn't know *how* doomed. None of them did, on the day the Listeners took them from their homes or their parents' homes, gave them a sanctuary and chopped off their ear and called them brother, promised the truth and offered everything but.

How could they know? They were just kids.

Like Katie was.

"Let me go back," says Daniel, so quietly he's not even sure he said it, or that he means it.

"Sorry?" says the colonel.

"Inside," says Daniel. He feels his heart pounding and his legs resisting, but he places a flat hand on the metal, even as the colonel stares at him, even as he shuts his own eyes and feels the breeze of *beyond-the-quarantine* on the back of his neck.

"Daniel—"

"They're just kids!" says Daniel, twisting his neck to look at the colonel without moving his frozen hand. "Some of them . . ." He shakes his head, then hangs it, nose pointed down at the gravel on the infected ground. "Some of them are just kids."

"We won't let you back out," says the colonel.

At that, Daniel shakes a little, the air snorting through his nostrils. But as his fingers squeal down along the solid metal, he says, "Then . . . then we'll be there." He turns to the colonel with eyes dark and wide. "We'll be there when it's over."

For a moment—a long, seemingly endless moment—the colonel doesn't move at all, simply breathing in and out, in and out, his mask inflating and deflating like a little white balloon. But then, his shoulders fall, and he types numbers into the keypad affixed to the side of the door.

The door opens. Daniel steps through.

He passes through sterile hallways and glass rooms.

A man in biohazard gear drives him through the sewer in a moped.

Daniel climbs a metal ladder.

He pushes against a heavy sewer cover.

A drizzle falls.

He holds his breath.

End of Second Part

The Beginning

The strange thing is that the pillows don't move. Katie holds hers between her head and the purple cushion, and Daniel's sits securely underneath his arm. His fingers grip the corner but he doesn't grab it. She's totally absorbed. She'd never see it, but he doesn't take the chance, because he's in as deep as she is.

They talk about a sickness. They talk about a quarantine. "Return to your homes," says the TV anchor in her deep red pantsuit with her short curled hair. "Stay indoors."

Then they show some footage from the borough, some places Daniel doesn't recognize, but some he does, like P.S. 128, American flag barely waving in the light wind. Katie sees it too, and then she sees Daniel, and she must think he's scared, because she scoots over and gives him a wide squirrel-girl smile.

"It's probably like that swine flu thingee, you know?" says Katie. "Just a lot of scared people."

A throat clears, but it's neither Daniel's nor Katie's. Behind the couch, leaning against the wall by the door of Katie's apartment, Daniel's mom folds her arms, the premature wrinkles lining her face standing out the paler she becomes. "We should . . ." she starts, glancing over at Katie's mom as she says it. "I guess we should go now," she says.

"Okay," Daniel says without moving. Beams of light, pushing out from behind a cloud or something, cut through the room and onto the TV screen until it's too bright to see the ticker crawling along the bottom of the screen or the anchors reporting the news—only to hear what they have to say.

After one of those long moments you wish was forever so you'd never have to face the one afterward, he turns to Katie and says, quietly, "What if it's not?"

"I'm not scared," says Katie. She smiles to prove it. "See? I'm not. You know why?"

The TV news speaks of sickness and quarantine. The experts expect it to last a few days at most. They urge borough residents to go directly home, regardless of supplies. But the television screen is a glowing haze, and Katie is bright and real and there as she says, "I won't be alone."

Daniel rubs his hands across his cheeks. His fingertips brush against his ears.

Katie smiles. "Because you'd come back," she says. "You'd come back."

The End

About the Author

Raised in Baltimore, Maryland on a steady diet of magical realism, literary fiction, science-fiction, and Spider-Man comics, Harrison Demchick spent most of his formative years inside his own head, working out strange thoughts and ideas that would eventually make their way into stories, screenplays, and songs.

He went to Oberlin College to attain one of today's most notoriously useless degrees, a BA in English with a creative writing concentration, but then actually used it, working the last seven years as a book editor.

Harrison is also a screenwriter, and the winner of the 2011 Baltimore Screenwriters Competition.

The Listeners was born in an independent study in fiction during Harrison's senior semester at Oberlin. Originally a series of interconnected short stories, it was adapted first into a screenplay, and then, from the screenplay, into his first novel. Harrison hopes ardently that *The Listeners* will catch on in such a way that he doesn't have to market it.

He lives still in Baltimore, working on a musical and various screenplays.

Harrison can be reached online at www.harrisondemchick.com and www.facebook.com/HarrisonDemchick. He's @HDemchick on Twitter, and he can be contacted by e-mail at hdemchick@gmail.com.

Acknowledgments

The *Listeners* has been seven years in the making. The fact that it exists today owes a lot to a great many people, and many great people, who are not me.

So I want to thank the following:

My parents, Neil and Barbara Demchick, who always encouraged me;

My brothers, Jonathan and Evan Demchick, who did nothing specifically to inhibit me;

Bonny Boto, my high school literary arts teacher for four years, whose boundless support and insight gave me (and so many others) the confidence to develop into the writer I am today;

Martha Collins, my creative writing professor and advisor at Oberlin, who encouraged that writer in his pursuit of a series of weird short stories about a bunch of people trapped in a quarantine;

Beth Gingles, whose lack of scathing and blistering criticism provided the first conclusive proof that my novel might not be all that bad (and who provided the personality for a certain main character's best friend);

The authors whose work I've had the opportunity to edit—Ron Cooper, Elizabeth Leiknes, Eden Unger Bowditch, Jonathon Scott Fuqua, and so many more—all of whom have made me a better writer;

The authors whose work I've had the opportunity to read—Salman Rushdie, Douglas Adams, John Marc DeMatteis, Kurt Vonnegut, and so many more—none of whom will ever really know how much they meant;

And perhaps most importantly, to Bruce Bortz, the editor, publisher, boss, and colleague who first suggested that a series of interconnected short stories could be a screenplay, and then that a screenplay could be a novel, and then that that novel should be published by Bancroft Press, and that all of this could be done during work hours.

Thank you all. I couldn't have done it without you.

Now please help me market my book.